John Timbs

Romance of London

Strange Stories, Scenes and Remarkable Persons of the Great Town: Vol.II.

John Timbs

Romance of London
Strange Stories, Scenes and Remarkable Persons of the Great Town: Vol.II.

ISBN/EAN: 9783744772945

Printed in Europe, USA, Canada, Australia, Japan

Cover: Foto ©Andreas Hilbeck / pixelio.de

More available books at **www.hansebooks.com**

ROMANCE OF LONDON:

STRANGE STORIES,
SCENES AND REMARKABLE PERSONS OF
THE GREAT TOWN.

BY

JOHN TIMBS, F.S.A.

AUTHOR OF 'A CENTURY OF ANECDOTE' ETC. ETC.

'Twas strange, 'twas passing strange.—SHAKSPEARE.

IN THREE VOLUMES.

VOL. II.

LONDON:
RICHARD BENTLEY, NEW BURLINGTON STREET,
PUBLISHER IN ORDINARY TO HER MAJESTY.

1865.

LONDON
PRINTED BY SPOTTISWOODE AND CO.
NEW-STREET SQUARE

CONTENTS

OF

THE SECOND VOLUME.

———•◦•———

ROGUERIES, CRIMES, AND PUNISHMENTS.

(Continued.)

LOVE AND MARRIAGE.

SUPERNATURAL STORIES.

SIGHTS AND SHOWS, AND PUBLIC AMUSEMENTS.

ROMANCE OF LONDON.

Rogueries, Crimes, & Punishments

(Continued).

THIS unfortunate lady, whose beauty and attractions proved her ruin, was fifth daughter of George, first Earl of Berkeley. Mary, her eldest sister, married, in the reign of Charles II., Ford, Lord Grey, of Werke—a nobleman of infamous memory, and to whose artifices the Lady Henrietta fell a victim. It seems that he had encouraged a passion for her when she was a girl, and basely taking advantage of the opportunities which his alliance with her family afforded, succeeded in effecting her ruin when she was little more than seventeen. After she had acknowledged an affection for him, the intrigue was continued about a year without discovery, but with great risk; and, on one occasion, as he himself confessed, he was two days locked in her closet without food, except a little sweetmeats. At length the suspicions of the Countess of Berkeley being excited by some trivial accident, she commanded her third daughter, the Lady Arabella, to search her sister's room; on which the latter delivered up a letter she had just been writing to Lord Grey, to this effect:—" My sister Bell did not suspect our being together last night, for she did not hear the noise. Pray come again on Sunday or Monday; if the last, I shall be very impatient."

This disclosure took place at Berkeley House, in London; and every precaution was taken to prevent correspondence or any clandestine meeting between the parties; notwithstanding which, Lady Henrietta contrived to elope from Durdanes, a seat of the Berkeleys near Epsom, and to join Lord Grey in London, with whom she resided, for a short time, in a lodging-house at Charing Cross.

The Earl of Berkeley then indicted him, and several other persons, for conspiring to ruin his daughter, by seducing her from her father's house. The trial came on in November 1682, at Westminster Hall; and, after a most affecting scene, the Lady Henrietta being herself present, and making oath that she had left home of her own accord, the jury were preparing to withdraw to consider their verdict, when a new tone was given to the proceedings by the lady declaring, in opposition to her father's claim of her person, that " she would not go with him, that she was married, and under no restraint, and that her husband was then in court." A Mr. Turner, son of Sir William Turner, then stepped forward and declared himself married to the lady. Sergeant Jeffreys then endeavoured to prove that Turner had been married before to another person, then alive, and who had children by him; but in this he failed. Turner then asserted there were witnesses ready to prove his marriage with Lady Henrietta, but the Earl of Berkeley disputed the Court having the cognizance of marriages, and desired that his daughter might be delivered up to him. The Lord Chief Justice saw no reason but his lordship might take his daughter; but Justice Dolben maintained they could not dispose of any other man's wife, and they said they were married. The Lord Chief Justice then declared the lady free for her father to take her; and that if Mr. Turner thought he had a right to the lady, he might take his course. The lady then declared she would go with her husband, to which the Earl replied, " Hussey, you shall go with me." It was then asked if Lord Grey might be discharged of his imprisonment. Sergeant Jeffreys objected; to which the Chief Justice replied:—" How can we do that, brother? The commitment upon the writ, *De Homine Replegiando*, is but till the body be produced; there she is, and says she is under no restraint." It was then argued that the lady was properly the plaintiff, that Lord Grey could not be detained in custody, but that he should give security to answer the suit. Accordingly he was bailed out. Then followed:—

Earl of Berkeley.—My Lord, I desire I may have my daughter again. *L. C. J.*—My Lord, we do not hinder you; you may take her. *Lady Henrietta.*— I will go with my husband. *Earl of Berkeley.*—Then, all that are my friends, seize her, I charge you. *L. C. J.*—Nay, let us have no breaking of the peace in the Court.

Despite, however, of this warning of the Chief Justice, Lord Berkeley, again claiming his daughter, and attempting to seize her by force in the Hall, a great scuffle ensued, and swords were drawn on both sides. At this critical moment the Court broke up, and the Judge, passing by, ordered his tipstaff to take Lady Henrietta into custody and convey her to the King's Bench, whither Mr. Turner accompanied her. On the last day of term she was released by order of the Court, and the business being, in some way, arranged among the parties during the vacation, the lawsuit was not persevered in.

Lady Henrietta herself is stated to have died, unmarried, in the year 1710; consequently, the claim of Turner must have been a mere collusion to save Lord Grey.—*Abridged from Sir Bernard Burke's Anecdotes of the Aristocracy,* vol. ii.

ASSASSINATION OF MR. THYNNE, IN PALL MALL.

As the visitor to Westminster Abbey passes through the south aisle of the choir, he can scarcely fail to notice sculptured upon one of the most prominent monuments a frightful scene of assassination, which was perpetrated in one of the most public streets of the metropolis, late in the reign of Charles II.

This terrible and mysterious transaction still remains among the darkest of the gloomy doings during the period of the Restoration, and the violence of faction consequent upon it. The murder of Thynne originated partly in a love affair, and partly, in all probability, from a secret political motive. The names and the interests of some of the proudest and most powerful families in the realm were involved in this nefarious homicide; and it is quite clear that while the actual assassins paid the forfeit of their crime, the instigator, or instigators, for there may have been more than one, were allowed to escape.

The interesting but innocent subject of the whole matter—the mainspring of the deed—was a daughter of the noble house of Percy, Lady Elizabeth, who, before she had completed her thirteenth year, was married, so far at least as the performance of the ceremony went, to Henry Cavendish, styled Earl of Ogle, the only son of Henry, second Duke of Newcastle of that house. But Lord Ogle, who had taken the name and arms of Percy, died in the beginning of November 1680, within a year after his marriage, leaving his father's dukedom without an heir, and the heiress of the house of Northumberland a prize for new suitors.

The fortunate man, as he was doubtless deemed, who, after only a few months, succeeded in carrying off from all competitors the youthful widow, was Thomas Thynne, Esq., of Longleat, in Wiltshire, from his large income called " Tom of Ten Thousand." The society in which he moved was the highest in the land. He had been at one time a friend of the Duke of York, afterwards James II.; but, having quarrelled with his Royal Highness, he had latterly attached himself with great zeal to the Whig or opposition party in politics, and had become an intimate associate of their idol, or tool for the moment, the Duke of Monmouth. He had sate as one of the members for Wiltshire in four parliaments. At Longleat, where he lived in a style of great magnificence, Thynne was often visited by Monmouth: he is the Issachar of Dryden's glowing description, in the Absalom and Achitophel, of the Duke's popularity-and-plaudit-gathering progresses:—

> From east to west his glories he displays,
> And, like the sun, the Promised Land surveys.
> Fame runs before him, as the morning star,
> And shouts of joy salute him from afar;
> Each house receives him as a guardian god,
> And consecrates the place of his abode.
> But hospitable treats did most commend
> Wise Issachar, his wealthy western friend.

A set of Oldenburg coach-horses, of great beauty, which graced the Duke's equipage, had been presented to him by Thynne.

The heiress of the house of Percy was nearly connected by affinity with the families both of Lord Russell
and Lord Cavendish; Lady Russell was a sister of her
mother; and the family of her late husband, Lord Ogle,
was a branch of that of the Earl of Devonshire; so
that it may be supposed Thynne was probably in part
indebted for his success in his suit to the good offices
of his two noble friends.   It would appear, however,
from an entry in Evelyn's Diary, that the Duke of
Monmouth was more instrumental than either.

The lady was fated to be a second time wedded only
in form: her marriage with Thynne appears to have
taken place in the summer or autumn of this year;
1681; and she was separated from him immediately
after the ceremony.   One account is, that she fled
from him of her own accord into Holland; another,
and more probable version of the story, makes Thynne ,
to have consented, at her mother's request, that she
should spend a year on the Continent.   It is to be
remembered that she was not yet quite fifteen.   The
legality of the marriage, indeed, appears to have been
called in question.

It was now, as some say, that she first met Count
Köningsmarck at the Court of Hanover; but in this
notion there is a confusion both of dates and persons.
The Count, in fact, appears to have seen her in England, and to have paid his addresses to her before she
gave her hand, or had it given for her, to Thynne: on
his rejection he left the country; but that they met
on the Continent there is no evidence or likelihood.

Köningsmarck appears to have returned to England
in the early part of the year 1681.   At this time Tom
of Ten Thousand, with the heiress of Northumberland,

his own by legal title, if not in actual possession, was at the height both of his personal and his political fortunes.

On the night of Sunday, the 12th of February 1682, all the Court end of London was startled by the news that Thynne had been shot passing along the public streets in his coach. The spot was towards the eastern extremity of Pall Mall, directly opposite to St. Alban's Street, no longer to be found, but which occupied nearly the same site with the covered passage now called the Opera Arcade. St. Alban's Place, which was at its northern extremity, still preserves the memory of the old name. King Charles at Whitehall might almost have heard the report of the assassin's blunderbuss; and so might Dryden, sitting in his favourite front room on the ground-floor of his house on the south side of Gerrard Street, also hardly more than a couple of furlongs distant.

Meanwhile, an active search continued to be made after Köningsmarck, in urging which Thynne's friends, the Duke of Monmouth and Lord Cavendish, are recorded to have been especially zealous.

About eight o'clock on the night of Sunday, the 19th, exactly a week after the commission of the murder, he was apprehended at Gravesend; and on the Monday following he was brought up, under a guard of soldiers, to London.

Thynne had survived his mortal wound only a few hours, during which the Duke of Monmouth sat by the bedside of his dying friend. He expired at six in the morning. Köningsmarck and the other three prisoners, after being examined, were lodged in Newgate; and, an indictment having been found against them by the grand jury, at Hicks's Hall, on Monday, the 27th of February 1681, they were the next day brought up to the bar at the Old Bailey to be arraigned and tried: Charles George Borosky, *alias* Boratzi, Christopher Vratz, and John Stern, as principals in the murder; and Charles John Count Königsmarck, as accessory before the fact.

The evidence, and indeed their own confessions, clearly proved the fact of Borosky shooting Thynne, and Vratz and Stern being present assisting him.

With respect to Königsmarck, besides the testimony of his accomplices, which of course went for nothing against him, the other evidence showed him living concealed in an humble lodging, and holding communication with the murderers before and almost at the time of the murder. He had also fled immediately after the offence was committed, and expressions of his in anger against Thynne for espousing Lady Ogle, were given by the witnesses. To this it was answered by Königsmarck, that the men accused were his followers and servants, and that of necessity he had frequent communion with them, but never about this murder; that when he arrived in London, he was seized with a distemper which obliged him to live privately till he was cured; and, finally, that he never saw, or had any quarrel with, Mr. Thynne. This defence, though morally a very weak one, was certainly strengthened by the absence of direct legal proof to connect the Count with the assassination; and also by the more than ordinarily artful and favourable summing up of Chief Justice Pemberton, who seemed determined to save him.

To the universal astonishment (save of Charles and

his court), the Count was acquitted, while his poor tools were hanged; the body of one of them, a Pole, being gibbetted " at Mile End,—being the road from the sea-ports where most of the northern nations do land." How the Count slipped his neck from the halter is pretty clearly indicated. Not only was the King's inclination in favour of the Count known; but " one Mr. B—, a woollen-draper in Covent Garden, who was warned to be on Count Koningsmarck's tryall jury, was askt if 500 guinies would do him any harm, if he would acquit the Count; but there being jurymen besides enough, he was not called; yet this he hath attested." This was a large sum to offer to a single juryman, for there is little doubt but the full pannel was as well paid.

The convicted prisoners were hanged in Pall Mall, the 10th of March following; and Borosky, who fired the blunderbuss, was suspended in chains near Mile-End, as above stated.

Evelyn tells us that " Vratz went to execution like an undaunted hero, as one that had done a friendly office for that base coward, Count Köningsmarck, who had hopes to marry his widow, the rich Lady Ogle, and was acquitted by a corrupt jury, and so got away." Vratz told a friend of Evelyn's, who accompanied him to the gallows, and gave him some advice, " that he did not value dying of a rush, and hoped and believed God would deal with him *like a gentleman.*"

Count Köningsmarck found it expedient to export himself from this country as fast as he could, after he had paid his fees and got out of the hands of the officers of justice at the Old Bailey.

According to the Amsterdam Historical Dictionary,

he went to Germany to visit his estates in 1683 ; was
wounded at the siege of Cambray, which happened that
same year ; afterwards went with his regiment to Spain,
where he distinguished himself at the siege of Gerona,
in Catalonia, and on other occasions ; and, finally, in
1686, having obtained the permission of the French
King, accompanied his uncle, Otho William, to the
Morea, where he was present at the sieges of Navarin
and Modon, and at the battle of Argos, in which last
affair he so overheated himself, that he was seized with
a pleurisy, which carried him off.

To end the story, we return to her with whom it
began, the heiress of the long line and broad domains
of the proud Percies.   Lady Ogle, as she was styled,
became an object of still greater public interest or
curiosity than ever, on the catastrophe of her second
husband.   Her third husband was Charles Seymour,
Duke of Somerset.

The life of his wife, the commencing promise of
which was so bright, and which was afterwards che-
quered with such remarkable incidents, not unmixed
with the wonted allotment of human sorrow, terminated
on the 23rd of November 1722.   The Duchess, when
she died, was in her fifty-sixth year.   She had brought
the Duke thirteen children, seven sons and six daughters, of whom only one son and three daughters arrived
at maturity.

MURDER OF MOUNTFORT, THE PLAYER.

THIS tragic scene, which can scarcely be called a
duel, is thus circumstantially related in Mr. Cunningham's excellent *Handbook of London.* In Howard
Street, between Surrey Street and Norfolk Street, in
the Strand, lived William Mountfort, the player, who
was murdered before his own door, on the night of the
9th of December 1692. " The story is an interesting
one. A gallant of the town, a Captain Richard Hill,
had conceived a passion for Mrs. Bracegirdle, the
beautiful actress. He is said to have offered her his
hand, and to have been refused. His passion at last
became ungovernable, and he at once determined on
carrying her off by force. For this purpose, he borrowed a suit of night-linen of Mrs. Radd, the landlady
in whose house in Buckingham Court he lodged; and
induced his friend, Lord Mohun, to assist him in his
attempt; he dodged the fair actress for a whole day
at the theatre, stationed a coach near the Horseshoe
Tavern in Drury Lane, to carry her off in, and hired
six soldiers to force her into it, as she returned from
supping with Mr. Page, in Prince's Street, (off Drury
Lane,) to her own lodging in the house of Mrs.
Dorothy Brown, in Howard Street. As the beautiful
actress came down Drury Lane, at ten at night, accompanied by her mother and brother, and escorted by
her friend Mr. Page, one of the soldiers seized her
in his arms, and endeavoured to force her into the
coach. Page resisting the attempt, Hill drew his sword,
and struck a blow at Page's head, which fell, however,
only on his hand. The lady's screams drew a rabble

about her, and Hill, finding his endeavours ineffectual, bid the soldiers let her go.

"Lord Mohun, who was in the coach all this time, now stept out of it, and with his friend Hill, insisted on seeing the lady home, Mr. Page accompanying them, and remaining with Mrs. Bracegirdle some time after for her better security. Disappointed in their object, Lord Mohun and Captain Hill remained in the street; Hill with his sword drawn, and vowing revenge, as he had done before to Mrs. Bracegirdle on her way home. Here they went to the Horseshoe Tavern in Drury Lane, for a bottle of canary, of which they drank in the middle of the street. In the meantime, Mrs. Bracegirdle sent her servant to Mr. Mountfort's house in Norfolk Street adjoining, to know if he was at home. The servant returned with an answer that he was not, and was sent again by her mistress to desire Mrs. Mountfort to send to her husband to take care of himself; "in regard my Lord Mohun and Captain Hill, who (she feared) had no good intention toward him, did wait him in the street." Mountfort was sought for in several places without success, but Mohun and Hill had not waited long before he turned the corner of Norfolk Street with, it is said by one witness (Captain Hill's servant), his sword over his arm. It appears, in the evidence before the coroner, that he had heard while in Norfolk Street, (if not before,) of the attempt to carry off Mrs. Bracegirdle, and was also aware that Lord Mohun and Hill were in the street, for Mrs. Brown, the landlady of the house in which Mrs. Bracegirdle lodged, solicited him to keep away. Every precaution was, however, ineffectual. He addressed Lord Mohun (who em-

braced him, it would appear, very tenderly), and said
how sorry he was to find that he (Lord Mohun) would
justify the rudeness of Captain Hill, or keep company
with such a pitiful fellow ("or words to the like
effect)," "and then," says Thomas Leak, the Captain's
servant, "the Captain came forward and said he would
justify himself, and went towards the middle of the
street, and Mr. Mountfort followed him and drew."
Ann Jones, a servant, (it would appear, in Mrs. Bracegirdle's house,) declared in evidence that Hill came
behind Mountfort, and gave him a box over the ear,
and bade him draw.   It is said they fought; Mountfort certainly fell with a desperate wound on the right
side of the belly, near the short rib, of which he died
the next day, assuring Mr. Page, while lying on the
floor in his own parlour, as Page declares in evidence,
that Hill ran him through the body before he could
draw his sword.   Lord Mohun affirmed they fought,
and that he saw a piece of Mountfort's sword lying on
the ground.   As Mountfort fell, Hill ran off, and the
Duchy watch coming up, Lord Mohun surrendered
himself, with his sword still in the scabbard.

"The scene of this sad tragedy was that part of
Howard Street, which lies between Norfolk Street
and Surrey Street.   Mountfort's house was two doors
from the south-west corner.   Mountfort was a handsome man, and Hill is said to have attributed his
rejection by Mrs. Bracegirdle to her love for Mountfort, an unlikely passion, it is thought, as Mountfort
was a married man, with a good-looking wife of his
own—afterwards Mrs. Verbruggen, and a celebrated
actress withal.   Mountfort, (only thirty-three when he
died,) lies buried in the adjoining church of St. Cle-

ment's Danes. Mrs. Bracegirdle continued to inhabit
her old quarters. 'Above forty years since,' says
Davies, 'I saw at Mrs. Bracegirdle's house in Howard
Street a picture of Mrs. Barry, by Kneller, in the
same apartments with the portraits of Betterton and
Congreve.' Hill's passionate prompter on the above
occasion was the same Lord Mohun who fell in a duel
with the Duke of Hamilton."

TWO EXTRAORDINARY SUICIDES AT LONDON BRIDGE.

A MELANCHOLY instance of suicide which took place
in 1689, is recorded by historians of London Bridge
as bearing testimony to the power of the torrent of
the Thames at that period. It is thus narrated in the
Travels and Memoirs of Sir John Reresby, Bart. :—
"About this time," says the Author, "a very sad
accident happened, which, for a while, was the discourse of the whole town: Mr. Temple, son to Sir
William Temple, who had married a French lady with
20,000 pistols; a sedate and accomplished young
gentleman, who had lately by King William been
made Secretary of War, took a pair of oars and drawing near the Bridge, leapt into the Thames, and
drowned himself, leaving a note behind him in the
boat to this effect: 'My folly in undertaking what I
could not perform, whereby some misfortunes have
befallen the King's service, is the cause of my putting
myself to this sudden end; I wish him success in all
his undertakings, and a better servant.'" Pennant, in
repeating this anecdote, adds, that it took place on
the 14th of April; that the unhappy man loaded his

pockets with stones to destroy all chance of safety, and instantly sank; adding that "his father's false and profane reflection on the occasion was, 'that a wise man might dispose of himself, and make his life as short as he pleased.' How strongly did this great man militate against the precepts of Christianity, and the solid arguments of a most wise and pious heathen!" (Cicero, in his *Somnium Scipionis.*)

The second suicide, of date about half a century later than that of Mr. Temple, was committed under a like mistaken influence and perverted reasoning. Eustace Budgell, who contributed to the *Spectator* the papers marked "X," through Addison's influence, obtained some subordinate offices under Government in Ireland. A misunderstanding with the Lord Lieutenant, Lord Bolton, and some lampoons which Budgell was indiscreet enough to write in consequence, occasioned his resignation. From that time he appears to have trodden a downward course: he lost 20,000*l.* in the South Sea Bubble, and spent 5,000*l.* more in unsuccessful attempts to get into Parliament. In order to save himself from ruin, he joined the knot of pamphleteers who scribbled against Sir Robert Walpole; and he was presented with 1,000*l.* by the Duchess of Marlborough. Much of the *Craftsman* was written by him, as well as a weekly pamphlet called *The Bee*, which commenced in 1733, and extended to 100 numbers. But his necessities reduced him to dishonest methods for procuring support, and he obtained a place in the *Dunciad*, not on account of want of wit, but want of principle, by appearing as a legatee in Tindal's will for 2,000*l.*, to the exclusion of his next heir and nephew; a bequest which Budgell is thought to have obtained surreptitiously; and the will was set aside. With this stain on his character, Budgell fought on for some time, but he became still deeper involved in lawsuits, his debts accumulated, and at last he dreaded an execution in his house. This prompted the alternative of suicide. In 1736, he took a boat at Somerset Stairs, and ordering the waterman to row down the river, he threw himself into the stream as they shot London Bridge. Having like Mr. Temple, taken the precaution of filling his pockets with stones, like him, Budgell rose no more. It is singular that Pennant should have overlooked this latter suicide; for, in his *London* he remarks, "of the multitudes who have perished in this rapid descent, (the torrent at the Bridge,) the name of no one, of any note, has reached my knowledge, except that of Mr. Temple, only son of the great Sir William Temple."

On the morning before that on which Budgell drowned himself, he had endeavoured to persuade a natural daughter, at that time not more than eleven years of age, to accompany him. She, however, refused; and afterwards entered as an actress at Drury Lane Theatre. Budgell left in his secretary a slip of paper, on which was written a broken distich, intended, perhaps, as an apology for his act:—

> What Cato did, and Addison approved,
> Cannot be wrong.

It is unnecessary to point out the fallacy of his defence of his conduct; there being as little resemblance between the cases of Budgell and Cato, as there is reason for considering Addison's *Cato* written with the view of defending suicide.

EXTRAORDINARY ESCAPE FROM DEATH.

SHERIFF HOARE, in his Journal of his Shrievalty, relates, that, on Monday, November 24, 1740, five persons were executed at Tyburn, when a most extraordinary event happened to one of them.—William Duell, aged seventeen years, indicted for a rape, robbery and murder, and convicted of the rape. Duell, after having been hung up by the neck with the others, for the space of *twenty-two minutes*, or more, was cut down, and being begged by the Surgeons' Company, was carried in a hackney-coach to their Hall, to be anatomised. But just as they had taken him out of the coach, and laid him on a table in the Hall, in order to make the necessary preparations for cutting him up, he was, to the great astonishment of the surgeon and assistants, heard to groan ; and, upon examination, finding he had some other symptoms of life, some of the surgeons let him blood ; after having taken several ounces, he began to stir, and in a short space of time was able to rear himself up, but could not immediately speak so as to be heard articulately. Messages were sent to the Sheriffs, and the news was soon spread about, insomuch that by five o'clock in the afternoon a great mob had gathered about Surgeons' Hall, in the Old Bailey, which intimidated the Sheriffs and their officers from attempting to carry Duell back the same day in order to hang him up again, and complete his execution ; " as," says Sheriff Hoare, " we might have done by virtue of our warrant, which was to execute him at any time in the day." Therefore they kept him till about twelve o'clock at night, when, the mob being dispersed, the Sheriff signed an order for his recommitment to Newgate, whither he was accordingly carried in a hackney-coach; being put into one of the cells, and covered up, and some warm broth given him, he began so far to recover as to be able to speak, and ask for more victual, but did not yet seem sensible enough to remember what had happened.

Two days afterwards, the Sheriffs waited on the Duke of Newcastle, Secretary of State, to know his Majesty's pleasure regarding the disposal of the criminal who had thus strangely escaped dissection and death; and who was then in Newgate, " fully recovered in health and senses." His Grace desired the Sheriffs to draw up a narrative of the circumstances in writing, which was accordingly done; and it was added, that the prisoner had been found guilty on no other evidence but his own confession before a Justice of the Peace.

The story of the lad's recovery now became known, and persons flocked to Newgate to see him and ask him questions; but he remembered nothing of his being carried to execution, or even of his being brought to trial; yet *Grub Street Papers,* cried about the streets, gave accounts of the wonderful discoveries he had made in the other world, of the ghosts and apparitions he had seen, "and such like invented stuff to get a penny." The conjectures of his not dying under the execution were various; some suggesting it was because he was not hung up long enough; others, that the rope was not rightly placed; others, from the light weight of his body. But the true reason, as Sheriff Hoare was informed, was accounted for physically,—he having been in a high fever since his commitment to Newgate, for the most part light-headed and delirious; and, consequently, having no impression of fear upon him, and his blood circulating with violent heat and quickness, might be the reason why it was the longer before it could be stopped by suffocation; and this likewise accounted for his not knowing anything that had happened (he being so ill) either at his trial or execution.

It does not appear from the Sheriff's Journal whether Duell received a pardon; but the *Gentleman's Magazine* for December, in the above year, informs us that he was transported for life. It also varies the statement of the resuscitation—that when one of the servants at Surgeons' Hall was washing the body for dissection, he found the breath to come quicker and shorter, on which a surgeon took some ounces of blood from him, and in two hours he was able to sit up in a chair.

That this was by no means the only instance of the resuscitation of the human body after it had been conveyed to Surgeons' Hall for dissection, is evident from the following curious order, made at a Court of Assistants, on the 13th of July 1587, which is copied from the minute-books of the Company, and here modernised: " Item. It is agreed that if any body which shall at any time hereafter happen to be brought to our Hall for the intent to be wrought upon by the anatomists of our Company, *shall revive or come to life again, as has of late been seen*, the charges about the same body so reviving, shall be borne, levied, and sustained by such person or persons who shall happen to bring home the body.   And further, shall abide such order or fine as this House shall award." Here we see that the *charges* were more attended to by the Court than any other consideration.

HUMAN HEADS ON TEMPLE BAR.

AFTER the remains of traitors ceased to be placed on London Bridge, when the right to dispose of the quartered remains of the subject devolved on the Crown, that right, as regards those who had suffered for high treason in London, was, with few exceptions, wholly or partially exercised in favour of Temple Bar. Thus the City Bar became the City Golgotha. The first person so exposed was Sir Thomas Armstrong, the last victim of the Rye House Plot. He was executed at Tyburn; his head was set up on Westminster Hall, and one of the quarters upon Temple Bar. Sir John Friend and Sir William Perkins, conspirators in the plot to carry off the King in 1695, on his return from Richmond to Kensington, were the next ornaments of the Bar; the head and limbs of Friend, and the headless trunk of Perkins, being placed upon its iron spikes. Evelyn refers to this melancholy scene " as a dismal sight, which many pitied. I think there never was such a Temple Bar till now, except once in the time of King Charles the Second, viz., Sir Thomas Armstrong." The head of Sir John Friend was set up on Aldgate; on account, it is presumed, of that gate being in the proximity of his brewery. Sir John Fenwick, nearly the last person to suffer on account of this conspiracy, is not associated with the Bar; but there is a remarkable coincidence in the death of King William being not altogether un-associated with the execution of this northern baronet. The King, on the morning of February 21, 1702, rode into the Home Park at Hampton Court, to inspect the progress of a new canal there, and was mounted on a sorrel pony, which had formerly been the property of

the unfortunate Sir John Fenwick. William having
reached the works, the pony accidentally placed his
foot in a molehill, and fell ; the King's collar-bone was
fractured by the fall, of the effects of which he expired
March 8. The adherents of James eulogised their beloved " Sorrel ; " and the wit of Pope was shown in the
following *jeu-d'esprit,* contrasting the safety of Charles .
in the oak at Boscobel, with the accident to William in
the gardens at Hampton :—

> Angels, who watched the guardian oak so well,
> How chanced ye slept when luckless Sorrel fell !

To return to Temple Bar. The next head placed on
its summit was that of Colonel Henry Oxburg, who
suffered for his attachment to the cause of the Pretender.
Next was the head of Christopher Layer, another of
the Pretender's adherents ; whose head frowned from
the crown of the arch for a longer period than any other
occupant. On the 17th of May 1723, nearly seven
months after his trial, he was conducted from the
Tower to Tyburn, seated in a ditch, habited in a full
dress suit, and a tie-wig ; and at the place of execution
he declared his adherence to King James (as he called
the Pretender), and advised the people to take up arms
on his behalf. " The day subsequent to his execution,
his head was placed on Temple Bar ; there it remained,
blackened and weather-beaten with the storms of many
successive years, until, as we have remarked, it became
its oldest occupant. Infancy had advanced into ma-
tured manhood, and still that head regularly looked
down from the summit of the arch. It seemed part of
the arch itself."* A curious story is told of Counsellor

---

* *Temple Bar ; the City Golgotha.* By a Barrister of the Inner
Temple. 1853.

Layer's head. One stormy night it was blown from
off the Bar into the Strand, and there picked up by
Mr. John Pearce, an attorney, who showed it to some
persons at a public-house, under the floor of which it
was stated to have been buried. Dr. Rawlinson, the
antiquary, meanwhile, having made inquiries after the
. head, with a wish to purchase it, was imposed upon with
another instead of Layer's head; the former the Doctor
preserved as a valuable relic, and directed it to be
buried in his right-hand; which request is stated to
have been complied with.

The heads of the victims of the fatal Rebellion of
'45 were the last placed upon the Bar; those being
Townley and Fletcher. Walpole writes to Montague,
August 16, 1746, " I have been this morning at the
Tower, and passed under the new heads at Temple
Bar, where people make a trade of letting spying-
glasses at a halfpenny a look." There is a scarce print,
in which the position of the heads is shown, and portraits cleverly engraved. For several weeks people
flocked to this revolting exhibition, which yielded to
some a savage pleasure. Dr. Johnson relates the
following impression from the sight. " I remember
once being with Goldsmith in Westminster Abbey.
While he surveyed Poets' Corner, I said to him:—

Forsitan et nostrum nomen miscebitur istis.

When we got to the Temple Bar, he stopped me,
pointed to the heads upon it and slily whispered me,

Forsitan et nostrum nomen miscebitur istis."

Johnson was a Jacobite at heart.

Another instance of political feeling is narrated.
On the morning of January 20, 1766, between 2 and

3 o'clock, a person was observed to watch his opportunity of discharging musket-balls, from a still cross-
bow, at the two remaining heads upon Temple Bar.
On his examination, he affected a disorder of his senses,
and said his reason for so doing was his strong attachment to the present government, and that he thought
it was not sufficient that a traitor should only suffer
death, and that this provoked his indignation; and that
it had been his constant practice for three nights
past, to amuse himself in the same manner; but the
account adds, " it is much to be feared that he is a near
relation to one of the unhappy sufferers." Another
account states that, " upon searching him, above 50
musket-balls were found wrapped in a paper with this
motto, *Eripuit ille vitam.*" It is added, that on March
31, 1772, one of the heads fell down; and that shortly
after, the remaining one was swept down by the wind.
The last of the iron poles or spikes was not removed
from the Bar until the commencement of the present
century.

Among persons living in the present century who recollected these grim tenants of the Bar were the following: J. T. Smith relates that in 1825, a person, aged 87,
remembered the heads being seen with a telescope from
Leicester Fields; the ground between which and Temple
Bar was then thinly built over. Mrs. Black, the wife of
the editor of the *Morning Chronicle* newspaper, when
asked if she remembered the heads on the spikes on
the Bar, used to reply, very collectedly, and, as usual
with her, without any parade of telling the story she
had to relate, " *Boys, I recollect the scene well!* I have
seen on that Temple Bar, about which you ask, two
human heads—men's heads—traitors' heads—spiked on

iron poles. There were two. I saw one fall. Women
shrieked as it fell; men, I have heard, shrieked: one
woman near me fainted. Yes, I recollect seeing human
heads upon Temple Bar."

The other person who remembered to have seen
human heads upon spikes on Temple Bar was one who
died in December 1856—Mr. Rogers, the banker-poet.
" I well remember (he said) one of the heads of the
rebels upon a pole at Temple Bar-a black shapeless
lump. Another pole was bare, the head having dropped
from it." Mr. Rogers, we take it, was the last surviving person who remembered to have seen a human
head on a spike on the Bar.

ADVENTURE WITH A FORGER.

Dr. Somerville, of Edinburgh, in his Second Journey
to London, relates the following singular adventure,
which is especially interesting for the portrait which
it gives of Sir John Fielding, the Police Magistrate.

" One of our travelling companions, whose behaviour
had excited various conjectures in the course of our
journey, was apprehended at the Bank of England the
day after our arrival on the charge of forgery. He
had, in fact, forged and circulated the notes of the
bank to a very large amount. He was carried before
Sir John Fielding, who in a few hours discovered the
lodgings of the several persons who had places in the
York coach along with the suspected forger. I happened to be in the gallery of the House of Commons
when one of Sir John's officers arrived at my sister's
house in Panton Square, requiring my immediate attendance at the Police Office; and it was not without

entreaty that the messenger was prevailed upon to desist from his purpose of following me to the House, upon the condition of one of my friends becoming security for my attendance in Catherine Street at eight o'clock next morning. The prisoner had during the night made an attempt to escape by leaping from the window of the room where he was confined; and having failed in this attempt, his resolution forsook him; and he made a voluntary confession of his guilt in the presence of Sir John Fielding, a few minutes before my arrival. Sir John, when informed of my being a minister of the Church of Scotland, desired me to retire with the culprit, whose name was Mathewson, to the adjoining chapel, and give him admonitions suitable to his unfortunate situation. In consequence of my advice, he made a more ample confession on returning to the bar. The circumstances which he added to his former confession were not, however, injurious to himself, otherwise I should not have urged him to mention them, but such as I thought could not be concealed consistently with the sincerity of that repentance which he now professed.

" I was so much amused and interested with the appearance of Sir John Fielding, and the singular adroitness with which he conducted the business of his office, that I continued there for an hour after the removal of Mathewson, while Sir John was engaged in the investigation of other cases. Sir John had a bandage over his eyes, and held a little switch or rod in his hand, waving it before him as he descended from the bench. The sagacity he discovered in the questions he put to the witnesses, and a marked and successful attention as I conceived, not only to the words, but to the accents and tones of the speaker, supplied the advantage which is usually rendered by the eye; and his skilful arrangement of the questions leading to the detection of concealed facts, impressed me with the highest respect for his singular ability as a police magistrate. This testimony I give not merely on the observation I had the opportunity of making on the day of my appearance before him.

"I frequently afterwards gratified my curiosity by stepping into Sir John Fielding's office when I happened to pass near Catherine Street. The accidental circumstance of my having been his fellow-traveller to London, gave me some interest in Mathewson, who, before his being removed from the office of Sir John Fielding, had addressed me in the most pathetic and earnest language, beseeching me to condescend to visit him in prison. I first saw him again in Clerkenwell, where he was committed till the term of the Old Bailey Sessions. The hardened, ferocious countenances of the multitude of felons all in the same apartment, the indecency and profaneness of their conversation, and the looks of derision which they cast upon me, awakened sensations of horror more than of pity, and made me request to be relieved from the repetition of this painful duty. I did not therefore return to Clerkenwell; but after Mathewson's trial and a few days before his execution (for he was executed), I made him a visit in Newgate. There I found him sitting in the condemned hold, with two other criminals under sentence of death. I requested the officer who superintended this department to permit me to retire with Mathewson to a private room, where he entered into a detailed confession of his guilt. Mathewson, at our interview in Sir

John Fielding's office, made known to me a circumstance which he thought gave him a strong claim to my humane services. He told me that his father had for a long time been in the service of Lord Minto, the Lord Justice-Clerk, and that he had been afterwards patronised by his Lordship and all his family on account of his diligence and fidelity. He had heard my name mentioned at the inn at Newcastle, a circumstance which determined him to take a place in the same coach; and, indeed, I had observed that he officiously clung to me in the progress of our journey. He attended Mr. Maclagan and me to the playhouse on Saturday evening after our arrival at York, to the Cathedral service on Sunday morning, and to Dr. Cappe's chapel in the afternoon—though, on account of his suspicious appearance, and the petulance of his manner, we gave him broad hints of our inclination to dispense with his company; and we were not a little surprised to find him seated in the stage-coach next morning, as, on our way from Newcastle, he had told us that he was to go no farther than York."

ECCENTRIC BENEVOLENCE.

EDWARD, sixth Lord Digby, who succeeded to the peerage in 1752, was a man of active benevolence. At Christmas and Easter, he was observed by his friends to be more than usually grave, and then always to have on an old shabby blue coat. Mr. Fox, his uncle, who had great curiosity, wished much to find out his nephew's motive for appearing at times in this manner, as in general he was esteemed more than a well-dressed man. On his expressing an inclination for this purpose, Major Vaughan and another gentleman undertook to watch his Lordship's motions. They accordingly set out; and observing him to go to St. George's Fields, they followed him at a distance, till they lost sight of him near the Marshalsea Prison. Wondering what could carry a person of his Lordship's rank and fortune to such a place, they inquired of the turnkey if a gentleman (describing Lord Digby) had not just entered the prison?

"Yes, masters," exclaimed the fellow, with an oath; "but he is not a man, he is an angel; for he comes here twice a year, sometimes oftener, and sets a number of prisoners free. And he not only does this, but he gives them sufficient to support themselves and their families till they can find employment. This," continued the man, "is one of his extraordinary visits. He has but a few to take out to-day."

"Do you know who the gentleman is?" inquired the Major.

"We none of us know him by any other marks," replied the man, "but by his humanity and his blue coat."

The next time his Lordship had on his almsgiving coat, a friend asked him what occasioned his wearing that singular dress. The reply was, by Lord Digby taking the gentleman shortly after to the George Inn, in the Borough, where seated at dinner were thirty individuals, whom his Lordship had just released from the Marshalsea Prison, by paying their debts in full.

THE EXECUTION OF LORD FERRERS.

In the last year of the reign of George II. (1760), our criminal annals received an addition, which, for atrocity, has few parallels. Horace Walpole, in his *Letters*, relates this event with his accustomed minuteness and spirit.

In January of the above year, Earl Ferrers, while residing at his seat, Staunton Harcourt, in Leicestershire, murdered Johnson, his steward, in the most barbarous and deliberate manner. The Earl had been separated by Parliament from his wife, a very pretty woman, whom he married with no fortune, for the most groundless barbarity, and then killed his steward for having been evidence for her. " He sent away all his servants but one," says Walpole, " and, like that heroic murderess, Queen Christina, carried the poor man through a gallery and several rooms, locking them after him, and then bid the man kneel down, for he was determined to kill him. The poor creature flung himself at his feet, but in vain; was shot, and lived twelve hours. Mad as this action was from the consequences, there was no frenzy in his behaviour; he got drunk, and at intervals talked of it coolly; but did not attempt to escape, till the colliers beset his house, and were determined to take him alive or dead. He is now in the gaol at Leicester, and will soon be removed to the Tower, then to Westminster Hall, and I suppose to Tower Hill; unless, as Lord Talbot prophesied, in the House of Lords, ' Not being thought mad enough to be shut up, till he had killed somebody, he will then be thought too mad to be executed ; ' but Lord Talbot

was no more honoured in his vocation than other pro-
phets are in their own country."

Lord Ferrers was tried by his peers in Westminster
Hall, and found guilty; he was condemned to be
hanged, and to the mortification of the peerage, to be
anatomised, according to the tenor of the new Act of
Parliament for murder. The night he received the
sentence he played at picquet with the Tower warders,
would play for money, and would have continued to
play every evening, but they refused. The governor
of the Tower shortened his allowance of wine after his
conviction, agreeably to the late strict Acts on murder.
This he much disliked, and at last pressed his brother,
the clergyman, to intercede, that, at least, he might
have more porter; for, said he, what I have is not a
draught. His brother protested against it, but at last
consenting (and he did obtain it), then said the Earl,
" Now is as good a time as any to take leave of you —
adieu ! "

On the return of the Earl from his trial and condemnation, and when the procession reached Thames
Street, a servant of some oilmen there, who had been
set to watch the boiling of some inflammable substances,
and who left his charge on the fire, went out to see the
pageant, and on his return the man found the whole of
the oilmen's premises in flames : seven dwelling-houses
were consumed, with all the warehouses on Fresh
Wharf, and the roof of St. Magnus Church; the whole
of the destruction being estimated at 40,000*l.*

On the last morning, May 5, the Earl dressed himself
in his wedding-clothes, saying he thought this at least
as good an occasion for putting them on as that for
which they were first made. He wore them to Tyburn :

this marked the strong impression on his mind. His courage rose on the occasion: even an awful procession of above two hours, with that mixture of pageantry, shame, and ignominy, nay, and of delay, could not dismount his resolution. He set out from the Tower at nine, amidst crowds, thousands. First went a string of constables; then one of the sheriffs in his chariot and six, the horses dressed with ribbons; next, Lord Ferrers, in his own landau* and six, his coachman crying all the way; guards at each side; the other sheriff's carriage following empty, with a mourning coach and six, a hearse, and the Horse Guards. Observe, that the empty chariot was that of the other sheriff, who was in the landau with the prisoner, and who was Vaillant, the French bookseller, in the Strand. Lord Ferrers at first talked on indifferent matters, and observing the prodigious confluence of people (the blind was drawn up on his side), he said — "But they never saw a lord hanged, and perhaps will never see another." One of the dragoons was thrown by his horse's leg entangling in the hind-wheel: Lord Ferrers expressed much concern, and said, "I hope there will be no death to-day but mine," and was pleased when Vaillant told him the man was not hurt. Vaillant made excuses to him on the office. "On the contrary," said the Earl, "I am much obliged to you. I feared the disagreeableness of the duty might make you depute your under-sheriff. As you are so good as to execute it yourself, I am persuaded the dreadful apparatus will be conducted with more expedition." The

---

* The carriage was, after the execution, driven to Acton, where it was placed in the coach-house, was never again used, but remained there until it fell to pieces. The Earl's wife was burned to death in 1807.

chaplain of the Tower, who sat backwards, then thought
it his turn to speak, and began to talk on religion; but
Lord Ferrers received it impatiently.

Meanwhile, the procession was stopped by the crowd.
The Earl said he was thirsty, and wished for some wine
and water. The Sheriff refused him. "Then," said
the Earl, "I must be content with this," and took some
pigtail tobacco out of his pocket. As they drew nigh,
he said, "I perceive we are almost arrived; it is time
to do what little more I have to do;" and then taking
out his watch, gave it to Vaillant, desiring him to
accept it as a mark of gratitude for his kind behaviour,
adding, "It is scarce worth your acceptance; but I
have nothing else; it is a stop watch, and a pretty
accurate one." He gave five guineas to the chaplain,
and took out as much for the executioner. Then
giving Vaillant a pocket-book, he begged him to
deliver it to Mrs. Clifford, his mistress, with what it
contained.

When they came to Tyburn, the coach was detained
some minutes by the conflux of the people; but as
soon as the door was opened, Lord Ferrers stepped out,
and mounted the scaffold : it was hung with black by
the undertaker, and at the expense of his family.
Under the gallows was a new invented stage, to be
struck from beneath him. He showed no kind of fear
or discomposure, only just looking at the gallows with
a slight motion of dissatisfaction. He spoke little,
kneeled for a moment to the prayer, said "Lord, have
mercy upon me, and forgive me my errors," and
immediately mounted the upper stage. He had come
pinioned with a black sash, and was unwilling to have
his hands tied, or his face covered, but was persuaded

to both. When the rope was put upon his neck, he turned pale, but recovered his countenance instantly, and was but seven minutes from leaving the coach to the signal given for striking the stage. As the machine was new, they were not ready at it; his toes touched it, and he suffered a little, having had time, by their bungling, to raise his cap; but the executioner pulled it down again, and they pulled his legs, so that he was soon out of pain, and quite dead in four minutes. He desired not to be stripped and exposed; and Vaillant promised him, though his clothes must be taken off, that his shirt should not. The decency ended with him: the sheriffs fell to eating and drinking on the scaffold, and helped up one of their friends to drink with them, as the body was still hanging, which it did for above an hour, and then was conveyed back with the said pomp to Surgeons' Hall, to be dissected: there is a print of "Lord Ferrers, as he lay in his coffin at Surgeons' Hall." The executioners fought for the rope, and the one who lost it cried. The mob tore off the black cloth as relics; "but," says Walpole, "the universal crowd behaved with great decency and admiration, as well they might; for sure no exit was ever made with more sensible resolution, and with less ostentation."

Earl Ferrers had petitioned George II. that he might die by the axe. This was refused. " He has done," said the old king, " de deed of de bad man, and he shall die de death of de bad man." One luxury, however, Lord Ferrers is reported to have secured for the last hour of his life—*a silken rope*.

The night before his death, he made one of his keepers read *Hamlet* to him, after he was in bed: he paid all his bills in the morning, as if leaving an inn ; and half an hour before the sheriffs fetched him, corrected some Latin verses he had written in the Tower.

His violence of temper and habitual eccentricities occasioned him to be set down as a madman by his contemporaries, and he is so held in the few historical records which name him. He hated his poor wife, and one of his modes of annoying her was to put squibs and crackers into her bed, which were contrived to explode just as she was dropping asleep. But she extricated herself through a separation by Act of Parliament, and obtained further atonement in a more congenial second union, many years after, with Lord Frederic Campbell, brother to the Duke of Argyll.

BALTIMORE HOUSE.

This noble mansion, in Russell Square, at the south corner of Guildford Street, was built for Lord Baltimore in the year 1759: subsequent to the formation of the Square, the house was divided into two handsome residences, after standing above forty years ; the premises comprising, with gardens, a considerable portion of the east side of the site of the Square.

Baltimore House acquired a celebrity, or rather notoriety, disgraceful to its titled owner, by a criminal occurrence there, which excited a considerable sensation at the time. Frederick, seventh Baron of Baltimore, who succeeded his father in his title and estates in 1751, was a man of dissolute character: he married

the daughter of the Duke of Bridgewater, but his
licentiousness and infidelity rendered the nuptial life a
scene of unhappiness. He is known to have kept
agents in various parts of the metropolis for the infamous purpose of providing him fresh victims to his
passion. Hearing through one of his agents, a Mrs.
Harvey, in November 1767, that a young Quaker
milliner, named Sarah Woodcock, keeping shop on
Tower Hill, was remarkably beautiful, Lord Baltimore
went there several times, under pretence of purchasing
lace ruffles, and other articles. At length, she was decoyed into his Lordship's carriage by one Isaacs, a
Jew, who had become an accomplice of Mrs. Harvey
in the vile conspiracy. Under pretence of taking
Woodcock to a lady, who would give her orders for
millinery, the carriage was driven rapidly from Tower
Hill, with the glasses up; and it being dark, Woodcock
was unaware of its being other than a hackney-coach,
until at length they arrived in the court-yard of Baltimore House. Upon alighting, she was ushered by
Mrs. Harvey through a splendid suite of rooms, when
Lord Baltimore made his appearance, and Woodcock
became greatly alarmed, as she recollected his calling
upon her at Tower Hill. Under pretext of his being
steward to the lady she was to be introduced to, the
poor milliner became more composed. Lord Baltimore
withdrew, and soon returned with a Mrs. Griffinburgh,
whom he represented as the lady about to order the
goods—this being another of the creatures of Lord
Baltimore ; she continued, under various pretences, to
detain Woodcock until a late hour, when she became
importunate to depart.

Keeping up the semblance of a steward, Lord Balti-

more took her over several apartments, and afterwards
insisted upon her staying to supper : after which, being
left alone with her, he made advances which she
indignantly repelled.   Doctor Griffinburgh, husband
of the woman of that name, with Mrs. Harvey, came
to assist his lordship in his vile arts; but Woodcock still
refused to consent, forced her way to the door, and
insisted upon going home. At a late hour, she was
conducted to a bed-room, where, with agonising distress, she continued walking about till morning,
lamenting her unhappy situation; the two women,
Griffinburgh and Harvey, being in bed in the same
room.   In the morning, Woodcock was conducted to
breakfast, but refused to eat, and demanded her liberty,
and wept incessantly; Lord Baltimore meanwhile vowing his excessive love, and urging it as an excuse for
detaining her; and whenever she went towards the
windows of the house, to make her distress evident to
passengers in the streets, the women forced her away.
Lord Baltimore persevered for some hours, by turns
soothing and threatening her: at length, under pretence
of taking her to her father, if she would dry her eyes,
and put on clean linen, (supplied to her by Mrs. Griffinburgh,) she was hurried into a coach, and conveyed to
Woodcote Park, Lord Baltimore's family seat, at
Epsom; the Doctor and the two infamous women
accompanying Woodcock, who, at Woodcote, yielded
to his lordship's wicked arts.

Meanwhile, Woodcock's friends had obtained a clue
to her detention at Woodcote, and, after a fortnight's
painful anxiety at her absence, a writ of Habeas Cor-
pus was obtained, and she was restored to her liberty.
Lord Baltimore and his two female accomplices were

tried at the assizes at Kingston-upon-Thames, 25th March 1768: after a long investigation of evidence, and much deliberation by the jury, Lord Baltimore was acquitted, the case appearing to have been one of seduction rather than violation, and the jury considering Woodcock not altogether guiltless; and there was an informality in her deposition, arising evidently from the agitation of her mind.

After the trial, Lord Baltimore, who was a man of some literary attainments, disposed of his property, and quitted the kingdom. He died at Naples, in September 1771; and his remains being brought to England, lay in state in one of the large rooms of Exeter Change, and were then buried in Epsom church, with much funeral pomp; the *cortège* extending from the church to the eastern extremity of Epsom.

After Lord Baltimore's tenancy had expired, this house was inhabited by the Duchess of Bolton; Wedderburne, Lord Chancellor Loughborough; Sir John Nicholl, Sir Vicary Gibbs, and by Sir Charles Flower, Bart. The mansion did not altogether lose its notoriety until its division into two residences: the unity of the house is still preserved in the pitch of the slated roof; one of the residences is named Bolton House, and the corner of Guildford-street, Bolton Gardens.

J. T. Smith tells us that he remembered, in 1777, going with his father and his pupils on a sketching party to what was subsequently called Pancras Old Church; and that Whitefield's Chapel in Tottenham Court Road, Montague House, Bedford House, and Baltimore House, were then uninterruptedly seen from the churchyard, which was at that time so rural, that it was only inclosed by a low and very old hand-railing, in some parts entirely covered with docks and nettles. Smith remembered also that the houses on the north side of Ormond Street, commanded views of Islington, Highgate, and Hampstead; including in the middle distance Copenhagen House, Mother Redcap's, the Adam and Eve, the Farthing Pie-house, the Queen's Head and Artichoke, and the Jew's-harp House.

THE MINTERS OF SOUTHWARK.

A LARGE portion of the parish of St. George the Martyr is called the Mint, from a "mint of coinage" having been kept there by Henry VIII., upon the site of Suffolk Place, the magnificent seat of Charles Brandon, Duke of Suffolk, nearly opposite the parish church. Part of the mansion was pulled down in 1557, and on the site were built many small cottages, to the increasing of the beggars in the Borough. Long before the close of the seventeenth century, the district called the Mint had become a harbour for lawless persons, who claimed there the privilege of exemption from all legal process, civil or criminal. It consisted of several streets and alleys; the chief entrance being from opposite St. George's Church by Mint Street, which had, to our time, a lofty wooden gate: there were other entrances, each with a gate; like Whitefriars, it had its Lombard Street. It thus became early an asylum for debtors, coiners, and vagabonds; and of "the traitors, felons, fugitives, outlaws, condemned persons, convict persons, felons, defamed, those put in exigent of outlawry, felons of themselves, and such as refused the law of the land," who had, from the time of Edward VI., herded in St. George's parish. The Mint at length became such a pest that its *privileges* were abolished by law; but it was not effectually suppressed until the reign of George I., one of whose statutes relieved all those debtors under 50*l.*, who had taken sanctuary in the Mint from their creditors. The Act of 1695–6 had proved inefficient for the suppression of the nuisance, though it inflicted a penalty of 500*l.* on anyone who should rescue a prisoner, and made the concealment of the rescuer a transportable offence. In 1705, a fraudulent bankrupt fled here from his creditors, when the Mint-men resisted a large body of constables, and a desperate conflict ensued at the gate before the rogue was taken. A child had been murdered within these precincts, when the coroner's officer was seized by the Mint-men, thrown into " the Black Ditch" of liquid mud; and, though rescued by constables, he was not suffered to depart until he had taken an oath on a brick, in their cant terms, never to come into that place again.

At the clearance of the place, in 1723, the exodus was a strange scene: " Some thousands of the Minters went out of the land of bondage, alias the Mint, to be cleared at the quarter sessions of Guildford, according to the late Act of Parliament. The road was covered with them, insomuch that they looked like one of the Jewish tribes going out of Egypt; the cavalcade consisting of caravans, carts, and wagons, besides numbers on horses, asses, and on foot. The drawer of the two fighting cocks was seen to lead an ass loaded with geneva, to support the spirits of the ladies upon

the journey. 'Tis said that several heathen bailiffs lay
in ambuscade in ditches on the road, to surprise some of
them, if possible, on their march, if they should strag-
gle from the main body; but they proceeded with so
much order and discipline that they did not lose a man
upon this expedition."

The Mint was noted as the retreat of poor poets.
When it was a privileged place, "poor Nahum Tate"
was forced to seek shelter here from extreme poverty,
where he died in 1716: he had been ejected from the
laureateship at the accession of George I. to make way
for Rowe.   Pope does not spare the needy poets:

> No place is sacred, not the church is free,
> E'en Sunday shines no Sabbath day to me:
> Then from the Mint walks forth the man of rhyme,
> Happy to catch me just at dinner-time.

Johnson has truly said: " The great topic of his
(Pope's) ridicule is poverty; the crimes with which he
reproaches his antagonists are their debts, their habi-
tation in the Mint, and their want of a dinner."

In Gay's *Beggar's Opera*, one of the characters,
Trapes, says: " The Act for destroying the Mint was
a severe cut upon our business. 'Till then, if a cus-
tomer stept out of the way, we knew where to have
her." Mat o' the Mint is one of Macheath's gang. This
was also one of the haunts of Jack Sheppard; and
Jonathan Wild kept his horses at the Duke's Head,
in Redcross Street, within the precincts of the Mint.
Marriages were performed here, as in the Fleet, the
Savoy, and in May Fair.   In 1715, an Irishman,
named Briand, was fined 2,000l. for marrying an or-
phan, about thirteen years of age, whom he decoyed
into the Mint.   The following curious certificate was

produced at his trial: "Feb. 16, 1715. These are therefore to whom it may concern, that Isaac Briand and
Watson Anne Astone were joined together in the holy
state of matrimony (*Nemine contradicente*) the day and
year above written, according to the rites and ceremonies of the Church of Great Britain.—Witness my
hand, Jos. Smith, Cler."

The Mint of the present century was mostly noted
for its brokers' shops, and its " lodgings for travellers ;"
and in one of the wretched tenements of its indigent
and profligate population occurred the first case of
Asiatic cholera, in 1832. Few of the old houses remain.

STEALING A DEAD BODY.

THE burial-ground of St. George the Martyr, Queen
Square, Bloomsbury, is a long and narrow slip of
ground behind the Foundling Hospital, to which a remarkable circumstance is attached. On October 9,
1777, the grave-digger and others were detected in the
act of stealing a corpse from this ground for dissection,
the only instance of this kind then ever known, and
which, in consequence, involved a difficulty in the de-
cision of the law, from its being the first indictment on
record for such a crime.

John Holmes, the grave-digger of St. George's;
Robert Williams, his assistant ; and Esther Donaldson,
were tried under an indictment for a misdemeanour,
before Sir John Hawkins, chairman, at Guildhall,
Westminster, 6th December 1777, for stealing the
dead body of one Mrs. Jane Sainsbury, who died in the

October preceding, and was interred in the burial-place of the said parish. Mr. Howarth, counsel for the prosecution, stated the case to the jury. Mr. Keys, counsel for the prisoners, objected to the indictment, and contended that if the offence was not felony, it was nothing, for it could not be a misdemeanour, therefore not cognizable by that court, or contrary to any law whatever. Sir J. Hawkins inquired of Mr. Howarth the reason for not indicting for a felony, as thereby the court was armed with power to punish as severely as such acts deserved. Mr. Howarth explained this, by saying, that to constitute a felony there must be a felonious act of taking away property; and if the shroud, or any other thing, such as the pillow, &c., or any part of it, had been stolen, it would have been a felony. In this case, he said, nothing of that kind had been done, the body only having been stolen; and though, in their hurry of conveying away the deceased, the thieves had torn off the shroud, and left pieces in the churchyard, yet there being no intention of taking them away, it was no felony, and, therefore, only a misdemeanour. Mr. Keys again insisted it was no misdemeanour; but Sir John Hawkins very ably refuted him, reminding him that if his objection was good, it was premature, for it would come as a motion for an arrest of judgment. The trial then went on.

Mr. Eustanston, who lived near the Foundling Hospital, deposed, that going by that hospital, about eight o'clock in the evening, with some other gentlemen, they met the prisoner, Williams, with a sack on his back, and another person walking with him. Having some suspicion of a robbery, he stopped Williams, and asked him what he had got there? to which he replied, " I don't know ;" but that pulling the sack forcibly from his back, he begged to be let go, and said he was " a poor man just come from harvest." Mr. Eustanston then untied the sack, and, to his astonishment, found the deceased body of a woman, her heels tied up tight behind her, her hands tied together behind, and cords round her neck, forcibly bending her head almost between her legs. They were so horrified as to be prevented securing the companion of Williams, but they took him to the Round House, where he was well known to be the assistant grave-digger to Holmes, and went by the name of Bobby. Next day, Holmes being applied to as he was digging in the burial-ground, denied all knowledge of Bobby, or Williams, or any such man. Neither could he recollect if any body had been buried within the last few days, or if there had, he could not tell where. However, by the appearance of the mould, they insisted on his running into the ground his long iron crow, and then they discovered a coffin, only six inches under ground, out of which the body had been taken. This coffin had been buried a few days before, very deep; the ground was further examined, and another coffin was discovered, out of which the body of Mrs. Jane Sainsbury had been stolen; and whilst this search was taking place, Holmes was detected hiding in his pockets several small pieces of shroud, which lay around the grave.

Mr. Sainsbury was under the painful necessity of appearing in court, when he identified the body found on Williams as that of his deceased wife. Williams was proved to have been constantly employed by Holmes, in whose house were found several sacks marked H. Ellis—the mark upon the sack in which

Mrs. Sainsbury was tied. The jury found the two men guilty, but acquitted Esther Donaldson. They were sentenced to six months' imprisonment, and each to be severely whipped twice in the last week of their confinement, from Kingsgate Street to Dyott Street, St. Giles's—full half a mile; but the whipping was afterwards remitted.

In St. George's burial-ground the first person interred was Robert Nelson, author of *Fasts and Festivals:* this was done to reconcile others to the place who had taken a violent prejudice to it. Dr. Campbell, author of the *Lives of the Admirals*, and Jonathan Richardson, the painter, and his wife, are buried here: also, Nancy Dawson, the famous hornpipe dancer, who died at Hampstead, May 27th, 1767: the tombstone to her memory in St. George's ground simply states: "Here lies Nancy Dawson."

THE EXECUTION OF DR. DODD.

"THE unfortunate Dr. Dodd," as he is called, was gifted with showy oratorical power; he shone in London, and when a young man, as a popular preacher. George III. made him his chaplain in ordinary; but, in 1774, he was indiscreet enough to write an anonymous letter to the wife of the Chancellor Bathurst, offering 2,000*l.* for the nomination to the rectory of St. George's, Hanover Square. On the writer being discovered, George III. struck him off the list of royal chaplains. In 1776, a chapel was built for Dodd, in Charlotte Street, Buckingham Gate; "great success attended the undertaking," writes the Doctor; "it pleased and it elated me."

Horace Walpole says: " Dodd was, undoubtedly,
a bad man, who employed religion to promote his
ambition; humanity to establish a character; and any
means to gratify his passions and vanity, and extricate
himself out of their distressing consequences. Having
all the qualities of an ambitious man, but judgment,
he gladly stooped to rise ; and married a kept mistress
of Lord Sandwich, and encouraged her love of drinking that he might be at liberty in the evenings to
indulge himself in other amours. The Earl of Chesterfield, ignorant of or indifferent to his character, committed his heir to his charge, and was exceedingly
partial to him ; nor was his pupil's attachment alienated
by the Doctor's attempt to make a simoniacal purchase of a crown-living from the Lord Chancellor.
Even his miscarriage in that overture he had in great
measure surmounted by varied activity, and by ostensible virtues in promoting all charitable institutions, in
particular that excellent one for discharging prisoners
for debt, of which he is said to have been the founder.
Still were his pleasures indecently blended with his
affected devotion ; and in the intervals of his mission,
he indulged in the fopperies and extravagance of a
young Maccaroni, both at Paris and the fashionable
watering-places in his own country. The contributions
of pious matrons did not, could not, keep pace with
the expense of his gallantries." In this state of things,
Dodd committed his last fatal act. Importuned by
creditors, he forged a draft on his own pupil, Lord
Chesterfield, for 4,200*l.*   He was instantly detected
and seized, not having had the discretion to secure
himself by flight ; nor did the Earl discover that tender
sensibility so natural and so becoming a young man.

From that moment the Doctor's fate was a scene of protracted horrors, and could but excite commiseration in every feeling breast. Yet he seemed to deserve it, as he at once abandoned himself to his confusion, shame, and terror, and had at least the merit of acting no parade of fortitude. He swooned at his trial, avowed his guilt, confessed his fondness for life, and deprecated his fate with agonies of grief. Heroism under such a character had been impudence. As the Earl was not injured, the case happened to be mitigated. An informality in the trial raised the prisoner's hopes ; and as the case was thought of weight enough to be laid before the judges, these hopes were increased ; but his sufferings were only protracted, for the judges gave, after some time, an opinion against him. Thus he endured a second condemnation.

" The malevolence of men and their good nature displayed themselves in their different characters against Dodd. His character appeared so bad to Dr. Newton, Bishop of Bristol, that he said, ' I am sorry for Dr. Dodd.' Being asked why, he replied, ' Because he is to be hanged for the least crime he ever committed.' Every unfavourable anecdote of his life was published, and one in particular that made deep impression. The young lord, his pupil, had seduced a girl, and when tired of her, had not forgotten the sacrifice she had made. He sent by Dr. Dodd her dismission and 1,000*l.* The messenger had retained 900*l.* for his trouble. On the other hand, the fallen apostle did not lose the hearts of his devotees. All his good deeds were set forth in the fairest light, and his labours in behalf of prisoners were justly stated in balance against a fraud that had proved innoxious. Warm and earnest sup-

plications for mercy were addressed to the throne in
every daily paper, and even some very able pleas were
printed in his favour. The Methodists took up his
cause with earnest zeal; Toplady, a leader of the sect,
went so far as to pray for him. Such application
raised the criminal to the dignity of a confessor in the
eyes of the people—but an inexorable judge had already
pronounced his doom. Lord Mansfield, who never
felt pity, and never relented unless terrified, had in-
directly declared for execution of the sentence even
before the judges had given their opinion. An incident
that seemed favourable weighed down the vigorous
scale. The Common Council of London had presented a petition of mercy to the King. Lord Mansfield urged rigour, and even the Chancellor seconded
it; though, as Dr. Dodd had offended him, it would
have been more decent to take no part, if not a lenient
one. The case of the Perreaus was cited, and in
one newspaper it was barbarously said that to pardon Dr. Dodd would be pronouncing that the Perreaus had been murdered. Still, the Methodists did
not despair, nor were remiss. They prevailed on
Earl Percy to present a new petition for mercy, which,
it was said, no fewer than 23,000 persons had sub-
scribed; and such enthusiasm had been propagated on
behalf of the wretched divine, that on the eve of his
death, a female Methodist stopped the King in his
chair and poured out volleys of execrations on his
inexorability. A cry was raised for Dodd's respite,
for the credit of the clergy; but it was answered that, if
the honour of the clergy was tarnished, it was by Dodd's
crime and not by his punishment. He appealed to Dr.
Johnson for his intercession, and Johnson compassion-

ately drew up a petition of Dr. Dodd to the King, and
of Mrs. Dodd to the Queen. He wrote *The Convict's
Address to his Unhappy Brethren*, a sermon which Dr.
Dodd delivered in the chapel of Newgate; also, Dr.
Dodd's *Last Solemn Declaration*, and other documents
and letters to people in power; all without effect. The
King was inclined to mercy; but the law was allowed
to take its course; and on the 27th of June 1777,
Dodd was conveyed, along with another malefactor, in
an open cart, from Newgate to Tyburn, and there
hanged, in the presence of an immense crowd. In apprehension of an attempt to rescue the criminal, 20,000
men were ordered to be reviewed in Hyde Park during
the execution, which, however, though attended by an
unequalled concourse of people, passed with the utmost
tranquillity."

A friend of George Selwyn (who delighted in wit-
nessing executions) has thus described the exit:—
" Upon the whole, the piece was not very full of
events. The Doctor, to all appearances, was rendered
perfectly stupid from despair. His hat was flapped all
round, and pulled over his eyes, which were never
directed to any object around, nor ever raised, except
now and then lifted up in the course of his prayers.
He came in a coach, and a very heavy shower of rain
fell just upon his entering the cart, and another just at
his putting on his nightcap. During the shower, an
umbrella was held over his head, which Gilly Williams,
who was present, observed was quite unnecessary, as
the Doctor was going to a place where he might be dried.

.   .   .   .   .   .

" The executioner took both the Doctor's hat and
wig off at the same time. Why he put on his wig

again, I do not know, but he did; and the Doctor took
off his wig a second time, and tied on a nightcap, which
did not fit him; but whether he stretched that, or took
another, I could not perceive. He then put on his
nightcap himself, and upon his taking it, he certainly
had a smile on his countenance, and very soon afterwards, there was an end of all his hopes and fears on
this side the grave. He never moved from the place
he first took in the cart; seemed absorbed in despair,
and utterly dejected; without any other signs of animation, but in praying. I stayed until he was cut
down, and put into the hearse." The body was hurried
to the house of Davies, an undertaker, in Goodge Street,
Tottenham Court Road, where it was placed in a hot
bath, and every exertion made to restore life—but in
vain."

Walpole tells us that the expected commiseration at
the execution was much drawn aside by the spectacle
of an aged father, who accompanied his son, one Harris,
who was executed for a robbery, at the same time.
The streaming tears, grey hairs, agony, and, at last,
the appearance of a deadly swoon in the poor old
man, who supported his son in his lap, deepened the
tragedy, but rendered Dr. Dodd's share in it less
affecting.

It may be added that, in 1772, Dr. Dodd wrote a
pamphlet entitled, *The Frequency of Capital Punish-
ments inconsistent with Justice, Sound Policy, and Religion*; and that two days before he forged the bond
on Lord Chesterfield, he preached for his last time, and
his text was, " Among these nations thou shalt find no
ease, neither shall the sole of thy foot have rest; but
the Lord shall give them a trembling heart and failing

of eyes, and sorrow of mind; and thy life shall hang in doubt before thee, and thou shalt fear day and night, and shalt have no assurance of thy life." (Dr. Doran: Horace Walpole's *Last Journals*.) How fearfully do these coincidences with Dr. Dodd's fate give evidence of the perturbed state of his mind.

Among the good service which he did to society, was his being an early promoter of the Magdalen Hospital, for whose benefit he preached a sermon in 1759; and again, in 1760, before Prince Edward, Duke of York: both sermons are eloquent compositions, were printed, and large editions were sold. Walpole describes his going to the first Magdalen House, beyond Goodman's Fields, with a party, in four coaches, with Prince Edward, to hear the sermon: he sketches the sisterhood, about 130, all in greyish-brown stuffs, broad handkerchiefs, and flat straw hats with a blue ribbon, pulled quite over their faces. "The chapel was dressed with orange and myrtle, and there wanted nothing but a little incense to drive away the devil or to invite him." After prayers, Dr. Dodd preached, in the French style, and very eloquently and touchingly. "He apostrophised the lost sheep, who sobbed and cried from their souls; so did my Lady Hertford and Fanny Pelham, till, I believe, the City dames took them both for Jane Shores." Dodd then addressed his Royal Highness, whom he called Most Illustrious Prince, beseeching his protection. After the service, the Governor kissed the Prince's hand, and then tea was served by the matron in the *parloir*. Thence the company went to the refectory, where the Magdalens, without their hats, were at tables, ready for supper. "I was struck and pleased," says Walpole, "with the modesty of two of

them, who swooned away with the confusion of being
stared at."

The " Story of the Unfortunate Dr. Dodd," related
by Mr. Percy Fitzgerald, and published in the spring of
1865, adds a bright relief in the person of the Rev.
Weedon Butler, who was associated with Dodd, and
was his amanuensis, and his assistant in his literary
work, and his church duty; but he did not participate
in any of Dodd's dissipation, or was he cognisant of his
villany.   His admiration for the popular author and
fashionable preacher must have been very great, even
to the last.   Weedon Butler was at Dodd's side during
his execution; and on the night after, he carried the
body to Cowley, there had it buried, and inscribed the
name over it; and often afterwards visited the grave.

THE STORY OF HACKMAN AND MISS REAY.

THIS romantic tale, Horace Walpole refers to as the
strangest story he had ever heard; " and which," adds
he, " I cannot yet believe, though it is certainly
true."   The gay Earl of Sandwich, First Lord of the
Admiralty during Lord North's administration, in
passing through Covent Garden, espied behind the
counter of a milliner's shop—No. 4, at the West-end
corner of Tavistock Court, on the South side of Covent
Garden Market—a beautiful girl, named Reay: one account states, his Lordship was purchasing some neck-
cloths.   She was the daughter of a labourer at Elstree;
others state that her father was a staymaker, in Holy-
well Street, Strand; she had been apprenticed to a
mantua-maker in Clerkenwell Close, with whom she

served her time out. A year or two after this, she was first seen by Lord Sandwich, who had her removed from her situation, had her education completed, rendered her a proficient in his favourite arts of music and singing, and then she became his Lordship's mistress. He was old enough to be her father.

Lord Sandwich took Miss Reay to his seat—Hinchinbrook, in Huntingdonshire, and there introduced her to his family circle, to the distress of Lady Sandwich. Here Miss Reay soon distinguished herself in the oratorios and other musical performances, at Hinchinbrook: her behaviour is described as very circumspect; she even captivated a bishop's lady, who was really hurt to sit directly opposite to her, and mark her discreet conduct, and yet to find it improper to notice her; " she was so assiduous to please, was so very excellent, yet so assuming," that the Bishop's lady was quite charmed with her. At this time Captain Hackman, 68th Foot, was recruiting at Huntingdon: he appeared at a ball, was invited to the oratorios at Hinchinbrook, and was much caressed there. The Captain was young and handsome: he fell in love with Miss Reay, and she is understood not to have been insensible to his passion. Hackman proposed marriage; but she told him she did not choose to carry a knapsack. Another account states that Miss Reay was desirous of marriage, but feared to hurt the feelings of the man who had educated her, in which sentiment Hackman, with all his passion, is said to have partaken. Walpole states that he was brother to a respectable tradesman in Cheapside; that he was articled to a merchant at Gosport, but, at nineteen, entered the army; during his acquaintance with Miss Reay, he exchanged the Army for the Church, and was presented to the living of Wyverton, in Norfolk. Meanwhile, Miss Reay had complained to Mr. Cradock, a friend of Lord Sandwich, of being alarmed by ballads, that had been sung, or cries that had been made, directly under the windows of the Admiralty, that looked into St. James's Park; adding, such was the fury of the mob, that she did not think either herself or Lord Sandwich was safe whenever they went out; the lady also represented to Mr. Cradock that her situation was precarious, that no settlement had been made upon her, that she was anxious to relieve Lord Sandwich of expense; that she had a good chance of success at the Italian Opera as a singer, and that 3,000*l.* and a free benefit had been offered to her.

A sudden stop was now put to Hackman's final expectations, and he became desperate; Lord Sandwich has placed Miss Reay under the charge of a duenna; Hackman grew more jealous; he was induced to believe that Miss Reay had no longer a regard for him, and he resolved to put himself to death. In this resolution, a sudden impulse of frenzy included the unfortunate object of his passion.

On the evening of April 7, 1779, Miss Reay went, with her female attendant, to Covent Garden Theatre, to see *Love in a Village.* She had declined to inform Hackman how she was engaged that evening: he appears to have suspected her intentions, watched her, and saw her carriage pass by the Cannon Coffee House (Cockspur Street, Charing Cross), where he had posted himself. Hackman followed. The ladies sat in a front box, and three gentlemen, all connected with the Admiralty, occasionally paid their compliments to them;

Mr. Hackman was sometimes in the lobby, sometimes in an upper side box, and more than once at the Bedford Coffee House to take brandy-and-water, but still seemed unable to gain any information. The dreadful consummation was, that at the door of the theatre, directly opposite the Bedford Coffee House, Hackman suddenly rushed out, and as a gentleman was handing Miss Reay into the carriage, with a pistol he first destroyed this most unfortunate victim.

' Another report states the catastrophe thus: " Miss Reay was coming out of Covent Garden Theatre, in order to take her coach, accompanied by two friends, a gentleman and a lady, between whom she walked in the piazza. Mr. Hackman stepped up to her without the smallest previous menace or address, put a pistol to her head, and shot her instantly dead. He then fired another at himself, which, however, did not prove equally effectual. The ball grazed upon the upper part of the head, but did not penetrate sufficiently to produce any fatal effect; he fell, however, and so firmly was he bent on the entire completion of the destruction he had meditated, that he was found beating his head with the utmost violence with the butt-end of the pistol, by Mr. Mahon, apothecary, of Covent Garden, who wrenched the pistol from his hand. He was carried to the Shakspeare, where his wound was dressed. In his pocket were found two letters; the one a copy of a letter which he had written to Miss Reay. When he had recovered his faculties, he inquired with great anxiety concerning Miss Reay; and being told she was dead, he desired her poor remains might not be exposed to the observation of the curious multitude. About five o'clock in the morning, Sir John

Fielding came to the Shakspeare, and not finding Hackman's wounds of a dangerous nature, ordered him to Tothill Fields Bridewell. The body of Miss Reay was carried into the Shakspeare Tavern for the inspection of the coroner."

Walpole details the assassination as follows: " Miss Reay, it seems, has been out of order, and abroad but twice all the winter. She went to the play on Wednesday night for the second time with Galli the singer. During the play, the desperate lover was at the Bedford Coffee House, and behaved with great calmness, and drank a glass of capillaire. Towards the conclusion he sallied into the piazza, waiting till he saw his victim handed by Mr. Macnamara (an Irish Templar, with whom Miss R. had been seen to coquet during the performance in the theatre). He (Hackman) came behind her, pulled her by the gown, and, on her turning round, clapped the pistol to her forehead, and shot her through the head. With another pistol he then attempted to shoot himself, but the ball only grazing his brow, he tried to dash out his brains with the pistol, and is more wounded by those blows than by the ball.

" Lord Sandwich was at home, expecting her to supper, at half an hour after ten. On her not returning an hour later, he said something must have happened: however, being tired, he went to bed half an hour after eleven, and was scarce in bed before one of his servants came in, and said Miss Reay was shot. He stared, and could not comprehend what the fellow meant; nay, lay still, which is full as odd a part of the story as any. At twelve came a letter from the surgeon to confirm the account. Now, is not the story full as strange as ever it was? Miss Reay has six children; the eldest son is 15, and she was at least three times as much."

Among the inquirers at the Admiralty, next morning, was Mr. Cradock, who described the scene of horror and distress, as told him by old James, the black. Lord Sandwich for a while stood, as it were, petrified, till, suddenly seizing a candle, he ran upstairs, and threw himself on the bed; and in an agony exclaimed, " Leave me for a while to myself—I could have borne anything but this !" [Walpole states that his Lordship was already in bed.]   Mr. Cradock doubted whether Lord Sandwich was aware there was any connexion between Mr. Hackman and Miss Reay.   She was buried in the church at Elstree, " where," says Leigh Hunt, very prettily, " she had been a lowly and happy child, running about with her blooming face, and little thinking what trouble it was to cost her." The Hertford-shire village, some five and forty years after, was brought into notice, in connexion with the murder of Weare, the gambler, whose body was thrown into the pond at Elstree.

Lord Sandwich retired for a few days to Richmond. On his return to the Admiralty, where the portrait of Miss Reay still hung over a chimney-piece, Mr. Cra-dock found his Lordship in ill health: he rarely dined out anywhere, and any reference to or reminder of Miss Reay greatly embarrassed him. He survived her twelve years.   She had borne him nine children, five of whom were then alive.   One of these attained to distinction,—namely, Mr. Basil Montague, the eminent lawyer and man of letters, who died in 1851, in his eighty-second year.

Hackman was tried at the Old Bailey for the murder. He confessed at the Bar that he had intended to kill himself, and protested that but for a momentary frenzy he should not have destroyed her, "who was more dear to him than life." He was, however, furnished with *two pistols*; which told against him on that point. Boswell, the biographer of Dr. Johnson, was at the trial, and tells us that the Doctor was much interested by the account of what passed, and particularly with Hackman's prayer for mercy of heaven. He said in a solemn, fervent tone, " I hope he *shall* find mercy." In talking of Hackman, Johnson argued as Judge Blackstone had done, that his being furnished with two pistols was a proof that he meant to shoot two persons. Mr. Beauclerk said, " No ; for that every wise man who intended to shoot himself, took two pistols, that he might be sure of doing it at once. Lord ——'s cook shot himself with one pistol, and lived ten days in great agony. Mr. ——, who loved buttered muffins, but durst not eat them because they disagreed with his stomach, resolved to shoot himself, and then he ate three buttered muffins for breakfast before shooting himself, knowing that he should not be troubled with indigestion; *he* had two charged pistols ; one was found lying charged upon the table by him, after he had shot himself with the other." " Well (said Johnson, with an air of triumph), you see here one pistol was sufficient." Beauclerk replied smartly, " Because it happened to kill him." It is impossible to settle this point.

Boswell addressed a long letter to the *St. James's Chronicle* upon this painful subject. He commences by observing: " I am just come from attending the Trial and Condemnation of the unfortunate Mr. Hackman, who shot Miss Reay, and I must own that I felt an unusual Depression of Spirits, joined with that Pause

which so solemn a Warning of the dreadful effects that
the passion of Love may produce, must give all of us
who have lively Sensations and Warm Tempers." He
goes on in a very apologetic strain:—

"As his (Mr. Hackman's) manners were uncommonly
amiable, his mind and heart seem to have been uncommonly Pure and Virtuous. It may seem strange at
first, but I can very well suppose that, had he been
less virtuous, he would not now have been so criminal.
His case is one of the most remarkable that has ever
occurred in the History of Human Nature; but it is
by no means unnatural. *The principle of it is very
philosophically explained and illustrated in the ' Hypo-
condriack,' a periodical paper peculiarly adapted to the
people of England, and which now comes out monthly in
the London Magazine.*"

He then quotes a passage from the paper, which is
too long to extract. The paper so praised Boswell
himself was the author of.

Walpole says: "On his trial, Hackman behaved
very unlike a madman, and wished not to live. He is
to suffer on Monday, and I shall rejoice when it is
over; for it is shocking to reflect that there is a human
being at this moment in so deplorable a situation."

Hackman was executed on April 19, 1779: he was
taken to Tyburn in a mourning-coach, containing besides the prisoner, a sheriff's officer, and James Boswell, who, like Selwyn, was fond of seeing executions.
The latter was not a spectator of Hackman's end; but
his friend, the Earl of Carlisle, attended the execution,
to give some account of Hackman's behaviour: "the
poor man behaved with great fortitude; no appearances of fear were to be perceived, but very evident

signs of contrition and repentance. He was long at his prayers; and when he flung down his handkerchief for the sign for the cart to move on, Jack Ketch, instead of instantly whipping on the horse, jumped on the other side of him to snatch up the handkerchief, lest he should lose his rights. He then returned to the head of the cart, and jehu'd him out of the world."

In the *St. James's Chronicle* of April 20, 1779, is the following fuller account of the execution :—" A little after five yesterday morning, the Rev. Mr. Hackman got up, dressed himself, and was at private meditation till near seven, when Mr. Boswell and two other gentlemen waited on him, and accompanied him to the chapel, when prayers were read by the Ordinary of Newgate, after which he received the Sacrament ; between eight and nine he came down from Chapel and was haltered. When the sheriff's officer took the cord from the bag to perform his duty, Mr. Hackman said, ' Oh! the sight of this shocks me more than the thought of its intended operation :' he then shed a few tears, and took leave of two gentlemen. He was then conducted to a mourning-coach, attended by Mr. Villette, the Ordinary; Mr. Boswell; and Mr. Davenport, the Sheriff's Officer—when the procession set out for Tyburn in the following manner, viz. Mr. Miller, City Marshal, on horseback, in mourning, a number of sheriff's officers on horseback, constables, &c., Mr. Sheriff Kitchen, with his Under-Sheriff, in his carriage ; the prisoner, with the afore-mentioned persons in the mourning-coach, officers, &c. ; the cart hung with black.

" On his arrival at Tyburn, Mr. Hackman got out of the coach, mounted the cart, and took an affectionate leave of Mr. Boswell and the Ordinary. When Mr.

Hackman got into the cart under the gallows, he immediately kneeled down with his face towards the horses, and prayed some time; he then rose and joined in prayer with Mr. Villette and Mr. Boswell about a quarter of an hour, when he desired to be permitted to have a few minutes to himself. The clergymen then took leave of him. His request being granted, he informed the executioner when he was prepared he would drop his handkerchief as a signal; accordingly, after praying about six or seven minutes to himself, he dropped his handkerchief, and the cart drew from under him."

A curious book arose out of this tragical story. In the following year was published an octavo, pretending to contain the correspondence of Hackman and Miss Reay. The work was entitled, *Love and Madness, or Story too True, in a Series of Letters between parties whose names would, perhaps, be mentioned, were they less known or less lamented.* London, 1780. The book ran through several editions. The author was Sir Herbert Croft, Bart. Walpole says of it: "I doubt whether the letters are genuine; and yet, if fictitious, they are executed well, and enter into his character; hers appear less natural, and yet the editors were certainly more likely to be in possession of hers than his. It is not probable that Lord Sandwich should have sent what he found in her apartments to the press. No account is pretended to be given of how they came to light." Walpole is frequently mentioned in a long letter by Hackman, pretending that Miss Reay desired him to give her a particular account of Chatterton; he gives a most ample one, but it is not probable that he went to Bristol, to collect the evidence.

•

ATTEMPTS TO ASSASSINATE GEORGE III.

Two desperate attempts were made upon the life of George III., in addition to attacks by the populace, and by individuals.

On the morning of August 2, 1786, as the King was stepping out of his post-chariot, at the garden entrance of St. James's Palace, a woman, who was waiting there, pushed forward, and presented a paper, which his Majesty received with great condescension. At that instant, she struck a concealed knife at the King's breast, which his Majesty happily avoided by bowing as he received the paper. As she was making a second thrust, one of the yeomen caught her arm, and, at the same instant, one of the King's footmen wrenched the knife out of the woman's hand. The King, with amazing temper and fortitude, exclaimed at the instant, " I have received no injury ; do not hurt the woman, the poor creature appears insane." This account is given by Mrs. Delany, in her *Letters*, who adds, "His Majesty was perfectly correct in his humane supposition. The woman underwent a long examination before the Privy Council, who finally declared that they were 'clearly and unanimously of opinion, that she was, and is, insane.' The instrument struck against the King's waistcoat, and made a cut, the breadth of the point, through the cloth. Had not the King shrunk in his side, the blow would have been fatal. Margaret Nicholson was committed to Bethlehem Hospital as a criminal lunatic, and was removed with the other inmates from the old hospital, in Moorfields, to the new hospital, in Lambeth, where she died May 14, 1828, in her ninety-ninth year, having been confined in Bethlehem forty-two years."

The second attempt of this diabolical nature was made by James Hadfield, in Drury Lane Theatre, on the night of May 15, 1800. In the morning, the King had been present at a field-day in Hyde Park, when, during the exercise, a shot wounded a young gentleman who stood near his Majesty. The event, which happened in the evening, added very much to the anxiety that had been felt from what had occurred in the morning. Their Majesties having announced their intention of going to Drury Lane Theatre, the house was extremely crowded. The Princesses first came into their box, as usual, the Queen next, and then the King. The audience had risen to receive and greet the royal family by clapping of hands, and other testimonies of affection, when at the instant his Majesty entered, and was advancing to bow to the audience, a man, who had placed himself about the middle of the second front row of the pit, raised his arm and fired a pistol, which was levelled towards the box. The flash and the report caused an instant alarm through the house: after an awful suspense of a few moments, the audience, perceiving his Majesty unhurt, a burst of most enthusiastic joy succeeded, with loud exclamations of " Seize the villain ! " " Shut the doors ! " The curtain was by this time drawn up, and the stage was crowded by persons of all descriptions from behind the scenes. A gentleman who stood next the assassin immediately collared him, and, after some struggling, he was conveyed over into the orchestra, where the pistol was wrenched from him, and delivered to one of the performers on the stage, who held it up to public view. There was a general cry of " Show the villain ! " who by this time was conveyed into the music-room, and given in charge of the Bow Street officers. The cry still continuing to seize him, Mr. Kelly, the stage manager, came forward to assure the audience that he was safe in custody. The band then struck up "God save the King," in which they were cordially joined, in full chorus, by every person in the theatre, the ladies waving their handkerchiefs and huzzaing. Never was loyalty more affectionately displayed. Mr. Sheridan, ever in attendance when the King visited the theatre, the moment the alarm was given, stepped into the green-room, and with that readiness of resource which rarely forsook him, in a few minutes wrote the following additional stanza, which was sung:—

> From every latent foe,
> From the assassin's blow,
>   Thy succour bring;
> O'er him thine arm extend,
> From every ill defend,
> Our Father, King, and Friend:
>   God save the King!

This extempore verse, inferred by the audience at once to have been written by Sheridan, was particularly gratifying to their feelings, and drew forth bursts of the loudest and most impassioned applause.

His Majesty, who at the first moment of alarm had displayed serenity and firmness, was now evidently affected by the passing scene, and seemed for a moment dejected. The Duke and Duchess of York, who were in their private box below, hastened to the King, who was eagerly surrounded by his family.

After the Duke of York had conversed for a few moments with the King, His Royal Highness and Mr. Sheridan went into the music-room, where the traitor was secured. Being interrogated, he said his name was

Hadfield, and it appears he formerly belonged to the 15th Light Dragoons, and served under the Duke of York in Flanders, where he was made prisoner. He was much scarred in the forehead, of low stature, and was dressed in a common surtout, with a soldier's jacket underneath.

In the music-room he appeared extremely collected, and confessed that he had put two slugs into the pistol. He said he was weary of life. Sir William Addington then came in, and at his request no further interrogations were made, and the man was conveyed to the prison in Coldbath Fields, where, in the course of the evening, the Prince of Wales, and the Dukes of York, Clarence, and Cumberland went to see him.

As soon as the event came to the knowledge of the ministers, a Privy Council was summoned, and at ten o'clock the traitor was carried to the Secretary of State's office, where the Cabinet ministers and principal law officers were assembled, and he continued under examination for some time.

Hadfield was brought to trial on June 26, following, and after an investigation of eight hours, a verdict of " Not Guilty " was returned. He was then remanded for safe custody to Newgate, and ultimately being proved of insane mind, he was committed to Bethlehem. Mr. N. P. Willis, when he visited the new hospital in 1840, conversed with Hadfield, whom he describes as quite sane, after having been in Bedlam for forty years. " He was a gallant dragoon, and his face," says Mr. Willis, " is seamed with scars, got in battle, before his crime. He employs himself with writing poetry on the death of his birds and cats, whom he has outlived in prison, and all the society he had in his long and weary imprisonment. He received us very courteously, and called our attention to his favourite canary, showed us his poetry, and all with a sad, mild, subdued resignation that quite moved me." Hadfield died in the year after Mr. Willis's visit.

TRIAL AND EXECUTION OF GOVERNOR WALL.

EARLY in the year 1802, great interest was excited by the trial of Lieut.-Colonel Wall, who was charged with murder committed twenty years before. It was while Governor and Commandant of Goree, an island on the coast of Africa, that Wall committed the offence which brought him to the scaffold—viz., the murder of one Benjamin Armstrong, by ordering him to receive eight hundred lashes on the 10th July 1782, of which he died in five days afterwards.

"Some time after the account of the murder of Armstrong reached the Board of Admiralty, a reward was offered for the apprehension of Wall, who had come to England, and he was taken. He, however, contrived to escape while in custody at Reading, and fled to the Continent: he sojourned there, in France and sometimes in Italy, under an assumed name, where he lived respectably, and was admitted into good society. He particularly associated with the officers of his own country who served in the French army, and was well known at the Scotch and Irish colleges in Paris. He now and then incautiously ventured into England and Scotland. While thus, at one time, in Scotland he made a high match. He wedded a scion of the great line of Kintail—viz., Frances, fifth daughter (by his wife, Lady

F 2

Mary Stewart, daughter of Alexander, sixth Earl of
Galloway) of Kenneth Mackenzie, Lord Fortrose,
M.P., and sister of Kenneth, last Earl of Seaforth.
Wall came finally to England in 1797. He was frequently advised by the friend who then procured him
a lodging to leave the country again, and questioned
as to his motive for remaining ; he never gave any
satisfactory answer, but appeared, even at the time
when he was so studiously concealing himself, to
have a distant intention of making a surrender, in
order to take his trial.

" His high-born wife showed him throughout his
troubles the greatest devotion : she was with him in
Upper Thornhaugh Street, Bedford Square, where he
lived under the name of Thompson when he was
apprehended. It is most probable that, had he not
written to the Secretary of State, saying he was ready
to surrender himself, the matter had been so long
forgotten, that he would never have been molested ;
but once he was in the hands of the law, the Government had but one obvious course, which was to bring
him to trial ; which was accordingly done, at the Old
Bailey, on the 20th January 1802. The main point
of Wall's defence was Armstrong's being concerned
in a mutiny, which, however, was not alluded to in a
letter from Wall to Government, on his return from
Goree. He was found guilty, and condemned to be
executed on the following morning. A respite was
sent, deferring his execution until the 25th. On the
24th he was further respited till the 28th. His wife
lived with him for the last fortnight prior to his conviction. During his confinement he never went out
of his room, except into the lobby to consult his counsel.

He lived well, and was sometimes in good spirits. He was easy in his manners and pleasant in conversation ; but during the night he frequently sat up in his bed and sung psalms, being overheard by his fellow-prisoners.

"From the time of the first respite until twelve o'clock on the night before his execution, Wall did not cease to entertain hopes of his safety. The interest made to save him was very great. The whole of the day previous occupied the great law-officers ; the Judges met at the Lord Chancellor's in the afternoon. The conference lasted upwards of three hours, but ended unfavourably to Wall. The prisoner had an affecting interview with his wife, the Hon. Mrs. Wall, the night before his death, from whom he was pain- fully separated about eleven o'clock.

"When the morning arrived, Wall ascended the scaffold accompanied by the Rev. Ordinary; there arose three successive shouts from an innumerable populace, the brutal but determined effusion of one common sentiment, for. the public indignation had never been so high since the hanging of Mrs. Brown- rigg, who had whipped her apprentices to death." *

John Thomas Smith, the well-known artist, who had made for the Duke of Roxburgh, the famous bibliomaniac, many drawings of malefactors, was com- missioned by the Duke to add to the collection a por- trait of Governor Wall. Smith had missed the trial at the Old Bailey; and the Duke failed to secure an order for the artist to see the criminal in the con- demned cell. However, Smith, by an introduction to Dr. Ford, the Ordinary of Newgate, succeeded in his

* *Celebrated Trials connected with the Army and Navy.* By Peter Burke, Serjeant-at-Law. 1865.

wishes. He found the Doctor in the club-room of a
public-house in Hatton Garden, pompously seated in
a superb masonic chair, under a crimson canopy,—
smoking his pipe! The introduction over, and its
object explained, the Doctor whispered (the room was
crowded with company), " Meet me at the felons' door
at the break of day." There Smith punctually applied: but, notwithstanding the order of the Doctor,
he found it necessary, to protect himself from an
increasing mob, to give half-a-crown to the turnkey,
who let him in. He was then introduced to a most
diabolical-looking little wretch, designated " the Yeoman of the Halter," Jack Ketch's head-man. Doctor
Ford soon arrived in his canonicals, with an enormous nosegay under his arm, and gravely uttered,
" Come this way, Mr. Smith," who thus describes the
scene he witnessed :—

" As we crossed the press-yard, a cock crew; and
the solitary clanking of a restless chain was dreadfully
horrible. The prisoner had not risen. Upon our entering a stone-cold room, a most sickly stench of green
twigs, with which an old, round-shouldered, goggle-
eyed man was endeavouring to kindle a fire, annoyed
me almost as much as the canaster fumigation of the
Doctor's Hatton Garden friends.

" The prisoner entered. He was death's counterfeit,
tall, shrivelled, and pale; and his soul shot so piercingly
through the port-holes of his head, that the first glance
of him nearly petrified me. I said in my heart, putting
my pencil in my pocket, ' God forbid that I should
disturb thy last moments.' His hands were clasped,
and he was truly penitent. After the yeoman had
requested him to stand up, ' he pinioned him,' as the

Newgate phrase is, and tied the cord with so little feeling, that the Governor, who had not given the wretch the accustomed fee, observed, ' You have tied me very tight;' upon which Dr. Ford ordered him to slacken the cord, which he did, but not without muttering. ' Thank you, sir,' said the Governor to the Doctor, ' it is of little moment.' He then observed to the attendant, who had brought in an immense shovelful of coals to throw on the fire, ' Ay, in one hour that will be a blazing fire; then, turning to the Doctor, questioned him : ' Do tell me, sir—I am informed I shall go down with great force; is it so ? ' After the construction and action of the machine had been explained, the Docter questioned the Governor as to what kind of men he had at Goree. ' Sir,' he answered, ' they sent me the very riffraff.' The poor soul then joined the Doctor in prayer; and never did I witness more contrition at a condemned sermon than he then evinced.

" The Sheriff arrived, attended by his officers, to receive the prisoner from the keeper. A new hat was then partly flattened on his head, for, owing to its being too small in the crown, it stood many inches too high behind. As we were crossing the press-yard, the dreadful execration of some of the fellows so shook his frame, that he observed, ' the clock had struck,' and, quickening his pace, he soon arrived at the room where the Sheriff was to give a receipt for his body, according to the usual custom. Owing, however, to some informality in the wording of this receipt, he was not brought out so soon as the multitude expected; and it was this delay which occasioned a partial exultation from those who betted as to a reprieve, and not from any pleasure in seeing him executed.

" After the execution, as soon as I was permitted to
leave the prison, I found the yeoman selling the rope
with which the malefactor had been suspended at *a
shilling an inch*; and no sooner had I entered Newgate
Street, than a lath of a fellow, past threescore years
and ten, and who had just arrived from the purlieus of
Black Boy Alley, exclaimed : ' Here's the identical rope
at sixpence an inch.' A group of tatterdemalions soon
collected round him, most vehemently expressing their
eagerness to possess bits of the cord. It was pretty
obvious, however, that the real business of this agent was
to induce the Epping buttermen to squeeze in their
canvas bags, which contained the *morning receipts*
in Newgate Market. A little further on, at the north-
east corner of Warwick Lane, stood Rosy Emma,
exuberant in talk and piping-hot from Pie Corner,
where she had taken in her morning dose of gin and
bitters. Her cheeks were purple, her nose of poppy-
red, or cochineal. Her eyes reminded me of Sheridan's remark on those of Dr. Arne, ' like two oysters
on an oval plate of stewed beet-root.' Emma, in her
tender blossom, I understand, assisted her mother in
selling rice-milk and furmety to the early frequenters
of Honey Lane Market : and in the days of her full
bloom, new-milk whey in White Conduit Fields, and
at the Elephant and Castle. Rosy Emma—for so she
was still called—was the reputed spouse of the Yeoman
of the Halter, and the cord she was selling as the identical noose, was for her own benefit :

> For honest ends, a most dishonest seeming.

Now, as fame and beauty ever carry influence, Emma's
sale was rapid. This money-trapping trick, steady

John, the waiter at the Chapter Coffee House, assured me, was invariably put in practice whenever superior persons or notorious culprits had been executed. Then to breakfast, but with little or no appetite. However, I made a whole-length portrait of the Governor, by recollection, which Dr. Buchan, the flying physician of the Chapter frequenters, and several of the Paternoster vendors of his *Domestic Medicine*, considered a likeness: at all events, it was admitted into the portfolio of the Duke of Roxburgh, with the following acknowledgment written on the back : ' Drawn by Memory.' " *

After hanging a full hour, Wall's body was cut down, put into a cart, and immediately conveyed to a building in Cowcross Street to be dissected. Wall was dressed in a mixed-coloured loose coat, with a black collar, swan-down waistcoat, blue pantaloons, and white silk stockings. He appeared a miserable and emaciated object, never having quitted the bed of his cell from the day of condemnation till the morning of his execution.

The body of the wretched Governor was not exposed to public view as usual in such cases. Mr. Belfour, Secretary to the Surgeons' Company, applied to Lord Kenyon, Lord Chief Justice of the Court of King's Bench, to know whether such exposure was necessary; and finding that the forms of dissection only were required, the body, after those forms had passed, was consigned to the relations of the unhappy man upon their paying fifty guineas to the Philanthropic Society. The remains were interred in the churchyard of St. Pancras-in-the-Fields.

* *A Book for a Rainy Day.* By J. T. Smith. Third Edition. 1861.

CASE OF ELIZA FENNING, THE SUSPECTED POISONER.

MANY are the cases in our criminal history of the extreme danger of convicting for capital offences on pre-
sumptive or circumstantial evidence alone; but in no
instance, within memory of the present generation, was
the public sympathy more intensely, and, as since
proved, more justly, excited than in the following case.
Elizabeth (Eliza) Fenning, cook in the family of Mr.
Olibar Turner, Law Stationer, of Chancery Lane, was
tried on April 11, 1815, at the Old Bailey, before the
Recorder, " that she, on the 21st day of March, felo-
niously and unlawfully did administer to, and cause to
be administered to, Olibar Turner, Robert Gregson
Turner, and Charlotte Turner his wife, certain deadly
poison (to wit, arsenick), with intent the said persons
to kill and murder." There were other counts, varying
the offence.   Mr. Gurney conducted the prosecution.
The poison, it was stated, had been mixed in some
yeast dumplings, of which the family, as also Eliza
Fenning, had freely partaken at dinner.   Although
violent sickness and excruciating pain was the result,
in no case, fortunately, did death ensue.   Of those who
suffered the most was Eliza Fenning.   Medical evidence proved that arsenic was mixed with the dough
from which the dumplings had been made.   No counsel
in criminal cases being then permitted to address the
jury on behalf of the prisoner (except on points of
law), poor Eliza Fenning could only assert her innocence, saying: " I am truly innocent of the whole
charge ; indeed I am !   I liked my place ; I was very
comfortable."   The jury in a few minutes returned a

verdict of Guilty, and the Recorder immediately passed sentence of death.

Had it not been for this calamitous event, in a very few days Eliza Fenning would have been married to one in her own position of life. Her bridal dress was prepared; with girlish pride she had worked a little muslin cap, which she proposed wearing on that joyous occasion. In this bridal dress, and little muslin cap, on the morning of the 25th of July, she followed the Ordinary of Newgate through the gloomy passages of the prison to the platform of death. Here again she firmly denied her guilt; and with the words on her lips, " I am innocent ! " her soul passed into eternity.

We quote these details from Mr. J. Holbert Wilson's privately-printed Catalogue: it is added, from a communication made to this gentleman by one acquainted with Mr. Fenning's family : " If my information be correct, Eliza Fenning was as guiltless of the crime for which she suffered as any reader of this note ; but some years elapsed before the proof of it was afforded. At length, however, Truth, the daughter of Time, unveiled the mystery. On a bed, in a mean dwelling at Chelmsford, in Essex, lay a man in the throes of death, his strong frame convulsed with inward agony. To those surrounding that bed, and watching his fearful exit from the world, he disclosed that he was the nephew of a Mr. Turner, of Chancery Lane; that many years since, irritated with his uncle and aunt, with whom he resided, for not supplying him with money, he availed himself of the absence for a few minutes of the servant-maid from the kitchen, stepped into it, and deposited a quantity of powdered arsenic on some dough he found mixed in a pan. Eliza

Fenning, he added, was wholly ignorant of these facts. He made no further sign, but, like the rich man in the Testament, 'he died and was buried.' I will not presume to carry the parallel further."

Mr. Hone published a narrative of the above case, with a portrait of the poor girl; this was replied to, and there was much contention upon the matter. The medical man who had given evidence on the trial suffered considerably in his practice. She was the last person condemned by Sir John Sylvester, Recorder.

It appears that the circumstance which gave colour to the case against the accused was, that she had often pressed her mistress to let her make some yeast dumplings, at which she stated herself to be a famous hand. On the 21st of March, the brewer left some yeast, and, instead of getting the dough from the baker's, the accused made it herself.*

WAINWRIGHT, THE POISONER.

THE system of defrauding insurance societies seems first to have manifested itself in the fraudulent destruction of ships, with their cargoes, or warehouses with their contents. Cases such as these are found often enough to have occupied the attention of our criminal lawyers towards the close of the last century. They were trivial, indeed, compared with the desperate lengths and deadly depths to which in a few short years this new form of crime extended itself. Formerly, we believe, in every office, all the benefits of insurance were forfeited in case of fraud, death by

* Abridged from *Walks and Talks about London.*

suicide, duelling, or the hands of the executioner. Gradually, but not wisely, most of these provisos for non-payment were abandoned, and soon we hear of various endeavours to deceive and defraud. Lives notoriously unsafe were insured. Suicides, that the premium might descend to the family, strange as it is, have more than once been known to occur; and at last, between the years 1830 and 1835, the various metropolitan offices began to realise the alarming extent to which they were open.to the machinations of clever, but unprincipled and designing, men and women.

The man by whom this lesson was taught was Thomas G. Wainwright. He was first known in the literary circles of the metropolis, as an able writer and critic in the *London Magazine*, under the *nom-de-plume* of Janus Weathercock. It is painful, now that after events have shown the fearful depths to which he fell, to trace in his writings the evil influences which were then plainly operating within. Passionate impulses, not only unchecked but fostered; a prurient imagination, rioting in the conception and development of luxurious and criminal pictures, intimate but too plainly to the moralist the fruit which the autumn of a summer so unhealthy might be expected to produce. Men of this class, it may truly be said, are ever trembling on the brink of a precipice; their hour of trial comes and they fall. So was it with Wainwright. Poverty, that most trying of earthly tests, came upon him, and found him not only unnerved and unarmed, but ready to adopt any means of escape from its galling assaults, however unscrupulous and deadly. An evil imagination, morbidly forced, and too prolific in the wildest suggestions, flattered him with the means of evasion—nay, of obtaining even wealth; and warily and deliberately, but unconscious of an avenger at his heels, he proceeded to carry them into effect.

At this period of his history (1825), Wainwright ceased to write. He and his wife (for by this time he was united to an amiable and accomplished woman) went to visit his uncle, to whose property he was believed to be the intended heir. During that visit the uncle died, leaving the property in question to his nephew, by whom it was speedily dissipated.

Shortly afterwards, Miss Helen and Miss Madeline Abercrombie, step-sisters to Mrs. Wainwright, fatally for the life of one, and destructively to the peace of all, became inmates of the family. It is impossible, whatever be our wish, to clear the memory of Helen Abercrombie from the very gravest suspicions. Be it supposed that, controlled by a power to which she had fatally rendered herself subservient, it was only intended, when these insurances were effected, that by a fictitious death the means should be obtained from the offices to linger out their lives alone in some foreign land. The supposition that Wainwright at this time really purposed compassing her death is scarcely tenable. She was the most prominent actress in the business, anxious to insure to a considerable extent, and hesitating not at falsehood in the endeavour. It is, therefore, impossible to acquit her of complicity. Insurances to the extent of 18,000*l.* or 20,000*l.* were effected, and then fearfully indeed were the tables turned on the unhappy dupe.

Meanwhile, Wainwright, like a chained tiger, was goaded by poverty. Time was requisite: time *must* elapse before the insurance card could be safely played. In the interim, money must be had; and, availing himself of the fact of some stock lying in the Bank of England, to the dividends only on which he and his wife were entitled, he proceeded to forge the names of the trustees to *six* several powers of attorney, authorising the sale of the principal. This, too, soon went, and the melancholy *dénouement* drew rapidly on.

Miss Abercrombie now professed her intention of going abroad, and made a will, leaving her property to her sister, and assigning her policy for 3,000*l.* in the Palladium—*which was only effected for a space of three years*—to Wainwright.

The very night following she was taken ill; in a day or two, Dr., now Sir Charles, Locock was called in; the usual probable causes were at once suggested and accepted; exposure to cold and wet, followed by a late and indigestible supper and gastric derangement, was the natural diagnosis. No danger was apprehended; but suddenly, when alone in the house, with the exception at least of her sister and domestics, Miss Abercrombie died. In justice to Wainwright, it should be remembered that he was not present. A *post-mortem* examination was held; and the cause of death was attributed to sudden effusion into the ventricles of the brain. This, it need scarcely be added, was only conjectural.

In due course, application was made to the several offices for the heavy amounts insured; and refused. This was an unexpected turn in the affair; and Wainwright, unable to remain longer in England, went abroad—after having brought an action, however, against one insurance office, which was decided against him. About this time, too, his forgery on the Bank of England was discovered, and to return to England was tantamount to encountering certain death. He remained, therefore, in France, and there his master apparently soon found other work for him to do. He insured the life of a countryman and friend, also resident at Boulogne, for 5,000l. in the Pelican office. After one premium only had been paid, this life too fell; and Wainwright was apprehended, and for nearly half a year incarcerated in Paris. It is said strychnine was found in his possession; but probably at that period no chemist, not even Orfila, would have ventured to attempt proving poisoning thereby.

Impelled, apparently, by that blind and inexplicable impulse which is said so often to draw criminals back again to the scenes of their past guilt, Wainwright, notwithstanding the imminent peril attendant on such a step, ventured to return to London. The reader who has followed the slight and imperfect clue we have endeavoured to supply, may conjecture the motive which attracted him into the meshes long woven and laid for him. He was recognised, and, in the course of a few hours, captured and lodged in Newgate; and now, seeing his case utterly desperate—his liberty, if not his life, hopelessly forfeited—he basely turns traitor to his surviving confederate, or confederates, and tenders information which may justify the offices in refusing to pay the various policies to Madeline Abercrombie. If we rightly apprehend the case, this is the key to the whole.

After a consultation held by all the parties interested, and with the sanction of the Government, it was determined to try him for the forgery on the Bank only. He was sentenced to transportation for life, and no long time after his arrival at Sydney he died in the General Hospital of that city.

RATCLIFFE HIGHWAY MURDERS.

THE murders of Marr and Williamson, in Ratcliffe Highway, are among the best remembered atrocities of the present century. Marr kept a lace and pelisse warehouse at 29 Ratcliffe Highway; and about midnight on Saturday, the 7th of December, 1811, had sent his female servant to purchase oysters for supper, whilst he was shutting up the shop-windows. On her return, in about a quarter of an hour, the servant rang the bell repeatedly without any person coming. The house was then broken open, and Mr. and Mrs. Marr, the shop-boy, and a child in the cradle (the only human beings in the house), were found murdered.

The murders of the Marr family were followed, twelve days later, by the murders of Williamson, landlord of the King's Arms public-house, in Gravel Lane, Ratcliffe Highway, his wife, and female servant. This was in the night, and a lodger, hearing a noise below, stole down stairs, and there, through a staircase-window, saw the murderers searching the pockets of their victims; he returned to his bed-room, tied the bedclothes together, and thus let himself down into the street, and escaped. The alarm was given, but the murderers escaped over some waste ground at the back of the house, and were never traced. Some circumstances, however, implicated a man named Williams, who was committed to prison, and there hanged himself. His body was carried on a platform, placed in a high cart, past the houses of Marr and Williamson, and was afterwards thrown, with a stake through his breast, into a hole dug for the purpose, where the New Road crosses, and Cannon Street Road begins.

Great was the terror throughout the metropolis and suburbs after these atrocities. " Many of our readers," says Macaulay, " can remember the terror which was on every face,—the careful barring of doors—the providing of blunderbusses and watchmen's rattles. We know of a shopkeeper, who, on that occasion, sold about three hundred rattles in about ten hours." It was very common to see from the street, placed in an upstairs window, a blunderbuss, with an inscription, in large letters, " Loaded," to terrify evildoers, though, in some cases, they were thus provided with a ready weapon for murder.

THE CATO STREET CONSPIRACY.

EARLY in the year 1820—a period of popular discontent—a set of desperate men banded themselves together with a view to effect a revolution by sanguinary means, almost as complete in its plan of extermination as the Gunpowder Plot. The leader was one Arthur Thistlewood, who had been a soldier, had been involved in a trial for sedition, but acquitted, and had afterwards suffered a year's imprisonment for sending a challenge to the minister, Lord Sidmouth. Thistlewood was joined by several other Radicals, and their meetings in Gray's Inn Lane were known to the spies Oliver and Edwards, employed by the Government. Their first design was to assassinate the Ministers, each in his own house; but their plot was changed, and Thistlewood and his fellow-conspirators arranged to meet at Cato Street, Edgware Road, and to proceed from thence to butcher the Ministers assembled at a Cabinet dinner, on February 23rd, at Lord Harrowby's, 39 Grosvenor Square, where Thistlewood proposed, as " a rare haul, to murder them all together." Some of the conspirators were to watch Lord Harrowby's house; one was to call and deliver a despatch-box at the door, the others were then to rush in and murder the Ministers as they sat at dinner; and, as special trophies, to bring away with them the heads of Lords Sidmouth and Castlereagh, in two bags provided for the purpose! They were then to fire the cavalry barracks; and the Bank and Tower were to be taken by the people, who, it was hoped, would rise upon the spread of the news.

This plot was, however, revealed to the Ministers by Edwards, who had joined the conspirators as a spy. Still, no notice was apparently taken. The preparations for dinner went on at Lord Harrowby's till eight o'clock in the evening, but the guests did not arrive. The Archbishop of York, who lived next door, happened to give a dinner party at the same hour, and the arrival of the carriages deceived those of the conspirators who were on the watch in the street, till it was too late to give warning to their comrades who had assembled at Cato Street, in a loft over a stable, accessible only by a ladder. Here, while the traitors were arming themselves by the light of one or two candles, a party of Bow Street officers entered the stable, when Smithers, the first of them who mounted the ladder, and attempted to seize Thistlewood, was run by him through the body, and instantly fell; whilst, the lights being extinguished, a few shots were exchanged in the darkness and confusion, and Thistlewood and several of his companions escaped through a window at the back of the premises; nine were taken that evening with their arms and ammunition, and the intelligence conveyed to the Ministers, who, having dined at home, met at Lord Liverpool's to await the result of what the Bow Street officers had done. A reward of 1,000*l*. was immediately offered for the apprehension of Thistlewood, and he was captured before eight o'clock next morning while in bed at a friend's house, No. 8 White Street, Little Moorfields. The conspirators were sent to the Tower, and were the last persons imprisoned in that fortress. On April 20th, Thistlewood was condemned to death after three days' trial; and on May 1st, he and his four principal accomplices, Ings, Brunt, Tidd, and Davidson, who had been severally tried and convicted, were hanged at the Old Bailey, and their heads cut off. The remaining six pleaded guilty; one was pardoned, and five were transported for life.

In 1830, three of these conspirators, — Strange, Wilson, and Harris,—were seen by Judge Therry, at Bathurst, New South Wales. Strange was living in 1862; he was for many years chief constable of the Bathurst district, and was then the terror of bush-rangers, for capturing several of whom he was rewarded by the Colonial Government. The reckless disregard of danger that, in a bad cause, made him an apt instrument for the deed that doomed him to transportation, made him, when engaged in a good cause, an invaluable constable. He obtained a *ticket-of-leave* soon after his arrival from Sir T. Brisbane, for capturing in a single-

handed struggle Robert Story, the notorious bushranger
of his time, and many other marauders of less note.
If it were known that "the Cato Street Chief" (the
title by which as chief constable he was known) was in
search of the plunderers who then prowled along the
roads, they fled from the district, and his name was
quite a tower of strength to the peaceable portion of
the community.   At present he is the head of a
patriarchal home on the banks of the Fish River, at
Bathurst, surrounded by children and grandchildren,
all industrious persons, in the enjoyment of a comfortable competence.   Wilson was also for some time an
active constable under Strange.   On obtaining the indulgence of a ticket-of-leave he married, and became
the fashionable tailor of the district, with a signboard
over his shop announcing him as "Wilson, Tailor,
from London."

VAUX, THE SWINDLER AND PICKPOCKET.

JAMES HARDY VAUX, remembered by his contribution
to convict literature, presented a strong instance of the
constant tendency to crime that some individuals exhibit.   He was, when very young, transported to New
South Wales, for life.   After the usual probationary
course, he obtained a conditional pardon, which placed
him in the position of a free citizen in New South
Wales, provided he did not leave the colony.   The
violation of the condition of residence subjected him to
be remitted to his first sentence—transportation for life.
He escaped, however, and, on his arrival in England,
had the hardihood to publish a book descriptive of his

carcer in the colony, which attracted some attention in London about the year 1818.

This is, by no means, an ordinary work: it is very minute; though it is hard to credit such a narrative, unreservedly. He tells us that he generally spent his mornings, from 1 to 5 o'clock, the fashionable shopping hours, in visiting the shops of jewellers, watchmakers, pawnbrokers, &c. Depending upon his address and appearance, he made a circuit of the town in the shops, commencing in a certain street and going regularly through it, on both sides of the way. His practice was to enter a shop, and request to look at gold seals, brooches, rings, or other small articles of value; and while examining them, and looking the shopkeeper in the face, he contrived, by sleight-of-hand, to conceal two or three, sometimes more, in the sleeve of his coat, which was purposely made wide. Sometimes he would purchase a trifling article, to save appearances; another time, he took a card of the shop, promising to call again; and as he generally saw the remaining goods returned to the window, a place from which they had been taken, before he left the shop, there was hardly a probability of his being suspected, or of the property being missed. In the course of his career, Vaux was never detected in the fact; though, once or twice, so much suspicion arose, that he was obliged to exert all his effrontery, and to use very high language, in order, as the cant phrase is, to *bounce* the tradesmen *out of it*; and Vaux's fashionable appearance, and affected anger at the insinuations, mostly convinced his accuser that he was mistaken, and induced him to apologise for the affront. He even sometimes carried away the spoil, notwithstanding what had passed; and he often paid a second

and a third visit to the same shop, with as good success
as the first.   To prevent accidents, however, he made
it a rule never to enter a second shop with any stolen
property about him ; for, as soon as he quitted the first,
he privately conveyed his booty to his assistant, Brom-
ley, who awaited him in the street, and who, for this
purpose, proved very useful.

By this course of depredation, Vaux acquired, on
the average, about ten pounds a week, though he sometimes neglected *shopping* for several days together.   This
was not, indeed, his only pursuit, but was his principal
morning occupation ; though, when a favourable opportunity offered for getting a guinea by any other means,
Vaux never let it slip.   In the evening, he generally
attended one of the theatres, where he mixed with the
best company in the boxes, and at the same time enjoyed the performance.   He frequently conveyed pocket-
books, snuff-boxes, and other portable articles from the
pockets of their proprietors into his own.   Here he
found the inconvenience of wanting a companion, who
might receive the articles, in the same manner as Brom-
ley did, in the street ; but, though he knew many of the
light-fingered gentry, whose appearance was good, yet,
their faces being well known to the police-officers who
attended the theatre, they would not have been allowed
to enter the house.   Here Vaux had the advantage, for
being just arrived in England, and a new face upon the
town, he carried on his depredations, under the very
nose of the officers, without suspicion.   Having, however, at first, no associate, he was obliged to quit the
theatre, and conceal his first booty in some private spot,
before he could make, with prudence, a second attempt.

Upon the whole, Vaux was very successful as to the

number of articles he filched—not so, as to their value.
He very frequently obtained nine or ten pocket-books,
besides other articles, in one evening; and these being
taken from well-dressed gentlemen, he had reason to
expect that he should some day meet with a handsome
sum in bank-notes; but fortune did not so favour him,
for, during nearly twelve months' almost nightly attendance at some public place did not yield more than 20*l*.
in a book, and that only on one occasion.   He several
times got five, ten, or eleven pounds, but commonly
one, two, or three pounds; and generally four books
out of the five contained nothing but letters or memo-
randa, or other useless papers. At the same time, Vaux
knew frequent instances of common street pickpockets
getting a booty of fifty, one hundred, and sometimes
three or four hundred pounds.   However, Vaux never
failed to pay the expenses of the night.   It sometimes
happened that the articles he got, particularly pocket-
books, were advertised by the losers, within a few
days, as "Lost," and a reward offered for their restoration; where the reward was worth notice, Vaux restored the property by means of a third person whom
he could confide in, and whom he previously tutored
for the purpose.

Vaux soon afterwards made his way to Dublin,
where he was again convicted of larceny, and transported for seven years, under the assumed name of
James Stewart.   On the arrival of the ship that conveyed him to New South Wales, this then somewhat
remarkable person is thus described: His address was
very courteous, and his voice was of a remarkably soft
and insinuating tone.   He expressed a deep contrition
for his past life, vowed amendment, poured forth his .

gratitude for the mercy that had been shown to him, expressing a hope that by his future conduct he might prove that it had not been unworthily bestowed. Perhaps he meant at the moment all that he uttered, but, so incapable had he become of resisting any temptation to crime, that within a twelvemonth after his arrival a second time as a convict, he committed a felony, for which he was sent to work for two years in irons on the public roads.

A MURDERER TAKEN BY MEANS OF THE ELECTRIC TELEGRAPH.

THE capture of the murderer Tawell, through the instrumentality of the Electric Telegraph, is among the earliest, as well as the most remarkable, instances of its marvellous achievements. Although the facts of this case may be in the recollection of some readers, we shall here narrate its main points, in so far as they show the wondrous working of the telegraph.

On Wednesday, the 1st of January 1845, a woman, named Sarah Hart, was found by her neighbours struggling in the agonies of death, in her cottage at Salthill, a short distance from the Slough station of the Great Western Railway. On the evening of the occurrence, the neighbour who overheard the poor woman's screams went into an adjoining garden, and there, by the dim light of a candle, which she carried in her hand, she distinctly saw a man, in the garb of one of the Society of Friends, retreating hastily from the cottage whence the screams proceeded; and further, this neighbour recognised the fugitive as bearing the appearance of a man who was an occasional frequenter of the house. He was seen to glance hurriedly about, and then to make for the Slough road. The neighbour, Mary Ashlee, who witnessed his precipitate flight, then entered the house, where she found Sarah Hart just upon the point of expiring. Having summoned surgical assistance, she communicated her suspicions to her neighbours; and the Rev. E. T. Champneys, vicar of Upton-cum-Chalvey, hearing of the mysterious death of the deceased, and that a person in the dress of a Quaker was the last man who had been seen to leave her cottage, he proceeded to the Slough station, thinking it likely the fugitive might proceed to town by the railway. The reverend gentleman saw the individual described pass through the railway booking-office, when he communicated his suspicions to Mr. Howell, the superintendent of the station. The man (Tawell) then left in a first-class carriage without interruption; and, at the same instant, Mr. Howell sent off, by the electric telegraph, a full description of his person, with instructions to cause him to be watched by the police, upon his arrival at Paddington.

The words of the communication were precisely as follows :—

The Message.

" A murder has just been committed at Salthill, and the suspected murderer was seen to take a first-class ticket for London by the train which left Slough at 7h. 42m. P.M. He is in the garb of a Quaker, with a brown great-coat on, which reaches nearly down to his feet; he is in the last compartment of the second first-class carriage."

Within a few minutes was received

The Reply.

" The up-train has arrived; and a person answering, in every respect, the description given by the telegraph, came out of the compartment mentioned. I pointed the man out to Sergeant Williams. The man got into a New Road omnibus, and Sergeant Williams into the same." Thus, while the suspected man was on his way to the metropolis at a fast rate, the telegraph, with still greater rapidity, sent along the wire which skirted the path of the carriage in which he sat the startling instructions for his capture!

On the omnibus arriving at the Bank, Tawell got out, crossed over to the statue of the Duke of Wellington, where he stopped for a short time, looking about, it is supposed, to see if any person was following him. He then proceeded to the Jerusalem Coffee-house; thence, over London Bridge, to the Leopard Coffee-house, in the Borough; then back again to Cannon Street, in the city, to a lodging-house in Scott's Yard, where he was apprehended, with 12*l*. 10*s*. in his pocket, and documents that led to his being identified.

Thus the capture was completed; and it was well observed, in a report of the inquest held upon the murdered woman, that " had it not been for the efficient aid of the electric telegraph, both at Slough and Paddington, the greatest difficulty, as well as delay, would have occurred in the apprehension of the party now in custody." Altogether, this application of the telegraph produced in the public mind an intense conviction of its vast utility to the moral welfare of society.

It need not be added how Tawell was tried, convicted, condemned, and executed for the murder; some

time after which few persons looked at the telegraph
station at Slough without feeling the immense import-
ance of this novel application of man's philosophy to
the protection of his race. The transmission of the
signals is practically instantaneous; and the conversation, by means of the keys, may be carried on by an
experienced person almost as rapidly as a familiar piece
of music could be played.

It is a curious, but perhaps not currently known
fact, that in the alphabet used by this electric telegraph
there are no separate signs or symbols for J, Q, or Z,
though each of these are represented by their syno-
nymes, or sister sounds, G, K, and S. This is occasionally found awkward. Its convenience, at any rate,
was illustrated in the particular case of Tawell, who
probably might have escaped, had it not been that the
manipulator at Paddington was aware of the adverse
results that might arise from the imperfection connected with the feature in question. It was the particular character or Quaker costume of Tawell that led
to his immediate detection. The manipulator at Slough
had to communicate the fact to the authority at Paddington, that the suspected party was a Quaker. This
puzzled him, from the fact of there being no exclusive
symbol for Q in the category of electric letters; and
the using of the letter K for this purpose might have
led to confusion and loss of time. While the clerks
were carrying on an interchange of " not understand,"
" repeat," &c. &c., six or seven times, the train might
have arrived, and Tawell have altogether escaped detection. It fortunately happened that the person then working the telegraph at Paddington knew the defect, and
comprehended at once, both mechanically and mentally,

what was intended to be conveyed. Of course, had Tawell got out between Slough and Paddington, and not at the latter terminus, he would have escaped, as the telegraph did not work at the intermediate stations.

John Tawell, it appears, from Judge Therry's work on Australia, published in 1864, was a returned convict, and a model specimen of prison reformation. Previous to his transportation to New South Wales, for forgery, upwards of forty years before, his occupation in England was that of a commercial traveller. His career in the colony exhibited a strange mixture of shrewdness and money-making talent, combined with an outward show of religion. On obtaining partial exemption from convict discipline, he became the principal druggist, and had one of the showiest shops of that kind in Sydney. After a prosperous career he sold his business to a respectable chemist for 14,000l. This sum he judiciously invested in buildings and other pursuits of profit. For nearly two years Tawell occupied the house opposite to Mr. Therry's in Sydney. He struck the late judge as being a remarkably well-conducted person. He was a member of the Society of Friends, and he wore the broad-brimmed hat, appeared always in a neat and carefully-adjusted costume, and his whole appearance and manner impressed one with the notion of his being a very saintly personage. He always sought the society in public of persons of reputed piety. Mr. Therry often met him in the street, accompanied by a secretary or collector to a charitable institution, whom he assisted in obtaining contributions for benevolent objects. At one time he took up the cause of temperance in such an intemperate spirit, that he ordered a puncheon of rum he had imported to be staved on the wharf in

Sydney, and its contents poured into the sea, saying
that he would "not be instrumental to the guilt of
disseminating such poison throughout the colony." At
another time his zeal took a religious turn, and he
built in Macquarie Street a commodious meeting-house
for the Society of Friends.

STORIES OF THE BANK OF ENGLAND.

THE traditions of the Bank of England present rack-
ings of human cunning, all which a little honesty might
have saved.   Several narratives of this class are related in Mr. Francis's popular *History* of the Bank.
Such are his stories of Stolen Notes.   For example, a
Jew having purchased twenty thousand pounds' worth
of notes of a felon banker's-clerk, the Jew, in six
months, presented them at the Bank, and demanded
payment ; this was refused, as the bills had been stolen.
The Jew, who was a wealthy and energetic man, then
deliberately went to the Exchange, and asserted publicly that the Bank had refused to honour their own
bills for 20,000*l.* ; that their credit was gone; their
affairs in confusion ; that they had stopped payment.
The Exchange wore every appearance of alarm; the
Hebrew showed the notes to corroborate his assertion ;
he declared they had been remitted to him from Holland: his statement was believed.   He then declared
he would advertise the refusal of the Bank ; information reached the directors, and a messenger was sent to
inform the holder that he might receive the cash in
exchange for the notes.   The fact is, the law could not
hinder the holder of the notes from interpreting the
refusal that was made of payment as he pleased—for

instance, as a pretext to gain time, and belief in this would have created great alarm; all which the directors foresaw—though this was at an early period, when the reputation of the company was not so firmly established as at the present time.

Of Lost Notes there are some entertaining narratives. Thus, in 1740, a bank director lost a 30,000l. banknote, which he was persuaded had fallen from the chimneypiece of his room into the fire. The Bank directors gave the loser a second bill, upon his agreement to restore the first bill, should it ever be found, or to pay the money itself, should it be presented by any stranger. About thirty years after this had occurred, the director having been long dead, and his heirs in possession of his fortune, an unknown person presented the lost bill at the Bank, and demanded payment. It was in vain that they mentioned to this person the transaction by which the bill was annulled; he would not listen to it; he maintained that it had come to him from abroad, and insisted upon immediate payment. The note was payable to bearer; and the thirty thousand pounds were paid him. The heirs of the director would not listen to any demands of restitution, and the Bank was obliged to sustain the loss. It was discovered afterwards that an architect, having purchased the director's house, had taken it down, in order to build another upon the same spot, had found the note in a crevice of the chimney, and made his discovery an engine for robbing the Bank.

The day on which a Forged Note was first presented at the Bank of England forms a memorable event in its history. For sixty-four years the establishment had circulated its paper with freedom; and, during this period, no attempt had been made to imitate it. He who takes the initiative in a new line of wrongdoing, has more than the simple act to answer for; and to Richard William Vaughan, a Stafford linendraper, belongs the melancholy celebrity of having led the van in this new phase of crime, in the year 1758. The records of his life do not show want, beggary, or starvation urging him, but a simple desire to seem greater than he was. By one of the artists employed, and there were several engaged on different parts of the notes, the discovery was made. The criminal had filled up to the number of twenty, and deposited them in the hands of a young lady to whom he was attached, as a proof of his wealth. There is no calculating how much longer bank-notes might have been free from imitation, had this man not shown with what ease they might be counterfeited. Thenceforth forged notes became common.

In the latter part of the last century and the earlier portion of the present, the cashier of the Bank was Abraham Newland, by whom all prosecutions for forgery of the notes of that establishment were instituted. Strange to say, the largest loss ever perhaps sustained by the Bank, through the dishonesty of a servant, was through Newland's nephew, Robert Astlett, a clerk in the establishment. It amounted to 320,000*l*., which consisted in plundered Exchequer Bills, and was equal to the entire half-yearly dividend of 1803, the year in which the fraud was perpetrated. Astlett escaped through the bungling of the Bank counsel in framing the indictment against him. He was tried under the Bank Act, to make his conviction the more certain; had he been tried under the ordinary law applicable to common cases of embezzlement, he would have been convicted.

Love and Marriage.

STORIES OF FLEET MARRIAGES.

THESE unlicensed marriages are said to have originated with the incumbents of Trinity, Minories, and St. James's, Duke's Place, who claimed to be exempt from the jurisdiction of the Bishop of London, and performed marriages without banns or license, till Elliot, Rector of St. James's, was suspended in 1616. The trade was then taken up by clerical prisoners living within the Rules of the Fleet, who, having neither money, character, nor liberty to lose, were just the men to adopt such a traffic. Mr. Burn, who has devoted much attention to these strange practices, enumerates 89 Fleet parsons, most of them lusty, jolly fellows, but thorough rogues and vagabonds, guilty of various offences, many of them too gross to be named. They openly plied their trade, as in the following specimens :—

"G.R.—At the true chapel, at the old Red Hand and Mitre, three doors up Fleet Lane, and next door to the White Swan, marriages are performed by authority by the Rev. Mr. Symson, educated at the university of Cambridge, and late chaplain to the Earl of Rothes.—*N.B.* Without imposition."

"J. Lilley, at ye Hand and Pen, next door to the China Shop, Fleet Bridge, London, will be performed the solemnisation of marriages by a gentleman regularly bred at one of our universities, and lawfully ordained according to the institutions of the Church of England, and is ready to wait on any person in town or country."

"Marriages with a license, certificate, and crown-

stamp, at a guinea, at the New Chapel, next door to
the China Shop, near Fleet Bridge, London, by a
regular bred clergyman, and not by a Fleet parson, as
is insinuated in the public papers; and that the town
may be freed mistakes, no clergyman being a prisoner
within the Rules of the Fleet, dare marry; and to
obviate all doubts, the chapel is not on the verge of the
Fleet, but kept by a gentleman who was lately chaplain on board one of his Majesty's men-of-war, and
likewise has gloriously distinguished himself in defence
of his King and country, and is above committing those
little mean actions that some men impose on people,
being determined to have everything conducted with
the utmost decorum and regularity, such as shall always
be supported on law and equity." (*Daily Advertiser.*)

There was great competition in the business. Thus,
at one corner might be seen in a window: " Weddings
performed cheap here;" and on another, " The Old
and True Register;" and every few yards along the
Ditch and up Fleet Lane, similar announcements.
But the great trade was at the " marriage-houses,"
whose landlords were also tavern-keepers. The Swan,
the Lamb, the Horse-shoe and Magpie, the Bishop
Blaire, the Two Sawyers, the Fighting Cocks, the
Hand and Pen, were places of this description; as were
the Bull and Garter, and King's Head (kept by warders of the Fleet Prison). The parson and landlord (the
latter usually acted as clerk) divided the fee between
them, after paying a shilling to the plyer, or tout, who
brought in the customers. The marriages were entered in a pocket-book by the parson, and on payment
of a small fee copied into the regular register of the
house, unless the interested parties desired the affair

to be kept secret. Marriages were performed in the
Fleet previously to 1754, in the Prison Chapel.

In the *Grub Street Journal* of January 1735, we
read : " There are a set of drunken, swearing parsons,
with their myrmidons, who wear black coats, and pretend to be clerks and registers of the Fleet, and who
ply about Ludgate Hill, pulling and forcing people to
some peddling alehouse or brandy-shop to be married;
even on a Sunday, stopping them as they go to church,
and almost tearing their clothes off their backs." Pennant confirms this : " In walking along the streets in
my youth, on the side next the Prison, I have often
been tempted by the question, ' Sir, will you be pleased
to walk in and be married ? ' Along this most lawless
space was frequently hung up the sign of a male and
female, with hands conjoined, with ' Marriages performed
within ' written underneath. A dirty fellow invited you.
The parson was seen walking before his shop; a squalid,
profligate figure, clad in a tattered plaid night-gown,
with a fiery face, and ready to couple you for a dram
of gin or roll of tobacco."

The following are a few cases : Since Midsummer
last, a young lady of birth and fortune was deluded
and forced from her friends, and by the assistance of a
wry-necked, swearing parson, married to an atheistical
wretch, whose life is a continued practice of all manner
of vice and debauchery. And since the ruin of my relative, another lady of my acquaintance had like to have
been trepanned in the following manner : This lady
had appointed to meet a gentlewoman at the Old Play
House, in Drury Lane ; but extraordinary business
prevented her coming. Being alone when the play
was done, she bade a boy call a coach for the city.

One dressed like a gentleman helps her into it, and jumps in after her. " Madam," says he, " this coach was called for me, and since the weather is so bad, and there is no other, I beg leave to bear you company ; I am going into the city, and will set you down wherever you please." The lady begged to be excused, but he bade the coachman drive on. Being come to Ludgate Hill, he told her his sister, who waited his coming but five doors up the court, would go with her in two minutes. He went, and returned with his pretended sister, who asked her to step in one minute, and she would wait upon her in the coach. The poor lady foolishly followed her into the house, when instantly the sister vanished, and a tawny fellow, in a black coat and a black wig, appeared. " Madam, you are come in good time; the doctor was just agoing !" " The doctor!" says she, horribly frighted, fearing it was a madhouse, " what has the doctor to do with me ?" " To marry you to that gentleman. The doctor has waited for you these three hours, and will be paid by you or that gentleman before you go !" " That gentleman," says she, recovering herself, " is worthy a better fortune than mine ;" and begged hard to be gone. But Doctor Wryneck swore she should be married; or, if she would not, he would still have his fee, and register the marriage for that night. The lady, finding she could not escape without money or a pledge, told them she liked the gentleman so well, she would certainly meet him to-morrow night, and gave them a ring as a pledge, " which," says she, " was my mother's gift on her death-bed, enjoining that, if ever I married, it should be my wedding-ring ;" by which cunning contrivance she was delivered from the black doctor and his tawny crew.

The indecency of these practices, and the facility they afforded for accomplishing forced and fraudulent marriages, were not the only evils. Marriages could be antedated, without limit, on payment of a fee, or not entered at all. Parties could be married without declaring their names. Women hired temporary husbands at the Fleet, in order that they might be able to plead coverture to an action for debt, or to produce a certificate in case of their being *enceinte*. These hired husbands were provided by the parson for five shillings each; sometimes they were women. And for half-a-guinea a marriage might be registered and certified that never took place. Sometimes, great cruelty was practised. In 1719, Mrs. Anne Leigh, an heiress, was decoyed from her friends in Buckinghamshire, married at the Fleet Chapel against her will, and barbarously ill-used by her abductors.

The following are a few extracts from the Register of the Fleet Marriages :—

" 1740. Geo. Grant and Ann Gordon, bachelor and spinster : stole my clothes-brush." In the account of another marriage, we find, " Stole a silver spoon."

" A wedding at which the woman ran across Ludgate Hill in her shift, ' in pursuance of a vulgar error that a man was not liable for the debts of his wife, if he married her in this dress.' "

" Married at a barber's shop next Wilson's, viz. one Kerrils, for half-a-guinea, after which it was extorted out of my pocket, and for fear of my life delivered."

" 5 Nov. 1742 was married Benjamin Richards, in the parish of St. Martin's-in-the-Fields, B^r and Judith Lance, do. sp. at the Bull and Garter, and gave [a guinea] for an ante-date to March ye 11th, in ye same year, which Lilley comply'd with, and put em in his book accordingly, there being a vacancy in the book suitable to the time."

" Mr. Comyngs gave me half-a-guinea to find a bridegroom, and defray all expenses. Parson, 2s. 6d. Husband, do., and 5s. 6d. myself. [We find one man married four times under different names, receiving five shillings on each occasion, ' for his trouble ! ' "]

" 1742, May 24.—A soldier brought a barber to the Cock, who, I think, said his name was James, barber by trade, was in part married to Elizabeth : they said they were married enough."

" A coachman came, and was half-married, and would give but 3s. 6d., and went off."

" Edward —— and Elizabeth —— were married, and would not let me know their names."

In one case, the parson was obliged to marry a couple, *in terrorem* : but " some material part was omitted."

All classes flocked to the Fleet, to marry in haste, from the barber to the officer in the Guards, from the pauper to the peer of the realm. Among the aristocratic patrons of its unlicensed chapels we find Lord Abergavenny ; the Hon. John Bourke, afterwards Viscount Mayo ; Sir Marmaduke Gresham ; Anthony Henley, Esq., brother of Lord Chancellor Northington ; Lord Banff ; Lord Montagu, afterwards Duke of Manchester ; Viscount Sligo ; the Marquis of Annandale ; William Shipp, Esq., father of the first Lord Mulgrave ; and Henry Fox, afterwards Lord Holland, of whose marriage Walpole thus writes to Sir Horace Mann : " The town has been in a great bustle about a private match ; but which, by the ingenuity of the ministry, has been made politics. Mr. Fox fell in love with Lady Caroline Lenox (eldest daughter of the Duke of Richmond), asked her, was refused, and stole her. His father was a footman ; her greatgrandfather, a king—*hinc illæ lachrymæ !* All the blood-royal have been up in arms."

In the Fleet, the errant Edward Wortley Montague (Lady Mary's son) was married; also Charles Churchill, the poet. In 1702, the ·Bishop of London interfered to prevent the scandalous practice, but with little effect; and it was not until the passing of the Act of Parliament, in 1754, that the practice was put an end to: on the day previously (March 24), in one register-book alone, were recorded 217 marriages, the last of the Fleet weddings. In 1821, a collection of the Registers of Fleet Marriages, and weighing more ·than· a ton, was purchased by the Government, and deposited in the Bishop of London's Registry, Doctors' Commons : the earliest date is 1674. They are not now, as formerly, received in evidence.

After the Marriage Bill of 1754, however, the Savoy Chapel came into vogue. On January 2, 1754, the *Public Advertiser* contained this advertisement : " By Authority.—Marriages performed with the utmost privacy, decency, and regularity, at the Ancient Royal Chapel of St. John the Baptist, in the Savoy, where regular and authentic registers have been kept from the time of the Reformation (being two hundred years and upwards) to this day. The expense not more than one guinea, the five-shilling stamp included. There are five private ways by land to this chapel, and two by water." The proprietor of this chapel was the Rev. John Wilkinson (father of Tate Wilkinson, of theatrical fame), who fancying (as the Savoy was extra-parochial) that he was privileged to issue licenses upon his own

authority, took no notice of the new law.   In 1755, he
married no less than 1,190 couples.   The authorities
began at last to bestir themselves, and Wilkinson
thought it prudent to conceal himself.   He engaged a
curate, named Grierson, to perform the ceremony, the
licenses being still issued by himself, by which arrangement he thought to hold his assistant harmless.   Among
those united by the latter were two members of the
Drury Lane company.   Garrick, obtaining the certificate, made such use of it that Grierson was arrested,
tried, convicted, and sentenced to fourteen years' transportation, by which sentence 1,400 marriages were declared void.

STORY OF RICHARD LOVELACE.

RICHARD LOVELACE, one of the most elegant of the
cavaliers of Charles I., will long be remembered by
his divine little poem, " To Althea, from Prison,"
which he composed in the Gate House, at Westminster; it begins with :

> When Love with unconfined wings
>   Hovers within my gates,
> And my divine Althea brings
>   To whisper at my grates—
> When I lie tangled in her hair,
>   And fetter'd in her eye,
> The birds that wanton in the air
>   Know no such liberty.
>
> . . . .
>
> Stone walls do not a prison make,
>   Nor iron bars a cage,
> Minds innocent and quiet take
>   That for an hermitage.
> If I am freedom in my love,
>   And in my soul am free :
> Angels alone, that soar above,
>   Enjoy such liberty.

This accomplished man, who is said by Wood to have been in his youth "the most amiable and beautiful person that eye ever beheld," and who was lamented by Charles Cotton, as an epitome of manly virtue, died at a poor lodging in Gunpowder Alley, Shoe Lane, in 1658, an object of charity.

Leigh Hunt, with the fellow-feeling of a poet, says: " He (Lovelace) had been imprisoned by the Parliament, and lived during his imprisonment beyond his income. Wood thinks that he did so in order to support the royal cause, and out of generosity to deserving men and to his brothers. He then went into the service of the French King, returned to England after being wounded, and was again committed to prison, where he remained till the King's death, when he was set at liberty. Having then," says his biographer, " consumed all his estate, he grew very melancholy (which brought him at length into a consumption), became very poor in body and purse, and was the object of charity, went in ragged clothes (whereas, when he was in his glory, he wore cloth of gold and silver), and mostly lodged in obscure and dirty places, more befitting the worst of beggars than poorest of servants," &c. " Geo. Petty, haberdasher in Fleet Street," says John Aubrey, " carried 20 shillings to him every Monday Morning from Sir —— Manny, and Charles Cotton, Esq., for —— months: but was never repaid." As if it was their intention he should be ! Poor Cotton, in the excess of his relish of life, lived himself to be in want; perhaps wanted the ten shillings that he sent. The mistress of Lovelace is reported to have married another man, supposing him to have died of his wounds in France. Perhaps this helped to make him careless of his fortune: but it is probable that his habits were naturally showy and expensive. Aubrey says he was proud. He was accounted a sort of minor Sir Philip Sydney. We speak the more of him, not only on account of his poetry (which, for the most part, displays much fancy, injured by want of selectness), but because his connection with the neighbourhood probably suggested to Richardson the name of his hero in *Clarissa*."

WYCHERLY AND HIS COUNTESS.

In lodgings on the west side of Bow Street, Covent Garden, over against the Cock Tavern, lived Wycherly, the dramatist, with his wife, the Countess of Drogheda. Here Wycherly happened to be ill of a fever. "During his sickness (says his biographer, Cibber), the King (Charles II.) did him the honour of a visit; when, finding his fever indeed abated, but his body extremely weakened, and his spirits miserably shattered, he commanded him to take a journey to the south of France, believing that nothing could contribute more to the restoring his former state of health than the gentle air of Montpelier during the winter season: at the same time, the King assured him, that as soon as he was able to undertake the journey, he would order five hundred pounds to be paid him to defray the expenses of it.

"Mr. Wycherly accordingly went to France, and returned to England the latter end of the spring following, with his health entirely restored. The King received him with the utmost marks of esteem, and shortly after told him he had a son, who he resolved should be educated like the son of a king, and that he could make choice of no man so proper to be his governor as Mr. Wycherly; and that, for this service, he should have fifteen hundred pounds a-year allotted to him; the King also added, that when the time came that his office should cease, he would take care to make such a provision for him as should set him above the malice of the world and fortune. These were golden prospects for Mr. Wycherly, but they were soon by a cross accident dashed to pieces.

" Soon after this promise of his Majesty's, Mr. Dennis tells us that Mr. Wycherly went down to Tunbridge, to take either the benefit of the waters or the diversions of the place, when, walking one day upon the Wells-walk with his friend, Mr. Fairbeard, of Gray's Inn, just as he came up to the bookseller's, the Countess of Drogheda, a young widow, rich, noble, and beautiful, came up to the bookseller and inquired for the *Plain Dealer*. ' Madam,' says Mr. Fairbeard, ' since you are for the *Plain Dealer*, there he is for you,' pushing Mr. Wycherly towards her. ' Yes,' says Mr. Wycherly, ' this lady can bear plain-dealing, for she appears to be so accomplished, that what would be a compliment to others, when said to her would be plain dealing.' ' No, truly, sir,' said the lady, ' I am not without my faults more than the rest of my sex: and yet, notwithstanding all my faults, I love plain-dealing, and am never more fond of it than when it tells me of a fault.' ' Then, madam,' says Mr. Fairbeard, ' you and the plain dealer seem designed by heaven for each other. ' In short, Mr. Wycherly accompanied her upon the walks, waited upon her home, visited her daily at her lodgings whilst she stayed at Tunbridge; and after she went to

London, at her lodgings in Hatton Garden: where, in
a little time, he obtained her consent to marry her.
This he did, by his father's command, without acquainting the King; for it was reasonably supposed, that
the lady's having a great independent estate, and noble
and powerful relations, the acquainting the King with
the intended match would be the likeliest way to prevent it.   As soon as the news was known at court, it
was looked upon as an affront to the King, and a contempt of his Majesty's orders; and Mr. Wycherly's conduct after marrying made the resentment fall heavier
upon him: for being conscious he had given offence,
and seldom going near the court, his absence was con-
strued into ingratitude.

"The Countess, though a splendid wife, was not
formed to make a husband happy: she was in her
nature extremely jealous; and indulged in it to such a
degree, that she could not endure her husband should
be one moment out of her sight.   Their lodgings were
over against the Cock Tavern, whither, if Mr. Wycherly
at any time went, he was obliged to leave the windows
open, that his lady might see there was no woman in
the company."

"The Countess," says another writer, "made him
some amends by dying in a reasonable time." His title
to her fortune, however, was disputed, and his circumstances, though he had property, were always con-
strained.   He was rich enough however to marry a
young woman eleven days before he died; but his
widow had no child to succeed to the property.   In
his old age he became acquainted with Pope, then a
youth, who vexed him by taking him at his word, when
asked to correct his poetry.   Wycherly showed a

candid horror at growing old, natural enough to a man who had been one of the gayest of the gay, very handsome, and a "Captain." He was captain in the regiment of which Buckingham was colonel.

Wycherly's acquaintance with the Duchess of Cleveland commenced oddly enough. One day, as he passed the Duchess' coach, in the Ring, in Hyde Park, she leaned from the window, and cried out, loud enough to be heard distinctly by him, "Sir, you're a rascal; you're a villain" [alluding to a song in his first play]. Wycherly, from that instant, entertained hopes.

<hr/>

STORY OF BEAU FIELDING.

BEAU FIELDING was thought worthy of record by Sir Richard Steele, as an extraordinary instance of the effects of personal vanity upon a man not without wit. He was of the noble family of Fielding, and was remarkable for the beauty of his person, which was a mixture of the Hercules and the Adonis. It is described as having been a real model of perfection. He married for his first wife, the Dowager Countess of Purbeck; followed the fortunes of James II., who is supposed to have made him a major-general, and perhaps a count; returned, married a woman of the name of Wadsworth, under the impression that she was a lady of fortune; and, discovering his error, addressed or accepted the addresses of the notorious Duchess of Cleveland, and married her; but she, discovering her mistake in time, indicted him for bigamy, and obtained a divorce. Before he left England to follow James, "Handsome Fielding," as he was called, appears to

have been insane with vanity and perverse folly. He
always appeared in an extraordinary dress: sometimes
rode in an open tumbril, of less size than ordinary, the
better to display the nobleness of his person; and his
footmen appeared in liveries of yellow, with black
feathers in their hats, and black sashes. When people laughed at him, he refuted them, as Steele says,
" by only moving." Sir Richard says he saw him one
day stop and call the boys about him, to whom he
spoke as follows :—

" Good youths,—Go to school, and do not lose your
time in following my wheels: I am loth to hurt you,
because I know not but you are all my own offspring.
Hark ye, you sirrah with the white hair, I am sure you
are mine, there is half-a-crown for you. Tell your
mother, this, with the other half-crown I gave her
. . . . comes to five shillings. Thou hast cost me
all that, and yet thou art good for nothing. Why,
you young dogs, did you never see a man before?"
" Never such a one as you, noble general," replied a
truant from Westminster. " Sirrah, I believe thee:
there is a crown for thee. Drive on, coachman." Swift
puts him in his list of Mean Figures, as one who " at
fifty years of age, when he was wounded in a quarrel
upon the stage, opened his breast and showed the
wound to the ladies, that he might move their love and
pity; but they all fell a laughing." His vanity, which
does not appear to have been assisted by courage,
sometimes got him into danger. He is said to have
been caned and wounded by a Welsh gentleman, in
the theatre in Lincoln's Inn Fields; and pressing forward once at a benefit of Mrs. Oldfield's, " to show
himself," he trod on Mr. Fulwood, a barrister, who

gave him a wound twelve inches deep. "His fortune, which he ruined by early extravagance, he thought to have repaired by his marriage with Mrs. Wadsworth, and endeavoured to do so by gambling; but he succeeded in neither attempt, and after the short-lived splendour with the Duchess of Cleveland, returned to his real wife, whom he pardoned, and died under her care. During the height of his magnificence, he carried his madness so far, according to Steele, as to call for his tea by beat of drum; his valet got ready to shave him by a trumpet to horse; and water was brought for his teeth, when the sound was changed to boots and saddle."

BEAU WILSON.

ONE of the gayest men about town, towards the end of the reign of William III., was a young man of fashion who lived in the most expensive style: his house was sumptuously furnished; his dress was costly and extravagant; his hunters, hacks, and racers were the best procurable for money; and he kept a table of regal hospitality. Now, all this was done without any ostensible means. All that was known of him was, that his name was Edward Wilson, and that he was the fifth son of Thomas Wilson, Esq., of Keythorpe, Leicestershire, an impoverished gentleman. Beau Wilson, as he was called, is described by Evelyn as a very young gentleman, "civil and good-natured, but of no great force of understanding," and "very sober and of good fame." He redeemed his father's estate, and portioned off his sisters. When advised by a friend to invest some of his money while he could, he replied,'

that however long his life might last, he should always
be able to maintain himself in the same manner, and
therefore had no need to take care for the future.

All attempts to discover his secret were vain; in his
most careless hours of amusement he kept a strict guard
over his tongue, and left the scandalous world to conjecture what it pleased.   Some good-natured people
said he had robbed the Holland mail of a quantity of
jewellery, an exploit for which another man had suffered death.   Others said he was supplied by the Jews,
for what purpose they did not care to say.   It was
plain he did not depend upon the gaming-table, for he
never played but for small sums.

How long he might have pursued his mysterious
career, it is impossible to say: it was cut short by
another remarkable man on the 9th of April 1694.
On that day, Wilson and a friend, one Captain Wight-
man, were at the Fountain Tavern, in the Strand, in
company with the celebrated John Law, who was then
a man about town.   Law left them, and the captain
and Wilson took coach to Bloomsbury Square.   Here
Wilson alighted, and Law reappeared on the scene;
as soon as they met, both drew their swords, and after
one pass, the Beau fell wounded in the stomach, and
died without speaking a single word.   Law was arrested, and tried at the Old Bailey for murder.   The
cause of the quarrel did not then come out, but Evelyn
says: "The quarrel arose from his (Wilson's) taking
away his own sister from lodging in a house where
this Law had a mistress, which the mistress of the house
thinking a disparagement to it, and losing by it, insti-
gated Law to this duel."   Law declared the meeting
was accidental, but some threatening letters from him

to Wilson were produced on the trial, and the jury believing that the duel was unfairly conducted, found him guilty of murder, and he was condemned to death. The sentence was commuted to a fine, on the ground of the offence amounting only to manslaughter; but Wilson's brother appealed against this, and while the case was pending a hearing, Law contrived to escape from the King's Bench, and reached the Continent in safety, notwithstanding a reward offered for his apprehension. He ultimately received a pardon in 1719.

Those who expected Wilson's death would clear up the mystery attached to his life, were disappointed. He left only a few pounds behind him, and not a scrap of evidence to enlighten public curiosity as to the origin of his mysterious resources.

While Law was in exile, an anonymous work appeared which professed to solve the riddle. This was *The Unknown Lady's Pacquet of Letters*, published with the Countess of Dunois' *Memoirs of the Court of England* (1708), the author, or authoress, of which pretends to have derived her information from an elderly gentlewoman, " who had been a favourite in a late reign of the then she-favourite, but since abandoned by her." According to her account, the Duchess of Orkney (William III.'s mistress) accidentally met Wilson in St. James's Park, incontinently fell in love with him, and took him under her protection. The royal favourite was no niggard to her lover, but supplied him with funds to enable him to shine in the best society, he undertaking to keep faithful to her, and promising not to attempt to discover her identity. After a time, she grew weary of her expensive toy, and alarmed lest his curiosity should overpower his discretion, and bring

her to ruin. This fear was not lessened by his accidental discovery of her secret. She broke off the connection, but assured him that he should never want for
money, and with this arrangement he was forced to be
content. The "elderly gentlewoman," however, does
not leave matters here, but brings a terrible charge
against her quondam patroness. She says, that having
one evening, by her mistress' orders, conducted a
stranger to her apartment, she took the liberty of playing eaves-dropper, and heard the Duchess open her
strong-box and say to the visitor: "Take this, and,
your work done, depend upon another thousand and
my favour for ever!" Soon afterwards poor Wilson
met his death. The confidant went to Law's trial,
and was horrified to recognise in the prisoner at the bar
the very man to whom her mistress addressed those
mysterious words. Law's pardon she attributes to the
lady's influence with the King, and his escape to the
free use of her gold with his jailers. Whether this story
was a pure invention, or whether it was founded upon
fact, it is impossible to determine. Beau Wilson's life
and death must remain among unsolved mysteries.
This compact story is from *Chambers' Book of Days*.

THE UNFORTUNATE ROXANA.

ONE of the earliest female performers was an actress
at the theatre at Vere Street: her name is not ascertained, but she attained an unfortunate celebrity in the
part of Roxana, in the *Siege of Rhodes*. She fell a
victim to Aubrey de Vere, the last Earl of Oxford of
that name, under the guise of a private marriage. The

story is told by Grammont, who, though apocryphal, pretends to say nothing on the subject in which he is not borne out by other writers. His lively account may be laid before the reader.

"The Earl of Oxford," says one of Grammont's heroines, "fell in love with a handsome, graceful actress, belonging to the Duke's Theatre, who performed to perfection, particularly the part of Roxana, in a very fashionable new play; insomuch that she ever after retained that name. This creature being both very virtuous and very modest, or, if you please, wonderfully obstinate, proudly rejected the presents and addresses of the Earl of Oxford. The resistance inflamed his passion; he had recourse to invectives and even spells; but all in vain. This disappointment had such an effect upon him, that he could neither eat nor drink; this did not signify to him; but his passion at length became so violent, that he could neither play nor smoke. In this extremity, Love had recourse to Hymen: the Earl of Oxford, one of the first peers of the realm, is, you know, a very handsome man: he is of the Order of the Garter, which greatly adds to an air naturally noble. In short, from his outward appearance, you would suppose he was really possessed of some sense; but as soon as ever you hear him speak, you are perfectly convinced to the contrary. This passionate lover presented her with a promise of marriage, in due form, signed with his own hand; she would not, however, rely upon this; but the next day she thought there could be no danger, when the Earl himself came to her lodgings attended by a sham parson, and another man for a witness. The marriage was accordingly solemnised with all due ceremonies, in the presence of

one of her fellow-players, who attended as a witness
on her part.   You will suppose, perhaps, that the new
countess had nothing to do but to appear at court
according to her rank, and to display the Earl's arms
upon her carriage.   This was far from being the case.
When examination was made concerning the marriage,
it was found to be a mere deception: it appeared that
the pretended priest was one of my Lord's trumpeters,
and the witness his kettle-drummer.   The parson and
his companion never appeared after the ceremony was
over; and as for the other witness, he endeavoured to
persuade her that the Sultana Roxana might have supposed, in some part or other of a play, that she was
really married.   It was all to no purpose that the poor
creature claimed the protection of the laws of God and
man ; both which were violated and abused, as well as
herself, by this infamous imposition: in vain did she
throw herself at the King's feet to demand justice; she
had only to rise up again without redress; and happy
might she think herself to receive an annuity of one
thousand crowns, and to resume the name of Roxana,
instead of Countess of Oxford."

MRS. CENTLIVRE, AND HER THREE HUSBANDS.

In Spring Gardens, Dec. 1, 1723, died Mrs. Centlivre,
the sprightly authoress of the *Wonder*, the *Busy Body*,
and the *Bold Stroke for a Wife*.   She was buried at St.
Martin's-in-the-Fields.   She is said to have been a beauty,
an accomplished linguist, and a good-natured friendly
woman.   Pope put her in his *Dunciad*, for having written,
it is said, a ballad against his *Homer* when she was a child!

But the probability is that she was too intimate with Steele and other friends of Addison while the irritable poet was at variance with them. It is not impossible, also, that some raillery of hers might have been applied to him, not very pleasant from a beautiful woman against a man of his personal infirmities, who was naturally jealous of not being well with the sex. Mrs. Centlivre is said to have been seduced when young by Anthony Hammond, father of the author of the *Love Elegies*, who took her to Cambridge with him in boy's clothes. This did not hinder her from marrying a nephew of Sir Stephen Fox, who died a year thereafter; nor from having two husbands afterwards. Her second was an officer in the army, of the name of Carrol, who, to her great sorrow, was killed in a duel. Her third husband, Mr. Centlivre, who had the formidable title of Yeoman of the Mouth, being principal cook to Queen Anne, fell in love with her when she was performing the part of Alexander the Great, at Windsor; for she was at one time an actress, though she never performed in London. Her *Bold Stroke for a Wife* was pre-condemned by Wilks, who said, coarsely enough,—" not only would her play be damned, but she herself for writing it."

STOLEN MARRIAGES AT KNIGHTSBRIDGE.

On the western outskirts of the metropolis, at Knightsbridge, formerly stood a little building called Trinity Chapel, near the French Embassy, on the site of a lazarhouse, or hospital, the foundation of which is hidden in obscurity: what is more remarkable, it is not exactly

known when the hospital ceased to exist; the last allusion to it is in 1720. The chapel itself, built in 1699, and
refaced in 1789, has been replaced by a more ecclesias-
tical structure. This was one of the places where
irregular marriages were solemnised, and it is accordingly often noticed by the old dramatists. Thus, in
Shadwell's *Sullen Lovers*, Lovell is made to say, "Let's
dally no longer; there is a person at Knightsbridge
that yokes all stray people together; we'll to him, he'll
despatch us presently, and send us away as lovingly as
any two fools that ever yet were condemned to marriage." Some of the entries in this marriage register
are suspicious enough—"secrecy for life," or "great
secrecy," or "secret for fourteen years" being appended
to the names. Mr. Davis, in his *Memorials of Knightsbridge*, was the first to exhume from this document the
name of the adventuress, "Mrs. Mary Aylif," whom
Sir Samuel Morland married as his fourth wife, in
1687. Readers of Pepys will remember how patheti-
cally Morland wrote, eighteen days after the wedding,
that when he had expected to marry an heiress, "I
was, about a fortnight since, led as a fool to the
stocks, and married a coachman's daughter not worth
a shilling." In 1699, an entry mentions one "Storey
at ye Park Gate." This worthy it was who gave his
name to what is now known as Story's Gate. He was
keeper of the Aviary to Charles II., whence was derived the name of the Birdcage Walk. In the same
year "Cornelius Van der Velde, Limner," was married here to Bernada Vander Hagen. This was a
brother of the famous William Van der Velde, the
elder, and himself a painter of nautical pictures, in the
employment of Charles II.—*Saturday Review.*

ABOUT the year 1730, Mr. Edward Walpole (after-wards Sir Edward, and brother of Horace Walpole) returned from his travels on the Continent, where the liberality of his father, the famous Sir Robert Wal-pole, had enabled him to make a brilliant figure; through his gallantries, he had no other appellation in Italy than " the handsome Englishman." On his return to London, Mr. Walpole had lodgings taken for him at a Mrs. Rennie's, a child's coat maker, at the bottom of Pall Mall. On returning from visits, or public places, he often passed a quarter of an hour in chat with the young women of the shop. Among them was one who had it in her power to make him forget the Italians, and even the beauties of the English court. Her name was Mary Clement; her father was, at that time or soon after, postmaster of Darlington, a place of 50l. per annum, on which he supported a large family. This young woman had been apprenticed to Mrs. Rennie, and discharged her duties with honesty and sobriety. Her parents, however, from their small means, could supply her very sparingly with clothes or money. Mr. Walpole observed her wants, and made her small presents in a way not to alarm the vigilance of her mistress, who exacted the strictest morality from the young persons under her care. Miss Clement is described as beautiful as an angel, with good but uncultivated sense. Mrs. Rennie had begun to suspect that a connection was forming which would not tend to the honour of her apprentice. She ap-prised Mr. Clement of her suspicions: he immediately came up to town, met his daughter with tears, expressed his fears; adding that he should take her home, where, by living prudently, she might chance to be married to some decent tradesman. The girl, apparently, acquiesced; but, whilst her father and her mistress were conversing in a little dark parlour behind the shop, the object of their cares slipped out, and, without hat or cloak, ran directly through Pall Mall to Sir Edward Walpole's house, at the top of the street, where, the porter knowing her, she was admitted, though the master was absent. She went into the parlour, where the table was laid for dinner, and impatiently awaited Sir Edward's return. The moment came: he entered, and was heard to exclaim, with great joy—" You here !" What explanation took place was in private; but the fair fugitive sat down that day, and never after left it.

The fruits of this connection were Mrs. Keppel; Maria, afterwards Lady Waldegrave, and subsequently Duchess of Gloucester; Lady Dysart; and Colonel Walpole, in the birth of whom, or soon after, the mother died. Never could fondness exceed that which Sir Edward cherished for the mother of his children; nor was it confined to her or them only, since he provided in some way or other for all her relations. His grief at his loss was great: he repeatedly declined overtures of marriage, and gave up his life to the education of his children. He had been prompted to unite himself to Miss Clement, by legal ties, but the threats of his father, Sir Robert, prevented his marriage; the statesman avowing that if he married Miss Clement, he would not only deprive him of his political interest, but exert it against him. It was, however, said by persons who had opportunity of knowing, that had Miss Clement survived Sir Robert, she would then have been Lady Walpole.

About the year 1758, the eldest daughter, Laura, became the wife of the Honourable and Reverend Frederick Keppel, brother to the Earl of Albemarle, and afterwards Bishop of Exeter. The Misses Walpole now took high rank in society. The sisters of Lord Albemarle were their constant companions; introduced them to persons of quality and fashion; in a word, they were received everywhere but at court. The shade attending their birth shut them out from the drawing-room, till marriage, as in the case of Mrs. Keppel, had covered the defect, and given them the rank of another family. The second daughter of the above union, Laura, married in 1784. " One of my hundred nieces," says Horace Walpole, " has just married herself by an expedition to Scotland. It is Mrs. Keppel's second daughter, a beautiful girl, and more universally admired than her sister or cousins, the Waldegraves. For such an exploit her choice is not a very bad one; the swain is eldest son of Lord Southampton. Mrs. Keppel has been persuaded to pardon her, but Lady Southampton is inexorable; nor can I quite blame her, for she has thirteen other children, and a fortune was very requisite; but both the bride and the bridegroom are descendants from Charles II., from whom they probably inherit stronger impulses than a spirit of collateral calculation." Lord Southampton was grandson of the Duke of Grafton ; the Bishop of Exeter's mother was Lady Anne Lenox, daughter of the first Duke of Richmond.

No one had watched the progress of Sir Edward Walpole's family upwards with more anxiety than

the Earl Waldegrave, who, though one of the proudest
noblemen in the kingdom, had long cherished a passion
for Maria Walpole. The struggle between his passion
and his pride was not a short one; and having con-
quered his own difficulties, it now only remained to
attack the lady, who had no prepossession; and Lord
Waldegrave, though not young, was not disagreeable.
They were married in 1759, and had issue three
daughters: Elizabeth Laura, married to her cousin,
George, fourth Earl Waldegrave; Charlotte Maria,
married to George, Duke of Grafton; and Anne
Horatia, married to Lord Hugh Seymour. In April
1763, Earl Waldegrave died of small-pox, and his lady
found herself a young widow. Had Lord Waldegrave possessed every advantage of youth and person,
his death could not have been more sincerely regretted
by his amiable relict. Again she emerged into the
world; she refused several offers; amongst others, the
Duke of Portland loudly proclaimed his discontent
at her refusal. But the daughter of Mary Clement
was destined for royalty; and it became within the
bounds of probability that the descendants of the postmaster of Darlington, and Mary Clement, the milliner
of Pall Mall, might one day have swayed the British
sceptre. Lady Waldegrave, after the Earl's decease,
became the wife of His Royal Highness William Henry,
Duke of Gloucester, by whom she was mother of the
late Duke of Gloucester, and of the Princess Sophia of
Gloucester.

Horace Walpole has recorded some amusing traits
of his brother, Sir Edward, who had a house at Englefield Green, and is styled by Horace, " Baron of Englefield." " He is very agreeable and good-humoured,

has some very pretty children, and a sensible and learned man that lives with him, one Dr. Thirlby, who, while in Sir Edward's house, is said to have kept a miscellaneous book of Memorables, containing whatever was said or done amiss by Sir Edward, or any part of his family. The master of the house," says Horace, " plays extremely well on the bass-viol, and has generally musical people with him." As to personal acquaintance with any of the Court beauties, little could be said; but to make amends, he was perfectly master of all the quarrels that had been fashionably on foot about Handel, and could give a very perfect account of all the rival modern painters. He was the first patron of Roubiliac, the sculptor, who, when a young man, chanced to find a pocket-book containing a considerable number of bank-notes, and some papers, apparently of consequence to the owner, Sir Edward Walpole, the prompt return of which was gracefully acknowledged by Sir Edward's commissions to the young sculptor. Horace Walpole did not live on good terms with his brother; for he says: " There is nothing in the world the Baron of Englefield has such an aversion for as for his brother."

Horace, writing January 8, 1784, says: " My brother, Sir Edward, is, I fear, dying : yesterday we had no hopes ; a sort of glimmering to-day, but scarcely enough to be called a ray of hope. He has, for a great number of years, enjoyed perfect health, and even great beauty, without a wrinkle, to seventy-seven; but last August his decline began by an aversion to all solids. He came to town in the beginning of November; his appetite totally left him ; and in a week he became a very infirm, wrinkled old man. We think that he imagined he could cure himself by almost total abstinence. With great difficulty he was persuaded to try the bark; it restored some appetite, and then he would take no more. In a word, he has starved himself to death, and is now so emaciated and weak, that it is almost impossible he should be saved, especially as his obstinacy continues; nor will he be persuaded to take sustenance enough to give him a chance, though he is sensible of his danger, and cool, tranquil, perfectly in his senses as ever. A cordial, a little whey, a dish of tea, it costs in all infinite pains to induce him to swallow. I much doubt whether entire tractability could save him!"

Walpole, in another letter, remarks: " I doubt my poor memory begins to peel off; it is not the first crack I have perceived in it. My brother, Sir Edward, made the same complaint to me before he died, and I suggested a comfort to him, that does not satisfy myself. I told him the memory is like a cabinet, the drawers of which can hold no more than they can. Fill them with papers; if you add more, you must shove out some of the former. Just so with the memory: there is scarce a day in our lives that something, serious or silly, does not place itself there, and consequently, the older we grow, the more must be displaced to make room for new contents. ' Oh!' said my brother, 'but how do you account for most early objects remaining?' Why, the drawers are lined with gummed taffety. The first ingredients stick; those piled higgledy-piggledy upon them, are tossed out without difficulty, as new are stuffed in; yet I am come to think that mice and time may gnaw holes in the sides, and nibble the papers too."

A MAYFAIR MARRIAGE.

In the autumn of 1748, a young fellow, called Handsome Tracy, was walking in the Park with some of his
acquaintance, and overtook three girls : one was very
pretty; they followed them; but the girls ran away,
and the company grew tired of pursuing them, all but
Tracy.   He followed to Whitehall Gate, where he
gave a porter a crown to dog them : the porter hunted
them—he, the porter.   The girls ran all round Westminster, and back to the Haymarket, where the porter
came up with them.   He told the pretty one she must
go with him, and kept her talking till Tracy arrived,
quite out of breath, and exceedingly in love.   He insisted on knowing where she lived, which she refused
to tell him ; and after much dispute, went to the house
of one of her companions, and Tracy with them.   He
there made her discover her family, a butter-woman in
Craven Street, and engaged her to meet him the next
morning in the Park; but before night he wrote her
four love-letters; and in the last offered two hundred
pounds a year to her, and a hundred a-year to her
mother !   Griselda made a confidence to a staymaker's
wife, who told her that the swain was certainly in love
enough to marry her, if she could determine to be
virtuous and refuse his offers.   " Ay," said she, " but
if I should, and lose him by it ?"   However, the measures of the cabinet council were decided for virtue ;
and when she met Tracy the next morning in the Park,
she was convoyed by her sister and brother-in-law, and
stuck close to the letter of her reputation.   She would
do nothing, she would go nowhere.   At last, as an instance of prodigious compliance, she told him, if he

would accept such a dinner as a butter-woman's daughter could give, he should be welcome. Away they
walked to Craven Street; the mother borrowed some
silver to buy a leg of mutton, and they kept the eager
lover drinking till twelve at night, when a chosen committee waited on the faithful pair to the minister of
Mayfair. This was the Rev. Alexander Keith, who
had a chapel in Curzon Street; at which marriages
(with a licence on a 5s. stamp and certificate) were
performed for a guinea. Keith was in bed, and swore
he would not get up to marry the King, but that he
had a brother over the way, who perhaps would, and
who did. The mother borrowed a pair of sheets, and
they consummated at her house; and the next day they
went to their own palace. In two or three days the
scene grew gloomy; and the husband coming home one
night, swore he could bear it no longer. " Bear ! bear
what?" " Why, to be teased by all my acquaintance
for marrying a butter-woman's daughter. I am determined to go to France, and will leave you a handsome allowance." " Leave me ! Why, you don't fancy
you shall leave me ? I will go with you." " What !
you love me, then ?" " No matter whether I love you
or not, but you sha'n't go without me."* And they
went.

GEORGE III. AND "THE FAIR QUAKERESS."

In the middle of the last century there dwelt in Market
Street, St. James's, a linendraper named Wheeler, a
Quaker, whose niece, Hannah Lightfoot, "the fair
Quakeress," served in her uncle's shop. The lady

* Walpole's *Letters and Correspondence*, ii. 127.

caught the eye of Prince George, in his walks and rides from Leicester House to St. James's Palace; and she soon returned the attractions of such a lover. The Duchess of Kingston is said to have arranged their meeting, through a member of a family living in Exeter Street, Knightsbridge. Hannah is stated to have been privately married to the Prince, in 1759, in Kew Church; another story gives it as a Mayfair marriage, by Parson Keith, at Curzon Street Chapel; and to this it was added that children were born of the union, of whom a son was sent, when a child, to the Cape of Good Hope, under the name of George Rex: now, in 1830 there was living in the colony a settler of this name, who was sixty-eight years of age, and the exact resemblance in features to George III.

Another version is that Prince George's intrigue alarming the royal family, it was contrived to marry the fair Quakeress to a young grocer, a former admirer, named Axford, of Ludgate Hill. The Prince was inconsolable; and a few weeks after, when Axford was one evening from home, a royal carriage was driven to the door, and the lady was hurried into it by the attendants and carried off. Where she was taken to, or what became of her, was never positively known; it is stated that she died in 1765, and that her death disturbed the royal mind. Axford, broken-hearted, retired into the country; he sought information about his wife at Weymouth and other places, but without effect. He married again, and had a family, and died about 1810.

There is a fine portrait of Hannah Lightfoot, by Sir Joshua Reynolds, at Knowle Park, Kent, which was, doubtless, painted by order of George III. In the catalogue she is called Mrs. Axford. In Sir Bernard Burke's

Dictionary of the Landed Gentry is the pedigree of "Prytherch of Abergole," by which it appears that the gentleman who is said to have married her granddaughter, has had by her no less than fourteen children. It is added that Hannah's father, Henry Wheeler, Esq., of Surrey Square, " was the last of the family who saw her on her going to Keith Chapel, in Mayfair, to be married to a person of the name of Axford, a person the family knew nothing of; *he* never saw her or heard of her after the marriage took place; every inquiry was made, but no satisfactory information was ever obtained respecting her."

GEORGE III. AND LADY SARAH LENOX.

LADY SARAH LENOX, born in 1745, was one of the numerous children of the second Duke of Richmond of his creation (grandson of King Charles II.) and Lady Sarah Cadogan, daughter of Marlborough's favourite general. Lady Sarah grew up an extraordinary beauty. Horace Walpole, in 1761, describes her as taking part in some private theatricals which he had witnessed at Holland House. The play selected to be performed by children and very young ladies was *Jane Shore*: Lady Sarah Lenox enacting the heroine; while the boy, afterwards eminent as Charles James Fox, was Hastings. Walpole praises the acting of the performers, but particularly that of Lady Sarah, who, he says, " was more beautiful than you can conceive . . in white, with her hair about her ears, and on the ground, no Magdalen by Correggio was half so lovely and expressive."

The charms of this lovely person had already made an impression on the heart of George III., then newly come to the throne at two-and-twenty. There seems no reason to doubt that the young monarch formed the design of raising his lovely cousin (for such she was) to the throne.

Early in the winter 1760–1, the King took an opportunity of speaking to Lady Sarah's cousin, Lady Susan Strangeways, expressing a hope at the drawing-room, that her ladyship was not soon to leave town. She said she should. "But," said the King, "you will return in summer for the coronation." Lady Susan answered that she did not know—she hoped so. "But," said the King again, "they talk of a wedding. There have been many proposals; but I think an English match would do better than a foreign one. Pray tell Lady Sarah Lenox I say so." Here was a sufficiently broad hint to inflame the hopes of a family, and to raise the head of a blooming girl of sixteen to the fifth heavens.

It happened, however, that Lady Sarah had already allowed her heart to be preoccupied, having formed a girlish attachment for the young Lord Newbottle, grandson of the Marquis of Lothian. She did not, therefore, enter into the views of her family with all the alacrity which they desired. According to a narrative of Mr. Grenville, "She went the next drawing-room to St. James's, and stated to the King, in as few words as she could, the inconveniences and difficulties in which such a step would involve him. He said that was his business: he would stand them all: his part was taken, he wished to hear hers was likewise. In this state it continued, whilst she, by advice of her

K 2

friends, broke off with Lord Newbottle, very reluc-
tantly on her part. She went into the country for a
few days, and by a fall from her horse broke her leg.
The absence which this occasioned gave time and
opportunities for her enemies to work; they instilled
jealousy into the King's mind upon the subject of Lord
Newbottle, telling him that Lady Sarah still continued
her intercourse with him, and immediately the marriage
with the Princess of Strelitz was set on foot; and, at
Lady Sarah's return from the country, she found herself deprived of her crown and her lover Lord Newbottle, who complained as much of her as she did of the
King. While this was in agitation, Lady Sarah used
to meet the King in his rides early in the morning,
driving a little chaise with Lady Susan Strangeways;
and once it is said that, wanting to speak to him, she
went dressed like a servant-maid, and stood amongst
the crowd in the Guard-room, to say a few words to him
as he passed by." Walpole also relates that Lady Sarah
would sometimes appear as a haymaker in the park at
Holland House, in order to attract the attention of the
King as he rode past; but the opportunity was lost.

It is believed that Lady Sarah was allowed to have
hopes till the very day when the young sovereign announced to his council that he had resolved on wedding
the Princess Charlotte of Mecklenburg-Strelitz. She
felt ill-used, and her friends were all greatly displeased.
With the King she remained an object of virtuous
admiration—perhaps also of pity. He wished to soften
the disappointment by endeavouring to get her established in a high position near his wife; but the impropriety of such a course was obvious, and it was not
persisted in.

Lady Sarah, however, was asked by the King to take a place among the ten unmarried daughters of dukes and earls who held up the train of his Queen at the coronation; and this office she consented to perform. It is said that, in the sober, duty-compelled mind of the sovereign, there always was a softness towards the object of his youthful attachment. Walpole relates that he blushed at his wedding service, when allusion was made to Abraham and *Sarah*.

Lady Sarah Lenox in 1764 made a marriage which proved that ambition was not a ruling principle in her nature, her husband being "a clergyman's son," Sir Thomas Charles Bunbury, Bart. Her subsequent life was in some respects infelicitous, her marriage being dissolved by Act of Parliament in 1776. By her next marriage to the Hon. Major-General George Napier, she became the mother of a set of remarkable men, including the late Sir Charles James Napier, the conqueror of Scinde; and Lieutenant-General Sir William Napier, the historian of the Peninsular War. Her ladyship died at the age of eighty-two, in 1826, believed to be the last surviving great granddaughter of Charles II.*

LOVE AND MADNESS.

ABOUT the year 1780, a young East Indian, whose name was Dupree, left his fatherland to visit a distant relation, a merchant, on Fish Street Hill. During the young man's stay, he was waited on by the servant of the house, a country-girl, Rebecca Griffiths, chiefly

----

* Abridged from Chambers's *Book of Days*.

remarkable for the plainness of her person, and the
quiet meekness of her manners. The circuit of pleasure
run, and yearning again for home, the visitor at length
prepared for his departure: the chaise came to the
door, and shaking of hands, with tenderer salutations,
adieus, and farewells, followed in the usual abundance.
Rebecca, in whom an extraordinary depression had for
some days previously been perceived, was in attendance, to help to pack the luggage. The leave-taking
of friends and relations at length completed, with a
guinea squeezed into his humble attendant's hand, and
a brief " God bless you, Rebecca!" the young man
sprang into the chaise, the driver smacked his whip,
and the vehicle was rolling rapidly out of sight, when a
piercing shriek from Rebecca, who had stood to all
appearance vacantly gazing on what had passed,
alarmed the family, then retiring into the house. They
hastily turned round: to their infinite surprise, Rebecca
was seen wildly following the chaise. She was rushing
with the velocity of lightning along the middle of the
road, her hair streaming in the wind, and her whole
appearance that of a desperate maniac!

Proper persons were despatched after her, but she
was not secured till she had gained the Borough; when
she was taken in a state of incurable madness to Beth-
lem Hospital, where she some years after died. The
guinea he had given her—her richest treasure: her
only wealth—she never suffered, during life, to quit
her hand; she grasped it still more firmly in her dying
moments, and at her request, in the last gleam of returning reason—the lightning before death—it was
buried with her. There was a tradition in Bedlam,
that through the heartless cupidity of the keeper, it

was sacrilegiously wrenched from her, and that her ghost might be seen every night, gliding through the dreary cells of that melancholy building, in search of her lover's gift, and mournfully asking the glaring maniacs for her lost guinea.

It was Mr. Dupree's only consolation, after her death, that the excessive homeliness of her person, and her retiring air and manners, had never even suffered him to indulge in the most trifling freedom with her. She had loved hopelessly, and paid the forfeiture with sense and life.

EMMA, LADY HAMILTON.

A CHARACTERISTIC letter of this extraordinary woman has been communicated to *Notes and Queries*, April 18, 1861. Mrs. Burt, the lady to whom the letter is addressed, was well acquainted with Emma Lyons when she was a barefooted girl residing at Hawarden, near Chester, and gaining a livelihood by driving a donkey, laden with coals and sand for sale. Mrs. Burt, having occasion to come to London, brought Emma with her at the request of Mrs. Lyons, then occupying some situation in the household of Sir W. Hamilton.* When, in the course of time, the little barefooted girl became Lady Hamilton, she, during her absence from England, occasionally wrote to her old friend and former protectress; but so far as is known, this is the only one of those letters now in

---

* Emma is also said to have begun life in the metropolis as a barmaid, at the Coach and Horses Inn, in Flood Street, Westminster, but to have been discharged for misconduct.

existence, and is in the possession of a grandson of Mrs. Burt:—

"Mrs Burt, at M^r
Boberts, no. 16 upper
John^s Street, Marlebone
London.

"Caserta, near Naples, dec^{br} 26th 1792.

"My dear Mrs. Burt, I Received your very kind Letter this morning & am surprised to hear my poor dear grandmother can be, in want, as I left her *thirty pound* when I Left england besides tea sugar & several thing^s & it is now five weeks since I wrote to a friend of ours & endeed a relation of my husbands to send twenty pound more so that my Grandmother must have had it on cristmas day, you may be sure I should never neglect that dear tender parent who I have the greatest obligations to, & she must have been cheated or she never cou'd be in want, but you did very Right my dearest friend to send her the four Guines which I will send you with enterest & a thousand thanks endeed I Love you dearly my dear Mrs Burt & I think with pleasure on those happy days I have pass'd in your Company, I onely wait for an answer from our friend with the account of my grandmothers having Received her twenty pounds & I will then send you an order on him for your money, & I send a piece of Silk to make you a Gown we send it in the ship Captain newman, who sails for england this month, but my next Letter I will send you a bill of Loading. I wrote you a Long Letter Last march, but I am affraid you never got it, which I am sorry for as their was a Long account of my reception at the Court of naples, endeed the Queen has been so Kind to me I cannot express to you she

as often invited me to Court & her magesty & nobility
treats me with the most kind and affectionate regard.
I am the happiest woman in the world my husband is
the best & most tender of husbands & treats me and
my mother with such goodness & tenderness, endeed I
love him dearly, if I cou'd have my dear grandmother
with me, how happy I shou'd be, but gods will be
done, she shall never want & if she shou'd wish for
any thing over above what I have sent her Let her
have it & I will repay you with entrest & thanks, you
see my dear Mrs Burt in a year and 2 months she will
have had fifty pounds theirfore I have nothing to Lay
to my charge, I write to Mrs Thomas who Lives on the
spot, & who I hope will see she is kindly used, I enclose
this in a friends Letter to save you the postage which
is very dear. I will write to you as soon as we have
Receved the answer that the twenty pounds are receved
& I then will say more about Mr Connor, my dear
mother desires her best Love to you & your Brother,
& pray present my Compliments to him & when you
write to Michell say every thing thats kind from us to
him. Miss Dodsworth, Mrs Greffor now, is brought to
bed & the King was god father and made her a present
of a Gold watch set in pearls twelve Sylver Candle-
sticks, a Sylver tea board & Sylver coffey pot Suger
Basen, &c. &c. She is a very good wife and M^r
Greffor is a good man & the King is very fond of him
when the Court is at Caserta we go with them and I
see Mrs Greffor often. Sir William is now on a shooting
party with the King, the Queen is at Caserta & and
our family is now there we onely Come to naples for
a few days. I am now at Caserta, we have a good
many english with us the duchess of ancaster Lord &

Lady cholmondly Lady plymouth Lady webster Lady
Forbes &c. &c. they all dined with me yesterday.   I
expect Sir William home to night.   God Bless you
my dear Mrs Burt, & thank you for all your goodness
write soon & believe me your ever true *and affectionate
friend*

" EMMY HAMILTON.
  " Direct for Lady Hamilton
     at naples."

The anxiety evinced in this letter by Lady Hamilton
for the comfort of her aged relative, places her in a
most pleasing light; and the mixing up of this matter
with the accounts of the distinguished circle of which
she was so brilliant an ornament, is very curious.   The
original is written in a bold hand, but not with the
freedom of a practised writer.

It is to the credit of Lady Hamilton, that in her
prosperity she was neither ashamed of her origin nor
unmindful of her friends.   Young Burt, the son of
Mrs. Burt, and articled to an engraver, was a frequent
guest at Merton, where he sat at table with the great
Nelson himself, and has heard Lady H. delight her
company with songs, celebrating the deeds of the hero,
and amuse them with reminiscences of her village life.

BREACHES OF PROMISE.

MR. PARKER, who had been a partner in Combe's
Brewery, was one of the oldest and dearest friends of
John Thomas Smith, of the British Museum.   Parker
died in 1828, at the advanced age of ninety ; and of him
Mr. Smith used to tell a remarkable story, which, says

the editor of *A Book for a Rainy Day,** we are rather surprised not to find recorded in his reminiscences. It was our fortune to be the first to communicate to Mr. Smith the fact of his old friend's decease, and that he had bequeathed to him a legacy of 100*l.* " Ah, sir ! " he said, in a very solemn manner, after a long pause, " poor fellow ! he pined to death on account of a rash promise of marriage he had made." We humbly ventured to express our doubts, having seen him not long before looking not only very un-Romeo-like, but very hale and hearty; and besides, we begged to suggest that other reasons might be given for the decease of a respectable gentleman of ninety. " No, sir," said Mr. Smith, " what I tell you is the fact, and sit ye down, and I'll tell you the whole story. Many years ago, when Mr. Parker was a young man, employed in the brewhouse in which he afterwards became a partner, he courted and promised marriage to a worthy young woman in his own sphere of life. But as his circumstances improved, he raised his ideas, and, not to make a long story of it, married another woman with a good deal of money. The injured fair one was indignant, but as she had no written promise to show, was, after some violent scenes, obliged to put up with a verbal assurance that she should be the next Mrs. Parker. After a few years the first Mrs. P. died, and she then claimed the fulfilment of his promise, but was again deceived in the same way, and obliged to put up with a similar pledge. A *second* time he became a widower, and a *third* time he deceived his unfortunate *first* love, who, indignant and furious beyond measure,

* See *A Book for a Rainy Day.* By John Thomas Smith. Third Edition. 1861.

threatened all sorts of violent proceedings. To pacify her, Mr. P. gave her a written promise that, if a widower, he would marry her when he attained the age of one hundred years ! Now he had lost his last wife some time since, and every time he came to see me at the Museum, he fretted and fumed, because he should be obliged to marry that awful old woman at last. This could not go on long, and as you tell me, he has just dropped off. If it had not been for this, he would have lived as long as Old Parr. And now," finished Mr. Smith, with the utmost solemnity, " let this be a warning to you. Don't make rash promises to women ; but, if you do so, *don't make them in writing.*"

MARRIAGE OF MRS. FITZHERBERT AND THE PRINCE OF WALES.

THE beautiful and accomplished Mrs. Fitzherbert was the daughter of Walter Smythe, Esq., of Brambridge, Hants, and was first married to Edward Weld, Esq., of Lulworth, Dorsetshire ; secondly, to Thomas Fitzherbert, Esq., of Swismerton, Staffordshire. She became a second time a widow, living on a handsome jointure, and greatly admired in society on account of her beauty and accomplishments ; when, in 1785, being twenty-nine years of age, she became acquainted with the Prince of Wales, who was six years younger. He fell distractedly in love with her, and was eager to become her third husband ; but she, well aware that the Royal Marriage Act made the possibility of anything more than an appearance of decent nuptials in this case very doubtful, resisted all importunities. It has been stated, on good authority, that to overcome her scruples, the Prince one day caused himself to be bled, put on the appearance of having made a desperate attempt on his own life, and sent some friends to bring her to see him. She was thus induced to allow him to engage her with a ring in the presence of witnesses; but she afterwards broke off the intimacy, went on the Continent, and for a long time resisted all the efforts made by the Prince to induce her to return. It is told as a curious fact in this strange love history, that one of the persons chiefly engaged in attempting to bring about this ill-assorted union was the notorious Duke of Orleans (Philip Égalité).

Towards the close of 1785, it was bruited that the heir-apparent to the British Crown was about to marry a Roman Catholic widow lady, named Fitzherbert. Even Horace Walpole is very mysterious about the rumour, for in February 1786, he writes to Sir Horace Mann: "I am obliged to you for your accounts of the House of *Albany* (Pretender family); but that extinguishing family can make no sensation here, when we have other guess-matter to talk of in a higher and more flourishing race; and yet, were rumour—ay, much more than rumour, every voice in England—to be credited, the matter, somehow or other, reaches even from London to Rome. I know nothing but the buzz of the day, nor can say more upon it; if I send you a riddle, fancy or echo from so many voices will soon reach you and explain the enigma, though I hope it is essentially void of truth, and that appearances rise from a much more common cause." Mr. Fox, to whose party the Prince had attached himself, wrote to his Royal Highness on the 10th of December a long letter, pointing out the dangerous nature of the course he was following. "Consider," said he, "the circumstances in which you stand: the King not feeling for you as a father ought; the Duke of York professedly his favourite, and likely to be married to the King's wishes; the nation full of its old prejudices against Catholics, and justly dreading all disputes about succession." Then the marriage could not be a real one. "I need not," said he, "point out to your good sense what source of uneasiness it must be to you, to her, and, above all, to the nation, to have it a matter of dispute and discussion whether the Prince is or is not married." The whole letter, written in a tone of sincere regard for the Prince, was highly creditable to the good sense of the writer.

The Prince answered on the instant, thanking Mr. Fox for his advices and warnings, but assuring him they were needless. "Make yourself easy, my dear friend; believe me, the world will now soon be convinced that there not only is [not], but never was, any ground for those reports which have of late been so malevolently circulated."

Ten days after the date of this letter, namely, on the 21st of December, the Prince and Mrs. Fitzherbert were married by an English clergyman, before two witnesses. Mr. Fox, misled by the Prince, on the next discussion of the subject in the House of Commons, contradicted the report of the marriage *in toto*, in point of fact as well as of law; it not only never could have happened legally, but it never did happen in any way whatever, and had, from the beginning, been a base and malicious falsehood. Horne Tooke, in a strong pamphlet which he wrote upon the subject,

. presumed so far on the belief of the marriage as to style Mrs. Fitzherbert " her Royal Highness." However, the public generally were not deceived. Mrs. Fitzherbert lived for several years with great openness as the wife of the Prince of Wales, and in the enjoyment of the entire respect of society, more especially of her husband's brothers. A separation only took place about 1795, when the Prince was about to marry (for the payment of his debts) the unfortunate Caroline of Brunswick. Mrs. Fitzherbert survived this event forty-two years, and never during the whole time ceased to be "visited." The lady occasionally resided at Brighton, in a neat stone-coloured villa, with verandas in front, at the south-east corner of Castle Square: this house was built by the architect, Mr. Porden, for Mrs. Fitzherbert, and was furnished in a superb style: here Mrs. Fitzherbert died on the 29th of March 1837, in her eighty-first year.

FLIGHT OF THE PRINCESS CHARLOTTE FROM WARWICK HOUSE.

THE marriage of the Princess Charlotte with the Prince of Orange was, in 1813, it is well known, most studiously desired by her royal father, the Prince Regent, who, however, appears to have been opposed in his wishes by the young lady herself, as well as certain members of her household. Miss Knight, the Princess's sub-governess or companion, in explanation to Sir Henry Halford, the Mentor sent by the Regent to forward his views, suggested that her beloved Princess was really somewhat intractable, and that they were not to blame if she showed a will of her own.

Thus, when the Princess was told, soon after that, she was to meet the Prince of Orange at Lady Liverpool's, she put on a blister prematurely, and kept away from the party. Yet, soon after, she went to Egham races, which Miss Knight thought more reprehensible; and she manifested a yet more obstinate will of her own when Sir Henry Halford, in addition to his usual prescriptions, proposed to her to *marry* the Prince of Orange aforesaid. "Marry I will," said she to the Princess of Wales, "and that directly, in order to enjoy my liberty, but not the Prince of Orange. I think him so ugly that I am sometimes obliged to turn my head away in disgust when he is speaking to me." She told Sir Henry she was willing to marry the Duke of Glocester, but not the Prince, and Miss Knight felt hurt that she should so commit herself; though this preference of her cousin was better received by the Regent than might have been expected.

Sir Henry returned to the charge on the subject of the Orange match, and he must have been a good diplomatist, for he speedily overcame the Princess's aversion. A long conference with her on the 29th of November appears to have turned the current, and she was soon receiving presents and meeting the would-be *futur.* The Princess said, "He is by no means so disagreeable as I expected;" and when the Regent took her aside one night at Carlton House, and said, "Well, it will not do, I suppose?" she answered, "I do not say that. I like his manner very well, as much as I have seen of it;" upon which the Prince was overcome with joy, and joined their hands immediately, and the Princess came home and told Miss Knight she was engaged.

Nevertheless, the Orange match was not to be, for it went off on the resolute determination of the Princess, if she did marry the Prince, not to quit England and live in Holland. Her father would probably have gladly settled her anywhere out of his own sight, but she was invincible upon this point. It is implied that the Grand Duchess Catherine secretly aided her determination, with a view to secure the Orange for a princess of Russia.

Miss Knight was now sent for by the enraged Regent, and ordered to admonish his daughter, which she did, though to very little purpose. The Regent expressed violent displeasure, but his daughter adhered to her stipulation. The Princess of Wales wrote with glee to Lady Charlotte Campbell that her daughter had declared " she would not see her father or any of the family till their consent to her remaining in this country had been obtained, or that otherwise the marriage would be broken off." The Princess took a course of her own, which no one was able to influence. Lord Liverpool, among others, made several fruitless attempts to induce her Royal Highness to waive her demands, and at length affected to yield to them. Thereupon the Princess of Wales was excluded from the Queen's Drawing-rooms because the Regent did not choose to meet her, and the waters were further troubled on this account. The Prince of Orange apparently consented to the Princess Charlotte's terms, but the Regent still pressed her, while the Queen went so far as to buy her wedding clothes, though the question was unsettled. When the Princess heard that it was the intention of the Regent to send for the Orange family and to have the wedding immediately, she was in a state of great alarm, and resolved to have a further explanation with the *futur* himself, and it finished by a definite rupture. The Emperor of Russia, then in this country, attempted to act as mediator, but failed. Of course, after him the Bishop of Salisbury failed also; though he intimated that unless Princess Charlotte would write a submissive letter to her father, and hold out a hope that in a few months she might be induced to give her hand to the Prince of Orange, arrangements would be made by no means agreeable to her inclinations. Her Royal Highness wrote to the Regent a most submissive and affectionate letter, but held out no hope of renewing the treaty of marriage; nor was it renewed.

Miss Knight had failed in enforcing the Regent's wishes upon his daughter. She asserts that some time previously the Regent tapped her on the shoulder and said, "Remember, my dear Chevalier, that Charlotte must lay aside this idle nonsense of thinking that she has a will of her own; while I live she must be subject to me as she is at present, if she were thirty, or forty, or five-and-forty." This programme must, however, under any circumstances, have failed. The Regent withdrew his support. The Duchess of Leeds sent in her resignation, and Miss Knight's dismissal followed.

The dismissal came in this wise. One day in July, about six o'clock, the Regent and the Bishop came to Warwick House, but the former alone came up, and desired Miss Knight would leave him with the Princess Charlotte. He was shut up with her alone for three-quarters of an hour, and then had another quarter of an hour assisted by the Bishop. But when the door opened, "she came out in the greatest agony," and told Miss Knight that she was wanted, and had only one instant to tell her that she and all the servants were to be dismissed, that she herself was to be confined to Carlton House for five days, then to go to Cranbourne Lodge, where she was to see no one but the Queen once a week, and that, if she did not go immediately, the Prince would sleep at Warwick House that night, as well as all the new ladies. Miss Knight begged her to be calm, but she fell on her knees in the greatest agitation, exclaiming, " God Almighty! grant me patience; " and then Miss Knight went up for her own share of the rating. The Prince apologised for putting a lady to inconvenience, but said he wanted her room that evening; and summary ejectment followed.

Then came the afterpiece, so frequently canvassed by other authorities. While this interview was taking place, the Princess Charlotte had slipped down the back stairs, called a hackney-coach, and fled to her mother's. The rush of great dignitaries after her has been recorded in many histories, with the irreverent expression of Lord Eldon, that " she kicked and bounced," but for a long time declined to leave her asylum.

The following version of the affair is from the pen of Lord Brougham : In a fine evening of July, about the hour of seven, when the streets are deserted by all persons of condition, the young Princess Charlotte rushed out of her residence in Warwick House, unattended, hastily crossed Cockspur Street, flung herself into the first hackney-coach she could find, and drove to her mother's house in Connaught Place. The Princess of Wales having gone to pass the day at her Blackheath villa, a messenger was despatched for her,

another for her law adviser, Mr. Brougham, and a
third for Miss Mercer Elphinstone, the young Princess's
bosom friend. Brougham arrived before the Princess
of Wales had returned; and Miss Elphinstone had
alone obeyed the summons.   Soon after the Royal
mother came, accompanied by Lady Charlotte Lindsay, her lady in waiting. It was found that the Princess
Charlotte's fixed resolution was to leave her father's
house, and that which he had appointed for her residence, and to live thenceforth with her mother.   But
Mr. Brougham is understood to have felt himself under
the painful necessity of explaining to her that, by the
law, as all the twelve judges but one had laid it down
in George I.'s reign, and as it was now admitted to be
settled, the King or the Regent had the absolute power
to dispose of the persons of all the Royal Family
while under age.   The Duke of Sussex, who had
always taken her part, was sent for, and attended the
invitation to join in these consultations. It was an un-
toward incident in this remarkable affair, that he had
never seen the Princess of Wales since the investigation
of 1806, which had begun upon a false charge brought
by the wife of one of his equerries, and that he had,
without any kind of warrant from the fact, been supposed by the Princess to have set on, or at least supported, the accuser.   He, however, warmly joined in
the whole of the deliberations of that singular night.
As soon as the flight of the young lady was ascertained,
and the place of her retreat discovered, the Regent's
officers of state and other functionaries were despatched
after her.   The Lord Chancellor Eldon first arrived,
but not in any particularly imposing state, or, " regard
being had " to his eminent station ; for, indeed, he

came in a hackney-coach. Whether it was that the example of the Princess Charlotte herself had for the day brought this simple and economical mode of conveyance into fashion, or that concealment was much studied, or that despatch was deemed more essential than ceremony and pomp—certain it is, that all who came, including the Duke of York, arrived in similar vehicles, and that some remained inclosed in them, without entering the Royal mansion. At length, after much pains and many entreaties, used by the Duke of Sussex and the Princess of Wales herself, as well as Miss Elphinstone and Lady C. Lindsay (whom she always honoured with a just regard), to enforce the advice given by Mr. Brougham, that she should return without delay to her own residence, and submit to the Regent, the young Princess, accompanied by the Duke of York and her governess, who had now been sent for, and arrived in a Royal carriage, returned to Warwick House, between four and five o'clock in the morning. There was then a Westminster election in progress, in consequence of Lord Cochrane's expulsion; and it is said that on her complaining to Mr. Brougham that he, too, was deserting her, and leaving her in her father's power, when the people would have stood by her—he took her to the window, when the morning had just dawned, and, pointing to the Park, and the spacious streets which lay before her, said that he had only to show her a few hours later on the spot where she now stood, and all the people of this vast metropolis would be gathered together on that plain, with one common feeling in her behalf—but that the triumph of one hour would be dearly purchased by the consequences which must assuredly follow in the next, when the troops poured in, and quelled all resistance to the clear and undoubted law of the land, with the certain effusion of blood—nay, that through the rest of her life she never would escape the odium which, in this country, always attends those who, by breaking the law, occasion such calamities. This consideration, much more than any quailing of her dauntless spirit, or faltering of her filial affection, is believed to have weighed upon her mind, and induced her to return home.

Warwick House, which was set apart for the residence of the Princess Charlotte, stood at the end of Warwick Street, which stretches from Cockspur Street towards Carlton House Terrace. It had once been the residence of Sir Phillip Warwick, the Royalist writer of the most picturesque memoirs of the times of the Civil War. It was out of repair and uncomfortable, "resembling a convent;" but here the Princess and Miss Knight looked upon themselves as settled, and the former thought herself emancipated and comparatively happy.*

GEORGE IV. AND HIS QUEEN.

IMMEDIATELY after the death of George III., Queen Caroline, although with more than suspicion hanging over her head, hastened to England to claim her right to the throne of a man who could hardly be considered her husband. His estrangement from her, the aversion he had manifested from the first moment of their ill-assorted marriage, was the only excuse the unfortunate woman could plead for her errors. The announcement

* Abridged, in part, from the *Times'* review of Miss Knight's *Autobiography*.

of her journey to England and the news of her demands for a regal reception caused a great sensation.. " Great bets," says Lord Eldon, " are laid about it. Some people have taken 50 guineas, undertaking in lieu of them to pay a guinea a day till she comes." 50,000*l.* a year were offered if she would consent to play the Queen of England at some continental court. She in her turn demanded a palace in London, a frigate, and the restoration of her name to the Church service. Nothing short of the prayers of the faithful would satisfy her craving for worldly distinction. Mr. Wilberforce, with characteristic indulgence, admired her for her spirit, though he feared she had been " very profligate." Her arrival in London was the signal for a popular ovation, " more out of hatred to the king than out of regard for her." For many weeks the stout lady in the hat and feathers was the favourite of the populace, and Alderman Wood's house in South Audley-street, where she had taken up her quarters, was at all hours of the day surrounded by a mob of noisy king-haters. Mr. Wilberforce, in a letter to Hannah More, recounts their proceedings: " A most shabby assemblage of quite the lowest of the people, who every now and then kept calling out, ' Queen! Queen!' and several times, once in about a quarter of an hour, she came out of one window of a balcony and Alderman Wood at the other." At which the crowd cheered prodigiously. When her trial was decided upon, this misguided woman, determined to brazen it out at all hazards, threatened to come daily to Westminster Hall in " a coach and six in *high style*," and she also insisted on being present at the coronation. " She has written to the king," says Mr. Th. Grenville,

" when and in what dress she should appear at the
coronation. I presume the answer will be: in a white
sheet, in the middle aisle of the Abbey."

The strictest orders were given for her exclusion, but
still she came, and among the extraordinary and disgraceful scenes of the time is that of a Queen of England " trying every door of the Abbey and the Hall,"
and at length withdrew.

" It is worthy of remark that no Diary or Journal
published since 1821 throws any new light upon the
question of the guilt or innocence of the Queen; but it
is significant that Lord Grenville, who had exculpated
her in 1806 upon the occasion of the *Delicate Investigation*, seems to have had no doubt as to her misconduct
in 1821, and both voted and spoke against her on the
second reading of the Bill. This is not the place to
discuss a nasty personal subject, with regard to which,
we suppose, most historians will not differ; but whatever may have been the sins of Caroline of Brunswick,
the behaviour of George IV. towards her had been of
such a kind that, in our judgment, political considera-
tions alone can account for the support which the ma-
jority of the House of Lords afforded him at the trial.
In fact, it is evident from many sources, that the real
issue in the case was lost sight of by all parties; and,
if it may be laid to the charge of the people that they
backed the Queen solely in the interest of revolution,
it is equally certain that the mass of the aristocracy
who sided with the King, only did so because they
thought that the constitution was in danger."*

* *Saturday Review.*

Supernatural Stories.

A VISION IN THE TOWER.

In the reign of Henry III., who far outwent his predecessors in his extensive additions to the Tower, there is recorded the following strange scene:—

In 1239, the King had accumulated within the walls of the fortress an enormous treasure, which he intended to use for its still greater strength and adornment. Fate, however—unless we choose to impute it to human design—seemed against him. The works were scarcely completed when, on the night of St. George in the following year, the foundations gave way, and a noble portal, with walls and bulwarks, on which much expense had been incurred, gave way and fell without a moment's warning, as if by the effect of an earthquake. Stranger still, no sooner were the works restored than, in 1241, the whole again fell down, on the very night and, as we are told, in the very self-same hour, which had proved so destructive to them in the year preceding. Matthew Paris—a most trustworthy and excellent historian—relates the whole occurrence in his Latin Chronicle, and gives a reason for the fall of the portal and rampart, which exhibits a famous character of the previous age in a light which to many of my audience is no doubt new. He relates how that as a certain priest was sleeping, a vision was granted to him. He saw a venerable figure in the robes of an archbishop, with the cross in his hand, walk up to the walls, and, regarding them with a stern and threatening aspect, strike them with the cross which he held, and forthwith they fell as if of some natural convulsion. He asked a priest, who seemed in attendance on the archbishop, who he was? and was answered, that the blessed martyr of Canterbury, the sainted Becket, by birth a Londoner, knowing that these walls were erected, not for defence of the kingdom, but for the injury and prejudice of the Londoners his brethren, had taken this summary mode of repressing the king's designs. On the following morning the vision was found to have been accompanied with palpable proof that, if not the archbishop, some all-powerful agency had effected the result desired. Becket was a warm defender and princely patron of the people; and the Londoners rejoiced at the destruction of these new buildings, which they said were a thorn in their eyes, and delighted to attribute their ruin to one whose memory they so greatly revered.—*The Rev. T. Hugo*, F.S.A.

THE LEGEND OF KILBURN.

KILBURN, a hamlet in the parish of Hampstead, is named from the priory situated near the spot subsequently occupied by a tavern, or tea-drinking house, at a fine spring of mineral water, called Kilburn Wells, at the distance of rather more than two miles from London, north-westward, on the Edgeware Road. It derived its origin from a recluse or hermit, named Goodwyn, who, retiring hither in the reign of Henry I., for the purpose of seclusion, built a cell near a little rivulet, called, in different records, Cuncburna, Keele-bourne, Coldbourne, and Kilbourne, on a site surrounded with wood. The stream rises near West End, Hampstead, and, after passing through Kilburn to Bayswater, it supplies the Serpentine reservoir in Hyde Park, and eventually flows into the Thames near the site of Ranelagh. Whether Goodwyn grew weary of his solitude, or from whatever cause, it appears, from documents yet extant, that between the years 1128 and 1134, he granted his hermitage of *Cuncburna*, with the adjoining lands, to the conventual church of St. Peter, Westminster, " as an alms for the redemption of the whole convent of brethren," under the same conditions and privileges with which " King Ethelrede had granted *Hamstede*," to which manor Kilburn had previously appertained, to the same church.

There is a curious traditionary relation connected with Kilburn Priory, which, however, is not traceable to any authentic source. The legend states, that at a place called Saint John's Wood, near Kilburn, there was a stone of a dark-red colour, which was the stain of the blood of Sir Gervase de Mertoun, which flowed upon it a few centuries ago. Stephen de Mertoun, being enamoured of his brother's wife, frequently insulted her by the avowal of his passion, which she, at length, threatened to make known to Sir Gervase; to prevent which, Stephen resolved to waylay his brother, and slay him. This he effected by seizing him in a narrow lane, and stabbing him in the back, whereupon he fell upon a projecting rock, which became dyed with his blood. In his expiring moments Sir Gervase, recognising his brother, upbraided him with his cruelty, adding, " This stone shall be thy death-bed."

Stephen returned to Kilburn, and his brother's lady still refusing to listen to his criminal proposals, he confined her in a dungeon, and strove to forget his many crimes by a dissolute enjoyment of his wealth and power. Oppressed, however, by his troubled conscience, he determined upon submitting to religious penance; and, ordering his brother's remains to be removed to Kilburn, he gave directions for their re-interment in a handsome mausoleum, erected with stone brought from the quarry where the murder was committed. The identical stone on which his murdered brother had expired formed a part of the tomb; and the eye of the murderer resting upon it, the legend adds, *blood was seen to issue from it!* Struck with horror, the murderer hastened to the Bishop of London, and, making confession of his guilt, demised his property to the Priory of Kilburn. Having thus acted in atonement for his misdeeds, grief and remorse quickly consigned him to the grave.

OMENS TO CHARLES I. AND JAMES II.

IN the career of these unfortunate monarchs we fall upon some striking prophecies, not verbal but symbolic, if we turn from the broad highway of public histories, to the by-paths of private memoirs. Either Clarendon, it is, in his Life (not his public history), or else Laud, who mentions an anecdote connected with the coronation of Charles I., (the son-in-law of the murdered Bourbon,) which threw a gloom upon the spirits of the royal friends, already saddened by the dreadful pesti-

lence which inaugurated the reign of this ill-fated
prince, levying a tribute of one life in sixteen from the
population of the English metropolis.   At the coronation of Charles, it was discovered that all London
would not furnish the quantity of purple velvet required for the royal robes and the furniture of the
throne.   What was to be done?   Decorum required
that the furniture should be all *en suite*.   Nearer than
Genoa no considerable addition could be expected.
That would impose a delay of 150 days.   Upon ma-
ture consideration, and chiefly of the many private
interests that would suffer amongst the multitudes
whom such a solemnity had called up from the country,
it was resolved to robe the King in *white* velvet.   But
this, as it afterwards occurred, was the colour in which
victims were arrayed.   And thus, it was alleged, did
the King's council establish an augury of evil.   Three
other ill omens, of some celebrity, occurred to Charles
I., viz. on occasion of creating his son Charles a Knight
of the Bath; at Oxford some years after; and at the
bar of that tribunal which sat in judgment upon him.

The reign of his second son, James II., the next
reign that could be considered an unfortunate reign,
was inaugurated by the same evil omens.   The day
selected for the coronation (in 1685) was a day memorable for England—it was St. George's day, the 23rd
of April, and entitled, even on a separate account, to
be held a sacred day as the birthday of Shakspeare in
1564, and his deathday in 1616.   The King saved a
sum of sixty thousand pounds by cutting off the ordinary cavalcade from the Tower of London to Westminster.   Even this was imprudent.   It is well known
that, amongst the lowest class of the English, there

is an obstinate prejudice (though unsanctioned by law)
with respect to the obligation imposed by the ceremony
of coronation.   So long as this ceremony is delayed,
or mutilated, they fancy that their obedience is a matter of mere prudence, liable to be enforced by arms,
but not consecrated either by law or by religion.   The
change made by James was, therefore, highly imprudent; shorn of its antique traditionary usages, the
yoke of conscience was lightened at a moment when it
required a double ratification.   Neither was it called
for on motives of economy, for James was unusually
rich.   This voluntary arrangement was, therefore, a
bad beginning; but the accidental omens were worse.
They are thus reported by Blennerhassett (*History of
England to the end of George I.*, vol. iv., p. 1760,
printed at Newcastle-upon-Tyne: 1751).   " The crown
being too little for the king's head, was often in a
tottering condition, and like to fall off."   Even this was
observed attentively by spectators of the most opposite
feelings.   But there was another simultaneous omen,
which affected the Protestant enthusiasts, and the
superstitious, whether Catholic or Protestant, still
more alarmingly.   " The same day the king's arms,
pompously painted in the great altar window of a London church, suddenly fell down without apparent cause,
and broke to pieces, whilst the rest of the window
remained standing."   Blennerhassett mutters the dark
terrors which possessed himself and others.   " These,"
says he, " were reckoned ill omens to the king."

PREMONITION AND VISION TO DR. DONNE.

In the crypt of St. Paul's cathedral is a monumental effigy, in a winding-sheet, a piece of sculpture which excites more curiosity than many a modern memorial in the church. This is the portrait in stone of John Donne, Dean of St. Paul's, and a poet of great power and touching sweetness, a writer of nervous prose, and an eloquent preacher. In Walton's Life of him, there is something remarkably affecting in that passage wherein there is the foreboding of ill in the mind of Donne's wife—and the account of the vision which appeared to him. At this time of Mr. Donne's and his wife's living in Sir Robert's house, in Drury Lane (Sir R. Drewry), the Lord Hay was, by King James, sent upon a glorious embassy to the French king, Henry IV.; and Sir Robert put on a sudden resolution to subject Mr. Donne to be his companion in that journey. And this desire was suddenly made known to his wife, ·who was then with child, and otherwise under so dangerous a habit of body, as to her health, that she protested an unwillingness to allow him any absence from her; saying her divining soul boded her some ill in his absence, and therefore desired him not to leave her. This made Mr. Donne lay aside all thoughts of his journey, and really to resolve against it. But Sir Robert became restless in his persuasions for it, and Mr. Donne was so generous as to think he had sold his liberty, when he had received so many charitable kindnesses from him—and told his wife so; who, therefore, with an unwilling willingness, did give a faint consent to the journey, which was proposed to be but for two months: within a few days after this resolve the Ambassador, Sir Robert, and Mr. Donne, left London, and were the twelfth day got safe to Paris. Two days after their arrival there, Mr. Donne was left alone in the room, where Sir Robert and he, with some others, had dined: to this place Sir Robert returned within half an hour, and as he left, so he found Mr. Donne alone, but in such an ecstacy, and so altered as to his looks, as amazed Sir Robert to behold him, insomuch as he earnestly desired Mr. Donne to declare what had befallen him in the short time of his absence? to which Mr. Donne was not able to make a present answer, but after a long and perplexed pause, said: " I have seen a dreadful vision since I saw you: I have seen my dear wife pass twice by me through this room, with her hair hanging about her shoulders, and a dead child in her arms; this I have seen since I saw you." To which Sir Robert replied, " Here, sir, you have slept since I saw you, and this is the result of some melancholy dream, which I desire you to forget, for you are now awake." To which Mr. Donne replied, " I cannot be surer that I now live, than that I have not slept since I saw you; and I am as sure that, at her second appearing, she stopped and looked me in the face and vanished."

Rest and sleep had not altered Mr. Donne's opinion the next day: for he then affirmed this vision with a more deliberate and so confirmed a confidence, that he inclined Sir Robert to a faint belief that the vision was true. It is well said that desire and doubt have no rest, and it proved so with Sir Robert; for he immediately sent a servant to Drury House, with a charge to hasten back, and bring him word whether

Mrs. Donne were alive, and if alive, in what condition
she was as to her health.   The twelfth day, the messenger returned with this account:—" That he found
and left Mrs. Donne very sad and sick in her bed; and
that, after a long and dangerous labour, she had been
delivered of a dead child.   And, upon examination, the
abortion proved to be the same day, and about the very
hour, that Mr. Donne affirmed he saw her pass by him
in his chamber."

There is much good sense and true feeling in the
observations of good Isaac Walton upon this case—
so delightful is the quaint style, which is the good plain
dress of truth : " This," he adds, " is a relation that
will beget some wonder, and it well may, for most of
our world are at present possessed with an opinion that
visions and miracles are ceased.   And though it is most
certain that two lutes, being both strung and tuned to
an equal pitch, and then one played upon, the other
that is not touched, being laid upon a table, will (like
an echo to a trumpet) warble a faint audible harmony
in answer to the same tune ; yet many will not believe
there is any such thing as a sympathy of souls ; and I
am well pleased that every reader do enjoy his own
opinion."

Walton says he had not this story from Donne himself, but from a " Person of Honour," who " knew
more of the secrets of his heart than any person then
living," and who related it " with such circumstance
and asseveration," that not to say anything of his
hearer's belief, Walton did " verily believe," that the
gentleman " himself believed it."

Drury House was in the parish of St. Clement's
Danes, in the Strand.   Donne, soon after his wife's

death, preached in the church a sermon, taking for his
text, " Lo, I am the man that have seen affliction." He
also had erected in the church his wife's tomb by
Nicholas Stone; it was destroyed when St. Clement's
church was rebuilt in 1680.

APPARITION IN THE TOWER.

AUBREY relates, in his *Miscellanies*, " Sir William
Dugdale did inform me that Major-General Middleton
(since Lord) went into the Highlands of Scotland, to
endeavour to make a party for Charles I., an old gentleman (that was second-sighted) came and told him, that
his endeavour was good, but he would not be successful:
and moreover, that they would put the King to death :
and that several other attempts would be made, but all
in vain ; but that his son would come in, but not reign ;
but at last would be restored."   This Lord Middleton
had a great friendship with the Laird Bocconi, and they
had made an agreement, that the first of them that died
should appear to the other in extremity.   The Lord
Middleton was taken prisoner at Worcester fight, and
was prisoner in the Tower of London, under three
locks.   Lying in his bed pensive, Bocconi appeared to
him : my Lord Middleton asked him if he were dead
or alive? he said, dead, and that he was a ghost ;
and told him, that within three days he would escape,
and he did so, in his wife's cloaths.   When he had done
his message, he gave a frisk, and said :—

> *Givenni, Givenni,* 'tis very strange,
> In the world to see so sudden a change.

And then gathered up and vanished. This account Sir William Dugdale had from the Bishop of Edinburgh. And this (says Aubrey) he hath writ in a book of miscellanies, which I have seen, and is now deposited with other books of his in the Museum of Oxford.

LILLY, THE ASTROLOGER.

LILLY lived in credulous times. He first acquired a taste for fortune-telling by accompanying his mistress to " a cunning or wise man," as to the chance of surviving her husband, with whom she was dissatisfied. When she died, Lilly, who had been her surgical attendant, found attached to her armpit a bag in which were several *sigils,* as he terms them; the obtaining of which contributed to strengthen his predilection for the occult sciences. He chanced to become acquainted with an eccentric personage named Evans, who gave him the first bent toward the studies which tinctured so strongly his future life. Lilly studied for some time under Evans, until they quarrelled regarding the casting of a figure, when the teacher and pupil parted. Our hero had already bought a great quantity of astrological books, and was so far initiated as to carry on his pursuit without assistance.

He retired to the country for four or five years; after which, in 1641, " perceiving there was money to be got in London," he returned thither, and began assiduously to labour in his vocation. He soon became known, more especially as he did not content himself with practising the arts of prophesying and magic in private, but also published a work, termed *Merlin the Younger,* which he continued subsequently to issue as a periodical almanack. This arrested the attention of men very speedily, and his fame became universal.

One of his trumpery bundles of periodical prophecies attracted the anxious attention of Parliament, whose members, not altogether approving of some of the author's dark sayings, ordered him to be imprisoned. As the sergeant-at-arms, however, was conveying him away, a personage stepped forward, who saved the astrologer from the distress of a long imprisonment, which, after he was once in gaol, might have been his doom. " Oliver Cromwell, lieutenant-general of the army, having never seen me, caused me to be produced again, where he steadfastly beheld me for a good space, and then I went with the messenger." Nevertheless he was not taken at that time to gaol, and though he gave himself up to custody next day from motives of deference to the Parliament, he was liberated again immediately by Cromwell's interposition. Whether or not Cromwell believed in the astrologer's power, it is impossible to say, but certainly he and his party owed some gratitude to Lilly. At the siege of Colchester, when the parliamentarian soldiers grew doubtful of the issue of the attack, and slackened somewhat in their exertions, Lilly and another person of the same character were sent for to encourage the besiegers, which they did by predicting the speedy surrender of the place, as it really fell out. Another example of the same kind occurred when Cromwell was in Scotland. On the eve of one of the battles fought by Oliver, a soldier mounted himself on an eminence, and as the troops filed past him, he cried out, " Lo, hear what Lilly saith; you are in this month promised victory; fight it out, brave boys—and then read that month's prediction!"

Our astrologer declares that, in the early part of the Civil War, his opinions leant decidedly to the side of the royalists, until they gave him some ground of offence. His sentiments in reality, however, appear to have been strongly guided by the circumstance of which party was at the time uppermost. He prophesied first for the King; when his cause declined, our hero prophesied stoutly for the Parliament; and when its influence waned, he put forth some broad hints of its approaching fall. King Charles himself put great confidence in the powers of Lilly; for at the time of his stay, or rather confinement, at Hampton Court, when he meditated an escape from the soldiery that surrounded him, he dispatched a secret messenger to the astrologer, desiring him to pronounce what would be the safest place of refuge and concealment. Lilly erected a figure and gave an answer, but the prediction was not put to the proof; the King, before it could be acted on, being removed to the Isle of Wight. In his *Memoirs*, Lilly boasts that he procured for Charles, when in Carrisbroke Castle, a file and a bottle of aqua-fortis, with which to sever the bars of his window asunder.

Next, the House of Commons, after the Great Fire of London, called the astrologer once more before them, and examined him as to his *fore-knowledge* of that calamity, which was then attributed to conspirators. Lilly answered them in the following words: " May it please your honours, after the beheading of the late King, considering that in the three subsequent years the Parliament acted nothing which concerned the settlement of the nation in peace; and seeing the generality

of the people dissatisfied, the citizens of London dis-
contented, and the soldiery prone to mutiny, I was
desirous, according to the best knowledge God had
given me, to make inquiry by the art I studied, what
might from that time happen unto the Parliament and
the nation in general.   At last, having satisfied myself
as well as I could, and perfected my judgment therein, I
thought it most convenient to signify my intentions and
conceptions thereof, in types, hieroglyphics, &c, without any commentary, that so my judgment might be
concealed from the vulgar, and made manifest only to
the wise—I herein imitating the examples of many
wise philosophers who had done the like. . . . Having
found that the city of London should be sadly afflicted
with a Great Plague, and not long after with an exorbi-
tant Fire, I framed these hieroglyphics as represented in
my book, which have in eff ·t proved very true." One
of the wiseacres of the Committee then asked him,
" Did you foresee the year ? "   " I did not," replied
Lilly, " nor was desirous; of that I made no scrutiny."
The astrologer then told them that he had found, after
much pains, that the fire was not of man, but of God.

   To give the reader some idea of the folly which could
believe him to. have predicted the Fire and Plague, we
may mention that, in the book where the prophecy is
said to occur, he gives sixteen pages of wood-cuts, being
enigmatical emblems of what was to befall the city for
many hundred years to come.   On the eighth page is
a set of *graves* and *winding-sheets*, and the thirteenth
some *houses on fire*, and this is the prediction !   The
Fire and Plague were almost in one year, and the
figures in the book are in very different places, though
he meant the emblems to indicate consecutive events.

Besides, a rebellion would have filled the graves, a burnt
warehouse would have answered the figure fire, just as
well as the plague or the burning of half the city.
The hieroglyphics, we may add, depicted every event
under the sun, so that the astrologer in no case could
have been put out. The inferior and uneducated
classes of the community followed, with blind super-
stition, the example set before them by their betters.
Love, sickness, trade, marriage, and on a thousand other
subjects, was the astrologer daily consulted, not only
by the citizens of London, but by residents in every
corner of the land. And so skilfully and equivocally
did he frame his responses, that he was very seldom
brought into annoyance from the failure of his predictions. This was fortunate for him, for though the courts
of law would not meddle with a true prophet, they did
not scruple to punish a bungler in the art. On one
occasion, a " half-witted young woman" brought him
before the courts to answer for having taken two-and-
sixpence from her for a prediction regarding stolen
goods. Lilly spoke for himself, and having satisfied
the court that astrology was a lawful art, he got easily
off by proving the woman to be half mad.

Of his success in deception, there exist abundance
of proofs. The number of his dupes was not confined
to the vulgar and illiterate, but included individuals of
real worth and learning, who courted his acquaintance
and respected his predictions. We know not whether
it "should more move our anger or our mirth" to see an
assemblage of British senators—the contemporaries of
Milton and Clarendon, of Hampden and Falkland—in
an age which roused into action so many and such
mighty energies, gravely engaged in ascertaining the

causes of a great national calamity, from the prescience of a knavish fortune-teller, and puzzling their wisdoms to interpret the symbolical flames which blazed in the mis-shapen wood-cuts of his oracular publications. From this disgrace to the wisdom of the seventeenth century, we have to make one memorable exception.

Butler, in his *Hudibras,* has inimitably portrayed Lilly under the character of Sidrophel; nearly all that the poet has ascribed to him, as Dr. Grey remarks, in his annotations, the reader will find verified in his autobiography :—

> Quoth Ralph, Not far from hence doth dwell
> A cunning man, hight Sidrophel,
> That deals in Destiny's dark Counsels,
> And sage Opinions of the Moon sells,
> To whom all People far and near
> On deep Importances repair;
> When Brass and Pewter hap to stray,
> And Linen slinks out of the way ;
> When Geese and Pullen are seduced,
> And Sows of Sucking Pigs are chows'd ;
> When Cats do feel indisposition
> And need the opinion of Physician ;
> When Murrain reigns in Hogs and Sheep,
> And Chickens languish of the Pip ;
> When Yeast and outward means do *fail*
> And have no power to work on Ale ;
> When Butter does refuse to come,
> And Love grows cross and *humoursome*,
> To Him with Questions and with Urine
> They for Discovery flock, or Curing.
>
> *Hudibras,* Part ii. Canto 3.

Of Lilly's *White King's Prophecy* eighteen hundred copies were sold in three days, and it was oft reprinted. Lilly left to a tailor, whom he had adopted, the copyright of this almanack, which he had continued to publish for thirty successive years.

TOUCHING FOR THE EVIL.

THE Touching for Disease by the royal hand is mentioned by Peter of Blois, in the twelfth century ; and it is stated to be traceable to Edward the Confessor. Sir John Fortescue, in his defence of the house of Lancaster against that of York, argued that the crown could not descend to a female, because the queen is not qualified by the form of anointing her, used at the coronation, to cure the disease called " the King's Evil." Aubrey refers to " the king's evill, from the king curing of it with his touch." This miraculous gift was almost reserved for the Stuarts to claim. Dr. Ralph Bathurst, one of the chaplains to King Charles I., " no superstitious man," says Aubrey, protested to him that " the curing of the king's evill by the touch of the king doth puzzle his philosophie ; for when they were of the House of Yorke or Lancaster, it did." The solemn words, " I touch, but God healeth," were always pronounced by the sovereign when he " touched" or administered " the sovereign salve," as Bulwer calls it. Then we read of vervain root and baked toads being worn in silken bags around the neck, as charms for the evil.

The practice of touching was at its full height in the reign of Charles II. ; and in the first four years after his restoration he " touched" nearly 24,000 persons. Pepys, in his *Diary*, June 23, 1666, records how he waited at Whitehall, " to see the king touch people for the king's evil." He did not come, but kept the poor persons waiting all the morning in the rain in the garden : " afterward he touched them in the banqueting-house." The practice was continued by Charles's successors. The Hon. Daines Barrington tells of an old man who was witness in a cause, and averred that when Queen Anne was at Oxford, she touched him, then a child, for the evil: the old man added, that he did not believe himself to have had the evil; but "his parents were poor, and he had no objection to a bit of gold." Again, Dr. Johnson, when a boy, was taken by his father from Lichfield to London, to be touched for the evil by Queen Anne, in 1712, and whom Johnson described as a lady in diamonds, and a long black hood. Mrs. Bray speaks of a "Queen Anne's farthing" being a charm for curing the king's evil in Devonshire.

At a late period, the use of certain coins was in common vogue, which, being touched by the king, were supposed to have the power of warding off evil or scrofula. These coins are called *Royal Touch-pieces*: several are preserved in the British Museum; and Mr. Roach Smith has one which has been so extensively used that the impression is quite abraded. The Pretender had his touch-pieces, and thought that he had a right to the English crown, and therefore had the power to confer the royal cure: probably, the claim, in either case, was equal.

" The practice was supposed to have expired with the Stuarts; but the point being disputed, reference was made to the library of the Duke of Sussex, and four several Oxford editions of the Book of Common Prayer were found, all printed after the accession of the House of Hanover, and all containing as an integral part of the service ' the office for the healing.'"—*Lord Braybrooke's Notes to Pepys's Diary.*

DAVID RAMSAY AND THE DIVINING-ROD.

AMONG the many strange tales told of the mysterious use of the Divining-rod is the following, in Lilly's *Life and Times*:—

"In the year 1634, David Ramsay, his Majesty's clock-maker, had been informed that there was a great quantity of treasure buried in the cloister of Westminster Abbey; he acquaints Dean Williams therewith, who was also then Bishop of Lincoln; the Dean gave him liberty to search after it, with this proviso, that if any was discovered, his church should have a share of it. Davy Ramsay finds out one John Scott, who pretended the use of the Mosaical rods, to assist him herein. I was desired to join with him, unto which I consented. One winter's night, Davy Ramsay, with several gentlemen, myself, and Scott, entered the cloisters; we played the hazel rod round about the cloister; upon the west side of the cloisters the rods moved one over another, an argument that the treasure was there. The labourers digged at least six feet deep, and there we met with a coffin; but in regard it was not heavy, we did not open, which we afterwards much repented. From the cloisters we went into the Abbey church, where, upon a sudden (there being no wind when we began), so fierce, so high, so blustering and loud a wind did rise, that we verily believed the west end of the church would have fallen upon us. Our rods would not move at all; the candles and torches, all but one, were extinguished, or burned very dimly. John Scott, my partner, was amazed, looked pale, knew not what to think or do, until I gave directions and command to dismiss the demons; which, when done, all was quiet again, and each man returned to his lodging late, about twelve o'clock at night. I could never since be induced to join with any in such like actions (Davy Ramsay brought a half-quartern sack to put the treasure in).

"The true miscarriage of the business was by reason of so many people being present at the operation, for there were about thirty, some laughing, others deriding us; so that if we had not dismissed the demons, I believe most part of the Abbey church had been blown down. *Secrecy and intelligent operators, with a strong confidence and knowledge of what they are doing, are best for this work.*"

LADY DAVIES, THE PROPHETESS.

THE prophetic Madame Davers, who is mentioned by Randolph, in 1638, is the notorious Lady Eleanor Davies, the youngest daughter of George, Earl of Castlehaven, and wife of Sir John Davies, Attorney-General for Ireland. She was a remarkable woman, but unfortunately believed that a prophetic mantle had descended upon her. The idea that she was a prophetess arose from finding that the letters of her name, twisted into an anagram, might be read, *Reveal, O Daniel!* For some of her prophetical visions, she was summoned before the High Commission Court. "Much pains," says Dr. Heylin, "was taken by the Court to dispossess her of this spirit; but all would not do till the Dean of Arches shot her with an arrow from her own quiver, and hit upon the real anagram,

Dame Eleanor Davies, *Never so mad a ladie !* She was subsequently prosecuted for " An enthusiastic epistle to King Charles," for which she was fined 3,000*l.*, and imprisoned two years in the Gatehouse, Westminster. Soon after the death of Sir John Davies, she married Sir Archibald Douglas, but seems not to have lived happily with either of her husbands. She died in the year 1652.

DR. LAMB, THE CONJUROR.

DR. JOHN LAMB, of Tardebigger, in Worcester, was a vile impostor who practised juggling, fortune-telling, recovering lost goods ; and likewise picked the pockets of lads and lasses by showing the earthly countenances of their future husbands and wives in his crystal glass. He was indicted at Worcester for witchcraft, &c., after which he removed to London, where he was confined for some time in the King's Bench Prison. He there practised as a doctor, with great success, till, having committed an outrage on a young woman, he was tried at the Old Bailey, but saved from punishment by the powerful influence of his patron and protector, Buckingham, whose confidential physician he was. The popular voice accused Lamb of several grave offences, particularly against women ; and on the very same day that the Duke was denounced in the House of Commons as the cause of England's calamities, his dependent and Doctor was murdered by an infuriated mob in the city of London. The story of his death, from a rare contemporary pamphlet, is worth transcribing :—

"On Friday, he (Dr. Lamb) went to see a play at the Fortune Theatre, in Golden Lane, Cripplegate, where the boys of the town, and other unruly people, having observed him present, after the play was ended flocked about him, and (after the manner of the common people, who follow a hubbub when it is once set on foot) began in a confused manner to assault and offer him violence. He, in affright, made towards the city as fast as he could, and hired a company of sailors that were there to be his guard. But so great was the fury of the people, who pelted him with stones and other things that came next to hand, that the sailors had much to do to bring him in safety as far as Moorgate. The rage of the people about that place increased so much, that the sailors, for their own sake, were forced to leave the protection of him; and then the multitude pursued him through Coleman Street to the Old Jewry, no house being able or daring to give him protection, though he attempted many. Four constables were there raised to appease the tumult; who, all too late for his safety, brought him to the Counter in the Poultry, where he was bestowed upon command of the lord mayor. For, before he was brought thither, the people had had him down, and with stones and cudgels, and other weapons, had so beaten him that his skull was broken, and all parts of his body bruised and wounded, whereupon, though surgeons in vain were sent for, he never spoke a word, but lay languishing till the next morning, and then died."

On the day of Lamb's death, placards containing the following words were displayed on the walls of London : " Who rules the kingdom ? — The King. Who rules the King ? — The Duke. Who rules the

Duke?—The devil. Let the Duke look to it, or he will be served as his doctor was served." A few weeks afterwards the Duke was assassinated by Felton.

In a very rare pamphlet giving an account of Lamb, is a woodcut of his " ignominious death," the citizens and apprentices pelting him to death, June 13, 1628.

MURDER AND AN APPARITION.

AUBREY relates, in his *Miscellanies*, that in 1647, the Lord Mohun's son and heir, (a gallant gentleman, valiant, and a great master of fencing and horsemanship,) had a quarrel with Prince Griffin; there was a challenge, and they were to fight on horseback in Chelsea Fields in the morning. Mr. Mohun went accordingly to meet him, but about Ebury Farm,* he was met by some, who quarrelled with him and pistoled him; it was believed, by the order of Prince Griffin; for he was sure that Mr. Mohun, being so much the better horseman, would have killed him had they fought.

* Ebury or Eybury Farm, "towards Chelsea," was a farm of 430 acres, meadow and pasture, let on lease by Queen Elizabeth, (when we hear of it for the first time,) to a person of the name of Whashe, who paid 21*l.* per annum, and by whom " the same was let to divers persons, who, for their private commodity, did inclose the same, and had made pastures of arable land; thereby not only annoying her Majesty in her walks and progresses, but to the hindrance of her game, and great injury of the common, which at Lammas was wont to be laid open " (*Strype*). Eybury Farm occupied the site of what is now Ebury Square, and was originally of the nature of Lammas-land, or land subject to lay open as common, after Lammas-tide, for the benefit of the inhabitants of the parish. The Neat at Chelsea was of the same description, and the owners of Piccadilly Hall and Leicester House paid Lammas-money to the poor of St. Martin's long after their houses were erected, as late as the reign of Charles II.—*Cunningham's Handbook of London,* 2nd edit. p. 172.

Now, in James Street, in Covent Garden, did then lodge a gentlewoman, a handsome woman, but common, who was Mr. Mohun's sweetheart. Mr. Mohun was murdered about ten o'clock in the morning; and at that very time, his mistress, being in bed, saw Mr. Mohun come to her bedside, draw the curtain, look upon her, and go away; she called after him, but no answer; she knocked for her maid, asked her for Mr. Mohun; she said she did not see him, and had the key of her chamber-door in her pocket. This account, (adds Aubrey,) my friend aforesaid had from the gentlewoman's own mouth, and her maid's.

A parallel story to this, is, that Mr. Brown, (brother-in-law to the Lord Coningsby,) discovered his murder to several. His phantom appeared to his sister and her maid in Fleet Street, about the time he was killed in Herefordshire, which was about a year since, 1693.

A VISION OF LORD HERBERT OF CHERBURY.

A PASSAGE in the life of this profound and original thinker, but of fanciful temperament, presents us with one of the most striking instances recorded, in modern times, of direct Divine interposition.

Lord Herbert, who lived in the reigns of James I. and Charles I., and who died in the same year as the latter monarch, is described by Leland to have been "of the first that formed deism into a system, and asserted the sufficiency, universality, and absolute perfection, of natural religion, with a view to discard all extraordinary revelation as useless and needless." He was inimical to every positive religion, but admitted

the possibility of immediate revelation from heaven,
though he denied that any tradition from others could
have sufficient certainty. Five fundamental truths
of natural religion he held to be such as all man-
kind are bound to acknowledge, and damned those
heathens who do not receive them as summarily as
any theologian.

These opinions are the groundwork of Herbert's
work *De Veritate*, &c., having completed which he
showed it to the great scholar, Hugo Grotius, who
having perused it, exhorted him earnestly to print and
publish it; "howbeit," says Herbert, in his Memoirs,
the earliest instance of autobiography in our language,
" as the frame of my whole book was so different from
anything which had been written heretofore, I found I
must either renounce the authority of all that had been
written formerly, concerning the method of finding out
truth, and consequently insist upon my own way, or
hazard myself to a general censure, concerning the
whole argument of my book; I must confess it did not
a little animate me that the two great persons above-
mentioned, (Grotius and Tieleners,) did so highly value
it, yet as I knew it would meet with much opposition,
I did consider whether it was not better for me a while
to suppress it; being thus doubtful in my chamber,
one fair day in the summer, my casement being opened
towards the south, the sun shining clear, and no wind
stirring, I took my book *De Veritate* in my hand, and
kneeling on my knees, devoutly said these words:—

" ' O thou eternal God, Author of the light which
now shines upon me, and giver of all inward illumina-
tions, I do beseech Thee of Thy infinite goodness to
pardon a greater request than a sinner ought to make;

I am not satisfied enough whether I shall publish this book *De Veritate*; if it be to Thy glory, I beseech Thee give me some sign from heaven; if not, I shall suppress it.'

"I had no sooner spoken these words, but a loud, though yet gentle noise came from the heavens, (for it was like nothing on earth), which did so comfort and cheer me, that I took my petition as granted, and that I had the sign I demanded, whereupon also I resolved to print my book; this (how strange soever it may seem) I protest before the eternal God is true, neither am I in any way superstitiously deceived herein, since I did not only clearly hear the noise, but in the serenest sky that I ever saw, being without all cloud, did to my thinking see the place from whence it came.

"And now I sent my book to be printed," &c.

Dr. Leland makes the following observations on this part of the narrative: "I have no doubt of his lordship's sincerity in the account. The serious air with which he relates it, and the solemn protestation he makes, as in the presence of the eternal God, will not suffer us to question the truth of what he relates; viz. that he both made that address to God which he mentions, and that in consequence of this, he was persuaded that he heard the noise he takes notice of, and which he took to come from heaven, and regarded as a mark of God's approbation of the request he had made; and accordingly, this great man was determined by it to publish the book. He seems to have considered it as a kind of *imprimatur* given to him from heaven, and as signifying the divine approbation of the book itself, and of what was contained in it."— *View of the Deistical Writers*, i. 27.

Lord Herbert "dyed (1648) at his house in Queen Street, in the parish of St. Giles's-in-the-Fields, very serenely; asked what was the clock, and then, sayd he, an hour hence I shall depart; he then turned his head to the other side and expired."—*Aubrey's Lives*, ii. 387.

A VISION ON LONDON BRIDGE.

IN a very rare and curious pamphlet in the Royal Library, in the British Museum, we find the following account of a Vision seen upon London Bridge, in March 1661. The book itself is only a small quarto, of four leaves; but the title is magnificent: " Strange News from the West, being Sights seen in the Air Westward, on Thursday last, being the 21 day of the present March, by divers persons of credit standing on London Bridge between 7 and 8 of the clock at night. Two great Armies marching forth of two Clouds, and encountering each other; but, after a sharp dispute, they suddenly vanished. Also, some remarkable Sights that were seen to issue forth of a Cloud that seemed like a Mountain, in the shape of a Bull, a Bear, a Lyon, and an Elephant and Castle on his back, and the manner how they all vanished."

The following are the details of the vision:—" Upon the 21st day of March, about, or between, 7 and 8 of the clock at night, divers persons living in the City, as they came over London Bridge, discovered several clouds in strange shapes, at which they suddenly made a stand, to see what might be the event of so miraculous a change in the motion of the Heavens. The first cloud seemed to turn into the form or shape of a

Cathedral, with a tower advancing from the middle of
it upwards, which continued for a small space, and
then vanished away.   Another turned into a tree,
spreading itself like an oak — as near as could be
judged—which, in a short space, vanished. Between
these two was, as it were standing, a great mountain,
which continued in the same form near a quarter of an
hour; after which, the mountain still remaining, there
appeared several strange shapes, one after another,
issuing out of the said mountain, about the middle of
the right side thereof; the first seemed to be formed
like a Crokedile, with his mouth wide open; this continued a very short space, and, by degrees, was trans-
formed into the form of a furious Bull; and, not long
after, it was changed into the form of a Lyon; but it
continued so a short time, and was altered into a Bear,
and soon after, into a Hog, or Boar, as near as those
could guess who were spectators. After all these shapes
had appeared, the mountain seemed to be divided and
altered into the form of two monstrous beasts, fastened
together by the hinder parts, drawing one apart from
the other: that which appeared on the left hand
resembled an Elephant with a castle upon his back;
that upon the right hand, we could not so well determine, but it seemed to us like a Lyon, or some such
like beast.

" The castle on the back of the Elephant vanished, the
Elephant himself loosing his shape; and, where the
castle stood, there rose up a small number of men, as we
judged, about some four or six; these were in conti-
nual motion. The other beast, which was beheld on the
right hand, seemed to be altered into the form of a
Horse, with a rider on his back, and, after a small pro-

portion of time, the whole vanished, falling downward.
Then arose another great cloud, and in small time it
formed itself into the likeness of the head of a great
Whale, the mouth of which stood wide open.   After
this, at some distance, on the right hand, appeared a
cloud, which became like unto a head or cap, with
a horn, or ear, on each side thereof, which was of a
very considerable length.   Between these two rose a
few men, who moved up and down with a swift motion;
and immediately after, they all vanished except one
man, who still continued moving up and down, with
much state and majesty.   In the meantime arose near
adjacent unto this head, or cap, another cloud, out of
which cloud issued forth an Army, or great body of
men ; and upon the left hand arose another Army, each
of which marched one towards the other; about this
time, the single man vanished away,—and the two
Armies seemed to approach very near each other, and
encounter, maintaining a combat one against the other,
and, after a short combat, all vanished.   During all
this time, there seemed to our best apprehension, a
flame of fire along the Strand, towards the city of
London."   Such is the account of these "strange
sights," as they are truly called.

This was the age for seeing *wonders in the air*, which
it was sometimes dangerous not to see.   The author of
the *History of the Great Plague* tells us that he was
in some danger from a crowd in St. Giles's, because he
could not discover an Angel in the air holding a drawn
sword in his hand.

The author of the *Chronicles of London Bridge*
well observes : " Minds of more weakness than piety
gave a ready faith to such visions; and in convulsed

or sorrowful times, were often hearing voices which
spake not, and seeing signs which were never visible:
willing to deceive, or be deceived, they saw, like Po-
lonius, clouds 'backed like an ousel,' or 'very like a
whale :'

> So hypochondriac fancies represent
> Ships, armies, battles, in the firmament;
> 'Till smaller eyes the exhalations solve,
> And all to its first matter, clouds, resolve."

STEPNEY LEGEND OF THE FISH AND THE RING.

THIS old tale is commemorated in a marble monu-
ment on the outer east wall of the chancel of the church
of St. Dunstan, at Stepney. It is to the memory of
Dame Rebecca Berry, wife of Sir Thomas Elton, of
Stratford Bow, and relict of Sir John Berry, 1696.
The inscription is as follows:—

> Come, ladies, ye that would appear,
> Like angels fine, come dress you here;
> Come, dress you at this marble stone,
> And make this humble grave your own,
> Which once adorn'd as fair a mind,
> As e'er yet lodg'd in womankind.
> So she was dress'd, whose humble life
> Was free from pride, was free from strife;
> Free from all envious brawls and jars,
> Of human life, the civil wars:
> These ne'er disturb'd her peaceful mind,
> Which still was gentle, still was kind.
> Her very looks, her garb, her mien,
> Disclos'd the humble soul within.
> Trace through her every scene of life,
> View her as widow, virgin, wife;
> Still the same humble she appears,
> The same in youth, the same in years;
> The same in low and high estate,
> Ne'er vex'd with this, or mov'd with that.

Go, ladies, now, and if you'd be
As fair, as great, as good as she,
Go learn of her Humility.

The arms on this monument are—Paly of six on a
bend three mullets (Elton) impaling a fish; and in
the dexter chief point an annulet between two bends
wavy. This coat of arms has given rise to the tradition that Lady Berry was the heroine of a popular
ballad called, " The Cruel Knight, or Fortunate Farmer's Daughter," the story of which is briefly this:
A knight, passing by a cottage, hears the cries of a
woman in labour, and his knowledge in the occult
sciences informs him that the child then born is destined
to be his wife; he endeavours to elude the decrees of
fate, and avoid so ignoble an alliance, by various attempts to destroy the child, which are defeated. At
length, when grown to woman's state, he takes her to
the sea-side, intending to drown her, but relents; at the
same time, throwing a ring into the sea, he commands
her never to see his face again, on pain of instant
death, unless she can produce that ring. She afterwards becomes a cook, and finds the ring in a cod-fish,
as she is dressing it for dinner. The marriage takes
place, of course. The ballad, it must be observed, lays
the scene of the story in Yorkshire.

DREAM TESTIMONY.

IN the year 1698, the Rev. Mr. Smythies, curate of
St. Giles, Cripplegate, published an account of the
robbery and murder of a parishioner, Mr. Stockden,
by three men, on the night of December 23, 1695, and

of the discovery of the culprits by several dreams of
Mrs. Greenwood, Mr. Stockden's neighbour. The main
points are these:—In the first dream Mr. Stockden
showed Mrs. Greenwood a house in Thames Street,
telling her that one of the men was there.   Thither
she went the next morning, accompanied by a female
neighbour, and learned that Maynard lodged there, but
was then out.   In .the second dream Mr. Stockden
represented Maynard's face to her, with a mole on the
side of the nose (he being unknown to Mrs. Greenwood), and also tells her that a wire-drawer must take
him into custody.   Such a person, an intimate of Maynard's, is found, and ultimately Maynard is apprehended.
In the third dream Mr. Stockden appeared with a
countenance apparently displeased, and carried her to
a house in Old Street where she had never been, and
told her that one of the men lodged there.   There, as
before, she repaired with her friend, and found that
Marsh often came there.   He had absconded, and was
ultimately taken in another place.   In the fourth
dream Mr. Stockden carried her over the bridge, up
the Borough, and into a yard, where she saw Bevil, the
third man, and his wife (whom she had never seen before).   Upon her relating this dream, it was thought
that it was one of the prison-yards; and she accordingly went to the Marshalsea, accompanied by Mr.
Stockden's housekeeper, who had been gagged on the
night of the murder.   Mrs. Greenwood there recognised
the man and woman whom she had seen in her dream.
The man, although not recognised at first by the housekeeper, being without his periwig, was identified by her
when he had it on.   The three men were executed,
and Mr. Stockden once more appeared in a dream to

Mrs. Greenwood, and said to her, "Elizabeth, I thank thee; the God of heaven reward thee for what thou hast done." After this, we are informed that she was "freed from these frights, which had caused much alteration in her countenance."

A MYSTERIOUS LADY.

In James Street, Covent Garden, towards the beginning of the last century, lived a mysterious lady, who died in the month of March 1720, and was then described as "unknown." She was a middle-sized person, with dark brown hair, and very beautiful features, and mistress of every accomplishment of high fashion. Her age appeared to be between 30 and 40. Her circumstances were affluent, and she possessed many rich trinkets, set with diamonds. Mr. John Ward, of Hackney, published several particulars of her in the newspapers; and amongst others, that a servant had been directed by her to deliver him a letter after her death; but as no servant appeared, he felt himself required to notice those circumstances, in order to acquaint her relations that her death occurred suddenly after a masquerade, where she declared she had conversed with the King; and it was remembered that she had been seen in the private apartments of Queen Anne, though, after the Queen's demise, she lived in obscurity. This unknown arrived in London from Mansfield, in 1714, drawn by six horses. She frequently said that her father was a nobleman, but that her elder brother dying unmarried, the title was extinct; adding, that she had an uncle then living, whose title was his least recommendation. It was conjectured that she might be the daughter of a Roman Catholic who had consigned her to a convent, whence a brother had released her and supported her in privacy. She was buried at St. Paul's, Covent Garden.

***

STORY OF THE COCK LANE GHOST.

Everyone has heard of this noted imposture, and most persons agree that it made much more noise in its day, than all the spirits in Queen Anne's reign put together. After the lapse of a hundred years, we hear it repeatedly referred to as a sort of climax of imposition; and the story will bear repetition. The scene is a narrow lane, over against Pie Corner, in Smithfield, where the Great Fire of London ended.

In the year 1762, Mr. Parsons, the clerk of St. Sepulchre's Church, lived in a house in Cock Lane, West Smithfield. Being a frugal man, Parsons let lodgings; and being an unlucky one, he let his lodgings to a lady who went by the name of Miss Fanny, and was the sister of the deceased wife of a Mr. K—, with whom Fanny cohabited. Miss Fanny took into her bed, " in the absence of the gentleman, who was in the country," her landlord's daughter, a child twelve years old. Some days afterwards, Miss Fanny complained to the family of violent knockings, which kept her awake at night. They were like the hammering of a shoemaker upon his lapstone, and were attributed to that cause; but the neighbour shoemaker ceased work on Sunday, and the hammerings were as loud as ever. The nuisance became serious. Mr. and Mrs. Parsons invited their neighbours to hear the noises, and everyone came away convinced that there was a ghost behind the wainscoting. The clergyman of the parish was invited to exorcise, but he prudently declined to come to knocks with such a ghost. Miss Fanny, who hardly cared to have so much public attention drawn upon her private arrangements, quitted, and went to live at Clerkenwell. She afterwards there died, and was buried in St. John's Church.

For eighteen months, quiet had reigned in Cock Lane; but immediately Miss Fanny died, the knockings recommenced. In whatever bed the child was placed, knockings and scratchings were heard underneath, and the girl appeared to be violently agitated as by fits. Parsons, the father, had now, either in fraud or in conviction, thoroughly taken the matter up. He undertook to question the ghost, and dictated how many knocks should serve for an answer affirmative or negative. By much cross-examination, it was discovered that the rapper was the ghost of Miss Fanny, who wished to inform the world that "the gentleman," whom we wot of, had poisoned her, by putting arsenic into her *purl* when she was ill of the small-pox.

The girl became alarmed; and the story getting wind, the house in Cock Lane, in which the father lived, was visited by hundreds and thousands of people,— many from mere curiosity, and others, perhaps, with a higher object in view. Indeed, it became a fashion to make up parties to visit the scene of the imposture. Horace Walpole, (January 29, 1762,) says, "I am ashamed to tell you that we are again dipped into an egregious scene of folly. The reigning fashion is a ghost—a ghost that would not pass muster in the paltriest convent in the Apennine. It only knocks and scratches; does not pretend to appear or to speak. The clergy give it their benediction; and all the world, whether believers or infidels, go to hear it." Again: "I could send you volumes on the ghost, and I believe, if I were to stay a little, I might send its *life*, dedicated to my Lord Dartmouth, by the ordinary of Newgate, its two great patrons. A drunken parish clerk set it on foot, out of revenge, the Methodists have adopted it, and the whole town think of nothing else.

"I went to hear it," says Walpole, "for it is not an *apparition*, but an *audition*. We set out from the Opera, changed our clothes at Northumberland House, the Duke of York, Lady Northumberland, Lady Mary Coke, Lord Hertford, and I, all in one hackney-coach, and drove to the spot: it rained in torrents; yet the lane was full of mob, and the house so full we could not get in; at last they discovered it was the Duke of York, and the company squeezed themselves into one another's pockets to make room for us. The house, which is borrowed, and to which the ghost has adjourned, is wretchedly small and miserable; when we opened the chamber, in which were fifty people, with no light but one tallow-candle at the end, we tumbled over the bed of the child to whom the ghost comes, and whom they are murdering by inches in such insufferable heat and stench. At the top of the room are ropes to dry clothes. I asked if we were to have rope-dancing between the acts? We heard nothing; they told us, as they would at a puppet-show, that it would not come that night till seven in the morning; that is when there are only 'prentices and old women. We stayed, however, till half-an-hour after one. The Methodists have promised their contributions; provisions are sent in like forage, and all the taverns and ale-houses in the neighbourhood make fortunes. The most diverting part is to hear people wondering *when it will be found out,* as if there was anything to find out—as if the actors would make their noises when they can be discovered."

Mrs. Montague writes to Mrs. Robinson—" As I suppose you read the newspapers, you will see mention of the ghost; but without you were here upon the spot, you could never conceive that the most bungling performance of the silliest imposture could take up the attention and conversation of all the fine world." Grave persons of high station, and not thought of as candidates for Bedlam, came away from Cock Lane shaking their heads thoughtfully. The clerk of St. Sepulchre's found the ghost the most profitable lodger he had ever had. The wainscots were pulled down, and the floor pulled up, but they saw no ghost, and discovered no trick. The child was removed to other houses, but the ghost followed, and distinctly rapped its declaration that it would never leave her.

As the noises were made for the detection, it is said, of some human crime, many gentlemen, eminent for their rank and character, were invited by the Rev. Mr. Aldrich, of Clerkenwell, to investigate the reality of the knockings ; and this was the more necessary, as the supposed spirit had publicly promised, by an affirmative knock, that one would attend any one of the gentlemen into the vault under the church of St. John, Clerkenwell, where the body was deposited, and give a token of her presence by a knock upon her coffin. This investigation took place on the night of the 1st of February 1762 ; and Dr. Johnson, one of the gentlemen present, printed at the time an account of what they

saw and heard:—About ten at night the gentlemen
met in the chamber in which the girl, supposed to be
disturbed by a spirit, had, with proper caution, been
put to bed by several ladies.   They sat rather
more than an hour, and hearing nothing, went down
stairs, when they interrogated the father of the girl,
who denied, in the strongest terms, any knowledge or
belief of fraud.   The supposed spirit had before publicly promised by an affirmative knock, that it would
attend one of the gentlemen into the vault under the
church of St. John, Clerkenwell, where the body is
deposited, and give a token of her presence there, by a
knock upon her coffin; it was therefore determined to
make this trial of the existence or veracity of the supposed spirit.   While they were inquiring and delibe-
rating, they were summoned into the girl's chamber by
some ladies who were near her bed, and who had heard
knocks and scratches.   When the gentlemen entered,
the girl declared that she felt the spirit like a mouse
upon her back, and was required to hold her hands out
of bed.   From that time, though the spirit was very
solemnly required to manifest its existence by appearance, by impression on the hand or body of any present,
by scratches, knocks, or any other agency, no evidence
of any preternatural power was exhibited.   The spirit
was then very seriously advertised, that the person to
whom the promise was made of striking the coffin was
then about to visit the vault, and that the performance
of the promise was then claimed.   The company at one
o'clock went into the church, and the gentleman to
whom the promise was made went with another into the
vault.   The spirit was solemnly required to perform
its promise, but nothing more than silence ensued: the

person supposed to be accused by the spirit then went down with several others, but no effect was perceived. Upon their return they examined the girl, but could draw no confession from her. Between two and three she desired and was permitted to go home with her father. It is, therefore, the opinion of the whole assembly, that the child has some art of making or counterfeiting a particular noise, and that there is no agency of any higher cause.

Of course the enquiry made the matter worse. Johnson had discovered, at the utmost, that the spirit told lies; whereas the point in dispute was whether the spirit made noises. As matter of probability, it could scarcely be less probable that the spirit should be a false spirit, than that it should be a spirit at all. Johnson was laughed at by the whole town, and fashion was beginning to tire of its toy.

Churchill ridiculed the enquiry in a poem in four books, called the " Ghost "—a poem whereof little is now remembered but the sketch of Johnson, under the name of Pomposo.

We quote the rest of the story from a contemporary :— It was now given out that the coffin in which the body of the supposed ghost had been deposited, or at least the body itself, had been displaced, or removed out of the vault. Mr. K——, therefore, thought proper to take with him to the vault the undertaker who buried Miss Fanny, and such other unprejudiced persons as, on inspection, might be able to prove the weakness of such a suggestion.

Accordingly, on February 25th, in the afternoon, Mr. K——, with a clergyman, the undertaker, clerk, and sexton of the parish, and two or three gentlemen, went into the vault, when the undertaker presently knew the coffin, which was taken from under the others, and easily seen to be the same, as there was no plate or inscription ; and, to satisfy further, the coffin being opened before Mr. K——, the body was found in it.

Others, in the meantime, were taking other steps to find out where the fraud, if any, lay. The girl was removed from house to house, and was said to be constantly attended with the usual noises, though bound and muffled hand and foot, and that without any motion in her lips, and when she appeared asleep: nay, they were often said to be heard in rooms at a considerable distance from that where she lay.

At last her bed was tied up, in the manner of a hammock, about a yard and a half from the ground, and her hands and feet extended as wide as they could without injury, and fastened with fillets for two nights successively, during which no noises were heard.

The next day, being pressed to confess, and being told that if the knockings and scratchings were not heard any more, she, her father, and mother, would be sent to Newgate; and half an hour being given her to consider, she desired she might be put to bed to try if the noises would come: she lay in her bed this night much longer than usual, but no noises. This was on a Saturday.

Sunday, being told that the approaching night only would be allowed for a trial, she concealed a board about four inches broad, and six long, under her stays. This board was used to set the kettle upon. Having got into bed, she told the gentleman she would bring F—— at six the next morning.

The master of the house, however, and a friend of

his, being informed by the maids that the girl had taken a board to bed with her, impatiently waited for the appointed hour, when she began to knock and scratch upon the board, remarking, however, what they themselves were convinced of, "that these noises were not like those which used to be made." She was then told that she had taken a board to bed, and on her denying it, searched, and caught in a lie.

The two gentlemen, who with the maids were the only persons present at this scene, sent to a third gentleman, to acquaint him that the whole affair was detected, and to desire his immediate attendance; but he brought another along with him.

Their concurrent opinion was, that the child had been frightened into this attempt by the threats which had been made the two preceding nights; and the master of the house also, and his friend, both declared "that the noises the girl had made that morning had not the least likeness to the former noises."

Probably the organs with which she performed these strange noises were not always in a proper tone for that purpose, and she imagined she might be able to supply the place of them by a piece of board.

At length Mr. K——, the paramour of Fanny, thought proper to vindicate his character in a legal way. On the 10th of July, the father and mother of the child, one Mary Frazer, who, it seems, acted as an interpreter between the ghost and those who examined her, a clergyman, and a reputable tradesman, were tried at Guildhall, before Lord Mansfield, by a special jury, and convicted of conspiracy against the life and character of Mr. K——; and the court, choosing that he who had been so much injured on this occasion should receive some reparation by the punishment of the offenders, deferred giving sentence for seven or eight months, in the hope that the parties might, in the meantime, make it up. Accordingly, the clergyman and tradesman agreed to pay Mr. K—— a round sum, some say between five and six hundred pounds, to purchase their pardon, and were thereupon dismissed with a severe reprimand. The father was ordered to stand in the pillory three times in one month, once at the end of Cock Lane, and after that one year in the King's Bench prison; Elizabeth, his wife, one year; and Mary Frazer, six months in Bridewell, with hard labour. But the father appearing to be out of his mind at the time he was first to stand on the pillory, the execution of that part of his sentence was deferred to another day, when, as well as on other days of his standing there, the populace, instead of pelting him, collected for him a considerable sum of money. Mr. Brown, of Amen Corner, who had published some letters on the affair, did not fare so well; for he was fined 50*l*. The mistress of the Ladies' Charity School, on Snow Hill, was a believer in the story; for, in the school minutes, 1763, the Ladies of the Committee censured the mistress for listening to the story of the Cock Lane Ghost, and " desired her to keep her belief in the article to herself."

In the course of the year, Oliver Goldsmith wrote for Newbury, the publisher, a pamphlet descriptive of the Cock Lane Ghost, for which he received three guineas: it is reprinted in Cunningham's edition of Goldsmith's Collected Works.

The trick is thought to have been carried on by means of ventriloquism, a faculty then little understood. The girl ultimately confessed as much. She died so

recently as 1807, having been twice married; her
second husband was a market-gardener at Chiswick.
(*London Scenes and London People*, 1863.)   Such is
the author's explanation; but the more probable story
is, that the bed-clothes being opened, the board was
found, upon which the girl had been accustomed to
rap; and this simple process annihilated the Cock Lane
Ghost.

Another explanation is, that K—— had incurred the
resentment of Parsons by pressing him for the payment
of some money he had lent him; and revenge for which
is supposed to have prompted the diabolical contrivance.
The Rev. Mr. Moore, to whom the spirit promised to
strike the coffin, and who accompanied Dr. Johnson in
the investigation, was so overwhelmed by the detection
of the imposture that he did not long survive it.

We have another circumstance to add relating to
the body of Fanny, which we have received from Mr.
Wykeham Archer.   When this artist was drawing in
the crypt of St. John's, in a narrow cloister on the
north side, (there being, at that time, coffins, and fragments of shrouds, and human remains lying about in
disorder,) the sexton's boy pointed out to Mr. Archer
one of the coffins, and said it was "Scratching Fanny."
Being thus reminded of the Cock Lane Ghost, Mr.
Archer removed the lid of the coffin, which was loose,
and saw therein the body of a woman, which had become *adipocere* : the face perfect, handsome oval, with
aquiline nose.   (Mr. Archer asked, "Will not arsenic
produce adipocere?")   She was said to have been
poisoned, although the charge is understood to have
been disproved.   Mr. A. was assured by one of the
churchwardens that the coffin had always been

understood to contain the body of the woman whose spirit was said to have haunted the house in Cock Lane.

In the *Liber Albus* (1419), we read that, in the Plantagenet times, loose women, and men who encouraged them, were led through the town—the men to the pillory, with mocking minstrels, and the women, with the same mockery, through Cheap and Newgate—to Cock Lane, there to take up their abode, just outside the City Walls. In Cock Lane, some sixty years since, wholesale whipmakers lived, and grew wealthy; the place being handy to Smithfield. •

A GHOST STORY EXPLAINED.

THE following account, from the *Diaries of a Lady of Quality*, of what was long considered, even by highly intellectual persons, a supernatural incident, shows that some *ghost stories*, however seemingly well authenticated, are capable of easy explanation, from natural and ordinary causes, when the circumstances are fully known.

At a meeting of the Literary Club, at which Dr. Johnson, Mr. Burke, and several other eminent characters of the day were present, it was observed that an old gentleman, who had never missed one of the meetings of the society, was that day absent. His absence was considered as the more extraordinary, because he happened to be president that day. While the company were expressing their surprise at this circumstance, they saw their friend enter the room, wrapped in a long white gown, his countenance wan and very much fallen. He sat down in his place, and when his friends wondered at his dress, he waved his hand, nodded to each separately, and disappeared from the room without speaking. The gentlemen, surprised at this circumstance, and determined to investigate it, called for the waiter, and asked whether anybody had been seen upon the staircase which led to the room where they were sitting. They were answered that no person had been seen either to enter the house or to mount the stairs, and that both the staircase and the entrance had been constantly filled with comers and goers. Not satisfied with this, they sent to the house of the gentleman whom they had just seen, to enquire whether he had been out. His residence happened to be very near the coffee-house where they were, and their messenger immediately returned with the following melancholy intelligence: their friend had died about ten minutes before, of a violent fever, which had confined him entirely to his bed for several days.

Some of the most eminent men of the club gave themselves great pains to discover the imposition which it was thought had been practised upon them; others firmly believed that their friend's ghost had actually appeared to them; and the latter opinion was confirmed by the total failure of all enquiries. All their efforts proved vain to remove the veil of mystery which hung over this transaction. At last they determined to remove the club to another part of the town, entering at the same time into an engagement never to reveal the circumstance which had occasioned this change.

Many years afterwards, as Mr. Burke was sitting at dinner with some friends at his own house, he was told that a poor old woman, who was dying in an obscure garret in the midst of the greatest wretchedness, had just said that she could not die in peace unless she could reveal a most important secret to Mr. Burke. This summons appeared so like a fraudulent means to extort money, that Mr. Burke refused to go. In a short time he received a second and still more pressing message, and, at the same time, such an account was given of the poor creature's extreme poverty and misery, that his compassion was excited, and he determined to go, in spite of the earnest entreaties of his friends, who still feared for his safety. They accordingly watched in the little obscure alley, saw him ascend the staircase which led to the garret in which he was told the poor woman was living, and reminded him that succour was at hand.

Mr. Burke soon returned. He told his friends that he had found everything as it had been represented; that the old woman had died after telling him a very extraordinary circumstance, which had given him great satisfaction. He then related all the former part of the story, and added that the dying woman had confessed that she had been guilty of a neglect which had cost an unfortunate man his life. She said that, upon her deathbed, she was determined to make all the atonement in her power, confess her error, and had therefore requested his presence, knowing him to be the most intimate friend of the deceased. She also said that, some years before, she was nurse to a gentleman who was ill of a dangerous fever, and named Mr. Burke's friend. On a particular day, which she named, she was told by the physician that the crisis of the disease was that day to be expected, and that the ultimate issue of the malady would very much depend on the patient's being kept perfectly quiet at that moment, which could only be done by incessant watching, as the delirium would run very high just before. In that case the physician directed that the patient should be forcibly detained in bed, as the least cold would prove fatal. He therefore ordered the nurse not to leave the room upon any account the whole of the day. The nurse added, that in the afternoon of that day a neighbour had called upon her; that seeing the gentleman perfectly quiet, she had ventured to leave the room for ten minutes: when she returned, she found her patient gone. In a few minutes he returned, and expired immediately. When she heard the enquiries made, she was well aware what had given birth to them, but was at that time prevented by shame from confessing the truth.

MARYLEBONE FANATICS:
SHARP AND BRYAN, BROTHERS AND SOUTHCOTE.

THE first of this quartette was *William Sharp*, the celebrated line-engraver; *Bryan* was an irregular Quaker, who had engrafted sectarian doctrines on an original stock of fervid religious feeling. Sharp, who possessed a fraternal regard for him, had him instructed in copper-plate printing, supplied him with presses, &c., and enabled him to commence business; but they soon quarrelled. Jacob Bryan had some intellectual pretensions, and a strong tide of animal spirits, which, when religion was launched on it, swelled to enthusiasm, tossed reason to the skies, or whirled her in mystic eddies. Sharp found him, one morning, groaning on the floor, between his two printing-presses, at his workshop in Marylebone Street, complaining how much he was oppressed, by bearing, after the example of the Saviour, part of the sins of the people; and he soon after had a vision, commanding him to proceed to Avignon, on a Divine mission. He accordingly set out immediately, in full reliance on Divine Providence, leaving his wife to negotiate the sale of his printing business: thus, Sharp lost his printer, but Bryan kept his faith. The issue of this mission was so ambiguous, that it might be combined into an accomplishment of its supposed object, according as an ardent or a cool imagination was employed on the subject; but the missionary (Bryan) returned to England, and then became a dyer, and so much altered, that a few years after he could even pun upon the suffering and confession which St. Paul has expressed in his text—" I die daily."

The Animal Magnetism of Mesmer, and the mysteries of Emanuel Swedenborg, had, by some means or other, in Sharp's time, become mingled in the imaginations of their respective or their mutual followers; and Bryan and several others were supposed to be endowed, though not in the same degree, with a sort of half-physical and half-miraculous power of curing diseases, and imparting the thoughts or sympathies of distant friends. De Loutherbourg, the painter, (one of the disciples,) was believed by the sect to be a very Esculapius in this divine art; but Bryan was held to be far less powerful, and was so by his own confession. Sharp had also some inferior pretensions of the same kind, which gradually died away.

But, behold! Richard Brothers arose! The Millennium was at hand! The Jews were to be gathered together, and were to re-occupy Jerusalem; and Sharp and Brothers were to march thither with their squadrons! Due preparations were accordingly made, and boundless expectations were raised by the distinguished artist. Upon a friend remonstrating that none of their preparations appeared to be of a marine nature, and enquiring how the chosen colony were to cross the seas, Sharp answered, " Oh, you'll see; there'll be an earthquake, and a miraculous transportation will take place." Nor can Sharp's faith or sincerity on this point be in the least distrusted; for he actually engraved *two* plates of the portrait of the prophet Brothers; having calculated that one would not print the great number of impressions that would be wanted when the important advent should arrive; and he added to each the following inscription : " Fully believing this to be the man appointed by God, I engrave his likeness : W. Sharp." The wags of the day, in reading it, generally chose to put the comma-pause in the wrong place, and to understand and interpret, that W. Sharp hereby made oath that he engraved the portrait of the man appointed, namely, Richard Brothers. But if the reader paused in the place where Sharp intended, the sentence expressed, " Fully believing this to be the man appointed by God "—to do what ? to head the Jews in their predestined march to recover Jerusalem ? or to die in a madhouse ? one being expressed as much as the other.

Brothers, however, in his prophecy, had mentioned *dates*, which were stubborn things. Yet the failure of the accomplishment of this prophecy may have helped to recommend " the Woman clothed with the Sun !" who now arose, as might be thought somewhat *mal-apropos*, in the West. Such was *Joanna Southcote*. The Scriptures had said, " The sceptre shall not de-

part from Israel, nor a lawgiver from between his feet,
until Shiloh come ; and to him *shall the gathering of
my people be.*"   When Brothers was incarcerated in a
madhouse in Islington, Joanna, then living in service
at Exeter, persuaded herself that she held converse
with the devil, and communion with the Holy Ghost,
by whom she pretended to be inspired.   When the
day of dread that was to leave London in ruins, while
it ushered forth Brothers and Sharp on their holy
errand, passed calmly over, the seers of coming events
began to look out for new ground, and to prevaricate
most unblushingly.   The *days* of prophecy, said Sharp,
were sometimes weeks or months ; nay, according to
one text, a thousand years were but as a single day, and
one day was but as a thousand years.   But he finally
clung to the deathbed prediction of Jacob, supported
as it was by the ocular demonstration of the coming
Shiloh.   In vain Sir William Drummond explained
that Shiloh was in reality the ancient Asiatic name of
a star in Scorpio ; or that Joanna herself sold for a
trifle, or gave away in her loving-kindness, the impression of a trumpery seal, which at the Great Day was
to constitute the discriminating mark between the
righteous and the ungodly.

> " The soul's dark cottage, batter'd and bewray'd,
>   Lets in new light through chinks that time has made ;"

but battered and bewrayed as Sharp's faith in modern
revelation might well be supposed to have become, no
new light streamed in at the chinks.   It was still the
soul's dark cottage when the corpse of the prophetess
lay in her house in Manchester Street.   When the
surgeons were proceeding to an anatomical investiga-

tion of the causes of her death, and the mob were gathering without-doors, in anticipation of a riot or a miracle, Sharp continued to maintain that she was not dead, but entranced! And, at a subsequent period, when he was sitting to Mr. Haydon for his portrait, he predicted to the painter, that Joanna would reappear in the month of July 1822. " But suppose she should not?" said Haydon. " I tell you she will," retorted Sharp; "but if she would not, nothing should shake my faith in her Divine mission." And those who were near Sharp's person during his last illness, state that in this belief he died at Chiswick, July 25, 1824. He is interred in Chiswick churchyard, near De Loutherbourg, for whom, at one period, he entertained mystic reverence.

Brothers had been a Lieutenant in the Navy: among other extravagances, he styled himself " the Nephew of God," and predicted the downfall of all sovereigns, of the Naval power of Great Britain, and the restoration of the Jews under him as Prince and Deliverer. All these events were to be accomplished between 1792 and 1798. His writings, founded on oral narrations of the Scriptures, at length led the Government to interfere; and on March 14, 1795, he was apprehended at his lodgings, No. 58 in Haddington Street, under a warrant from the Secretary of State. After a long examination before the Privy Council, in which Brothers persisted in the divinity of his legation, he was committed to the custody of a State messenger. In a few days he was declared a lunatic, by a jury appointed under a commission, and was subsequently removed to a private asylum at Islington, where he remained till 1806, when he was discharged by the authority of Lord Chancellor Erskine. He died of consumption, in Upper Baker Street, in 1824.

Joanna Southcote was a native of Exeter, and commenced her delusions early in life. In 1792, she assumed to be a prophetess, and of the Woman of the Wilderness, and began to give to her followers scaled papers—called *seals*,—which were to protect both from the judgments of the present and a future life, and thousands were caught in the snare. Her predictions were delivered in prose and in doggerel rhyme, and related to the denunciation of judgments on the surrounding nations, and promised a speedy approach of the Millennium. In the course of her mission, as she called it, she employed a boy, who pretended to see visions, and attempted, instead of writing, to adjust them on the walls of her chapel, " the House of God." A schism took place among her followers, one of whom, named Carpenter, took possession of the place, and wrote against her; not denying her mission, but asserting that she had exceeded it.

Early in her last year, she secluded herself from male society, and fancied that she was with child—by the Holy Spirit!—that she was to bring forth the Shiloh promised by Jacob Bryan, and which she pretended was to be the second appearance of the Messiah ! This child was to be born before the end of harvest; as she was certain it was impossible for her to survive undelivered till Christmas. The harvest, however, was ended, and Christmas came, without the fulfilment of her predictions. Some months previously, Joanna had declared her pretended situation, and invited the opinion of the faculty. Several medical men admitted her pregnancy, among whom was Dr. Reece; others doubted;

and some, among whom was Dr. Sims, denied it. Her followers, however, were confident, and some of them made her costly presents, among which was a Bible, which cost 40*l.*; and a superb cot or cradle, 200*l.*; besides a richly-embroidered coverlid, etc. About ten weeks before Christmas, she was confined to her bed, and took very little sustenance, until pain and sickness greatly reduced her. Mr. Want, a surgeon, warned her of her approaching end; but she insisted that all her sufferings were only preparatory to the birth of the Shiloh. At last she admitted the possibility of a temporary dissolution, and expressly ordered that means should be taken to preserve warmth in her for four days, after which she was to revive, and be delivered; or, in failure, she gave permission to be opened. On December 27th, 1814, she actually died, in her sixty-fifth year: in four days after, she was opened in the presence of fifteen medical men, when it was demonstrated that she was not pregnant, and that her complaint arose from bile and flatulency, from indulgence and want of exercise. In her last hours, she was attended by Ann Underwood, her secretary; Mr. Tozer, who was called her high-priest; Colonel Harwood, and some other persons of property; and so determined were many of her followers to be deceived, that neither death nor dissection could convince them of their error. Her remains were removed to an undertaker's in Oxford Street, whence they were interred, with great secrecy, in the cemetery of St. John's Wood Chapel. Here is a tablet to her memory with these lines:—

> " While through all thy wondrous days,
> Heaven and Earth enraptur'd gaz'd—

> While vain Sages think they know
> Secrets Thou Alone canst show,
> Time alone will tell what hour
> Thou'lt appear to 'Greater' Power.
>   SABINEUS."

Another tablet, erected by her friends fourteen years after her decease, bears, in letters of gold, three Scripture texts.

For some years, her followers, Southcotonians, continued to meet and commit various extravagances.   In 1817, a party of the disciples, conceiving themselves directed by God to proclaim the coming of the Shiloh on earth, for this purpose marched in procession through Temple Bar, and the leader sounded a brazen trumpet, and declared the coming of Shiloh, the Prince of Peace; while his wife shouted, " Wo! wo! to the inhabitants of the earth, because of the coming of Shiloh!" The crowd pelted the fanatics with mud, some disturbance ensued, and some of the disciples were taken into custody, and had to answer for their conduct before a magistrate. A considerable number of the sect appeared to have remained in Devonshire, Joanna's native county.

The whole affair was one of the most monstrous delusions of our time. " It is not long since," says Sir Benjamin Brodie, "no small number of persons, and not merely those belonging to the uneducated classes, were led to believe that a dropsical old woman was about to be the mother of the real Shiloh." The writer, however, adds that Joanna was " not altogether an impostor, but in part the victim of her own imagination."—*Psychological Inquiries*, 3rd edit.

HALLUCINATION IN ST. PAUL'S.

Dr. Arnould, of Camberwell, relates a singular case of a gentleman, about thirty-five years of age, of active habits and good constitution, living in the neighbourhood of London, who, being subject to hallucinations, was, by Dr. Arnould's advice, sent to a private asylum, where he remained about two years. His delusions gradually subsided, and he was afterwards restored to his family. The account which he gave of himself was as follows:—

One afternoon, in the month of May, feeling unsettled, and not inclined to business, he took a walk into the City; and having strolled into St. Paul's Churchyard, he stopped at the shop-window of Bowles and Carver, and looked at the prints, one of which was a view of the Cathedral. He had not been there long before a short, grave-looking elderly gentleman, dressed in dark-brown clothes, came up and began to examine the prints, and soon entered into conversation with him, praising the print of St. Paul's in the shop-window; relating some anecdotes of Sir Christopher Wren, the architect; and asking if he had ever been "up St. Paul's." He replied in the negative. The stranger then proposed they should dine together, and then ascend the Cathedral: this was agreed to, and having dined at a tavern in a court in the neighbourhood, they very soon left the table, and ascended to the ball just below the cross, which they entered alone. They had not been there many minutes, when, while he was gazing on the extensive prospect, and delighted with the splendid view below him, the grave old gentleman pulled out from an inside coat pocket something like a compass, having round the edges some curious figures; then having muttered some unintelligible words, he placed it in the centre of the ball. He felt a great trembling and a sort of horror come over him, which was increased by his companion asking him if he should like to see any friend at a distance, and to know what he was at that moment doing, for if so, the latter could show him any such person. Now his father had been for a long time in bad health, and for some weeks past he had not visited him. A sudden thought came into his mind that he should like to see his father. He had no sooner expressed his wish than the exact person of his father was immediately presented to his sight on the mirror, reclining in his arm-chair, and taking his afternoon sleep. He became overwhelmed with terror at the clearness of the vision; and entreated his mysterious companion to descend, as he felt very ill. The request was complied with; and in parting under the northern portico, the stranger said to him, " Remember! you are the slave of the man of the mirror!"

He returned in the evening to his house: he felt unquiet, depressed, gloomy, apprehensive, and haunted with thoughts of the stranger: for the last three months he had been conscious of the power of the latter over him. Dr. Arnould inquired of him in what way this power was exercised. He cast on the Doctor a look of suspicion, mingled with confidence, took his arm, and after leading him through two or three rooms, and then into the garden, exclaimed: " It's of no use—there is no concealment from him, for all places are alike open to him—he sees and he hears us *now*!" the Doctor says: " I asked him where the man was that heard us? He replied, in a voice of deep agitation, ' Have I not told you that he lives in the ball below the cross on the top of St. Paul's, and that he only comes down to take a walk in the churchyard, and get his dinner in the house in the dark alley?   Since the fatal interview with the necromancer,' he continued, ' for such I believe him to be, he is continually dragging me before him on his mirror, and he not only sees me every moment of the day, but he reads all my thoughts, and I have a dreadful consciousness that no action of my life is free from his inspection, and no place can afford me security from his power.'   On my replying that the darkness of the night would afford him protection from these machinations, he said, ' I know what you mean, but you are quite mistaken.   I have only told you of the mirror; ' but in some part of the building which he passed in coming away, he showed me what he called a great bell, and I heard sounds which came from it, and which went to it; sounds of laughter, and of anger, and of pain; there was a dreadful confusion of sounds, and as I listened with wonder and affright, he said, ' This is my organ of hearing; this great bell is in communication with all other bells within the circle of hieroglyphics, by which every word spoken by those under my control is made audible to me.'   Seeing me look surprised at him, he said, 'I have not yet told you all; for he practises his spells by hieroglyphics on walls and houses, and wields his power, like a detestable tyrant as he is, over the minds of those whom he has enchanted, and who are the objects of his constant spite, within the circle of the hieroglyphics.'   I asked him what these hieroglyphics were, and how he perceived them? He replied, ' Signs and symbols which you, in your ignorance of their true meaning, have taken for letters and words, and reading as you have thought, *Day and Martin* and *Warren's Blacking!*   Oh, that is all nonsense! they are only the mysterious characters which he traces to mark the boundary of his dominion, and by which he prevents all escape from his tremendous power.   How have I toiled and laboured to get beyond the limits of his influence!   Once I walked for three days and nights, till I fell down under a wall exhausted by fatigue, and dropped asleep; but on waking I saw the dreadful signs before my eyes, and I felt myself as completely under his infernal spells at the end as at the beginning of my journey.'" *

Dr. de Boismont, who, in his clever work *On Hallucinations*, gives the above, considers that there cannot be an instance of an hallucination more completely followed out in detail, or better adapted to produce a conviction in the minds of persons not acquainted with these singular phenomena, than the one which is here related by Prichard.   In the Middle Ages this person would have been considered as possessed, and would doubtless have been subjected to the ceremonies of exorcism.   Even in the present day, a similar tale would find many believers.

It is highly probable that this person had formerly visited St. Paul's, but, having become insane, his recollections of previous occurrences were mixed up in a very extravagant manner.   As they grew more and more vivid, they became depicted by the imagination in a manner which caused the eye to mistake them for realities.

* A Treatise on Insanity, and other Disorders affecting the Mind, by James Cowles Prichard, p. 455. London: 1835.

THE GHOST IN THE TOWER.

In that storehouse of interesting and serviceable information, *Notes and Queries*—to which we are often indebted for enlightenment upon curious and out-of-the-way subjects—we find the following circumstantial account of an apparition which has excited considerable discussion upon its several points.

The narrator, in the first instance, is Mr. Edward Lenthal Swifte, who, at the period of the occurrence, was Keeper of the Crown Jewels in the Tower, and resident upon the spot where the apparition took place. Mr. Swifte relates: " One Saturday night in October 1817, about ' the witching hour,' I was at supper with my then wife, our little boy, and her sister, in the sitting-room of the Jewel-house, which is said to have been the doleful prison of Anne Boleyn, and of the ten Bishops whom Oliver Cromwell piously accommodated therein. For an accurate picture of the *locus in quo* my scene is laid, I refer to George Cruikshank's woodcut in Ainsworth's *Tower of London*; and I am persuaded that my gallant successor in office, General Wyndham, will not refuse its collation with my statement.

" The room was—as it still is—irregularly shaped, having three doors and two windows, which last are cut nearly nine feet deep into the outer wall; between these is a chimney-piece projecting far into the room, and (then) surmounted with a large oil-picture. On the night in question, the doors were all closed, heavy and dark cloth curtains were let down over the windows, and the only light in the room was that of two candles on the table. I sate at the foot of the table, my son

on my right hand, his mother fronting the chimney-
piece, and her sister on the opposite side.   I had offered
a glass of wine-and-water to my wife, when, on putting
it to her lips, she paused, and exclaimed, 'Good God!
what is that?'   I looked up, and saw a cylindrical
figure, like a glass tube, seemingly about the thickness
of my arm, and hovering between the ceiling and the
table ; its contents appeared to be a dense fluid, white
and pale azure, like to the gathering of a summer-cloud,
and incessantly rolling and mingling within the cylin-
der.   This lasted about two minutes ; when it began
slowly to move before my sister-in-law ; then, following
the oblong shape of the table *before* my son and myself;
passing *behind* my wife, it passed for a moment over
her right shoulder, [observe, there was no mirror
opposite to her, in which she could then behold it.]
Instantly, she crouched down, and with both hands,
covering her shoulder, she shrieked out, 'Oh Christ!
it has seized me!'   Even now, while writing, I feel the
fresh horror of that moment.   I caught up my chair,
struck at the wainscot behind her, rushed upstairs to
the other children's room, and told the terrified nurse
what I had seen.   Meanwhile, the other domestics had
hurried into the parlour, where their mistress recounted
to them the scene, even as I was detailing it above
stairs.

" The marvel—some will say the absurdity—of all
this is enhanced by the fact that *neither my sister-in-
law, nor my son, beheld this appearance*—though to their
mortal vision it was as apparent as to my wife's demise.
When I, the next morning, related the night's horrors
to our chaplain, after the service in the Tower Church,
he asked me, Might not some person have his natural

senses deceived? And if one, why not *two*? My answer was, If *two*, why not two thousand?

" I am bound to add, that shortly before this strange event, some young lady-residents in the Tower had been, I know not wherefore, suspected of making phantasmagorial experiments at their windows, which, be it observed, had no command whatever on any windows in my dwelling. An additional sentry was accordingly posted, so as to overlook any such attempt.

" Happen, however, as it might, following hard at heel the visitation of my household, one of the night-sentries at the Jewel-office was, as he said, alarmed by a figure like a huge bear, issuing from underneath the door; he thrust at it with his bayonet, which stuck in the door, even as my chair dinted the wainscot; he dropped in a fit, and was carried senseless to the guard-room. His fellow-sentry declared that the man was neither asleep nor drunk, he himself having seen him the moment before, awake and sober. Of all this I avouch nothing more than that I saw the poor man in the guard-house prostrated with terror, and that in two or three days the fatal result—be it of fact or of fancy—was—that *he died*." To the truth of the above, Mr. Swifte pledges his faith and honour.

This statement is succeeded by the following from Mr. George Offor: " This unfortunate affair took place in Jan. 1816, and shows the extreme folly of attempting to frighten with the shade of a supernatural appearance the bravest of men. Before the burning of the Armouries, there was a paved yard in front of the Jewel-house, from which a gloomy and ghost-like doorway led down a flight of steps to the Mint. Some strange noises were heard in this gloomy

corner; and on a dark night, at twelve, the sentry saw
a figure like a bear cross the pavement, and disappear
down the steps. This so terrified him that he fell, and
in a few hours, after having recovered sufficiently to
tell the tale, he died. It was fully believed to have
arisen from phantasmagoria, and the Governor, with
the Colonel of the regiment, doubled the sentry, and
used such energetic precautions that no more ghosts
haunted the Tower from that time. The soldier bore
a high character for bravery and good conduct. I was
then in my thirtieth year, and was present when his
body was buried with military honours in the Flemish
burial-ground, St. Katherine's." (*Notes and Queries*,
2nd S. No. 245.)

To this communication, Mr. Swifte replies that the
Jewel-house guard had been doubled *before* the fatal
night—and there—*nec post nec propter hoc*—for the
surer supervising the phantasmagorean pranks; that
on the morrow he saw the soldier in the main-guard
room with his fellow-sentinel, who testified " to his
being awake and sober, and that he spoke to him on
the previous night just before the alarm; that the
latter distinctly said, the ' figure ' did not ' cross the
pavement, and disappear down the steps ' of the sally-
post, but issued from underneath the Jewel-house
door; which was beneath a stone archway as utterly
out of the reach of any phantasmagorean apparatus (if
such there were) as of Mr. Swifte's windows." Mr.
Swifte saw the sentry on the following day; and in
another day or two—*not* "in a few hours "—the sentry
died.

At the suggestion of the chaplain, who conceived
the possibility of the phantasmagoria having been *in-
tromitted* at the windows of Mr. Swifte's room, a scien-

tific friend inspected the parlour, but could not solve the mystery. Subsequently, a professor of the Black Art offered to produce any "cylindrical figure" on the ceiling or elsewhere in the room, *provided* that he might have his own apparatus on the table; or (with the curtains drawn back) on the seven-gun battery, fronting the window—where, by the bye, a sentry is posted day and night. His *provisos* were, of course, declined. Mr. Swifte adds that Sir John Reresby, when Governor of York Castle, in the reign of James II., relates that one of the night-sentries was grievously alarmed by the appearance of a huge black animal issuing upon him from underneath a door in the castle. (*Notes and Queries*, 2nd S. No. 247.) Sir John Reresby's story is as follows: "One of my soldiers being on guard, about eleven in the night, at the gate of Clifford Tower, the very night after the witch was arraigned, he heard a great noise at the Castle; and going to the porch, he there saw a scroll of paper creep from under the door, which, as he imagined, by moonlight, turned first into the shape of a monkey, and thence assumed the form of a turkey-cock, which passed to and fro by him. Surprised at this, he went to the prison, and called the under-keeper, who came and saw the scroll dance up and down, and creep under the door, where there was scarce an opening of the thickness of half-a-crown. This extraordinary story I had from the mouth of both one and the other." (*Memoirs of Sir John Reresby*, p. 238.)

In reply to an inquiry, Mr. Swifte states that the phantom did not assume any other form; but at the moment of his wife's exclamation, and his striking at it with the chair, it crossed the upper end of the table, and disappeared in the recess of the opposite window.

Upon this, Prof. De Morgan refers to a version of the above narrative in Dr. Gregory's *Letters on Animal Magnetism*, in which some account is given of a court-martial held on the sentry, evidence that he was not asleep, but had been singing a minute or two before the phantom appeared—the declaration of the sergeant that such appearances were not uncommon, &c.—all which details were new to Mr. Swifte, who, being resident on the spot, may be presumed to have had the best information. Nor had he been aware of Dr. Gregory's publication, or communicated with him: he received his account from Sir David Brewster.

Another Correspondent remarked that, up to a certain point, Mr. Swifte's narrative bears a striking resemblance to a story, related by the Baron de Guldenstubbé, of an apparition seen by him at Paris, in 1854, and quoted in Mr. Owen's *Footfalls on the Boundary of another World*. Another Correspondent writes: " While reading the case of the Baron de Guldenstubbé, the *Spectre of the Brocken* rushed into my mind: and further reflection convinced me that two apparitions so closely resembling each other as those of Mr. Swifte and the Baron must be due to natural causes. The latter case also resembles one which recently (December 1860) occurred at Bonchurch, and was described in the *Times*. I would ask—Is it known whether the figure seen by the Baron in the column of vapour resembled himself? Whether the external air was very damp? and whether there had recently, or ever, been a fire in the stove in front of which the ghost appeared? It seems to have kept the line between the Baron and the fire-place, and the doorway was in a line also. As a faggot is mentioned, I suppose the fire-place in the saloon was an open one. My reason tells me that the similarity of these two visitations is strong evidence against their being supernatural: while we have the testimony, &c., of the tourists on the Brocken, the gentleman at Bonchurch, Ulloa on Pichincha, and the host of Scotch second-sight seers, as to such effects in the open air. Then, why may not the same have occurred in a column of fog descending a damp chimney?"

Mr. Swifte's case is more difficult to account for, particularly as regards the sentinel; still, if one case be solved, the other may, the clue once given.

"One word as to the Baron's 'electric shocks.' Can these be accounted for by atmospheric causes? His frame seems not to have been in a healthy state, as he could not sleep. Were they not simply those twitchings of the muscles, or prickings in the veins, which are not uncommon in ailing persons? We know how a state of semi-sleep magnifies every sound and feeling, and hence, I think, the truth of the Baron's electric shocks may be doubted." (*Notes and Queries*, 2nd S. No. 259.)

Mr. Swifte, it should be added, cannot supply the precise date of the sentinel's alarm; the "morrow," when he saw the poor fellow in the Tower guard-room, had reference to his visitation, not Mr. Swifte's; which he submits is the more difficult of solution.

The appearance in the Jewel-house did not suggest to Mr. Swifte the Brocken spectre; and the Gulden-stubbé phantom fails, in its parallel. "We were not," says Mr. Swifte, "favoured by any 'portly old man' detaching himself from our vaporous column, and re-solving himself into it again; no 'electric shocks,' or 'muscular twitchings,' had predisposed us; and the densest fog that had ever descended a damp chimney could hardly have seized one of us by the shoulder."

In conclusion, Mr. Swifte adds: "The only 'natural

cause ' which has occurred to me, is *phantasmagoric* agency; yet—to say nothing of the local impediments in the Jewel-house—the most skilful operator, with every appliance accorded him, could not produce an appearance, visible to one-half the assembly, while invisible to the other half, and bodily laying hold of one individual among them. The causation of non-natural, preternatural, or supernatural effects passes my scholarship; and the anomalies of a formless, purposeless phantom, foretelling nothing, and fulfilling nothing, is better left to the adepts in psychology."

We all remember Dean Swift's words: " One argument to prove that the common relations of ghosts and spectres are generally false, may be drawn from the opinion held, that *spirits are never seen by more than one person at a time*; that is to say, it seldom happens to above one person in company, to be possessed with any high degree of spleen or melancholy."

Now, at the Tower, the phantom was seen by more than one person at a time, though not by all the party; neither of whom seems to have been in the melancholy mood which Swift considered requisite to realise a spectre.

The Tower, which presents us with the *scaffolding* of our mediæval and later history, has, of course, its legendary whisperings, and its midnight stillness, broken even by the moaning wind, must be very suggestive in association with the history of the fortress: there is more than one tradition of the spirit of Raleigh hovering about the prison-house, whose nooks and corners smell of blood: the sentinel had, in all probability, heard of Raleigh's re-visitation, and it may have had some share in the poor sentinel's frightful end.

Sights and Shows, and Public Amusements.

THE following ballad, detailing, pleasantly enough, a "Bumpkin's Visit to London," may be safely assigned to a period as early as the reign of Charles I. It is transcribed from a MS. in the British Museum (Harleian MS. 3,910, fol. 37), and Mr. Peter Cunningham has, in communicating it to the *Builder*, added a few notes. The references and other allusions to the Lord Mayor on horseback (in his robes, of course), carry us back to the days of Holinshed and Stow; while the Tabor, in Fleet Street, speaks of holiday and Tarlton mirth in London:—

> When I came first te London Towne,
> I was a novice as most men are:
> Methought y⁰ King dwelt at y⁰ sign of y⁰ Crown,
> And the way to Heaven was through y⁰ Starr.
>
> I sett up my horse, and walkt to Paule's,
> "Lord," thought I, "wᵗ a Church is heere!"
> And then I swore by all Christen soules,
> 'Twas a myle long or very neere.*
>
> Nay, methought, 'twas as high as a hill.
> "A Hill!" quoth I, "nay, as a Mountayn;"
> Then up I went wᵗʰ a very good will,
> But gladder was to come down againe.
>
> For on the topp my head turn'd round;
> For be it knowne to all Christen people,
> The man's not a little way from the ground
> That's on the top of all Paule's steeple.

---

* The nave of Old St. Paul's was very long.

To Ludgate, then, I ran my race :
   When I was past I did backward looke ;
Ther I spyed Queen Elizabeth's grace,*
   Her picture guylt, for all gould I tooke.

And as I came down Ludgate-hill;
   Whome should I meet but my good Lord Mayor,
On him I gap'd, as yongsters still
   Gape on toyes in Bartelmew faire.

I know not wch of 'em to desire,
   The Mayor or ye horse, they were both so like ;
Their trappings so rich you would admjre,
   Their faces such non could dislike.

But I must consider perforce
   The saying of ould, so true it was,—
" The gray mare is the better horse,"—
   And " All's not gould that shines lyke brass."

In Fleet Street then I heard a shoote ;
   I put of my hutt, and I made no staye;
And when I came unto the rowte,
   Good lord ! I heard a Tuber playe.

For, so God save mee, a Morrys Daunce :
   Oh ! ther was sport alone for mee,
To see the hobby horse, how he did praunce
   Among the gingling company.

I proffer'd them money for their coats,
   But my conscience had remorse ;
For my father had no oates,
   And I must haue had the hobbie horse.

To see the Tombes was my desire,
   And then to Westminster I went :
I gave one twoepence for his hyre,
   'Twas the best twopence y^t e'er I spent.

" Here lyes," quoth hee, " King Henry the Third."
   " 'Tis false," said I, " hee speaks not a word."
" And here is King Richard ye Seacond inter'd ;
   And here is good King Edward's sword.

---

* The statue of Queen Elizabeth, formerly at Ludgate, now at St.
Dunstan's, Fleet Street.

And this," quoth he, "is Jacob's stone,
    This very stone here under y⁰ chuire."
            *   *   *   *

I tooke a Boate, and would stay no longer;
    And as I towards y⁰ Bridge did rowe,
I and myself began to wonder
    Howe that it was built belowe.

But then my friend, John Stow, I remember,
    In's Booke of London call'd the Survay
Saith that, on the fifthe daye of September,
    With wooll-sacks they did it underlay.

Then through y⁰ Bridge to the Tower I went,
    With much adoe I wandred in;
And when my penny* I had spent,
    Thus the spokesman did begin :—

"This Lyon's the King's, and this is the Queene's,
    And this is the Prince's yᵗ stands by him."
I drew nere, not knowing wᶜʰ hee means.
    " Wᵗ ayle you, my frend, to go so nigh him ? "

"Doe you see y⁰ Lyon this yᵗ lyes downe ?
    It's Henry the Great, twoe hondred years olde."
"Lord bless us ! " quoth I, " How hee doth frown ! "
    "I tell you," quoth he, " hee's a lyon boulde."

Now was it late, I went to my Inne ;
    I supt, and I slept, and I rose betymes,
Not wak't wᵗʰ crowes, nor ducks quackling,
    But wᵗʰ the noyse of Cheapside chymes.†

THE WALLS OF ROMAN LONDON.

Mr. Tite, the architect of the Royal Exchange, who
has enjoyed several opportunities of tracing the remains of the walls of Roman London, in 1853, had

* Our ballad-monger lived in the days when Peacham published his
"Worth of a Penny," and a penny peep was a penny's worth.

† Bow bells.

the good fortune to find a beautiful tesselated pavement under Gresham House, in Old Broad Street;
which discovery led Mr. Tite to believe that similar
remains existed in the same neighbourhood, further
strengthened by the fact that in Trinity Square, not
far distant, a portion of the ancient wall still existed
above ground, which, though not Roman, was supposed
to rest on Roman foundations.   In 1841, the Black-
wall Railway, much further north than this point, cut
through Roman remains of the great wall; 'but it was
not until the autumn of 1864 that further traces were
found.   Then, in some large works in Cooper Row,
was discovered a very extensive fragment of a Norman wall, with narrow slits for archers to shoot their
arrows.   This fragment was 110 feet long, and in
height, from the bottom of the foundation to the top of
the parapet, 41 feet.   All the foundations, and a considerable portion of the lower wall, were undoubtedly
Roman, built of square stones, in regular courses,
with bonding courses of Roman brick of intense hard-
ness, and excellent cement, as hard as any red earthen-
ware, and was, as was always the case with the Roman,
more of what we should call a tile, being about 1 foot
square, and $1\frac{1}{2}$ in. thick.   The mortar between the
bricks was nearly as thick as the bricks themselves,
and abounding in portions of pounded brick.   The
exact place of these remains is shown in an ancient plan
of London in the reign of Elizabeth, when the walls
and gates were in existence.   Undoubted Roman remains of these walls are traceable in Camomile Street,
the street called London Wall, and near Moorgate.

In referring to the history of Roman London, Mr,
Tite proceeds to point out that there could have been

no walls at the time when Suetonius abandoned it in
A.D. 61. Some Norman historians referred the walls
to a period as late as the Empress Helena, but Mr.
Tite is of opinion that they date about the second
century of our era. The distinctly Norman work
above this level, Mr. Tite attributes to the period
when Archbishop Langton and William Marshall,
Earl of Pembroke, had failed in their first endeavours
to prevail on King John to restore the ancient laws
contained in the Great Charter; the associated Barons
assumed their arms, and with their forces marched
first to Northampton and thence to Bedford. They
were favourably received there by William de Beau
champ; and there also came to them messengers from
London, who privately advised them immediately to
go thither. On this they advanced to Ware, and
arrived at Aldgate after a night march on the 24th of
May 1215, the Sunday before Ascension Day. Finding the gates open, says Roger de Wendover, they
entered the city without any tumult, while the inhabitants were performing Divine service; for the
rich citizens were favourable to the Barons, and the
poor ones were afraid to complain of them. After
this, the walls being in a ruinous state, they restored
them, using the materials of the Jews' houses existing
in the neighbourhood, and then destroyed to build up
the defences, which, as chroniclers relate, were in a
subsequent reign in a high state of excellence.

Mr. Tite pursues his history of the wall of London
through its various phases of ruin and revival until the
patriotic Lord Mayor, citizen, and draper, Ralph Josce-
lyne, in 1477, completely restored all the walls, gates,
and towers, in which work he was assisted by the

Goldsmiths' and other Companies, and by Sir John
Crosby, a member of the Grocers' Company. The
gradual increase of the necessities of the citizens for
more space, and the Great Fire of 1666, completed
the destruction of these once important defences, and
but few remains now exist to show their extent and
value. Mr. Tite states that the total area enclosed by
the walls which still constitutes the great " City of
London " is only about 380 acres.

THE DANES IN LONDON.

THE marriage of the Prince of Wales to a Princess
of the royal family of Denmark invests, with fresh
interest, our historical association with that country,
which has ever been a popular subject with the
Danes. Mr. Worsae, by desire of King Christian
VIII. of Denmark, in 1846, made an archæological
exploration of Scotland and the British Isles with the
view of illustrating the connection of the two coun-
tries, which has been productive of interesting results.
Thus, we are reminded that, besides Denmark Court,
Denmark Street, Copenhagen Street, indicative of the
connection between England and Denmark in modern
times, we possess numerous memorials of the earlier
occupation of London by the Danes and Northmen.
The most popular of these associations is in the history
of the church of St. Clement Danes, in the Strand,
which, though not 150 years old, occupies a Danish
site of eight centuries since. In some curious regu-
lations for the prevention of fire in the metropolis, in

the year 1189, we read of a great conflagration which
"happened in the first year of King Stephen (1135),
when, by a fire which began at London Bridge, the
church of St. Paul was burnt, and then that fire spread,
consuming houses and buildings, even *unto the church
of St. Clement Danes.*" Stow's account is that the
church was so called "because Harold, a Danish King,
and other Danes were buried here." Strype gives
another reason—"that the few Danes left in the
kingdom married English women, and compulsorily
lived between Westminster and Ludgate, and there
built a synagogue, called *Ecclesia Clementis Dano-
rium.*" This account Fleetwood, the antiquary, reported to the Lord Treasurer Burghley, who lived at
Cecil House, in the parish.

Mr. Worsae, the Danish antiquary, however, thus
relates the history— that here "the Danes in London had
their own burial-place, in which reposed the remains
of Canute the Great's son and next successor, Harold
Harefoot. When, in 1040, Hardicanute ascended the
throne after his brother, Harold, he caused Harold's
corpse to be disinterred from its tomb in Westminster
Abbey and thrown into the Thames, where it was found
by a fisherman, and afterwards buried, it is said, in the
Danes' churchyard in London. From the churchyard
it was subsequently removed into a round tower which
ornamented the church before it was rebuilt at the
close of the seventeenth century. It was taken down in
1680, and rebuilt by Edward Pierce, under the super-
intendence of Wren, the old tower being left; but this
was taken down, and the present tower and steeple
built by Gibbs in 1719. By a strange coincidence, the
first person buried in this church, after it was rebuilt,

was Nicholas Byer, the painter, a Norwegian, employed by Sir William Temple at his house at Shene."

Mr. Worsae considers the church to have been named, not because so many Danes were buried in it, but because, as it is situated close by the Thames, and must originally have lain outside the City walls, the Danish merchants and mariners, who for the sake of trade were then established in London, had here a place of their own, in which they dwelt together as fellow-countrymen. This church, too, like others in commercial towns, as at Aarhuus in Jutland, at Trondjem in Norway, and even in the city of London (in Eastcheap), was consecrated to St. Clement, who was especially the seaman's patron saint. The Danes naturally preferred to bury their dead in this church, which was their proper parish church. The present church bears in various parts the emblems of St. Clement's martyrdom—the anchor, with which about his neck he is said to have been thrown into the sea. The name of Southwark is of Danish or Norwegian origin. The Sagas relate that in the time of King Svend Tveskjœg the Danes fortified this trading-place, hence its Saxon name *Sudivercher*, the South-work of London. It is called *Surder-virke* in a Danish account by a battle fought here by King Olaf in 1008. Notwithstanding this Saxon etymology, there is abundant proof that Southwark was an extensive station and cemetery of the Romans during an early period of their dominion in Britain, as attested by vases and pavements, portions of Roman homes, found in Southwark. Even Mr. Lindsay's ninety-seven etymologies will not invalidate this tangible evidence.

Lambeth, formerly Lambythe, was, in the Danish

time, a village; and here, in 1042, a Danish jarl celebrated his marriage, King Hardicanute and his followers being present at the banquet.

The Danish church, in Wellclose Square, is a modern
edifice, built in 1696, by Cibber, the sculptor, at the
expense of Christian V., King of Denmark, for the
use of his subjects, merchants and seamen accustomed
to visit the port of London; and here is " the Royal
Pew," in which sat Christian VII., King of Denmark,
when on a visit to England in 1768.

Somerset House, in the Strand, was, in 1616, when
the Queen (Anne of Denmark) feasted the King here,
commanded by him to be called Denmark House.

The characteristic conviviality of the Danes appears
to have given a name to certain houses of public entertainment in England, as Great and Little Denmark
Halls, at Camberwell, whence is named Denmark Hill.
Denmark Street, originally built in 1689, was, when
Hatton wrote, in 1708, " a pretty though small street,
on the west side of St. Giles's church." Zoffany, the
celebrated painter, lived at No. 9; the same house is
also the scene of Bunbury's caricature, " A Sunday
Evening Concert." (Dr. Rimbault, *Notes and Queries*,
No. 15.) From a house in this street Sir John Mur-
ray, late Secretary to the Pretender, was, in 1771,
carried off by a party of strange men.

Memorials of the Danes in other parts of the kingdom
are by no means rare; and, in 1846, Mr. Worsae, by
desire of King Christian VIII. of Denmark, made an
archæological exploration of Scotland and the British
Isles, the interesting results of which were published
in a volume in 1852.

Among the old traces of Danish rule here was the

Dane gild, a contribution originally paid to the King for the purpose of pacifying the Danes. It was still levied long after the Danish times, and was only abolished by King Henry II. (*Liber Albus*, note.)

CITY REGULATIONS IN THE PLANTAGENET TIMES.

It is curious to note that in the *Guildhall White Book* milk is nowhere mentioned as an article of sale or otherwise; it was perhaps little used, if at all, by the City population. The same negative evidence will scarcely warrant a corresponding suggestion in the article of " drunkenness," coupled in the same sentence with milk, because, like that innocent beverage, the subject of drunkenness is " nowhere " in these pages. It is inferred that intoxication was probably not deemed an offence by the authorities if unattended with violence. " The best ale, too, which was no better than *sweet-wort*, was probably so thin that it might be drunk in ' potations pottle deep,' without disturbing the equilibrium of the drinker." Ale-houses were to be closed at Curfew, under heavy penalties, as also were wine-taverns,—to prevent persons of bad character from meeting to concoct their " criminal designs." No allusion occurs to wine in bottles or flasks; it would seem to have been consumed wholly in draught. The price of Rhenish in Richard II.'s time was 8*d.* a gallon; Malmsey, then called Malvesie, was just double that price. " It seems to have been a prevalent custom with knavish bakers to make bread of fine quality on the outside and coarse within; a practice which was forbidden by enactment, it being also forbidden to

make loaves of bran or with any admixture of bran."
The servants of *bons gens* were legally entitled to be
present when the baker kneaded his dough. Fines
were at one time extensively exacted from the baking
trade, but, "by a civic enactment *temp.* Edward II.,
it is ordered that from henceforth the Sheriffs shall
take no fines from bakers and breweresses, but shall
inflict upon them corporal punishment (by pillory) instead." For a first offence, against the required
weight or quality of his loaves, the culprit was drawn
upon a hurdle—shoeless and stockingless, and his
hands tied down by his side—from Guildhall, through
the dirtiest and most densely peopled streets, the short-
weight loaf pendent from his neck. For the second,
he was dragged by the same conveyance to the pillory
in Cheap, to air himself for an hour, and receive the
mob's voluntary contributions, animal, vegetable, and
nondescript. For the third, he had a third journey on
the hurdle, his oven was ignominiously pulled to pieces,
and himself compelled to abjure baker's business in the
City of London for evermore. The hurdle appears,
however, to have been discontinued in Edward II.'s
reign, and the pillory substituted for it in first offences.

ST. PAUL'S DAY IN LONDON.

In the metropolis, the day of St. Paul, Jan. 25, the
patron saint of the City, was formerly observed with
picturesque ceremonies.

In the reign of Philip and Mary (1555), this day was
observed in the metropolis with great processional state.
In the *Chronicle of the Grey Friars of London,* we read

that " on St. Paul's Day there was a general procession
with the children of all the schools in London, with all
the clerks, curates, and parsons and vicars, in copes, with
their crosses; also the choir of St. Paul's ; and divers
bishops in their habits, and the Bishop of London, with
his pontificals and cope, bearing the sacrament under
a canopy, and four prebends bearing it in their gray
amos; and so up into Leadenhall, with the mayor and
aldermen in scarlet, with their cloaks, and all the crafts
in their best array; and so came down again on the
other side, and so to St. Paul's again.   And then the
King, with my Lord Cardinal, came to St. Paul's, and
heard masse, and went home again; and at night great
bonfires were made through all London, for the joy of
the people that were converted likewise as St. Paul
was converted."

Down to about this time there was observed, in connection with St. Paul's Cathedral, a custom arising
from an obligation incurred by Sir William Baud in
1375, when he was permitted to enclose twenty acres
of the Dean's land, in consideration of presenting the
clergy of the cathedral with a fat buck and doe yearly
on the days of the Conversion and Commemoration of
St. Paul. " On these days, the buck and the doe were
brought by one or more servants at the hour of the
procession, and through the midst thereof, and offered
at the high altar of St. Paul's Cathedral : after which
the persons that brought the buck received of the Dean
and Chapter, by the hands of their Chamberlain, twelve
pence sterling for their entertainment; but nothing
when they brought the doe.   The buck being brought
to the steps of the altar, the Dean and Chapter, apparelled in copes and proper vestments, with garlands

of roses on their heads, sent the body of the buck to be baked, and had the head and horns fixed on a pole before the cross, in their procession round about the church, till they issued at the west door, where the keeper that brought it blowed the death of the buck, and then the horns that were about the city answered him in like manner; for which they had each, of the Dean and Chapter, three and fourpence in money, and their dinner: and the keeper, during his stay, meat, drink, and lodging, and five shillings in money at his going away; together with a loaf of bread, having in it the picture of St. Paul."

CHRISTMAS FESTIVITIES IN WESTMINSTER HALL.

OUR early kings kept this great Christian festival in the Grand Hall at Westminster—" Rufus's Roaring Hall " —from the Anglo-Norman times. Here John held his Christmas feasts in 1213 and 1214 ; and Henry III. in 1234, 1238, and 1241; and in 1248, whilst Henry himself kept Christmas at Winchester, he commanded his treasurer " to fill the King's great hall from Christmas Day to the Day of Circumcision (January 1st) with poor people, and feast them there." In the next (Edward I.) reign, in 1277, Llewellyn, Prince of Wales, sat a guest at the Christmas feast in Westminster Hall. In 1290, 1292, and 1303, Edward I. also kept Christmas here ; as did Edward II. in 1317, when, however, few nobles were present, " because of discord between them and the King; " but in 1320, he kept Christmas here " with great honour and glorie."

Edward III. was a right royal provider of Christmas

cheer.   The art of cookery was now well understood;
and the making of blancmanges, tarts, and pies, and
the preparing of rich soups of the brawn of capons,
were among the cook's duties at this period.   French
cooks were employed by the nobility; and in the merchants' feast we find jellies of all colours, and in all
figures—flowers, trees, beasts, fish, fowl, and fruit.
The wines were " a collection of spiced liquors; " and
cinnamon, grains of paradise, and ginger were in the
dessert confections.   Edward kept his Christmas in
Westminster Hall, in 1358, and had for his guests at
the banquet the captive King of France, and David,
King of Scotland.   And, in 1362, King David and the
King of Cyprus met here at two grand entertainments
given by King Edward.

Richard II., according to Stow, gave "a house-
warming in this hall," upon the completion of this
magnificent edifice, of " profuse hospitality," when he
feasted 10,000 persons.   We need not wonder, then,
that Richard kept 2,000 cooks: they were learned in
their art, and have left to the world " The Form of
Cury; or a Roll of English Cookery, compiled about
the year 1390, by the Master Cook of Richard II."
In 1399, Richard kept Christmas sitting in the great
hall, in cloth-of-gold, garnished with pearls and precious
stones, worth 3,000 marks.

In 1478, Edward IV. kept Christmas here with
great pomp, wearing his crown, and making costly
presents to his household.   Richard III., although his
reign was short and turbulent, kept two Christmases
here in sumptuous state : one in 1488, when, chronicles
Philip de Comines, " he was reigning in greater splendour than any King of England for the last hundred

years." Next year he solemnised the festival most splendidly, and so attentive was the King to trivial matters, that we find a warrant for the payment of "200 marks for certain New Year's gifts against the feast of Christmas." The festivities continued till the day of Epiphany, when they terminated with an extraordinary feast: "the King himself," says the historian of Croyland, "wearing his crown, and holding a splendid feast in the great hall, similar to that of his coronation."

Henry VII., though little inclined to spending money, kept the ninth Christmas of his reign with great magnificence in Westminster Hall; feasting the Lord Mayor and Aldermen of London, and showing them sports on the night following, in the hall, hung with tapestry; which sports being ended *in the morning*, the King, Queen, and Court sat down at a table of stone to 120 dishes, placed by as many knights and squires; while the Mayor was served with twenty-four dishes, and abundance of wines. And, finally, the King and Queen being conveyed with great lights into the palace, the Mayor and his company, in barges, returned to London by break of the next day. Henry VIII. mostly kept his Christmas at Richmond, Greenwich, and Eltham. Edward VI., at Christmas, 1552, kept one of the most magnificent revellings on record; but in Queen Mary's short and gloomy reign the Christmas festivities were neglected. They were, however, renewed by Queen Elizabeth, when plays and masques were specially patronised, and the children of St. Paul's and Westminster often performed before the Queen.

We part from these pictures of the Royal Christmas of centuries since, as from one of Time's stately pageants; which bring the picturesqueness of the past into

vivid contrast with the more widely-spread hospitalities
of the present age; reminding us that, although Westminster Hall may be void and gloomy on the coming
Christmas Day, greater enjoyment than was yielded by
the prodigal heaps of luxury once consumed within
those walls, is now, with each returning festival, scat-
tered through the length and breadth of the land, and
the national wealth of Christmas is thus brought home
to every Englishman's fireside.

For the celebrations at Colleges and Inns of Court,
the Great Halls were specially adapted. In 1561,
the Christmas revels at the Inner Temple were very
splendid: brawn, mustard, and malmsey were served
for breakfast, and the dinner in the Hall was a grand
affair; between the two courses, first came the master
of the game, then the ranger of the forests; and having
blown three blasts of the hunting-horn, they paced
three times round the fire, then in the middle of the
Hall. Certain courtesies followed, nine or ten couple
of hounds were brought in, with a fox and cat, both
which were set upon by the dogs, amid blowing
of horns, and killed beneath the fire. At the close of
the second course, the oldest of the masters of the
revels sang a song: after some repose and further
revels, supper was served, which being over, the
marshal was borne in by four men, on a sort of scaffold, three times round the fire, crying, " A lord," &c.,
after which he came down, and went to dance. The
Lord of Misrule then addressed himself to the banquet, which ended with minstrelsy, mirth, and dancing.
The Christmas masque at Gray's Inn, in 1594, was
very magnificent. In 1592, the heads of colleges at
Cambridge acted a Latin comedy at Christmas before

Queen Elizabeth; and in 1607, there was a celebrated exhibition of the Christmas Prince at St. John's College, Oxford.

LONDON COCKPITS.

BRITISH COCKS are mentioned by Cæsar; but the first notice of English cockfighting is by Fitzstephen, in the reign of Henry II.; and it was a fashionable sport from *temp.* Edward III. almost to our time. Henry VIII. added a cockpit to Whitehall Palace, where James I. went to see the sport twice a week. There were also cockpits in Drury Lane, Shoe Lane, Jewin Street, Cripplegate, and " behind Gray's Inn ; " and several lanes, courts, and alleys are named from having been the sites of cockpits. The original name of the *pit* in our theatres was the *cock-pit,* which seems to imply that cockfighting had been their original destination. One of our oldest London theatres was called the *Cockpit*; this was the Phœnix, in Drury Lane, the site of which was Cockpit Alley, now corruptly written Pitt Place. Southwark has several cockpit sites. The cockpit in St. James's Park, leading from Birdcage Walk into Dartmouth Street, was only taken down in 1816, but had been deserted long before. Howell, in 1657, described " cockfighting a sport peculiar to the English, and so is bear and bull baitings, there being not such dangerous dogs and cocks anywhere." Hogarth's print best illustrates the brutal refinement of the cockfighting of the last century; and Cowper's " Cockfighter's Garland," greatly tended to keep down this modern barbarism, which is punishable by statute. It was, not many years since, greatly indulged in through

Staffordshire; and " Wednesbury (Wedgbury) cockings" and their ribald songs were a disgrace to our times.

Pepys has this entry of his visit to the Shoe Lane cockpit: " December 21. To Shoe Lane to a cockfighting at a new pit, but Lord! to see the strange variety of people, from Parliament men, to the poorest 'prentices, bakers, brewers, butchers, draymen, and what not; and all these fellows, one with another, cursing and betting. Strange that such poor people, that look as if they had not bread to put in their mouths, shall bet three or four pounds at a time, and lose it, and yet bet as much the next battle, so that one of them will lose 10*l.* or 20*l.* at a meeting! I soon had enough of it."

The Whitehall Cockpit, after the fire in 1697, was altered into the Privy Council Office—a conversion which has provoked many a lively sally. Hatton describes the Cockpit as " between the gate into King Street, Westminster, and the gate by the banqueting-house;" the former was designed by Holbein, and known as the Cockpit Gate. The old place had some interesting historical associations. Philip Herbert, Earl of Pembroke and Montgomery, from a window of his apartments in the Cockpit, saw his sovereign, Charles I., walk from St. James's to the scaffold. Monk, Duke of Albemarle, died here, 1669-70; and Villiers, Duke of Buckingham, 1673. And here, in the Council Chamber, Guiscard stabbed Harley, Earl of Oxford. The Cockpit retained its original name, long after the change in its uses. Mr. Cunningham says: " The Treasury Minutes, circ. 1780, are headed ' Cockpit;' " the *Picture of London*, edit. 1806 and 1810, refers to the Council-chamber as

" commonly called the Cockpit;" and we remember to have read at the foot of a printed proclamation at Whitehall, " Given at the Cockpit," &c.

STORY OF THE BOOK OF ST. ALBAN'S.

THE visitor to the British Museum who pauses at Show-case VIII., in the King's Library, where specimens of the early English press are displayed, may notice quite at the end an open volume, bearing the following label :—

" The book of St. Alban's. The bokys of Haukyng and Huntyng, and also of Coot armuris. Written by Dame Juliana Barnes, or Berners, Prioress of Sopwell Nunnery. Printed at St. Alban's in 1486. Bequeathed by the Rt. Hon. Thomas Grenville."

The following adventures which befel this very volume before it found its present secure resting-place, are worthy of a place in the first rank of bibliographical romance.

The story originally formed part of a letter written on bibliographical matters by the Rector of Pilham, in 1847, to the Rev. S. R. Maitland :—

" In June 1844, a pedlar called at a cottage at Blyton, and asked an old widow, named Naylor, whether she had any rags to sell. She said ' No,' but offered him some old paper, and took from a shelf *The Book of St. Alban's* and others, weighing 9 lbs., for which she received ninepence. The pedlar carried them through Gainsboro', tied up in a string, past a chemist's shop, who, being used to buy old paper to wrap drugs in, called the man in; and, struck by the

appearance of *The Boke*, gave him three shillings for
the lot. Not being able to read the colophon, he took
it to an equally ignorant stationer and offered it to him
for a guinea; at which price he declined it, but proposed that it should be exposed in his window as a
means of eliciting some information about it. It was
accordingly placed there, with the label—' Very old
curious work.' A collector of books went in, and
offered 2s. 6d. for it. This excited the suspicion of
the vendor. Soon after Mr. Bird, the Vicar of Gainsboro', went in and asked the price, wishing to have a
very early specimen at a reasonable price; not knowing, however, the great value of the book. While he
was examining the book, Stark, a very intelligent
bookseller, came in, to whom Mr. Bird at once ceded
the right of pre-emption. Stark betrayed such visible
anxiety that the vendor, Smith, declined settling a
price. Soon after, Sir C. —— came in, and took the
book to collate, and brought it back in the morning,
having found it imperfect in the middle, and offered 5l.
for it. Sir Charles had no book of reference to guide
him to its value; but, in the meantime, Stark had
employed a friend to obtain for him the refusal of it,
and had undertaken to give a little more than Sir
Charles might offer. On finding that at least 5l. could
be got for it, Smith went to the owner and gave him
two guineas, and then proceeded to Stark's agent and
sold it for 7l. 7s. Stark took it to London, and sold
it to the Rt. Hon. T. Grenville for 70 or 80 guineas.

" It must now be stated how it came to pass, that a
book without covers of such extreme age was preserved.
About fifty years since, the Library of Thonock Hall,
in the parish of Gainsboro', the seat of the Hickman

family, underwent great repairs; and the books were sorted over by a most ignorant person, whose selection seems to have been determined by the coat. All books without covers were thrown into a great heap, and condemned to all the purposes which Leland laments in the sack of the Conventual Libraries by the visitors. But they found favour in the eyes of a literate gardener, who begged leave to take what he liked home. He selected a large quantity of Sermons before the House of Commons, local pamphlets, tracts from 1680 to 1710, opera books, &c. &c. He made a list of them, which was afterwards found in his cottage; and No. 43, was ' Cotarmouris.' The old fellow was something of a herald, and drew in his books what he held to be his coat. After his death, all that could be stuffed into a large chest were put away in a garret; but a few favourites, and, *The Boke* among them, remained on the shelves of the kitchen for years, till his son's widow grew so *stalled* of dusting them that she determined to sell them."

Here ends the material part of the story. The volume was afterwards splendidly bound, and is now the only copy in the British Museum.—*Notes and Queries*, 3rd S., No. 97.

RACES IN HYDE PARK.

In Cromwell's time, Hyde Park was noted for sporting matches, such as coach and foot races, hurling, and wrestling. In the *Moderate Intelligencer* we find that there was " a hurling of a great ball by fifty Cornish gentlemen of the one side, and fifty of the other; one

party played in red caps, and the other in white;" and
that there were present " his Highness the Lord Protector, many of his Privy Council, and divers eminent
gentlemen, to whose view was presented great agility of
body, and most neat and exquisite wrestling at every
meeting of one with the other, which was ordered with
such dexterity, that it was to show more the strength,
vigour, and nimbleness of their bodies than to endanger
their persons.   The ball they played withal was silver,
and designed for that party which did win the goal."

" Evelyn went to see a coach-race in Hyde Park."
Pepys wrote—" To Hyde Park by coach, and saw a
fine foot race three times round the park, between an
Irishman and Joseph Crow, that was once my Lord
Claypole's footman." It was in this Hyde Park racing-
ground that " his Highness the Lord Protector" met
with an accident which might have cost him his life.
Ludlow tells us that " the Duke of Holstein made him
(Cromwell) a present of a set of gray Friesland coach-
horses, with which, taking the air in the park attended
only by his secretary Thurlow, he would needs take
the place of the coachman, not doubting but the three
pairs of horses he was about to drive would prove as
tame as the three nations that were ridden by him, and
therefore, not content with their ordinary pace, he
lashed them very furiously.   But they, unaccustomed
to such a rough driver, ran away in a rage, and stopped
not till they had thrown him out of the box, by which
fall his pistol fired in his pocket, though without any
hurt to himself; by which he might have been instructed how dangerous it was to meddle with those
things wherein he had no experience."

OLD PALL MALL SIGHTS.

PALL MALL had early its notable sights and amusements. In 1701 were shown here models of William
the Third's palaces at Loo and Hunstaerdike, " brought
over by outlandish men," with curiosities disposed of
" on public raffling days." In 1733, " a holland smock,
a cap, checked stockings, and laced shoes," were run
for by four women in the afternoon, in Pall Mall; and
one of its residents, the High Consable of Westminster, gave a prize laced hat to be run for by five men,
which created so much riot and mischief, that the
magistrates " issued precepts to prevent future runs to
the very man most active in promoting them." Here
lodged George Psalmanazar, when he passed for an
islander of Formosa, and invented a language which
baffled the best philologists in Europe. Here lived
Joseph Clark, the posture-master, celebrated for per-
sonating deformities : now deceiving, by feigned dislo-
cated vertebræ, the great surgeon, Moulins ; then per-
plexing a tailor's measure with counterfeit humps and
high shoulders. To this class of notorieties belongs
Dr. Graham's " Celestial Bed," and his other impostures, at Schomberg House, advertised by two gigantic
porters stationed at the entrance, in gold laced cocked-
hats and liveries: of these we shall presently say more.

At the Chinese Gallery was exhibited, in 1825, " the
Living Skeleton" (Anatomie Vivante), Claude Am-
broise Seurat, a native of Troyes, in Champagne, 28
years old. His health was good, but his skin resembled
parchment, and his ribs could be counted and handled
like pieces of cane : he was shown nude, except about
the loins : the arm, from the shoulder to the elbow, was

like an ivory German flute; the legs were straight, and the feet well formed. (See Hone's *Every-day Book*.)

In the old Star and Garter house, westward of Carlton House, was exhibited, in 1815, the *Waterloo Museum* of portraits and battle-scenes, cuirasses, helmets, sabres, and fire-arms, state-swords, truncheons, rich costumes, and trophies of Waterloo; besides a large picture of the battle, painted by a Flemish artist; and at No. 59, Salter spent five years in painting his great picture of the Waterloo Banquet at Apsley House.

ROMANCE OF SCHOMBERG HOUSE.

THIS celebrated historic house, on the south side of Pall Mall, was, when entire, one of the most interesting of the few remaining mansions of the seventeenth century in the metropolis. With the history of this mansion are associated many of the most remarkable passages in the lives of those distinguished persons who occupied it at successive periods. The house was built about the year 1650, during the government of Cromwell; and was, at that time, considered " a fair mansion enclosed with a garden abutting on the Pall Mall, and near to Charing Cross." At the period of its erection, Pall Mall was planted with elm trees to the number of 140, which the Survey Commissioners described as standing " in a very regular and decent manner on both sides of the walk." In 1660, on the Restoration of Charles II., the house was occupied by several of the Court favourites; and, subsequently, by Edward Griffin, Treasurer of the Chamber, and by the Countess of Portland.

The houses at the south side of Pall Mall, of which there were not more than half-a-dozen, were surrounded " by large meadows, always green, in which the ladies walked in summer time." The Royal gardens, now the private grounds of Marlborough House, stretched immediately behind; and here it was that Charles amused himself by feeding his pet animals, and " discoursing familiarly," as Evelyn writes, with Mrs. Nellie, an " impudent comedian," and the Duchess of Cleveland, " another curse of our nation." Nell Gwyn then resided in the house now No. 79, next door to Schomberg House, as we have already related.

In the reign of William III., Schomberg House was thoroughly repaired and beautified by Frederick, Duke of Schomberg, who employed Peter Berchett to paint the staircase. The third duke, who was killed at the battle of the Boyne, also made it his residence: and here it was that the Duke of Cumberland—the " hero " or the " butcher " of Culloden, as the case may be — passed many years of his life. During the rebellion of Lord George Gordon the house was twice threatened with demolition ; and that, too, at a moment when the King's troops were encamped under canvas in the Park at the rear of the building. The mansion, however, survived the troubles of the period, and was spared for many years, to become a store-house for the arts, and a rallying point for much that was celebrated in the world of literature and *belles lettres*. " Astley, the Beau," as he was termed, lived here for many years, and divided the house into three portions, retaining the centre himself. He was a portrait-painter, of little merit, but of much eccentricity ; the group of " Painting " over the central doorway was his work. He planned in the

upper story, a suite of apartments accessible only to
himself, and built on the roof a large painting-room
facing the park, which he called his " Country House."
To this room he was in the habit of repairing; and, as
he had several smaller apartments, and a separate staircase adjoining, he used to shut himself up for several
weeks, without being visible to any but special friends.
Astley was succeeded in his tenancy by Richard Cos-
way, the miniature-painter: here his wife, also a
painter, gave her musical parties. She made a pil-
grimage to Loretto, which she had vowed to do if
blessed with a living child.

When Gainsborough returned to London, in 1774,
he rented the western wing of the mansion at 300*l.*
a year. Before he had been many months in London,
George III. and Queen Charlotte sat to him for their
portraits; and here the painter received as sitters for
their portraits some of the most eminent churchmen,
lawyers, statesmen, players, sailors, and naturalists of
his time. Here Gainsborough painted his large landscape, " in the style of Reubens," says Walpole; " and
by far the finest landscape ever painted in England,
and equal to the great masters." Here, too, Sir Joshua
Reynolds consented to sit to Gainsborough for his portrait. Sir Joshua sat once; but being soon afterwards
afflicted by slight paralysis, he was obliged to go to
Bath. On his return to town, perfectly restored to
health, he sent word to Gainsborough, who only replied
he was glad to hear he was well; and never after desired him to sit, or call upon him, or had any further
intercourse with him until he was dying, when he sent
and thanked him for the very handsome manner in
which he had always spoken of him—a circumstance

which Sir Joshua has thought worth recording in his Fourteenth Discourse. Gainsborough was so enamoured of his art, that he had many of the pictures he was then working upon brought to his bedside to show them to Reynolds, and flattered himself that he should live to finish them.

However, towards the middle of July 1788, when Gainsborough rapidly became worse, he felt that there was one whom he had not treated with courtesy—it was Sir Joshua Reynolds; and to him he wrote, desiring to see him once more before he died. " If any little jealousies had subsisted between us," says Reynolds, " they were forgotten in those moments of sincerity; and he turned towards me as one who was engrossed by the same pursuits, and who deserved his good opinion by being sensible of his excellence." The two great painters were alone in a second-floor chamber at Schomberg House: Gainsborough said he did not fear death, but regretted leaving his art, more especially as he now began to see what his deficiencies were. His words began to fail, and the last he uttered to Reynolds were : " We are all going to Heaven, and Vandyke is of the company." A few days afterwards Gainsborough died.

Part of the house was subsequently occupied by Bowyer, for his *Historic Gallery*; and by Dr. Graham for his quackeries, of which we shall presently say more. Payne and Foss, the booksellers, lived here till 1850.

The uniformity of this fine specimen of a ducal mansion of the seventeenth century has been spoiled by the eastern wing and centre being taken down, and rebuilt in another style ; but *Gainsborough's wing* remains.

DR. GRAHAM AND HIS QUACKERIES.

IN the year 1780 there appeared in London one of the
most extraordinary empirics of modern times, named
Graham. He was a graduate of Edinburgh, wrote in
a bombastic style, and possessed great fluency of elocu-
tion. He occupied part of Schomberg House, just
described, which he designated the Temple of Health.
The front was ornamented with an enormous gilt sun,
a statue of Hygeia, and other emblematic devices ; and
the suites of rooms in the mansion were superbly furnished, and the walls decorated with mirrors, so as to
confer on the place an effect like that of enchantment.
Here Dr. Graham delivered Lectures on Health and
Procreation, at the extravagant price of two guineas
per lecture, which, with the novelty of the subjects,
drew considerable audiences of the wealthy and dissipated. He enlisted a woman, of beautiful figure,
whom he called the Goddess of Health ; and it was her
business to deliver a concluding discourse after the
Doctor himself had finished his lecture. As a further
means of attraction, he hired two men of extraordinary
stature, who wore enormous cocked hats and showy
bulky liveries, whose part it was to distribute bills of
advertisement from house to house through the town.

Dr. Graham became an object of universal curiosity,
but all his visitors were not duped by him. Horace
Walpole, who was not likely to be thus deceived,
writing to the Countess of Ossory, Aug. 23, 1780,
thus describes his visit to the quack : " In the evening
I went to Dr. Graham's. It is the most impudent
puppet-show of imposition I ever saw, and the mounte-
bank himself the dullest of his profession, except that

he makes the spectators pay a crown a-piece. We were eighteen. A young officer of the Guards affected humour, and tired me still more. A woman, invisible, warbled to clarionets on the stairs. The decorations are pretty and odd; and the apothecary, who comes up a trap-door, for no purpose, since he might as well come upstairs, is a novelty. The electrical experiments are nothing at all singular; and a poor air-pump, that only bursts a bladder, pieces out the farce. The Doctor is like Jenkinson in person, and as flimsy a puppet."

As Graham's two-guinea auditors were soon exhausted, he dropped the admission-money to his lectures successively, to one guinea, half-a-guinea, and five shillings; and, as he said, " for the benefit of all," to half-a-crown ; and when he could no longer draw at this price, he exhibited the Temple itself for one shilling to daily crowds, for several months. Among his properties, or furniture, was a Celestial Bed, as he called it, standing on glass legs, and provided with the richest hangings. He pretended that married pairs, without children, might have heirs by sleeping in this bed, for which he demanded one hundred pounds per night; and such was the folly of wealth, that persons of high rank were named who acceded to his terms. He then pretended to have discovered the Elixir of Life, by taking which a person might live as long as he pleased; he modestly demanded one thousand pounds for a supply of it, and more than one noble person was reported to have paid this enormous price to be cured of his folly.

Having worn out his character in these various impositions, Graham then recommended Earth-bathing, and undertook to sanction it by his own practice.

During one hour every day he admitted spectators, first at a guinea, and then descended to a shilling, to view him and the Goddess of Health in the *warm* earth to their chins; the Doctor having his hair full dressed and powdered, and the Goddess' head being dressed also in the best fashion of the time.

When no more money was to be drained from the population of London, the Doctor visited the great provincial towns, and lectured and exhibited in the above manner, wherever he could obtain permission of the magistrates. But the Goddess of Health nearly fell a victim to the earth-bathing; and the Doctor, retiring from public life, died in poor circumstances, in spite of his Elixir of Life, at the early age of fifty-two. His brother married the celebrated Mrs. Macauley, who, in consequence, is generally styled Mrs. Macauley Graham; and his sister was married to Dr. Arnold, of Leicester, the author of an able treatise on Insanity. It is generally understood that the lady who personated the Goddess of Health was Emma, afterwards the wife of Sir William Hamilton, the personal favourite of Lord Nelson. The Goddess is also said to have been a lady named Prescott.

Southey tells us that Graham was half-mad; and his madness, at last, contrary to the usual practice, got the better of his knavery. Latterly he became wholly an enthusiast, would madden himself with ether, run out into the streets, and strip himself to clothe the first beggar whom he met.

It is curious to find this earth-bath used as a remedy for drunkenness by the Irish rebel, Shane O'Neill, in Elizabeth's days:—" Subtle and crafty he was, especially in the morning; but in the residue of the day

very uncertain and unstable, and much given to excessive gulping and surfeiting. And, albeit he had
most commonly two hundred tuns of wines in his cellar
at Dundrun, and had his full fill thereof, yet was he
never satisfied till he had swallowed up marvellous
great quantities of usquebagh, or aqua vitæ of that
country; whereof so unmeasurably he would drink and
brase, that for the quenching of the heat of the body,
which by that means was most extremely inflamed and
distempered, he was eftsoons conveyed (as the common
report was) into a deep pit, and, standing upright in the
same, the earth was cast round about him up to the
hard chin, and there he did remain until such time as
his body was covered to some temperature."—*Holinshed*, vol. iv. p. 331.

After many failures, Graham turned a regular M.D.,
and repaired to Glasgow, where, in 1784, as mentioned
in " Sir James Mackintosh's Memoirs," Graham was
a fellow-student with him at the University. Graham
is said to have realised a large fortune by a most successful practice as a physician in England, Scotland,
and America; but the immense sums he had lavished
in the sumptuous decorations of the Temple of Health
involved him in difficulties from which he never recovered. He died in June 1794, in his house opposite
the Archers' Hall, Edinburgh, and was buried in the
Grey Friars Churchyard. His latter days were cheered
by an annuity of 50*l.*, settled upon him by a Genevese
gentleman, who derived benefit from reading one of his
tracts—an instance of generosity rare enough to merit
notice here.

Dr. Graham appears to have been a fanatic as well
as an empiric. He published almost numberless tracts,

full of folly and extravagance, but free from immorality and obscenity, which, however, he combined in his private lectures. He was, certainly, one of the most remarkable of a class of quacks, who succeeded in winning reputation, not among the uneducated and vulgar, but among persons of education and distinction.

There can be little doubt of his fanaticism. In 1787 he styled himself " The Servant of the Lord, O. W. L.," meaning by the initials, Oh, Wonderful Love, and dated his bills and other publications, " In the first year of the New Jerusalem Church." The magistrates of Edinburgh not relishing this new system of chronology, caused him to be confined in his own house as a lunatic; but he wandered away to the North of England, where he discovered such marks of insanity, that he was secured, and sent back to Edinburgh. Among his works are " Travels and Voyages in Scotland, England, and Ireland, including a Description of the Temple of Health, 1783."—" The Christian's Universal Prayer, with a Discourse on the Duty of Praying, and a short Sketch of Dr. Graham's Religious Principles and Moral Sentiments."—" Hebe Vestina's Celebrated Lectures; as delivered by her from the Electrical Throne, in the Temple of Health in London."

In the Catalogue of a bookseller at Edinburgh, dated 1825, is the following work:—

" Graham (James, M. D., the celebrated Earth-Bather, Lecturer, &c.)—A Discourse delivered in the Tolbooth of Edinburgh, on Sunday, August 17, 1783, on Isaiah, chap. xi. verse 6 : ' All flesh is grass.'- -A Lecture on the Greatness, Increase, and Improvement of the Human Species ! with a Description of the Structure and most Irresistible Genial Influences of the celebrated Celestial Bed!!! .... The Blazing Star; or, Vestina, the Gigantic, Rosy Goddess of Health; a Defence of the Fair Sex, delivered by the Priestess of the Temple.—The Celestial Bed; or, a Review of the Votaries of the Temple of Health and Temple of Hymen (in verse, with curious notes).—A Clear, Full, and Faithful Portraiture of a certain most Beautiful and Spotless Virgin Princess. With several others; consisting of Advertisements, &c., folio broadsides: a Curious and Genuine Letter, in the Handwriting of the Doctor; a Print, by Kay, of Ditto, lecturing to the Sons of Mirth and Pleasure in Edinburgh; including also a curious *Manuscript*, written expressly to Dr. Graham, regarding his Religious Concerns, by Benjamin Dockray, a Quaker, at Newtown, near Carlisle, in 1790, &c. &c. 20 pieces, folio, qto., 8vo. and duodecimo. A very singular and rare collection."

This remarkable volume was purchased by Sir Walter Scott, and is now in the library at Abbotsford. Another odd tract is " A New and Curious Treatise on the Nature and Effects of Simple Earth, Water, and Air, when applied to the Human Body : How to Live for many Weeks, Months, or Years without Eating anything whatever; with the Extraordinary Histories of many Heroes, Male and Female, who have so subsisted." " This," says a Correspondent of *Notes and Queries*, " is a most extraordinary book, showing to what extent of delusion the human mind is capable of being carried, and the amount of credulity to be found in the general public. The pamphlet opens by giving a copy of an affidavit which he appears to have made at the Mansion House, London, 3rd .

April 1793, before James Sanderson, Mayor, in which he swears ' on the Holy Evangelists,' that ' from the last day of December 1792, till the 15th day of January 1793, being full 14 successive days, and 14 successive nights,' he did not eat, nor drink, nor receive into the body anything whatever, ' not even the smallest particle or drop, except some cold, raw, simple water, and that life was sustained by wearing cut-up turfs to the naked body, admitting air into his rooms night and day, and by rubbing his limbs with his own ' Nervous Etherial Balsams,' and that by these means, without either food or drink, he was enabled to bear the wear and tear of an extensive medical practice, and of lecturing two hours almost every night."

ORIGIN OF HACKNEY-COACHES.

THERE is an old story in French *ana*, referring " the Origin of Hackney-Coaches " to Paris in the year 1662. The reader, we dare say, remembers the incident, which occurred in the ministry of Colbert, through whom the Duke de Roannes obtained the Royal privilege, or license, the carriage being the suggestion of Blaise Pascal. The success of the scheme was aided when the King and Queen being caught in a shower, his Majesty made the Queen and her ladies enter one of the new calèches, which happened to be plying for passengers, and the King mounted the box, and, himself taking the reins, drove to the palace. This is a pleasant story enough ; but, unfortunately for the French claim, we had hackney-coaches in London in 1625, or thirty-seven years before the Paris scheme. They were first kept at inns, but got into the streets in 1634, as appears from *Stafford's Letters*. Captain Bailey had the first stand, near the Maypole, in the Strand, where St. Mary's Church now is; and immediately adjoining there was a stand in our day.

In 1637, Charles I. granted a special commission to his Master of the Horse to license hackney-coaches; and the Board of Commissioners had a snug location at the bottom of Essex Street until our day; a commissioner-ship being one of the good things of the good old times. In this respect there is a remarkable coincidence between the English and French origins; in each case it became a Court or Government favour. To the recent version of the Paris anecdote is this rider—that the speculation was anything but profitable till the reign of Louis XV., when it came into the hands of a coach-painter, named Martin, who turned it to good account. This latter invented a new varnish (ever since known as the Vernis-Martin) to imitate Chinese lacquer, which was used not only for carriages, but also for furniture and boxes, which are still highly valued; for not long since a snuffbox of the Vernis-Martin was sold at a Paris auction for 3,000f.

Hackney-coaches were first excluded from Hyde Park in 1695, when " several persons of quality having been affronted at the Ring by some of the persons that rode in hackney-coaches with masks, and complaint thereof being made to the Lord Justices, an order is made that no hackney-coaches be permitted to go into the said Park, and that none presume to appear there in masks." (*Post-Boy*, June 8, 1695.) And the exclusion continues to this day.

By coach was the usual mode of sight-seeing: " I took (*Tatler*, June 18, 1709) three lads, who are under my guardianship, a-rambling in a hackney-coach, to show them the town; as the lions, the tombs, Bedlam," &c.

THE PARISH CLERKS OF CLERKENWELL.

There is a very curious matter connected with the parish of Clerkenwell, namely, the History of the Stroud Green Corporation. From the little that is known of it, it appears that when the Comic Muse took refuge in theatrical buildings, the ancient Society of Parish Clerks became divided—some turned their genius to wrestling and mimicry at Bartholomew Fair, whilst others, for their better administration, formed themselves into the Society of the Mayor, Aldermen, and Recorder of Stroud Green, assembling at the Old Crown, in Merry Islington; but still saving their right to exhibit at the Old London Spaw, formerly Clerks' Well, when they might happen to have learned sheriffs and other officers to get up their sacred pieces as usual. Even so late as the year 1774 (according to Lewis's *Islington*, p. 281), the members of this ancient Society were accustomed to meet annually in the summer time at Stroud Green, near Hornsey Wood House, and to regale themselves in the open air; the number of persons drawn to the spot on these occasions producing a scene similar to that of a country wake or fair.

SEDAN-CHAIRS IN LONDON.

Sedans were first used in England by the Duke of Buckingham, in 1623, when Prince Charles, returning from Spain, brought with him three curiously wrought sedans, two of which the Prince gave to the Duke, who, first using one in London, was accused of "degrading Englishmen into slaves and beasts of burden." Massinger, in his play of the *Bondman*, produced a few weeks after, refers to ladies—

> For their pomp and ease being borne
> In triumph *on men's shoulders*;

doubtless, in allusion to Buckingham's sedan, which was borne like a palanquin. The popular clamour was ineffectual; and in 1634, Sir Sanders Duncombe, who had named the chair from having first seen it at Sedan, on the Meuse, in France, obtained a patent from the King " for carrying people up and down in close chairs," and had "forty or fifty making ready for use." The coachmen and chairmen soon quarrelled; and in 1636 appeared a tract, entitled *Coach and Sedan pleasantly disputing for Place and Precedence*. The chairmen, however, no longer bore the sedan on their shoulders, but suspended by straps, as in our time; and the form of the chair was also changed.

Among the Exchequer papers has been found a bill for a sedan-chair made for Nell Gwyn, 34*l*. 11*s*., the several items being charged separately; besides a bill for chair-hire, 1*l*. 11*s*. 6*d*.

Defoe, writing in 1702, says : "We are carried to these places (the coffee-houses of Pall Mall and St. James's Street) in chairs (or sedans), which are here very cheap—a guinea a week, or a shilling per hour; and your chairmen serve you for porters, to run on errands, as your gondoliers do at Venice." Dryden has, " close mew'd in their sedans; " and Gay,

At White's the harnessed chairman idly stands.—*Trivia*.

" Two pages and a chair" are the outfit of Pope's
Belinda (*Rape of the Lock*). Swift thus describes a
fop in a sedan during a " City Shower: "

> Box'd in a chair, the beau impatient sits,
> While spouts run clattering o'er the roof by fits;
> While ever and anon, with frightful din,
> The leather sounds;—he trembles from within!

In St. James's Palace is the " Chair Court; " Hogarth's picture of " The Rake arrested by Bailiffs "
shows us the arrival of chairs at the Palace Gate; and
in Hogarth's " Beer Street " we have a pair of chairmen
calling for a foaming mug. The chairmen of the aristocracy wore embroidered liveries, cocked-hats, and
feathers: and the chair had its crimson velvet cushions
and damask curtains, such as Jonathan Wild recovered
for the Duchess of Marlborough, when two of his
rogues, in the disguise of chairmen, carried away her
chair from Lincoln's Inn Chapel, while " the true
men were drinking." There exists a curious print of
Leicester Square in the reign of George II., showing
the Prince of Wales borne in his sedan towards St.
James's, attended by halberdiers and his suite.

Hannah More, during the Westminster election, in
1784, was carried in a chair from Henrietta Street
through Covent Garden, when a great crowd followed
her, crying out, " It is Mrs. Fox: none but Mr. Fox's
wife would dare to come into Covent Garden in a chair.
She is going to canvass in the dark ! " " Though not
a little frightened," says Hannah, " I laughed heartily
at this: but shall stir out no more in a chair for some
time.

Sedans are now very rare: the Duchesses of Gloucester, Hamilton, and Dowager Northumberland, and

the Marchioness of Salisbury, are stated to have been the last persons who retained this antiquated mode of conveyance. In entrance-halls is occasionally kept the old disused family sedan, emblazoned with arms. The sign of "the Two Chairmen," exists in Warwick Street, Cockspur Street; and on Hay Hill.

Perhaps the longest journey ever performed in a sedan was the Princess Amelia being carried by eight chairmen from St. James's to Bath, between April 13 and April 19, 1728. The chairmen were relieved in their turns, a coach and six horses attending to carry the men when not on service.

A LONDON NEWSPAPER OF 1667.

THE *London Gazette* was first issued shortly after the Restoration; and it is curious to read in its "home news," usually dated from Whitehall, and supplying the place of the Court Circular, the following records.

First, we view in familiar guise a historical character, better known to us by heading charges of cavalry at Naseby—a daring cavalier, a valiant soldier; though now we see him *en deshabille*, and only as Prince Rupert, who, poor gentleman, has lost his pet dog! "Lost," says the advertisement—"lost on Friday last, about noon, a light fallow-coloured greyhound, with a sore under her jaw, and a scar on her side; whoever shall give notice of her at Prince Rupert's apartments at Whitehall shall be well rewarded for their pains." The next month we find the Prince assisting at a launch. "This day (3rd March) was happily launched at Deptford, in presence of his Majesty, his Royal

Highness Prince Rupert, and many persons of the court, a very large and well-built ship, which is to carry 106 great guns, and is like to prove a ship of great force and excellent service, called Charles the Second."

A little later, we find an account of the visit of " Madam," Duchess of Orleans, and sister to Charles II. Her reception, her return, and her death, follow quickly one upon another; so sudden, indeed, was her decease, that her death was not, says history, without suspicion of poison. 'Dover, *May* 21, 1670.—The 15 ins., about six in the morning, arrived here Her Royal Highness the Duchess of Orleans, attended, among other persons of quality, by the Mareshal de Plessis Praslin; her brother, Bishop of Tournay; Madame de Plessis, the mareshal's son's lady; and the Countess of Grammont; having the day before, at about the same hour, embarked with her train upon the men-of-war and several yachts under the command of the Earl of Sandwich, vice-admiral of England, &c."

" The same evening, the court was entertained with a comedy, acted by his Royal Highness's servants, who attend here for their diversion."

" Yesterday was acted, by the said servants, another comedy, in the midst whereof Madam and the rest of the ladies were entertained with an excellent banquet."

Confining ourselves to home news, there appears an edict from Whitehall, commanding the Duke of York's (James II.) absence. " Whitehall, 3 *Mar.* 1678.—His Majesty, having thought fit to command the Duke to absent himself, his Royal Highness and the Duchess took leave of their Majestys, and embarked this morning, intending to pass into Holland." But three years afterwards, he must have stood better with the City, for in 1681 we find the Lord Mayor and Court of Aldermen offering a reward of 500*l.* for the discovery of the person who offered an indignity to the picture of his Royal Highness in the Guildhall, to show their deep resentment at that " insolent and villainous act."

AMBASSADORS' SQUABBLE.

PEPYS records the following amusing scene to have occurred at York House in his time :—

" 30th (September 1661). This morning up *by moonshine,* at five o'clock " (here was one of the great secrets of the animal spirits of those times), " to Whitehall, to meet Mr. More at the Privy Seale, and there I heard of a fray between the two embassadors of Spaine and France, and that this day being the day of the entrance of an embassador from Sweeden, they intended to fight for the precedence. Our King, I heard, ordered that no Englishman should meddle in the business, but let them do what they would. And to that end, all the soldiers in town were in arms all the day long, and some of the train bands in the city, and a great bustle through the city all the day. Then we took coach (which was the business I came for) to Chelsey, to my Lord Privy Seale, and there got him to seal the business. Here I saw by daylight two very fine pictures in the gallery, that a little while ago I saw by night; and did also go all over the house, and found it to be the prettiest contrived house that ever I saw in my life. So back again; and at Whitehall light, and saw the soldiers and people running up and down the streets. So I went to the Spanish embas-

sador's and the French, and there saw great preparations
on both sides; but the French made the most noise and
ranted most, but the other made no stir almost at all;
so that I was afraid the other would have too great a
conquest over them. Then to the wardrobe and dined
there; and then abroad, and in Cheapside hear, that
the Spanish hath got the best of it, and killed three of
the French coach-horses and several men, and is gone
through the city next to our King's coach; at which, it
is strange to see how all the city did rejoice. And,
indeed, we do naturally all love the Spanish and hate
the French. But I, as I am in all things curious,
presently got to the water side, and there took oars to
Westminster Palace, and ran after them through all
the dirt, and the streets full of people; till at last, in
the Mews, I saw the Spanish coach go with fifty drawn
swords at least to guard it, and our soldiers shouting
for joy. And so I followed the coach, and then met it
at York House, where the embassador lies; and there
it went in with great state. So then I went to the
French house, where I observe still, that there is no
men in the world of a more insolent spirit where they
do dwell, nor before they begin a matter, and more
abject if they do miscarry, than these people are; for
they all look like dead men, and not a word among
them, but shake their heads. The truth is, the
Spaniards were not only observed to fight more desperately, but also they did outwitt them; first in lining
their own harnesse with chains of iron that they could
not be cut, then in setting their coach in the most
advantageous place, and to appoint men to guard every
one of their horses, and others for to guard the coach,
and others the coachmen. And, above all, in setting

upon the French horses and killing them, for by that means the French were not able to stir. There were several men slaine of the French, and one or two of the Spaniards, and one Englishman by a bullet. Which is very observable, the French were at least four to one in number, and had near one hundred cases of pistols among them, and the Spaniards had not one gun among them, which is for their honour for ever, and the others' disgrace. So having been very much daubed with dirt, I got a coach and home; where I vexed my wife in telling her of this story, and pleading for the Spaniards against the French."

DRYDEN CUDGELLED.

STEELE has well said that, " the life of a wit is a warfare upon earth." Dryden fell a victim to this sort of brutality. On the evening of December 18, 1679, as he was returning to his house in Long Acre, over against Bow Street, he was barbarously assaulted and wounded by three persons hired for the purpose by Wilmot, Earl of Rochester, who had mistaken Dryden for the author of the *Essay on Satire*, really by Lord Mulgrave, but in which his lordship had received some assistance from Dryden. Rochester says, in one of his letters :—" You write me word that I am out of favour with a certain poet, whom I have admired for the disproportion of him and his attributes. He is a rarity which I cannot but be fond of, as one would be of a hog that could fiddle, or a singing owl. If he falls on me at the blunt, which is his very good weapon in wit, I will forgive him if you please, and *leave the reparation to black Will with a cudgel.*"

In pursuance of this infamous resolution, upon the above night, Dryden was waylaid by hired ruffians, and severely beaten, as he passed through Bow Street. A reward of fifty pounds was in vain offered in the *London Gazette* and other newspapers, for the discovery of the perpetrators of this outrage. The town was, however, at no loss to pitch upon Rochester as the employer of the bravos, with whom the public suspicion joined the Duchess of Portsmouth, equally concerned in the supposed affront thus avenged.

" It will certainly be admitted, that a man, surprised in the dark, and beaten by ruffians, loses no honour by such a misfortune. But if Dryden had received the same discipline from Rochester's own hand, without resenting it, his drubbing could not have been more frequently made a matter of reproach to him : a sign, surely, of the penury of subjects for satire in his life and character, since an accident, which might have happened to the greatest hero that ever lived, was resorted to as an imputation on his honour. The Rose Alley Ambuscade became almost proverbial ; and even Mulgrave, the real author of the satire, and upon whose shoulders the blows ought in justice to have descended, mentions the circumstance in his *Art of Poetry*, with a cold and self-sufficient sneer :—

> Though praised and punished for another's rhymes,
> His own deserve as great applause *sometimes.*

To which is added, in a note, ' A libel for which he was both applauded and wounded, though entirely ignorant of the whole matter.' This flat and conceited couplet, and note, the noble author judged it proper to omit in the corrected edition of his poem. Otway

alone, no longer the friend of Rochester, and, perhaps,
no longer the enemy of Dryden, has spoken of the
author of this dastardly outrage with the contempt
it deserved:—

> Poets in honour of the truth should write,
> With the same spirit brave men for it fight;
> And though against him causeless hatreds rise,
> And daily where he goes of late, he spies
> The scowls of sudden and revengeful eyes;
> 'Tis what he knows with much contempt to bear,
> And serves a cause too good to let him fear;
> He fears no poison from incensed drab,
> No ruffian's five-foot sword, nor rascal's stab;
> Nor any other snares of mischief laid,
> *Not a Rose-alley cudgel ambuscade;*
> From any private cause where malice reigns,
> Or general pique all blockheads have to brains."

FUNERAL OF DRYDEN.

LITERARY impostures have a wonderful vitality, especially if they are of a romantic hue, such as that we
are about to relate. Dryden died in his house, now
No. 43, in Gerard Street, Soho, on the 1st of May
1700. Connected with his funeral is a " memorable
romance," or wild story, of which there is more than
one version, but the following are its chief points:—

" On the Sunday morning after the poet's death,
when the hearse was at the door and the poet's body
in it, whilst eighteen mourning coaches were attending, a party of young rakes rode by the door, and one
of them, Lord Jeffreys, seeing the procession, which
had begun to move, asked whose funeral it was. He
was told it was Mr. Dryden, whereupon he declared
that so great a poet should not be buried in so private.

a manner, and he declared he would take upon himself
the honour of interment, and give a thousand pounds
for a monument.   After a time he persuaded the servants to show him up to the room where Lady Elizabeth Dryden was still in bed: they complied, and he
unfolded his wishes; Lady Elizabeth refusing, he fell
on his knees and declared he would never rise till she
granted his request.   Poor Lady Elizabeth fainted
away, and Jeffreys pretending that he had gained her
consent, went down stairs, and ordered the body to be
taken to Cheapside, to a Mr. Russell's, an undertaker,
there to await further orders.   Meantime the choirs
and the Abbey were lighted up, the grave was dug,
and yawned to receive the dead.   The Bishop awaited
the corpse, and awaited for hours in vain.   The following day Charles Dryden went to the Bishop, and Lord
Halifax, and stated the whole case to them.   The
undertaker repaired also three days afterwards—having
heard nothing—to Lord Jeffreys for orders; but was
told that his lordship remembered nothing of the
matter, and supposed it was a drunken frolic:—and
added he might do what he liked with the body.   Mr.
Charles Dryden, in consternation, wrote to Lord
Halifax and the Bishop of Rochester, who now refused
to have anything to do with the affair, and the body
remained unburied three weeks, until Dr. Garth,
Dryden's intimate friend, sent for it to the College of
Physicians. . . . One heart throbbed with passionate
grief and anger as the body of John Dryden was thus
lowered into the earth.   It was that of Charles Dryden;
that ill-fated, high-spirited young man, whose nativity
his father had cast. . . . No sooner were the funeral
obsequies over than he sent a challenge to Lord

Jeffreys. It was not answered. Several others were sent. At last the young man went himself. Charles Dryden, receiving no reply, waited and watched for the young lord; but waited and watched in vain; for Lord Jeffreys found it best to depart from London, and the insulted family of Dryden found no redress; and the matter was settled, as many disputes are, by the great arbitrator, death."—*Mrs. A. Thomson.*

Dr. Johnson, in his *Life of Dryden*, quotes a more lengthy version of the story than the above; adding, " This story I intended to omit, as it appears with no great evidence; nor have I met with any confirmation, but in a letter of Farquhar, and he only relates that the funeral of Dryden was tumultuary and confused."

The whole story was but a Grub Street invention of the notorious " Corinna " of the *Dunciad*, and first appeared in one of Curll's Grub Street pamphlets. Malone, in his *Life of Dryden*, long since exposed its absurdity. Ned Ward, in his *London Spy*, published in 1706, relates that at Dryden's funeral there was a performance of solemn music at the College of Physicians; and that at the procession, which he himself saw, standing at the end of Chancery Lane, Fleet Street, there was a concert of hautboys and trumpets. He also describes the musical service in Westminster Abbey; but strangely refers to Lord Jeffreys, as " concerned chiefly in the pious undertaking," which was written in 1706. We have seen how Johnson, with slight reservation, adopted this invention of Mrs. Thomson's romantic brain, which was believed for nearly a century to be true.

GAMING-HOUSES KEPT BY LADIES.

THE following curious piece of evidence, probably an extract from the Journals of the House of Lords, although there is no reference to the subject in the published "Parliamentary Debates," was found not long since by the Editor of the *Athenæum* amongst a mass of contemporary MSS:—

"Die Lunæ, 29° Aprilis, 1745.—GAMING.—A Bill for preventing the excessive and deceitful use of it having been brought from the Commons, and proceeded on so far as to be agreed to in a Committee of the whole House with Amendments,—information was given to the House that Mr. Burdus, Chairman of the Quarter Session for the city and liberty of Westminster, Sir Thomas de Veil, and Mr. Lane, Chairman of the Quarter Sessions for the county of Middlesex, were at the door ; they were called in, and at the Bar severally gave an account that claims of Privilege of Peerage were made and insisted on by the Ladies Mordington and Cassillis, in order to intimidate the peace officers from doing their duty in suppressing the public Gaming-Houses kept by the said ladies. And the said Burdus thereupon delivered in an instrument in writing under the hand of the said Lady Mordington, containing the claim she made of Privilege for her officers and servants employed by her in her said Gaming-House.—And then they were directed to withdraw.—And the said instrument was read as follows :—' I, Dame Mary, Baroness of Mordington, do hold a house in the Great Piazza, Covent Garden, for and as an Assembly, where all persons of credit are at liberty to frequent and play at such diversions as are used at other Assemblys. And I have hired Joseph Dewberry, William Horsely, Ham Cropper, and George Sanders as my servants or managers (under me) thereof. I have given them orders to direct the management of the other inferior servants, (namely) John Bright, Richard Davids, John Hill, John Vandenvoren, as box-keepers,—Gilbert Richardson, housekeeper, John Chaplain, regulator, William Stanley and Henry Huggins, servants that wait on the company at the said Assembly, William Penny and Joseph Penny as porters thereof—And all the above-mentioned persons I claim as my domestick servants, and demands all those Privileges that belong to me as a Peeress of Great Britain appertaining to my said Assembly.—M. MOR-DINGTON.—Dated 8th Jan. 1744.'—Resolved and declared that no person is entitled to Privilege of Peerage against any prosecution or proceeding for keeping any public or common Gaming-House, or any house, room, or place for playing at any game or games prohibited by any law now in force."

ROYAL GAMING AT CHRISTMAS.

GAMING was formerly a Royal pastime of the Christmas holidays which the subjects of the Sovereign were permitted to witness. The play run high in Charles II.'s time, and it lasted almost to our day. George I. and George II. played on certain days at hazard in public at the groom-porter's in St. James's Palace, where the nobility and even the Princesses staked considerable sums. This gaming in public was discontinued some time in the reign of George III. The office of groom-porter, we are told, still occurs in the enumeration of the palace household.

The groom-porter of old is described as an officer of the Royal household whose business it was to see the King's lodging furnished with tables, stools, chairs, and firing; as also to provide cards, dice, &c., and to decide disputes arising at cards, dice, bowling, &c. Formerly he was allowed to keep an open gambling-table at Christmas. In Ben Jonson's *Alchymist* we have—

> He will win you
> By irresistible luck, within this fortnight,
> Enough to buy a barony. They will set him
> Upmost at the groom-porter's all the Christmas,
> And for the whole year through at every place.

Basset—a game at cards said by Dr. Johnson to have been invented at Venice—was certainly known in Italy as early as the end of the thirteenth century. It appears to have been a fashionable game in England at the end of the seventeenth century. Who does not recollect Pope's charming eclogue, the Basset-table?—

> But of what marble must that breast be form'd,
> To gaze on Basset, and remain unwarm'd?
> When Kings, Queens, Knaves, are set in decent rank;
> Exposed in glorious heaps the tempting bank,
> Guineas, half-guineas, all the shining train;
> The winner's pleasure, and the lover's pain;
> In bright confusion open rouleaus lie;
> They strike the soul and glitter in the eye.
> Fired by the sight, all reason I disdain;
> My passions rise, and will not bear the rein.
> Look upon Basset, you who reason boast,
> And see if reason must not there be lost.
> *   *   *   *   *   *   *
> At the Groom-porter's batter'd bullies play,
> Some Dukes at Mary-bone bowl time away;
> But who the bowl or rattling dice compares
> To Basset's heavenly joys and pleasing cares?

Mr. Hawkins, the numismatist, possesses a silver token, marked to the amount of ten pounds, which appears to have passed among the players for the groom-porter's benefit at basset. It is within the size of half-a-crown; in the centre of the obverse is L-X; legend round, AT · THE · GROOM-PORTER'S · BASSET; mint-mark, a fleur-de-lis. On the reverse, a wreath and gold coronet; the coronet being of gold let in; legend, NOTHING · VENTURE · NOTHING · WINNS; mint-mark again, a fleur-de-lis.

Theodore Hook, in one of his novels, has this note of experience upon the above subject:—" The room at St. James's formerly appropriated to hazard was remarkably dark, and conventionally called by the inmates ' Hell!' whence, and not, as generally supposed, from their own demerits, all the gaming-houses in London are designated by the same fearful name. Those who play, or have played, English hazard, will recollect that, for a similar inconsequent reason, the man who raked up the dice and called the odds was designated ' the groom-porter.' "

PUNCH AND JUDY.

THE street-play of Punch has amused crowds in London for two centuries; but in a French illuminated MS. in the Bodleian Library, there is a coloured illustration, four centuries old, exactly corresponding with the puppets and the itinerant show of the present day; showing the famous puppet to have amused the world long before he reached England. He is as popular in Egypt, Syria, and Turkey, as in London or Naples.

The earliest date of Punch in our metropolis was found by Mr. Peter Cunningham, in the overseers' book of St. Martin's-in-the-Fields, being four entries, in 1666 and 1667, of " Ree. of Punchinello, ye Italian popet player, for his booth at Charing Cross," sums varying from 2*l.* 12*s.* 6*d.* to 1*l.* 2*s.* 6*d.* Next are quoted some lines on why it was so long before the statue of Charles I. was put up at Charing Cross, the last line being,

Unless Punchinello is to be restored.

" These," says Mr. Cunningham, " are the earliest notices of Punch in England."

Another early reference is that made by Granger, who, speaking of one Philips, a noted merry-andrew in the reign of James II., says, " this man was some time fiddler to a puppet-show, in which capacity he held many a dialogue with Punch, in much the same strain as he did afterwards with the mountebank-doctor, his master, upon the stage."

Sir Richard Steele, in the *Tatler*, immortalises Powel, the famous puppet-showman, who exhibited his wooden heroes under the Little Piazza in Covent Garden, opposite St. Paul's Church, as we learn from the letter of the sexton in the *Spectator* (No. 14), attributed to Steele, who complains that the performances of Punch thinned the congregation in the church; and that, as Powel exhibited during the time of prayer, the tolling of the bell was taken by all who heard it for notice of the commencement of the exhibition. The writer, in another letter, decides that the puppet-show was much superior to the opera of *Rinaldo and Armida* in the Haymarket; he adds, that too much encouragement cannot be given to Mr. Powel, who has so well disciplined his pig, that he and Punch dance a minuet together.

In No. 44 of the *Tatler*, Isaac Bickerstaff, Esq., complains that he has been abused by Punch in a prologue, supposed to be spoken by him, but really delivered by his master, who stood behind, "worked the wires," and by "a thread in one of Punch's chops" gave to him the appearance of animation. No. 50 of the same work contains a real or supposed letter from the showman himself, insisting on his right of control over his own puppets, and denying all knowledge of the "original of puppet-shows, and the several changes and revolutions that have happened in them since Thespis." A subsequent No. (115) shows that Punch was so attractive, particularly with the ladies, as to cause the opera and Nicolini to be deserted. Here also we learn that then, as now, Punchinello had "a scolding wife;" and that he was attended besides by a number of courtiers and nobles.

Punchinello was part of the Bartholomew Fair revels:

'Twas then, when August near was spent,
That Bat, the grilliado'd saint,
Had usher'd in his Smithfield revels,
Where Punchinelloes, popes, and devils
Are by authority allowed,
To please the giddy, gaping crowd.
Hudibras Redivivus, 1707.

Hence we collect that the popularity of Punch was completely established in 1711-12, and that he materially lessened the receipts at the opera, if not at the regular national theatres. Still, no writer of the reign of Queen Anne speaks of him as a novelty, which may

be established from poetry as well as prose. Gay, in
his *Shepherd's Week* (Saturday), distinguishes between
the tricks of " Jack-Pudding, in his parti-coloured
jacket," and " Punch's feats ; " and adds, that they
were both known at rustic wakes and fairs. But the
most remarkable account of Punch is given in No. 3 of
the *Intelligencer*.

Nevertheless, the exact date of Punch's arrival in
England is uncertain. Mr. Payne Collier concludes
that he and King William came in together, and that
the Revolution is to be looked upon as the era of the
introduction of the family of Punch, and of the glorious
" House of Orange."

Mr. Collier humorously speculates on " the character
of Punch," and attempts to prove it to be " a combina-
tion or concentration of two of the most prominent and
original delineations on the stage "—King Richard III.
and Falstaff: his costume closely resembles the Eliza-
bethan peascod-bellied doublets.

At various periods the adventures of Punch have
been differently represented, and innovations have been
introduced to suit the taste and to meet the events
of the day. Thus, in Fielding's time, in consequence
of the high popularity of *The Provoked Husband*, he
complains (*Tom Jones*, book xii. chap. v.) that a puppet-
show witnessed by his hero included " the fine and
serious part " of the above comedy. Here is a later in-
terpolation: after the battle of the Nile, Lord Nelson
figured on one of the street stages, and held a dialogue
with Punch, in which he endeavoured to persuade him,
as a brave fellow, to go on board his ship, and assist in
fighting the French : " Come Punch, my boy," said the
naval hero, " I'll make you a captain or a commodore,

if you like it." " But I don't like it," replied the puppet-show hero; "I shall be drowned." " Never fear that," answered Nelson; " he that is born to be hanged, you know, is sure not to be drowned."

During one of the elections for Westminster, Sir Francis Burdett was represented kissing Judy and the child, and soliciting Mr. Punch for his vote.

Punch has amused ages. " We ourselves," says Mr. Collier, " saw the late Mr. Windham, then one of the Secretaries of State, on his way from Downing Street to the House of Commons, on a night of important debate, pause like a truant boy until the whole performance was concluded, to enjoy a hearty laugh at the whimsicalities of the motley hero."

Porsini and Pike were celebrated Punch exhibitors in our time: the former is said to have frequently taken 10l. a day, but he died in St. Giles's workhouse. Porsini used a trumpet.

FANTOCCINI.

EXHIBITIONS of Puppets have always been amongst the favourite amusements of the British public. We do not here refer to that most popular of wooden performers, Mr. Punch, but of such entertainers as have aimed at the representation of more regularly constructed dramas. The allusions to them in our older writers are numerous, as a *motion*. Thus, the chief part of the fifth act of Ben Jonson's *Bartholomew Fair*, relates to a motion, or puppet-show, where is the exquisitely humorous portrait of Lanthorn Leatherhead, with his *motions* of *Hero and Leander*, and *Damon and Pythias.* In Shakspeare's *Winter's Tale* having compassed a motion of the Prodigal Son is one of the many callings which the merry rogue Autolycus had followed. In the *Knave in Grain*, 1640,

D.—Where's the dumbe shew you promis'd me?
J.—Even ready, my lord; but may be called a motion, for puppits will speak but such corrupt language you 'll never understand.

A large circle of readers of another class will remember how in the next century Steele and Addison celebrated the "skill in motions" of Powel, whose place of exhibition was under the arcade in Covent Garden. In April 1751, the tragedy of *Jane Shore* was advertised for representation at "Punch's Theatre in James Street, in the Haymarket," by puppets; Punch's Theatre being, of course, located in Hickford's Room. Strutt, writing before 1801, says: "A few years back a puppet-show was exhibited at the court end of the town, with the Italian title, *Fantoccini,* which greatly attracted the notice of the public, and was spoken of as an extraordinary performance: it was, however, no more than a puppet-show, with the motions constructed upon better principles, dressed with more elegance, and managed with greater art, than they had formerly been." In Piccadilly, "Italian Fantoccini" were also exhibited in 1780, by which comedies and comic operas were performed, the latter with music by Pergolesi, Jomelli, and other composers; followed by a dance, and an entertainment, in which "Harlequin, while refreshing himself with a dish of maccaroni, is surprised by the appearance of a Spaniard from a remote corner, who sings a favourite comic song;" the flight of Harlequin, &c.

The reader, we dare say, will remember Fantoccini

in pantomimes at Drury Lane Theatre; Marionettes
at the Adelaide Gallery; and George Cruikshank's
admirable delineation of the itinerant Fantoccini shown
in the streets of the metropolis in 1825.—*Condensed
chiefly from Notes and Queries*, 3rd S. v. 52.

MRS. SALMON'S WAX-WORK.

MRS. SALMON's moving Wax-work was one of the
curiosities of Fleet Street which lasted to our time. It
was originally established at the Golden Salmon, St.
Martin's, near Aldersgate (*Harl. Ms.*, 5931, British
Museum), and delighted the sight-seeing public of the
days of Queen Anne, as we gather from the 28th
paper of the *Spectator*, April 2, 1711 : " It would have
been ridiculous for the ingenious Mrs. Salmon to have
lived at the sign of the Trout." Her handbill runs :
" Mrs. Salmon's Wax-work—Royal Court of England—
the moving Wax-work—140 figures as big as life, all
made by Mrs. Salmon, who sells all sorts of moulds
and glass eyes, and teaches the full art," &c. In what
year she removed to Fleet Street is unknown: her
collection was shown near the Horn Tavern (now An-
derton's), in a house with the sign of the Salmon, which
has been engraved by J. T. Smith. Thence the wax-
work was removed to 198 Fleet Street, to a house on
the site of the present banking-house of Messrs. Praed
& Co. She died at the age of ninety, when her death
was thus announced: " March 1760: Died Mrs.
Steers, aged 90, but was generally known by the name
of her former husband, Mrs. Salmon. She was famed
for making several figures in wax, which have been
long shown in Fleet Street." Upon her death, the

collection was purchased by Mr. Clark, a surgeon, who lived in Chancery Lane. Mrs. Clark, after the decease of her husband, continued the exhibition in the name of Salmon, until the close of 1794, when, the premises occupied by her on the north side of Fleet Street having been purchased by Messrs. Praed & Co. as a site for their banking-house, she removed to No. 17, on the south side, as thus announced in the *Morning Herald* of January 28, 1785:

" The house in which Mrs. Salmon's Wax-work has, for above a century, been exhibited, is pulling down : the figures are removed to the very spacious and handsome apartments at the corner of the Inner Temple gate, which was once the Palace of Henry Prince of Wales, the eldest son of King James the First, and they are now the residence of many a royal guest. Here are held the courts of Alexander the Great, of King Henry the Eighth, of Caractacus, and the present Duke of York. Happy ingenuity to bring heroes together, maugre the lapse of time! The levées of each of these personages are daily very numerously attended, and we find them all to be of very easy access, since it is insured by a shilling to one of the attendants."

At a very advanced age, Mrs. Clark was seriously injured by falling upon the steps of the altar after receiving the sacrament. She was confined to her bed many weeks; during which her son constantly attended his venerable parent. For some years before this accident, the exhibition of Wax-work had ceased to attract, and had become no longer a source of profit; but Mrs. Clark could never be prevailed on to quit the premises and reside with her family.

Here the Wax-work was exhibited until Mrs. Clark's

death, in the year 1812 : the figure of Ann Siggs on
crutches, at the door, we well recollect, but not the
kick which Mother Shipton gave the visitor on going
out, and of which J. T. Smith had so vivid an impression. When the frail establishment was broken up,
the wax-folk were sold, it is said, for less than 50*l.*
Many of the figures were removed to a house at the
west corner of Water Lane, and there exhibited for a
few pence, by which the proprietor realised a considerable sum. However, one night, in July 1827, some
thieves broke open the premises, and stole a sum of
money and several articles of wearing apparel; destroyed some of the figures, stripped part of their
clothes, and tore the gold lace and trinkets from
others ; they then smashed the heads of the figures to
pieces, and piled them up until they nearly reached the
ceiling : the loss was set down at 150*l.* Still, the Wax-
work, with repairs and additions, lingered here until
1831, when the fine folk—emperors, kings, and princes—
were sold under an execution for rent !

It may be as well to notice Mrs. Salmon's misde-
scription of the old house in Fleet Street, as well as
the misinscription upon the house itself, as " formerly
the palace of Henry VIII. and Cardinal Wolsey."
Mrs. Salmon is nearer probability when she styles the
house as " once the palace of Henry Prince of Wales,
son of King James I." The first-floor front-room has
an enriched plaster ceiling, inscribed P. (triple plume)
H., which, with part of the wainscoting, denotes the
structure to be of the time of James I. Still, we do
not find in the lives of Prince Henry any identification
of this house as a royal palace. It appears, however,
that the house, though never the residence of Prince

Henry, was the *office in which the Council for the Management of the Duchy of Cornwall Estates held their sittings*; and in the Calendar of State Papers, edited by Mrs. Green, is the following entry of the time of Charles, created Prince of Wales four years after the death of Henry: " 1619, Feb. 25; Prince's *Council Chamber, Fleet Street*," and other entries to the same effect; thus settling the appropriation of the old house in Fleet Street, but stripping it of about a century of its boasted antiquity.

The finest Wax-work collection of the present day is Tussaud's, stated to be the oldest exhibition in Europe. It was commenced on the Boulevard du Temple, at Paris, in 1780, and was first shown in London, at the Lyceum, Strand, in 1802. It now consists of upwards of two hundred figures in wax, in the costume of their time, and several in the dresses which they actually wore; besides a large collection of paintings and sculpture. Thus, it not only contains fine specimens of modelling in wax, but a curious assemblage of costume and personal decoration, memorials of celebrated characters, historical groups, &c.

Madame Tussaud was born at Berne, in Switzerland, in 1760. When a child she was taught to model figures in wax, by her uncle, M. Curtius, at whose house she often dined with Voltaire, Rousseau, Dr. Franklin, Mirabeau, and La Fayette, of whose heads she took casts. She taught drawing and modelling to the Princess Elizabeth, and many of the French noblesse, just before the Revolution of 1789. She also modelled in wax Robespierre, Marat, and Danton; and often took models of heads severed on the scaffold. Madame Tussaud died in London, 15th April 1850, aged 90.

THE RAGGED REGIMENT IN WESTMINSTER ABBEY.

This was, until some thirty years since, one of the sights of London, and consisted mostly of the wax effigies of noted persons which had been carried in their funeral processions to Westminster Abbey, and were, after the interment, deposited there. It may here be remarked that a waxen image was a part of the paraphernalia of a witch, by means of which she was supposed to torment her unfortunate victims. In Ben Jonson's *Sad Shepherd*, we find the witch sitting in her dell, " with her spindle, threads, and images: " the practice was, to provide the waxen image of the person intended to be tormented, and this was stuck through with pins, and melted at a distance from the fire.

These wax effigies were formerly called " The Play of the Dead Volks," and " The Ragged Regiment." They represented " princes and others of high quality " who were buried in the Abbey. In a description of them a century since, we are told: " These effigies resembled the deceased as near as possible, and were wont to be exposed at the funerals of our princes and other great personages in open chariots, with their proper ensigns of royalty or honour appended. The most ancient that are here laid up are the least injured, by which it would seem as if the costliness of their clothes had tempted persons to partly strip them; for the robes of Edward VI., which were once of crimson velvet, now appear like leather; but those of Queen Elizabeth (who is said to have been arrayed in her coronation robes) and King James I. are entirely stript, as are all the rest, of everything of value. In two handsome wainscot presses are the effigies of King William, and Queen Mary, and Queen Anne, in good condition. The figure of Cromwell is not mentioned in the list; but in the account of his lying-in-state, the effigy is described as made to the life in wax, and apparelled in velvet, gold-lace, and ermine. This effigy was laid upon the bed of state, and carried upon the hearse in the funeral procession: both were then deposited in Westminster Abbey; but at the Restoration, the hearse was broken to pieces, and the effigy was destroyed, after it had been hung from a window at Whitehall." In the prints of the grand state funeral procession of General Monk, Duke of Albemarle, in 1670, his effigy, clad in part-armour and ducal robes and coronet, is borne upon an open chariot beneath a canopy, and surrounded by a forest of banners; on reaching the Abbey, the effigy was taken from the car, and placed upon the body, beneath a lofty canopy bristling with bannerets, and richly dight with armorial escutcheons.

Nollekens, the sculptor, describes the collection as " the wooden figures, with wax masks, all in silk tatters, that the Westminster boys called ' The Ragged Regiment,' from the tattered state of the costumes." Among the later additions were the figures of the great Earl of Chatham and Lord Nelson.

To what may be styled the legitimate wax figures at Westminster were added, from time to time, those of other celebrities, as, for example, Mother Shipton: this strange collection was shown until 1839, when it was very properly removed.

There was formerly a similar wax-work exhibition in France. Mr. Cole, of Milton, upon his visit to the

Abbey of St. Denis, near Paris, November 22, 1765, says, in his diary:

" Mr. Walpole had been informed by M. Mariette, that in this treasury were several wax figures of some of the later kings of France, and asked one of the monks for leave to see them, as they were not commonly shown or much known. Accordingly, in four cupboards, above those in which the jewels, crosses, busts, and curiosities were kept, were eight ragged figures of as many monarchs of this country to Louis XIII., which must be very like, as their faces were taken off in wax immediately after their decease. The monk told us, that the great Louis XIV.'s face was so excessively wrinkled, that it was impossible to take one off from him."

THE PIG-FACED LADY.

THE mythical existence of a pig-faced lady is common to the nursery literature of several European languages. The story generally is that of a newly-married lady of rank and fashion, in reply to the entreaties of a wretched beggar-woman with a squalling child, exclaiming, " Take away your nasty pig, I will not give you anything!"—whereupon the enraged beggar retorted: " May your own child, when it is born, be more like a pig than mine!" Shortly after this, the lady gave birth to a girl, beautifully formed, save that its face, some say the whole head, exactly resembled that of a pig. The child grew to be a woman: its fond and wealthy parents had it fed out of a silver trough; and a small fortune was paid annually as wages to the waiting-maid upon this creature. The greatest perplexity, however, was to the parents, what would become of the creature after their decease. It was determined that she should be married, the father giving a large dowry, and settling a handsome annuity on the husband. However, this money-bait failed to lure anyone to the unfortunate creature : even old fortune-hunters were glad to retreat. Then it was proposed to found a hospital, the trustees of which were bound to cherish and protect the "pig-faced" until death did them part. Such are the features of the conventional stories of pig-faced ladies.

But we have only to treat of London specimens. In 1641, there was published *A certain Relation of the Hog-faced Gentlewoman*, named Tanakin Skinkery, having all the limbs and lineaments well featured and proportioned, save having the nose of a hog, or swine; forty thousand pounds were offered to the man who would consent to wed her, and gallants came from all parts of England and the Continent, but soon gave up the idea of marrying her, and fled.

We have a distinct recollection of a pig-faced lady of the present century. In 1815, there appeared a portrait of the lady, with her silver trough of food. She was then twenty years of age, lived in Manchester Square, and on her life and issue by marriage a very large property depended. The account sold with the print stated : " Her person is most delicately formed, and of the greatest symmetry ; her hands and arms are delicately modelled in the happiest mould of nature ; and the carriage of her body indicative of superior birth. Her manners are, in general, simple and unoffending ; but when she is in want of food, she articulates, certainly, something like the sound of pigs

when eating, and which, to those who are not acquainted with her, may perhaps be a little disagreeable." *

Her attendant, though receiving 1,000*l.* a year, soon
grew tired of the situation, when there appeared the
following advertisement in the *Times* of Thursday,
the 9th of February 1815:

" *For the Attention of Gentlemen and Ladies.*—A
young gentlewoman having heard of an advertisement
for a person to undertake the care of a lady, who is
heavily afflicted in the face, whose friends have offered
a handsome income yearly, and a premium for residing
with her for seven years, would do all in her power
to render her life most comfortable; an undeniable
character can be obtained from a respectable circle of
friends; an answer to this advertisement is requested,
as the advertiser will keep herself disengaged. Address, post paid, to X. Y., at Mr. Ford's, Baker, 12,
Judd Street, Brunswick Square."

Another advertiser, aspiring to become the husband
of the pig-faced lady, thus advertised in the *Morning
Herald* of February 16, 1815:

' *Secrecy.*—A single gentleman, aged thirty-one, of
a respectable family, and in whom the utmost confidence may be reposed, is desirous of explaining his
mind to the friends of a person who has a misfortune
in her face, but is prevented for want of an introduction. Being perfectly aware of the principal particulars, and understanding that a final settlement would
be preferred to a temporary one, presumes he would
be found to answer to the full extent of their wishes.
His intentions are sincere, honourable, and firmly re-

* See a paper in Chambers's *Book of Days*, vol. ii. pp. 255–257.

solved.   References of great respectability can be
given.   Address to M. D., at Mr. Spencer's, 22,
Great Ormond Street, Queen Square."   .

The story of the London pig-faced lady was, from
beginning to end, a catchpenny hoax, founded upon
the old myth: there was no actual lady, but there
were printed accounts of her, and these were the source
of profit.   The advertisements, we suppose, kept up
the deception.

There is a story of this kind associated with Steevens's
Hospital, in Dublin, but no one can tell why: the
foundress, Miss Steevens, whose portrait hangs in the
library, is a well-favoured lady.   Parties came to see
the portrait and the silver trough; but the matron·
was forbidden to show them, though the visitors gave
a fee for the information.   In Dublin, too, is a story
of a boar's head crest, engraved upon a silver punch
bowl, leading to its being called the pig-trough.

COUNT BORUWLASKI AND GEORGE IV.

WHEN this celebrated Dwarf visited England, he
was graciously received by the Duke and Duchess of
Devonshire, was presented to the King and Queen,
patronised by the Prince of Wales and the nobility,
and became the sort of lion, on a smaller scale, which
General Tom Thumb afterwards became, on less pretensions.

Among the memorable persons with whom the Count
came in contact was "a stupendous giant, eight feet
three or four inches high," who was then exhibiting himself. This must have been O'Byrne, the Irish giant, whom

we shall notice presently. "Our surprise," says Boruwlaski, "was mutual; the giant remained a moment
speechless with astonishment; then stooping half way
he presented his hand, which could easily have contained a dozen of mine, and made me a very pretty
compliment." When they stood beside each other, the
giant's knee was very nearly on a level with the dwarf's
head. They both resided together some time at an inn
at Epping, where they often walked out together,
greatly to the amusement of the townsfolk.

Mathews, the comedian, was a friend and admirer
of Boruwlaski; and Mrs. Mathews, in the *Memoirs*
of her husband, describes the dwarf as a most fasci-
nating person, full of accomplishments and good sense,
playful as an infant, and altogether the most charming
of companions. He had written his *Memoirs*, which
he earnestly desired to present in person to His Majesty George the Fourth, who had previously desired,
many years before, that they should be dedicated to
him. The *Memoirs* were published in 1788 ; they are
written in bad French, accompanied by a very bad
translation, and headed by a list of very aristocratic
subscribers. Mathews contrived to get an interview
arranged between His Majesty and the Count. "At
the hour appointed," says Mrs. Mathews, " my husband and his little charge were ushered into the presence of the sovereign, who was seated in his domestic
circle. On the announcement of his expected visitors,
the King rose from his chair, and met Boruwlaski at
the entrance, raising him up in his arms in a kind of
embrace, saying, ' My dear old friend, how delighted
I am to see you!' and then placed the little man upon
a sofa. But the Count's loyalty not being so satisfied,

he descended, with the agility of a schoolboy, and threw himself at his master's feet, who, however, would not suffer him to remain in that position for a minute, but raised him again upon the sofa. When the Count said something about sitting in the presence of his sovereign, he was graciously told to 'remember for the time there was no sovereign *there.*' . . . In the course of the conversation, the Count, addressing the King in French, was told that his English was so good it was quite unnecessary to speak in any other language; for His Majesty, with his usual tact, easily discerned that he should be a loser in resigning the Count's prettily-broken English, which (as he always thought in his native language, and literally translated its idioms,) was the most amusing imaginable, and totally distinct from the imperfect English of other foreigners. . . . The King, in the course of conversation, said, 'But, Count, you were married when I knew you: I hope madame is still alive, and as well as yourself.' 'Ah, no! Majesty; Isolina die thirty year! *Fine* woman! *sweet, beauty* body! You have no *idea*, Majesty.' 'I am sorry to hear of her death. Such a charming person must have been a great loss to you, Count.' 'Dat is very true, Majesty; *indid, indid*, it was great sorrow for me!' Just at this moment he recollected that it might be improper to lay further stress on so melancholy a subject on so pleasing a visit. Resuming, therefore, a cheerful tone, the Count playfully observed that 'he had throughout been *great* philosophy,' and quoted the Frenchman's epitaph upon *his* departed wife:—

Ci-gît ma femme! ah qu'elle est bien,
Pour son repose, et pour le mien!

which sally surprised the King into a hearty laugh, while everybody present doubtless felt that such an allusion to wives might have been made at a more safe moment. Boruwlaski afterwards confessed to my husband that he was himself conscious, though too late, of the impropriety of it at that particular juncture. . . . His Majesty then inquired how old the Count was, and on being told, with a start of surprise, observed, ' Count, you are the finest man of your age I ever saw. I wish you could return the compliment.' To which Boruwlaski, not to be outdone in courtesy, ludicrously replied, ' Oh! Majesty, *fine* body! *indid, indid; beauty body!* ' "

The King, on accepting the book which the Count wished to present, turned to the Marchioness of Conyngham, and took from her a little case containing a beautiful miniature watch and seals, attached to a superb chain, the watch exquisitely embossed with jewels. This he begged the Count to accept, saying, as he held the *Memoirs* in the other hand, " My dear friend, I shall read and preserve this as long as I live, for your sake ; and in return I request you will wear this for mine." The King said to Mathews, in the absence of the Count, " If I had a dozen sons, I could not point out to them a more perfect model of good breeding and elegance than the Count; he is really a most accomplished and charming person." He also inquired if the Count were really at ease in his circumstances, and was glad to be informed that this was the case. For we have omitted to mention that, after many years of ineffectual concert-giving, the Count, having no Barnum to manage his affairs, and make a fortune out of his figure, had finally resolved on a visit to America, when two charitable ladies of Durham, named Metcalfe, made up a sum which purchased an annuity for him, thus securing him independence for the remainder of his life.—*Abridged from Fraser's Magazine.*

THE IRISH GIANTS.

ALL the fossils hitherto discovered, and supposed to belong to giants, have, on inspection, been proved to belong to brutes. All the evidence by which a colossal race of men was once accredited disappears; and no one scientifically educated now belives that giants ever existed as a *race*, although individual giants have been far from rare. Men of seven feet are not so rare but that many readers must have seen such; and a visit to the Museum of the Royal College of Surgeons in Lincoln's Inn Fields, will convince anyone that even eight feet have been reached. Among the osteological curiosities of that collection stands the skeleton of the Irish giant, O'Byrne, *eight feet* high; and beside it stands the skeleton of Mademoiselle Crachami, only *twenty-three inches* high: two striking types of the giant and dwarf, not belonging to fable, not liable to the scepticism which must ever hang over the reports of travellers, but standing there in naked reality, measurable by a prosaic foot-rule. We read, indeed, of eight feet and a half, and even of nine feet having been attained; but here, at any rate, is O'Byrne, a solid, measurable fact, admitting of no doubt. That one must generally doubt all reported measurements of wondrous types, is illustrated, even in the case of O'Byrne. The *Annual Register*, in its obituary for June 1783, vol. xxvi. p. 209, gives this account of him :—

" In Cockspur Street, Charing Cross, aged only twenty-two, Mr. Charles Byrne, the famous Irish giant, whose dèath is said to have been precipitated by excessive drinking, to which he was always addicted, but more particularly since his late loss of almost all his property, which he had simply invested in a single bank-note of 700*l.*

" Our philosophical readers may not be displeased to know, on the credit of an ingenious correspondent who had opportunity of informing himself, that Mr. Byrne, in August, 1780, measured eight feet ; that in 1782 he had gained two inches ; and after he was dead he measured eight feet four inches.

" Neither his father, mother, brother, nor any other person of his family, was of an extraordinary size."

Nothing can be more precise than the measurements here given : eight feet four he is said to have been, and such Boruwlaski reported him to have been, in his published *Memoirs* ; yet there stands his skeleton, measuring, upon the testimony of Professor Owen (in the Catalogue of the Osteology of the Hunterian Museum), " eight feet in a straight line from the vertex to the sole." This is, of course, only the height of the skeleton ; and we must allow about two inches more for the scalp and hair, and the soft cushion below the heel, which gives us eight feet two inches as the absolute height of the living man.

There was also another " Irish Giant," Patrick Cotter, otherwise O'Brien, a plaster cast of whose hand is shown in the Museum of the College of Surgeons. He was born in 1761, in the town of Kinsale. His

parents were of the common stature.   At eighteen his
great size attracted the notice of a showman, who hired
him for exhibition in England for three years at 50*l.*
per annum.   Quarrelling with this man, O'Brien was
arrested for an imaginary debt at Bristol.   Getting
assistance, he exhibited on his own account in a fair at
St. James's, in the same town.   In three days he received 30*l.*   At the age of twenty-six he measured
eight feet seven inches, and was proportionably stout.
His hand, including the palm and middle finger, measured twelve inches ; and his shoe was seventeen inches
long.   His limbs, however, were clumsy, and not well
knit. Every motion seemed attended with inconvenience
and even pain.   When he stood up he usually placed
both hands on the small of his back, and bent forward
evidently with difficulty.   His usual seat was a table
covered with a cushion.   He exhibited himself for upwards of twenty-five years, and was seldom absent
from Bartholomew Fair.   He took exercise in the
streets at two or three o'clock in the morning.   When
he wished to light his pipe he commonly took off the
top of a street-lamp for the purpose.   He could scarcely
manage to walk up an incline, and rested his hands on
the shoulders of two men for support in passing up
Holborn Hill.   Once on a journey in his own carriage
he was stopped by a highwayman, on which he looked
from the window, when the thief, terrified at his prodigious size, rode off in great alarm.   There was a box
sunk to a considerable depth below the bottom of the
vehicle to receive his legs and feet.   His last appearance in London was in 1804.   Here is a copy of the
placard then posted :—

    " Just arrived, and to be seen at No. 61, Haymarket,

the celebrated Irish Giant, Mr. O'Brien, indisputably the tallest man ever shown—is a lineal descendant of King Brien Borom, and resembles that great potentate. All the members of the family are distinguished by their immense size. The gentleman alluded to measures near nine feet high. Admittance one shilling."

Having realised a considerable fortune, he declined exhibiting, and resided for about two years at Bristol. He died of consumption in 1800, being then in his forty-sixth year. He bequeathed his clothes to a servant, who dressed up a huge figure in resemblance of his master, which was exhibited in various parts of London.

A NORFOLK GIANT.

In the year 1863, there died Robert Hales, " the Norfolk giant," who was, in 1851, one of the " curiosities of London." Hales was born at Westlomerton, near Yarmouth, in 1820, and was therefore only forty-three years of age. He came of a family remarkable for their great stature, his father (a farmer) being 6ft. 6in. in height, and his mother 6ft. It is traditionally said that an ancestor of his mother was the famous warder of King Henry VIII., who stood 8ft. 4in. high. Of such Patagonian parents the family—five daughters and four sons—all attained extraordinary stature, the males averaging 6ft. 5in. in height, and the females 6ft. 3½in. Robert Hales stood 7ft. 6in. in height; weight, 33 stone (462lb.); measurement across the chest, 62in.; round the abdomen, 64in.; across the shoulders, 36in.; round the thigh, 36in.; round the calf of the leg, 21in. These were his dimensions in

1851.   In 1848, Hales visited the United States, and
remained there about two years.   Barnum made a
" speculation " of the giant, and 28,000 persons flocked
to see him in ten days.   In January 1851, he returned
to England, and took the Craven Head Tavern, in
Wych-street, Strand.   On April 11th he had the
honour of being presented to the Queen and Royal
Family, when Her Majesty gave him a gold watch and
chain, which he wore to the day of his death.   His
health had been much impaired by the close confinement of the caravans in which he exhibited.   He died
of consumption.   Hales was cheerful and well-informed.
He had visited several continental capitals, and was
presented to Louis Philippe, King of the French.

CELEBRATED DWARFS.

STOW, in his Chronicle, dated 1581 (24th of Queen
Elizabeth), has recorded the extraordinary exhibition
of two Dutchmen in London, in that year, one of
whom was seven feet seven inches in height, and the
other only three feet.   The " giant" was " in breadth
betwixt the shoulders, three-quarters of a yard and
an inch, the compasse of his breast one yard and a half
and two inches; and about the waist, one yard, quarter,
and one inch; the length of his arm to the hand, a full
yard."   He was " a comely man of person, but lame
of his legges," which he had broken " with lifting a
barrel of beer."   The dwarf was without knees, and
had " never a good foot, and yet could he daunce a
galliard."   He had no arms, and " but a stumpe to
the elbow, or little more, on the right side, on the
which, singing, he would daunce across, and after tosse

it about three or four times, and every time receive the same upon the said stumpe: he would shoote an arrow neare to the marke, flourish with a rapier, throw a bowle, beate with a hammer, hew with an axe, sound a trumpet, and drinke every day ten quarts of the best beere—if he could get it." Stow adds: " I myselfe saw the taller man sitting on a bench, bareheaded, and the lesser, standing on the same bench, and having on his head a hat with a feather, was yet lower. Also, the taller man standing on his feet, went upright between his legs, and touched him not."

The dwarfs usually kept in great houses, were often the subject of merriment. James I. had in his court a dwarf, a giant, and a jester; and the King often amused himself by fomenting quarrels amongst them. In the time of Charles, a dwarf named Richard Gibson, who was a page at the back stairs, was married to Anne Shepherd, who was equally diminutive. The King gave away the bride, and Waller wrote a poem on the occasion—

Design or chance make others wive,
But nature did this match contrive.
Eve might as well have Adam fled,
As she denied her little bed
To him, for whom heav'n seem'd to frame,
And measure out his only dame.
Thrice happy is that humble pair,
Beneath the level of all care !
Over whose heads those arrows fly
Of sad distrust and jealousy;
Secured in as high esteem,
As if the world had none but them.

They each measured three feet three inches. The little pair were painted at full length, by Sir Peter Lely. They had nine children, five of whom attained maturity. Gibson was an artist of considerable merit; he taught Queen Anne drawing; he reached the age of seventy-five years, and his wife died in 1709, at the age of eighty-nine, having survived her husband twenty years.

Another famous Court Dwarf was Jeffrey Hudson, who was born in 1619, at Oakham, in Rutlandshire. When seven years of age, he was scarcely eighteen inches in height, yet without any deformity, and wholly proportionable. At about the age of eight years he was taken into the service of the Duchess of Buckingham, at Burleigh-on-the-Hill, where " he was instantly heightened (not in stature, but) in condition, from one degree above rags to silks and satins, and had two tall men to attend him." Shortly after he was served up in a cold pye, at an entertainment given to Charles I. and his consort, Henrietta Maria, in their progress through Rutlandshire: and was then, most probably, presented to the Queen, in whose service Jeffrey continued many years. At a masque, given at court, the King's gigantic porter drew Hudson out of his pocket, to the amazement of all the spectators. At the commencement of the Civil Wars, Jeffrey became a Captain of Horse in the Royal Army, and in that capacity he accompanied the Queen to France, where he killed his antagonist in a duel, and was, in consequence, imprisoned, and then expelled the court. He was then thirty years old; and, as he affirmed, had never increased anything considerable in weight since he was seven years old. He now endured a number of hardships, which are said to have added to his stature. Wright, in his *History of Rutland*, tells us that Jeffrey " shot up in a little time to that height of stature which he remained at in his old age, about three feet and nine inches;" the cause of which he attributed to the severity of treatment during his captivity. After his release he returned to England, and lived for some time on small pensions allowed him by the Duke of Buckingham, and other persons of rank. During the excitement of the Titus Oates' Plot, Hudson was arrested as a Papist, and committed to the Gatehouse, where he lay a considerable time. He died in 1682, shortly after his release, in the sixty-third year of his age. We possess, in London, a curious memorial of Jeffrey Hudson. Over the entrance of Bull Head Court, Newgate Street, is a small stone, portraying, in low relief, sculptures of William Evans, the gigantic porter of Charles I., and Hudson, his diminutive fellow-servant. On the stone are cut these words: " The King's Porter and the Dwarf," with the date 1680. Evans is described as having been full six feet and a half in height, though knock-kneed, splay-footed, and halting ; yet he danced in an antimask at Court, where he drew little Jeffrey, the dwarf, out of his pocket, much to the wonder and laughter of the company. Among the curiosities of the Ashmolean, at Oxford, are preserved the waistcoat, breeches, and stockings (the two latter in one piece) of Jeffrey: they are of blue satin, the waistcoat being slashed with figured white silk. And in the Towneley collection was a rare tract, or " New Yere's Gift," 1636, containing a portrait of Hudson; the binding of the book is a piece of Charles I.'s waistcoat.

In 1773, a remarkable female dwarf was exhibited in the metropolis: she was a native of Corsica, and named

Madame Teresa, or the Corsican fairy. She was only thirty-four inches high, and weighed but twenty-six pounds. Her form was highly symmetrical and pleasing, and her features were considered very beautiful. She was full of vivacity, could speak Italian and French, and danced with great elegance.

PLAYING ON THE SALT-BOX.

THE middle-aged reader may remember to have seen the odd performance with a rolling-pin and salt-box, beaten together, and the noise being modulated so as to resemble a sort of " music." It was formerly played by Merry-Andrews at country fairs; and in Croker's *Boswell*, we find Johnson praising the humour of Bonnell Thornton's burlesque *Ode on St. Cecilia's Day*, and repeating these lines :—

> In strains more exalted the salt-box shall join,
> And clattering, and battering, and clapping combine;
> With a rap and a tap, while the hollow side sounds,
> Up and down leaps the flap, and with rattling rebounds.

In a note Mr. Croker quotes from Dr. Burney a passage which well illustrates this subject :—

" In 1769, I set for Smart and Newbury, Thornton's burlesque *Ode on St. Cecilia's Day*. It was performed at Ranelagh in masks, to a very crowded audience, as I was told; for I then resided in Norfolk. Beard sang the salt-box song, which was admirably accompanied on that instrument by Brent, the fencing-master; Skeggs on the broomstick as bassoon, and a remarkable performer on the Jew's harp,

> Buzzing twangs the iron lyre."

A SHARK STORY.

In the United Service Museum, Whitehall Yard, are exhibited " the jaws of a shark," wide open and enclosing a tin box. The history of this strange exhibition is as follows:—A ship, on her way to the West Indies, fell in with and chased a suspicious-looking' craft, which had all the appearance of a slaver. During the pursuit the chase threw something overboard. She was subsequently captured, and taken into Port Royal to be tried, as a slaver. In absence of the ship's papers, and other proofs, the slaver was not only in a fair way to escape condemnation, but her captain was anticipating the recovery of pecuniary damages against his captor for illegal detention. While the subject was under discussion, a vessel came into port which had followed closely in the track of the chase above described. She had caught a shark; and in its stomach was found a tin box, which contained the slaver's papers. Upon the strength of this evidence, the slaver was condemned. The written account is attached to the box.

TOPHAM, THE STRONG MAN OF ISLINGTON.

In Upper Street, Islington, was formerly a public-house with the sign of the Duke's Head, at the south-east corner of Gadd's. Row (now St. Alban's Place), which was remarkable, towards the middle of the last century, on account of its landlord, Thomas Topham, " the strong man of Islington." He was brought up to the trade of a carpenter, but abandoned it soon after the term of his apprenticeship had expired; and about the age of twenty-four became the host of the Red Lion, near the old Hospital of St. Luke, in which house he failed. When he had attained his full growth, his stature was about five feet ten inches, and he soon began to give proof of his superior strength and muscular power. The first public exhibition of his extraordinary strength was that of pulling against a horse, lying upon his back, and placing his feet against the dwarf wall that divided Upper and Lower Moorfields. He afterwards pulled against two horses, but, his legs being placed horizontally instead of rising parallel to the traces of the horses, he was jerked from his position; it was, nevertheless, the opinion of Dr. Desaguliers, the eminent mechanic and experimental philosopher, that, had Topham been in a proper position, he might have kept his situation against the pulling of four horses, without inconvenience.

The following are among the feats which Dr. Desaguliers says he himself saw Topham perform:— By the strength of his fingers, he rolled up a very strong and large pewter dish. Among the curiosities of the British Museum, some years ago, was a pewter dish, marked near the edge, " April 3, 1737, Thomas Topham, of London, carpenter, rolled up this dish (made of the hardest pewter) by the strength of his hands, in the presence of Dr. John Desaguliers, &c." He broke seven or eight pieces of a tobacco-pipe, by the force of his middle finger, having laid them on his first and third fingers. Having thrust the bowl of a strong tobacco-pipe under his garter, his legs being bent, he broke it to pieces by the tendons of his hams, without altering the position of his legs. Another bowl of this kind he broke between his first and second finger, by pressing them together sideways. He took an iron kitchen poker, about a yard long, and three inches round, and bent it nearly to a right angle, by striking upon his bare left arm between the elbow and the wrist. Holding the ends of a poker of like size in his hands, and the middle of it against the back of his neck, he brought both extremities of it together before him; and, what was yet more difficult, pulled it almost straight again. He broke a rope of two inches in circumference; though, from his awkward manner, he was obliged to exert four times more strength than was necessary. He lifted a rolling stone of eight hundred pounds' weight with his hands only, standing in a frame above it, and taking hold of a chain fastened thereto.

It is probable that Topham kept the Duke's Head at the time he exhibited the exploit of lifting three hogsheads of water, weighing one thousand eight hundred and thirty-one pounds, in Coldbath Fields, May 28, 1741, in commemoration of the taking of Porto Bello by Admiral Vernon; and which he performed in the presence of the Admiral and thousands of spectators. He then removed to Hog Lane, Shoreditch. His wife proved unfaithful to him, which so distressed him that he stabbed her, and so mutilated himself that he died, in the flower of his age.

THE POPE'S PROCESSION, AND BURNING OF THE POPE.

AFTER the discovery of the pretended Meal Tub Plot, in 1679, the people became indignant against the Roman Catholics.

Each anniversary of Queen Elizabeth's accession

(Nov. 17) was for many years celebrated by the
citizens of London in a manner expressive of their
detestation of the Church of Rome.   A procession—at
times sufficiently attractive for royal spectators—pa-
raded the principal streets, the chief figure being an
effigy of

The Pope, that pagan full of pride,

well executed in wax, and expensively adorned with
robes and a tiara.   He was accompanied by a train of
cardinals and Jesuits; and at his ear stood a buffoon in
the likeness of a horned devil.

In the latter part of Charles II.'s reign, these anti-pa-
pistical solemnities were employed as engines to excite
"the popular resentment against the Duke of York and
his religion," and they were performed with great state
and expense.   The most famous of these processions
were those of 1679, 1680, and 1681, to which Dryden
thus alludes at the conclusion of his epilogue to
Œdipus :—

> Yet as weak states each other's powers assure,
> Weak poets by conjunction are secure.
> Their treat is what your palates relish most,
> Charm! Song! and Show! a Murder and a Ghost.
> We know not what you can desire or hope,
> To please you more, but *Burning of a Pope*.

From a very scarce pamphlet, and an equally rare
broadside, we gather that, on the 17th of November,
the bells began to ring about 3 o'clock in the morning,
in the city.   In the evening, the *Solemn Procession*
began from Moorgate, and so to Bishopsgate Street,
and down Houndsditch to Aldgate, through Leadenhall
Street, Cornhill, by the Royal Exchange, through
Cheapside to Temple Bar, in order following :—

1. Six whifflers, to clear the way, in pioneers' caps and red waistcoats. 2. A bellman, ringing his bell, and with a dolesome voice, crying all the way, "Remember Justice Godfrey." 3. A dead body representing Justice Godfrey, in a decent black habit, and the cravat wherewith he was murdered about his neck, with spots of blood on his wrists, breast, and shirt, and white gloves on his hands, his face pale and wan, riding upon a white horse, and one of his murderers behind him, to keep him from falling, in the same manner as he was carried to Primrose Hill. 4. A priest came next, in a surplice, and a cope embroidered with dead men's skulls and skeletons, who give out pardons very plentifully to all that would murder Protestants; and proclaiming it meritorious. 5. Then a Protestant alone, with a great silver cross. 6. Four Carmelite friars, in white and black habits. 7. Four Grey friars, in the proper habits of their order. 8. Six Jesuits, carrying bloody daggers. 9. Four wind-musick, called the waits, playing all the way. 10. Four bishops in purple, with lawn sleeves, with golden crosses on their breasts, and croziers in their hands. 11. Four other bishops, *in pontificalibus*, with surplices and richly embroidered copes, and golden mitres on their heads. 12. Six cardinals, in scarlet robes and caps. 13. Then followed the Pope's chief physician, with jesuits, powder, &c. 14. Two priests, in surplices, with two golden crosses.

Lastly, the Pope himself, in a chair of state, covered with scarlet, richly embroidered and fringed, and bedecked with golden balls and crosses. At his feet, a cushion of state and two boys in surplices, with white silk banners, painted with red crosses and daggers, with an incense pot before them, censing his Holiness, who was arrayed in a splendid scarlet gown, lined with ermine and daubed with gold and silver lace; on his head a triple crown of gold, a collar of gold and precious stones, St. Peter's keys, a number of beads, &c. At his back, the degraded Seraphim, instructing him to destroy his Majesty, to forge a Protestant plot, and to fire the city again, for which purpose he held in his hand an infernal torch.

The whole procession was attended with one hundred and fifty flambeaux and lights, besides thousands of volunteers. The balconies, windows, and houses were crowded, and the streets thronged with people, all expressing their abhorrence of Popery, with shouts and acclamations; in all not fewer than 200,000 spectators.

Thus, with slow and solemn pace, they proceeded to Temple Bar; the houses being converted into heaps of men and women and children, for whose diversion there were provided great quantities of fireworks.

The statue of Queen Elizabeth in Temple Bar was, in regard to the day, crowned with gilded laurel, and in her hand a golden shield inscribed "The Protestant Religion and Magna Charta." Before this shield were placed flambeaux; and the Pope being brought up here, a song was sung in parts, characterising the statues in the Bar, part one representing the English cardinal, and others the people.

Then the spectators were entertained with fireworks, and a bonfire just over the Inner Temple Gate, into "the impartial flames of which his Holiness was toppled;" the devil laughing heartily at his ignominious end; and then arose a prodigious shout that might be heard far beyond Somerset House, and echoed to Scotland, France, and even Rome itself.

Lord North, in describing one of these "Pope-burn-

ing tumults," mentions the *Green Ribbon Club,* styling
it "the more visible administration, mediate, as it were,
between the Earl of Shaftesbury (at the head of the
direction) and the greater and lesser vulgar who were
to be the immediate tools." This Club held its evening sittings at the King's Head Tavern, over against
the Inner Temple; and from the signal of a *Green
Ribbon,* agreed to be worn in their hats, on the days of
their street engagements, they were called the *Green
Ribbon Club.* Their seat was in a sort of *Carfour*
at Chancery Lane end, the house being double-bal-
conied in the front, for the Clubsters to issue forth in
fresco, with hats and no peruques, pipes in their
mouths, merry faces, and diluted throats.

In describing the Pope-burning Procession of the
17th of November 1680, North says that "the rabble
first changed their title, and were called the *mob* in
the assemblies of the above Club. It was their Beast
of Burthen, and called, first, *mobile vulgus,* but fell
naturally into the contraction of one syllable, and ever
since it is become proper *English.*"

North thus describes the procession of 1681 :—

" When we had posted ourselves," he says, " at
windows, expecting the play to begin " (he had taken
his stand in the Green Dragon Tavern), " it was very
dark; but we could perceive the street to fill, and
the hum of the crowd grew louder and louder; and
at length, with help of some lights below, we could
discern, not only upwards towards the bar, where the
squib-war was maintained, but downwards towards .
Fleet Bridge; the whole street was crowded with
people, which made that which followed seem very
strange; for about eight at night we heard a din from

below, which came up the street, continually increasing
till we could perceive a motion; and that was a row of
stout fellows, that came, shouldered together, cross the
street, from wall to wall on each side. How the people
melted away, I cannot tell; but it was plain those
fellows made clear board, as if they had swept the
street for what was to come after. They went along
like a wave; and it was wonderful to see how the
crowd made away: I suppose the good people were
willing to give obedience to lawful authority. Behind
this wave (which, as all the rest, had many lights attending) there was a vacancy, but it filled apace, till
another like wave came up; and so four or five of
these waves passed, one after another; and then we
discerned more numerous lights, and throats were
opened with hoarse and tremendous noise; and with
that advanced a pageant, borne along above the heads
of the crowd, and upon it sat a huge Pope, *in pontificalibus*, in his chair, with a seasonable attendance for
state: but his premier minister, that shared most of
his ear, was Il Signior Diavolo, a nimble little fellow,
in a proper dress, that had a strange dexterity in
climbing and winding about the chair, from one of the
Pope's ears to the other."

The description concludes with a brief mention of
burning the effigies, which, on these occasions, appear
to have been of pasteboard.

One of the great figures in this ceremony was the
doleful image of Sir Edmond Berry Godfrey, the magistrate, supposed to have been killed by the Papists
during the question of the Plot. Dryden has a fine
contemptuous couplet upon it in one of his prologues:

> Sir Edmondbury first in woful wise,
> Leads up the show, *and milks their maudlin eyes.*

On the discovery of the Rye House Plot, the Pope's Procession was discontinued; but was resuscitated on the acquittal of the Seven Bishops and dethronement of James II. Sacheverel's trial added a new interest to the ceremony; and besides a popular dread of the Church being in danger—from the listlessness of the ministers and the machinations of the Pretender—there was a general opposition to the Peace with France, for which the Tories were intriguing. The party cry of " No Peace " was shouted in the same breath with " No Popery."

The Whigs were determined, it was said, to give significance and force to these watchwords by getting up the anniversary show of 1711 with unprecedented splendour. No good Protestant, no honest hater of the French, could refuse to subscribe his guinea for such an object; and it is said that upwards of a thousand pounds were collected for the effigies and their dresses and decorations alone, independent of a large sum for incidental expenses. The Pope, the devil, and the Pretender were, it was asserted, fashioned in the likeness of the obnoxious cabinet ministers. The procession was to take place at night, and " a thousand mob " were to be hired to carry flambeaux at a crown apiece, and as much beer and brandy as would inflame them for mischief. The pageant was to open with " twenty-four bagpipes marching four and four, and playing the memorable tune of Lillibullero. Presently was to come a figure representing Cardinal Gaulteri (lately made by the Pretender protector of the English nation), looking down on the ground in sorrowful posture; his train supported by two missionaries from Rome, supposed to be now in England."—" Two pages throwing beads, bulls, pardons, and indulgences."—

" Two jackpuddings sprinkling holy water."—" Twelve
hautboys playing the Greenwood Tree."—Then were
to succeed " six beadles with Protestant flails; " and
after a variety of other satirical mummery, the grand
centrepiece was to show itself:—" The Pope under a
magnificent canopy, with a right silver fringe, accompanied by the Chevalier St. George on the left, and
his councillor the devil on his right." The whole procession was to close with twenty streamers displaying,
this couplet wrought on each:

> God bless Queen Anne, the nation's great defender,
> Keep out the French, the Pope, and the Pretender.

To be ready for this grand spectacle, the figures were
deposited in a house in Drury Lane, whence the procession was to march (with proper reliefs of lights at
several stations) to St. James's Square, thence through
Pall Mall, the Strand, Drury Lane, and Holborn to
Bishopsgate Street, and return through St. Paul's
Churchyard to the bonfire in Fleet Street. " After
proper ditties had been sung, the Pretender was to
have been committed to the flames, being first absolved
by the Cardinal Gaulteri. After that the said Cardinal
was to be absolved by the Pope, and burnt. And then
the devil was to jump into the flames with his Holiness
in his arms." This programme is from a folio half-sheet
published at the time.

The Tories spread exaggerated reports of these preparations, as of certain accidents which were contrived
beforehand by the conspirators. But all this was harmless as compared with the threatened sequel. On the
diabolical programme were said to be inscribed certain
houses that were to be burnt down. That of the Com-

missioners of Accounts in Essex Street was to form the first pyre, because in it had been discovered and completed Marlborough's commissorial defalcations. The Lord Treasurer's was to follow. Harley himself was to have been torn to pieces, as the Dutch pensionary De Witt had been. Indeed, the entire city was only to have escaped destruction and rapine by a miracle.

These were the coarse excuses which the Tories put forth for spoiling the show in 1711. At midnight on the 16—17th of November, a posse of constables made forcible entry into the Drury Lane temple of the waxen images, and, by force of arms, seized the Pope, the Pretender, the cardinals, the devil and all his works, a chariot to have been drawn by six of his imps, the canopies and bagpipes, the bulls, the pardons, the Protestant flails, the streamers,—in short, the entire paraphernalia. At one fell swoop the whole collection was carried off to the Cockpit at Whitehall, then the Privy Council Office. That the City apprentices should not be wholly deprived of their expected treat, fifteen of the group were exhibited to the public gratis. Swift wrote to Stella: "I saw to-day the Pope, the devil, and the other figures of cardinals, &c., fifteen in all, which have made such a noise. I hear the owners of them are so impudent, that their design is to replevy them by law. The images are not worth forty pounds, so I stretched a little when I said a thousand. The Grub Street account of that tumult is published. The devil is not like lord treasurer: they are all in your old antic masks bought in common shops." (See *Wills's Notes to Sir Roger de Coverley.*)

THE GIANTS AT GUILDHALL.

" THE Two Giants in Guildhall" are supposed to have been originally made for carrying about in pageants, a custom not peculiar to the City of London; for the going of the giants at Midsummer " occurs among the ancient customs of Chester, before 1599." We read of Midsummer pageants in London, in 1589, " where, to make the people wonder, are set forth great and uglie gyants, marching as if they were alive," &c. Again, " one of the gyant's stilts," that stalks before my Lord Mayor's pageants, occurs in a play of the year 1663.

In 1415, when Henry V. returned in the flush of triumph, after his victory of Agincourt, he entered London by Southwark, when a male and female giant stood at the entrance of London Bridge; in 1432, here " a mighty giant" awaited Henry VI.; in 1554, at the entry of Philip and Mary, Corinœus and Gog-Magog stood upon London Bridge; and when Elizabeth passed through the City the day before her coronation, these two giants were placed at Temple Bar. The Lord Mayor's pageant in 1672 had " two extreme great giants, at least 15 feet high," that did sit and were drawn by horses in two chariots, talking and taking tobacco, as they rode along, to the great admiration and delight of the spectators.

Ned Ward describes the Guildhall Giants, in his *London Spy*, 1699; and, among the exhibitions of fire-works upon the Thames in honour of the coronation of James II. and his queen, in 1685, " were placed the statues of the two giants of Guildhall, in lively colours and proportions, facing Whitehall, the backs of which were all filled with fiery materials." Bragg, in his

Observer, Dec. 25, 1706, tells us that when the colours taken at Ramilies were put up in Guildhall, "the very giants stared with all the eyes they had, and smiled as well as they could."

In a very rare book, entitled *The Gigantick History of the Two Famous Giants in Guildhall*, 3rd edit. 1741, we read that "before the present giants inhabited Guildhall, there were two giants made only of wickerwork and pasteboard, put together with great art and ingenuity ; and these two terrible giants had the honour yearly to grace my Lord Mayor's Show, being carried in great triumph in the time of the pageants ; when that eminent annual service was over, they remounted their old stations in Guildhall—till, by reason of their great age, old Time, with the help of a number of City rats and mice, had eaten up all their entrails. The dissolution of the two old weak and feeble giants gave birth to the two present substantial and energetic giants; who, by order, and at the City charge, were formed and fashioned. Captain Richard Saunders, an eminent carver, in King Street, Cheapside, was their father, who, after he had completely finished, clothed, and armed these his two sons, they were immediately advanced to those lofty stations in Guildhall, which they have peaceably enjoyed since the year 1708."

The *Gigantick History* was published within Guildhall, when shops were permitted there; so that the publisher had the best means of obtaining correct information. It is further stated in his work, that "the first honour which the two ancient wickerwork giants were promoted to in the City, was at the Restoration of King Charles II., when, with great pomp and majesty, they graced a triumphal arch which was erected

on that happy occasion, at the end of King Street, in
Cheapside.   This was before the Fire of London, by
which Guildhall was 'much damnifyed' but not burned
down; for the conflagration was principally confined to
the wooden roof; and, according to the accounts, the
wicker giants escaped till their infirmities and the de-
vastations of the ' City rats ' rendered it necessary to
supersede them."   The City accounts, in the Chamberlain's office, show a payment of 70*l.* to Saunders, the
carver, in 1707, which, doubtless, includes the charge
for the two giants.

Stow describes these giants as an ancient Briton
and Saxon, which is, perhaps, as orthodox as the information that, every day when the giants hear the clock
strike twelve, they come down to dinner.   The *Gigantick History* supposes that the Guildhall Giants repre-
sent Corinæus and Gog-Magog, whose history is related
by Geoffrey of Monmouth.   It includes the adventures
of Brutus and his band of Trojans, under Corinæus,
who, arriving at Totness, in Devonshire, in the Island
of Albion,

> More mightie people borne of giant's brood
> That did possesse this ocean-bounded land,
> They did subdue, who oft in battle stood
> 'Gainst them in field, until by force of hand
> They were made subject under Bruce's command :
> Such boldness then did in the Briton dwell,
> That they in deeds of valour did excell.

Unable to cope with these experienced warriors, none
escaped,

> Save certain giants, whom they did pursue,
> Which straight to caves in mountains did them get.
> So fine were woods, and floods, and fountaines set,
> So cleare the aire, so temperate the clime,
> They never saw the like before that time.

Perceiving that this was the country denoted by the oracle, wherein they were to settle, Brutus divided the island among his followers, which, with reference to his own name, he called Britain:

> To Corinœus gave he frank and free,
> The land of Cornwall for his service done,
> And for because from giants he it won.

Corinœus was the better pleased with this allotment, inasmuch as he had been used to warfare with such terrible personages. The employment he liked fell afterwards to his lot. On the sea-coast of Cornwall, while Brutus was keeping a peaceable anniversary of his landing, a band of the old giants made their appearance, and broke up the mirth and rejoicing. The Trojans flew to their arms, and a desperate battle was fought, wherein the giants were all destroyed, save Corinœus, the hugest among them, who, being in height twelve cubits, was reserved alive, that Corinœus might try his strength with him in single combat. Corinœus desired nothing more than such a match, but the old giant in a wrestle caught him aloft, and broke three of his ribs. Upon this, Corinœus being desperately enraged, collected all his strength, heaved up Gog-Magog by main force, and bearing him on his shoulders to the next high rock, threw him headlong, all shattered, into the sea, and left his name on the cliff, which has ever since been called Lan-Goegmagog, that is to say, the Giant's Leap. Thus perished Gog-Magog, the last of the giants. Brutus afterwards built a city in a chosen spot, and called it Troja Nova, which changed in time to Trinovantum, and is now called London. An ancient writer records these achievements

in Britain to have been performed at the time when
Eli was the high priest in Judæa.

The Rabbins make the giant Gog, or Magog, contemporary with Noah, and convinced by his preaching,
so that he was disposed to "take the benefit" of the
Ark. But here lay the distress—it by no means suited
his dimensions; therefore, as he could not enter in, he
contented himself to ride upon it ; and although you
must suppose that in stormy weather he was more than
" half boots over," he kept his seat, and dismounted
safely when the Ark reached Ararat. (*Warburton's
Letters.*) This same Gog had, according to the Rabbins,
a thigh-bone so long, that a stag, pursued by the
hunters, employed half a day in running along it.
(*Note to Thaumaturgus.*)

Their story is briefly told by Archdeacon Nares.
" One of them was called Gogmagog (the patron, I
presume, of the Gogmagog Hills, near Cambridge),
and his name divided, now serves for both; the other,
Corinœus, the hero and giant of Cornwall, from whom
that country was named, here are thus mentioned on a
broad-sheet, printed in 1660 :—

> And such stout Coronæus was, from whom
> Cornwall's first honor, and her name doth come.
> For though he showeth not so great nor tall,
> In his dimensions set forth as Guildhall,
> Know 'tis a poet only can define
> A gyant's posture in a gyant's line.
>
> .   .   .   .
>
> And thus attended by his direful dog
> The gyant was (God bless us) Gogmagog.

Each of the giants in Guildhall measures upwards of
14 feet in height: the young one is set down as Corinœus,
and the old one Gog-Magog. They are made of wood,

and hollow within, and from the method of joining and gluing the interior, are evidently of late construction; but they are too substantially built for the purpose of being carried or drawn, or any way exhibited in a pageant. Their habiliments were renewed, and their armour polished in 1837.

LORD MAYOR'S DAY.

THE procession of the Lord Mayor from the Guildhall to Westminster, on the 9th of November, is the only state exhibition of the metropolis that remains of the splendid City pageants. It is now exclusively a procession by land, the aquatic portion having been discontinued since the Conservancy of the Thames has been taken out of civic administration; so that we can no longer

> Stand in Temple Gardens, and behold
> London herself on her proud stream afloat;
> For so appears this fleet of magistracy,
> Holding due course to Westminster.
> *Shakspeare's Henry V.*

The procession was by land until the year 1435, in the reign of Henry VI., when Sir John Norman built a sumptuous barge for going by water, which custom lasted for four centuries and a quarter. Fabyan alludes to a roundell or songe, made by the watermen, in praise of Sir John Norman, Lord Mayor; and Dr. Rimbault believes that he has found the original music to which this roundell was sung.

The Inauguration Banquet in the Guildhall remains a splendid spectacle, with traces of feudal character in its magnificence.

The Lord Mayor and his distinguished guests advance to the feast by sound of trumpet : and the superb dresses and official costumes of the company, about 1,200 in number, with the display of costly plate, is very striking.   The Hall is divided : at the upper, or hustings tables, the courses are served hot ; at the lower tables the turtle only is hot.   The baron of beef is brought in procession from the kitchen into the Hall in the morning, and being placed upon a pedestal, at night is cut up by " the City carver." The kitchen, wherein the dinner is dressed, is a vast apartment ; the principal range is 16 feet long, and 7 feet high, and a baron of beef (3 cwt.) upon the gigantic spit is turned by hand. There are 20 cooks, besides helpers ; 14 tons of coals are consumed ; some 40 turtles are slaughtered for 250 tureens of soup ; and the serving of the dinner requires about 200 persons, and 8,000 plate-changes.   Next morning the fragments of the Great Feast are doled out at the kitchen-gate to the City poor.

In this noble Hall have been held the Inauguration dinners of the Lord Mayors since 1501.   Here Whittington entertained Henry V. and his queen, when he threw the King's bonds for 60,000*l.* into a fire of spice wood.   Charles I. was feasted here in 1641, with a political object, which failed.   Charles II. was *nine times* entertained here ; and from 1660, with only three exceptions, our Sovereign has dined at Guildhall on the Lord Mayor's Day, after his or her accession or coronation.   The exceptions were James II., who held the City Charter upon a writ of *quo warranto* at his accession ; George IV., who was rendered unpopular by his quarrel with his queen ; and William IV., who apprehended political tumult.   But George IV. (when

Regent) was entertained here June 18th, 1814, with
Alexander, Emperor of Russia, and Frederick-William
III., King of Prussia, when the banquet cost 25,000*l.*,
and the value of the plate used was 200,000*l.** On
July 9th following, the Duke of Wellington was entertained in Guildhall. The banquet to George III. cost
6,898*l.*, when 1,200 guests dined in the Hall; that to
Queen Victoria, November 9th, 1837, cost 6,870*l*; and an
evening entertainment to Her Majesty, July 9th, 1851,
to celebrate the Great Exhibition, cost 5,120*l.* 14*s.* 9*d.*,
being 129*l.* 5*s.* 3*d.* less than the sum voted; invitations,
1,452. (*Curiosities of London.*)

The *Show* is now modern: its last ancient feature
was the poor men of the Company to which the Lord
Mayor belonged, wearing their long gowns and close
caps, of the Company's colour, and wearing painted
shields; there being as many men as years in the Lord
Mayor's age. The Show, in its earliest years, consisted
of a procession of minstrels and beadles on horseback.
For a time water spectacles, chiefly sham fights, grew
popular. In 1566, on the Mayor-day of Sir William
Draper, a pageant was arranged which had no scenic
representations, but had " a foist, or barge, with ten
pair of oars and masts," but whether they had sails or
flags does not appear. " The Queen's arms flowed
from the maintop, and a red crosse from the foretop;
long pendants were added to these, and two ancients
displayed on the pope (poop) or baste." This vessel
" had a master and a gunner, with squibs sufficient for

---

* It has been little noticed that on the anniversary of this day, June
18, 1815, was fought the battle of Waterloo, precisely a year after the
above banquet, in commemoration of the conclusion of our war with
France.

the time, well painted and trimmed, with 20 pavases and two half-barrels of gunpowder on board." A little later, on the same occasion, in the Grocers' pageant "there was a large ship, rigged and manned, with Galatea at its bows, a sea nymph, drawn on a sea chariot by dolphins, accompanied by syrens, tritons, sea lions, which saluted the Lord Mayor on the river, near the Temple."

In 1568, Sir Thomas Rae, a Merchant Taylor, being elected Mayor, the Company voted him 40*l*. for his expenses. The wardens were charged to see the tables at Guildhall properly arranged for the feasts, and " sixteen " of the Bachelors' Company were ordered to carry up the service to table. The pageant embodied an allegorical representation of the patron saint, John Baptist. He was attended by four boys, whose duty it was to deliver complimentary speeches. St. John's speech began thus: " I am that voyce in wilderness which once the Jews did call."

Sir Thomas Middleton, Grocer and Mayor, 1613, was among the first who attempted a scenic representation. He gave a water spectacle, with five islands, artfully garnished with all manner of Indian fruit, fruit-trees, drugs, spices, and the like. The centre island was embellished with " a faire castle, especially beautified," probably in allusion to the East India Company, then newly established.

From this period to 1708 the Lord Mayor's show derived its chief magnificence from the great Livery Companies, and assumed a dramatic tone.

END OF THE SECOND VOLUME.

PRINTED BY SPOTTISWOODE AND CO., NEW-STREET SQUARE, LONDON.

www.ingramcontent.com/pod-product-compliance
Lightning Source LLC
Chambersburg PA
CBHW060517030726
47498CB00004B/979